AFTER
THE
FIRE

AFTER
THE
FIRE

JOHN LOCKLEY

WORD PUBLISHING
WORD ENTERTAINMENT LTD
Milton Keynes, England

AFTER THE FIRE

99 00 01 02 / 10 9 8 7 6 5 4 3

Acknowledgements

Grateful thanks to Susie Barnes, Wendy Berliner, Mike Colley, Chris Garraway, John Goddard, Andrew Lockley, Philip Lockley, John Metcalf, Andy Mott, Niall Quinn, Ryder Rogers, Jeff Solomons, Douglas Tate and Colin Wood for their assistance and encouragement. Special thanks to Mary Watkin, my secretary, for all her hard work; to the Wyvern Shipping Company; the staff of the BBC Three Counties Radio; Jeff Berliner, formerly of TV-am; and to all those in Ampthill who so kindly afforded me access to their houses and establishments whilst researching this book. (May I emphasise that the fictional inhabitants of Ampthill are in no way any representation of the real-life inhabitants of these buildings!)

Author's note

'Peter Abraham's' trial is a fictionalised account of a real-life trial in which I was the medical witness. To the shame of our legal system it really happened. So did the second trial in that chapter, though not in the same court.

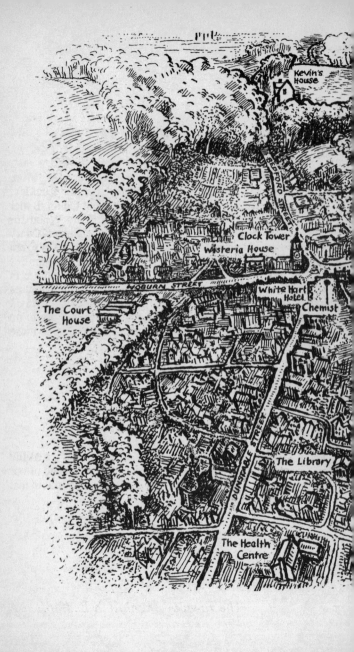

Kevin's House

Clock Tower

Wisteria House

WOBURN STREET

The Court House

White Hart Hotel

Chemist

The Library

The Health Centre

The Town of Ampthill in Bedfordshire

Part I

-1-

Friday, 5.15 p.m.

*I*t all began with a mouse.

The future seldom turns out to be what we expect. We *think* we can predict what will happen, but our predictions merely look like a slightly altered version of the present, as a quick look at old science-fiction films demonstrates. In reality the future is often very different from what we imagine: yet on looking back we always *feel* we should have been able to predict it.

Before the catastrophe, doomwatchers had been expecting that the end of the world would involve some sort of man-made cataclysm—a nuclear war; the greenhouse effect getting out of hand; the hole in the ozone layer extending to cover the whole earth.

But when the catastrophe finally occurred it came from an entirely different direction, though—as always—looking back it was quite obvious. It all happened through a mouse—and a little bit of human error: or, to be more blunt about it, laziness and negligence. Most people have got away with worse, but this particular bit of negligence, though tiny, was crucial.

The mouse in question lived in a laboratory. It wasn't even a *laboratory* mouse—that might have been predictable—but merely a member of the secret flora and fauna that inhabit all buildings.

The laboratory in question was an ordinary-looking building in the grounds of Southill Hospital in southwest London. Originally built as a storeroom, eventually, owing to pressure of space, it had been brought into service as an addition to the bacteriology department. The hospital needed a separate, hermetically sealed building for the more virulent organisms they dealt with, and as money was tight (when wasn't it?) the hospital management decided that rather than paying for a custom-built lab it would convert the storeroom instead. Chief among the alterations was a purification system to suck air away from the faces of the laboratory staff, and filter out pathogenic bacteria, before venting it to the outside world.

The conversion worked surprisingly well. The lab serviced the old fever hospital for many years: when it was taken over to become southwest London's main isolation hospital it continued its sterling service, processing samples from patients with contagious diseases in order to identify the organism causing the illness.

The lab dealt with all sorts of infectious material—TB, smallpox, hepatitis A, B and C; the AIDS virus; even Lassa fever and Green Monkey disease (but on the one occasion they actually acquired a case they passed the samples on to the government installation at Porton Down *very* quickly!)

The lab continued working in this fashion for decade after decade—until the year of the mouse. No—the mouse didn't catch a disease from the laboratory rats, or the samples in the Petri dishes—that would have been too obvious, and the doom-watchers would have thought of that. Nor did it carry contaminated material on its coat into the hospital kitchens—the doomwatchers had thought of that, too. Instead, it continued on with its short and happy life behind the skirting boards, feeding, mating, and rearing its young, litter by litter, until one day it came across something really juicy to eat.

*   *   *

The lab handyman was Bob Harris, a balding, weary man of fifty-two, with a face lined from smoking too many cigarettes. He'd had the same job for the past twenty years and loathed every boring minute of it. He couldn't wait to get back home to his pigeons. He spent every minute thinking of them—about breeding them, racing them, cleaning them, feeding them. As far as he was concerned, every minute spent away from the pigeon-loft was a minute wasted.

Today being Friday, he couldn't wait to put down his tools and go home to his pigeons. It was quarter past five, he was late, they didn't pay him overtime, and he still wasn't finished. His last job each week was to replace the filters in the ventilation system. There were seven of them, each looking much like an air-filter for a car engine, only larger—corrugated, fibre-like paper, quite flimsy in itself, but supported on a tough plastic rim which fitted snugly into its housing inside the air ducts.

Unfortunately for Bob Harris, because the laboratory had been cobbled together out of the storeroom, these filters had had to be put in widely separated ducts situated in the tiny roof-space and were only accessible to someone crawling on hands and knees along the rafters. Worse, because they were potentially infectious—*very* infectious in some cases—Harris had to do the whole job masked and gowned in a complete plastic safety suit, which created its own jungle micro-climate next to his skin. Five minutes' effort in that lot and the sweat poured down inside the suit, unable to get away. Not only did he have to negotiate the cramped loft space, but he also had to carry the replacement filters, the old filters and a bag of tools. Crawling along the roof space in that suit was a fittingly diabolical end to each dreadful week.

On this particular Friday he wriggled through the trapdoor into the loft and along the crawling boards between the rafters. There was little enough space to move, let alone stand up as, navigating by torch, he wormed his way awkwardly between the rafters and the roof trusses. Within two minutes he was perspiring freely.

After twenty minutes he had reached the furthest point of his journey, filter number five, in the darkest and most cramped recess of all. Perspiration streamed down his face as he lowered himself awkwardly into the corner, but he couldn't wipe it away from his eyes because of the protective headgear.

In the darkness he leaned across to remove the old filter. To do this he had to unscrew the central wing nut, as well as three restraining bolts round the edges. One by one he undid them, but the filter stuck in its housing and took a good few minutes of considerable effort to loosen.

Eventually sweating profusely, he levered it free, and replaced it with a new one. With some difficulty he extricated himself from the corner of the roof and crawled to filter number six, carrying the new filter in his right hand. On the way he had to negotiate a particularly awkward change of direction amid the trusses, and as he did so, he lost his balance temporarily. He flung out his right arm to grab the nearest truss and steady himself, but as he did so the new filter in his hand snagged against a protruding nail.

He swore. He had visions of crawling back the fifty feet to

the entrance hatch, finding a new filter (he *knew* he hadn't got one in the lab, so he'd have to go over to stores, which he was sure would be locked . . .). Thoughts like these were followed shortly after by happier thoughts of his pigeons. He looked down at the half-centimetre hole in the filter, and pulled the ripped corrugated black paper back into place. Miraculously, it seemed to go together and stick to itself so the break wasn't noticeable. He smoothed the felt-like paper into itself, then put his torch behind it: no light came through. It would do, he thought. Removing the old filter, he dropped it into place, screwed the bolts up tightly, and moved on to the last filter housing.

By the time he emerged from the roof space he was dripping with sweat inside his protective plastic suit. Gratefully he disposed of the old filters into a sealed waste-disposal bag, peeled off his protective garments, washed and then, switching off the lights, went home to his beloved pigeons.

*   *   *

An hour after Bob Harris had been wrestling with the filters, Mary Harper was preparing to go out. A large, portly, grey-haired woman of fifty-five, she had that strange intensity common to ladies of that age who have never married, and who have sublimated their sexual energy into something quite different, which they pursue with the exuberance and intensity of a passionate affair. Mary's concern was the environment. She was incensed with the way that mankind was dominating the earth, destroying it in the process: not only had we damaged the environment almost irretrievably, we couldn't even manage to feed our own kind, even though other parts of the world were cutting back on farming to keep up prices. Disgusted with the materialism of Western society, she had turned avidly to New Age thinking as a reaction against all she saw as evil within society.

Mary was a New Ager down to the tip of her little finger. Perhaps that was being a little kind: in practice she had developed a cynical disdain for those who didn't agree with New Age thinking; they were selfish, scientific materialists, interested only in themselves and the profit they could make from manipulating the planet, out of tune with the environment, out of tune with the spirit of life, out of tune with the spiritual aspects of the Universe—in fact, out of tune with just about everything.

Her position as librarian in the London suburb of Ealing allowed her considerable leeway to organise exhibitions and meetings consistent with her ideas. She had just put the finishing touches to one that afternoon, an elegantly illustrated display of craft work using renewable materials—flax, straw and vegetable dyes. The exhibits were excellent, and to add to the effect she had arranged for them to display symbolic aspects of another New Age truth—the reality of Gaia, the spirit of Earth. It was a good display—artistically pleasing and tastefully laid out. She hoped that it would create even more interest than the previous exhibition two weeks earlier, on 'Astrology Through the Ages'.

She was already planning her next event—a display of library books on alternative medicines. As she put on her coat she reflected that homoeopathy and acupuncture were almost orthodox now: perhaps instead she should concentrate on some of the more abstruse ones: crystal science; radionics; perhaps even pyramidology.

As part of her New Age approach she was also an avid vegetarian, convinced that raising and killing animals for food was quite unprincipled, unnecessary and an affront to nature. As well as being vegetarian herself, she had introduced it to her dog Howler, an appropriately named mongrel of extremely indeterminate parentage that she'd acquired from the animal rescue agency. She was teaching him to be vegan. Howler didn't think much of the idea, if he thought at all (to say which in our anthropomorphic-based society seems like heresy), but seeing as the food came free (to him), and he didn't have to bother chasing and killing it, he put up with the idea—not that he got the chance to eat anything else.

Mary felt happy in the knowledge that she and her household weren't responsible for slaughtering off innocent animals merely in order to eat. As she went out of the front door—the talk this evening was to be on the plight of the Amazonian Indians now the rainforest was being cut down—she reflected once again on the stupidity and arrogance of man in trying to dominate the world and profit out of it. Live naturally, she thought, as she closed the door. If only everyone would.

*   *   *

Shortly after Mary left for her meeting the mouse had begun exploring yet another nook behind the laboratory walls when it found something most interesting—a long, grey, string-like object snaking invitingly across his path. The mouse sniffed at it, and then chewed it in a disinterested way. It had potential. The mouse nibbled a bit more: it was different to what it normally ate and seemed quite good to the taste. The sharp teeth bit deeper and deeper.

The mouse didn't know anything about what happened next. As it bit into the cable its teeth finally touched the live wire inside and with a blue flash and a slight fizzing noise, 250 volts of alternating current discharged itself up one canine, across the mouse's brain and down the other canine. The animal was thrown back, dead, from the wire, and two seconds later, all was as it had been before, except for the smell of burning flesh.

In the junction box high on the laboratory wall, the fuse on that circuit blew, cutting off the current and protecting against fire.

-2-

Sunday Morning

*T*hat Sunday morning at 10.20 a.m. the Reverend Martin Freeman ascended the pulpit of All Souls Church, Heston to deliver the sermon at Matins. A single man in his early thirties, he was likeable, but curiously uneasy and uncertain of himself. He was handsome in a boyish sort of way, tall and gangling, with straight fair hair, of which one strand seemed perpetually to be falling across his eyes.

His congregation was not large, and since he had come to the parish three years ago had dwindled progressively despite his enthusiastic approach. In practice, however, his enthusiasm was very unidirectional. Whatever text he preached from, he really had only one sermon: love your neighbour, turn the other cheek and, above all, disarm. A passionate CND supporter for most of his life, he was obviously enthused by his message, but sadly, he reflected, its impact on his parishioners seemed to be small. As he stood in the stone pulpit waiting for the end of the hymn he looked around at the twenty-five or so parishioners scattered in the pews of the draughty Victorian church and wondered why it was that preaching our Lord's gospel of peace seemed to produce such a poor response. Still, he thought, there was a very direct message that day from the Sermon on the Mount. 'Blessed are the peacemakers'—a godsend, literally, of a verse to preach on.

Martin waxed lyrical. He denounced wars and armies and reminded his congregation yet again that the world would be able to feed all its occupants if it gave up its spending on weaponry. Peace on earth was what our Saviour had come to tell us about and only when we learned that message could we have a truly happy society. Nation should speak peace unto nation. Swords should be beaten into ploughshares. What was more, we should start here in England, getting rid of our weapons even if no one else followed suit. Arms were no longer needed in a civilised world—an unhelpful complication to life, an unnecessary drain on national expenditure, a waste. All that was needed was love—the love expressed by Jesus who always turned the other cheek.

It was undoubtedly one of the best sermons that he had ever preached, yet afterwards, as he stood at the door bidding each member of the congregation good day and listening to their comments of 'Lovely sermon Vicar', 'Thank you', and so on, he had within him a nagging fear that very little of what he had said had gone home.

The service over, he closed the church door and walked back through the churchyard to the adjoining vicarage—like the church, a Victorian red-brick affair with tall windows and a steeply sloping roof. Once it had been a very grand building indeed, but the delapidation of age (it was a very long time since it had been painted) meant that it was now gloomy, draughty and dark. Although it was far too big for just one man, the Church Commissioners hadn't got round to doing anything about it, so Martin continued to live there on his own, often reflecting on the fact that although he didn't have an enemy in the world, there didn't seem to be many who would listen to him either.

*   *   *

After the mouse shorted out the cable, not much appeared to happen. As it had been a Friday evening, no one was there to notice anything different—not that there was much to notice. The cable had supplied one of the refrigerators, and when the power went off, it shuddered to a halt in the peculiar way that they do, and then stayed silent.

Inside the fridge were Petri dishes and conical flasks with growth support media for bacteria. Although bacteria are encouraged to grow into colonies so that they can be identified, there is a point beyond which further growth is unhelpful, so plates which have been 'developed' are transferred to the fridge to 'mark time' and stop growth, prior to being tested. One set of samples in the fridge was from a Peter Elliot who had died a week earlier in the hospital. He'd flown in two days before from Central Africa, and shortly after his arrival had become unwell with an odd set of symptoms which didn't seem to be related to any specific disease. He was obviously ill, and was put in a side cubicle on the ward. Embarrassingly for the hospital (and very embarrassingly for Peter who was only twenty-eight) he was found dead in bed next morning.

None of the doctors could say precisely why he'd died, so a postmortem was arranged. The pathologist immediately discovered that Elliot had died of a pneumonia-like disease because the lungs were soggy, like a sponge filled with water instead of air. He took samples, some of which were streaked on to Petri dishes, and others which were inoculated into nutrient broth: all were placed in incubation cubicles and kept at body heat for two days.

As the laboratory had been busy, there hadn't been time for the bacteriologist to do a full work-up on the specimens before the weekend. There was no urgency—after all, the poor chap was dead—so he put the samples in the fridge to keep them in suspended animation until they could be tested. The flask containing the broth went in as well. Often flasks are open-topped, with a pledget of cotton wool in the top to allow air in but keep airborne bacteria from falling in and contaminating the specimen. On this occasion, however, the culture medium was in a screw-top flask.

Because of lack of space in the lab, the refrigerator had been situated by the side of one of the incubation booths, so its cooling unit had to work harder to keep the internal temperature down. However, it was well within its capacity—so long as the electricity was switched on.

When the power went off that Friday evening the temperature inside the refrigerator began to rise slowly as warmth from the lab, and particularly from the adjacent incubation booth, seeped in. By midday on Saturday it was just under room temperature, and the bacteria were starting to multiply again.

Biochemical processes double their speed with every ten degrees centigrade increase in temperature. Whilst most bacteria multiply only sluggishly at 4°C, at room temperature they are active: at body temperature they will have quadrupled their rate of multiplication.

By the time that Martin delivered his sermon that Sunday, the temperature inside the fridge had crept up to 23°C and the bacteria in the Petri dishes and conical flasks were multiplying at an alarming rate. Eventually, as the fridge got warmer and warmer, the multiplication processes got completely out of hand.

＊   ＊   ＊

There is an old story about a Chinese man who had bravely saved the life of the Emperor's daughter. The Emperor, much pleased, said to the peasant that he could have anything he asked for in the whole of China—he was only to ask and it was to be given him. The peasant picked up a nearby chessboard and said to the Emperor, 'May it please your Majesty, would you arrange for one grain of rice to be put on the first square, two grains on the second square, four on the third, eight on the fourth, and continue in this way until all sixty-four squares have been used.'

'Don't you want anything more?' asked the Emperor. 'It seems very little for the life of my daughter.'

'Your Majesty, it will be quite sufficient,' replied the peasant.

The Emperor commanded his courtiers to carry out the peasant's wishes. Half an hour later they returned. 'Your Majesty,' they said, 'we cannot do it. By the time we reach the sixty-fourth square the amount of rice involved will be greater than China's entire harvest for the year.'

History does not record what the Emperor did or said at that moment, but the story is a graphic reminder that repeated doubling soon produces an amount which is overwhelmingly large.

So it was with the contents of the conical flask. At room temperature each bacterium split into two in about half an hour. Although there were only a few thousand bacteria at the start, by midday on Saturday there were millions swimming in the nutrient broth. By noon the next day the temperature had risen to 25°C, so not only were a large number of bacteria continuing to double every so often, but the rise in temperature had speeded up the biochemical processes, and the time taken for them to double had halved, thus multiplying the already staggering speed of increase in numbers of bacteria. By Sunday evening the bacteria had overgrown the Petri dishes: and the nutrient broth in the conical flask was packed with a mixture of organisms from Peter Elliot's lungs.

It wasn't a pure culture. There were the organisms that had killed Peter Elliot directly, but there were contaminants also— bacteria that produced a lot of carbon dioxide as a breakdown product. As the temperature rose and the numbers of bacteria grew exponentially, large quantities of carbon dioxide were given off.

By midnight the bacteria had used up all the nutrient in the broth, so they stopped growing—which was perhaps a good job as the conical flask was already under considerable pressure from the excess carbon dioxide.

The disaster was waiting to happen.

-3-

Monday, 6.00 a.m.

It was six o'clock on Monday morning and at AM-TV in Camden the day's broadcasting had just begun—a marathon stint of three and a half hours, the longest continuous TV programme anywhere in the world. The production company for the

Independent TV Network's morning programme, AM-TV had come into being after yet another shake-up within the volatile world of ITV franchises. With its acquisition of the original TV-am studios at Camden Lock, the wheel (and even the name) had turned full circle.

The AM-TV complex was situated in a large converted warehouse which nestled inside a crescent of the Grand Union Canal as it traversed North London. At six a.m. an outsider might have expected the whole building to be humming with energy as the programme went on air, but the vast open-plan production office was deserted, except for an occasional figure moving around purposefully. The only site of real activity was at the porter's desk where guests for the programme were being checked in. The whole place had the same sort of atmosphere as the City of London on a Sunday morning—it's there, it can do things, but it isn't quite ready to do them just yet.

The inactivity of the offices was definitely not mirrored within the studios; here there was an electric air of expectancy. The studios were tucked away on one side of the ground floor, almost as an afterthought—a strange state of affairs for an organisation whose existence is justified solely by their output. There are two studios: the main programme studio is just what a visitor might imagine—spacious, with lights strung overhead and four cameras shuttling around on the floor. The news studio is quite different—a tiny room, not much bigger than the average front lounge, with a single newsreader sitting in front of a remote controlled camera.

Each studio has its own gallery, a separate room where the producer and her assistants sit in semidarkness facing a bank of monitors. The production team sits in a line in front of them, at the production desk, from which they control cameras, sound, and videotapes. The size and complexity of the gallery bears an inverse relationship to the size of the studio it controls: the gallery to the main studio is less complex, as most of the activity it controls is live discussion interspersed with fairly long videotapes, but the news gallery is just the opposite: here the accent is on short videotaped reports, and the newsreader is only a small part of the whole operation, so the technical back-up in the news gallery needs to be much greater.

Although to the viewer the programmes seem relaxed and informal, they are timed to the last second. Their smoothness depends on the studio presenter's ability to wind up a conversation and lead effortlessly into the next subject whilst keeping strictly to time, and still asking sensible questions. The presenter's job is made more difficult because he has to accommodate changes of timing or running order, videotape failures, and all the other last-minute adjustments that can occur in a live current affairs programme. Each presenter has an earpiece through which he or she can hear instructions from the gallery: so, while he is interviewing the Secretary of State for Transport he may also be listening in his earpiece for timing checks, and receiving instructions from the producer on additional questions to ask. At the same time, the presenter has to keep up a relaxed, yet probing conversation with the studio guest: not an easy task!

If the organisation of the programme sounds complicated in the main studio, it's ten times worse in the news studio, because here short videotapes are shown every few moments and the linking between them has to be exact. There must be no embarrassing pauses while someone presses the 'Play' button. The videotapes are either started as instant roll or with a three-second start-up. Instant roll is easier in a fast-moving show such as the news but it can be clumsy, and occasionally goes wrong when the picture hasn't been started quickly enough and is seen for a moment, frozen, on-screen; so where there's not as much pressure, a three-second roll is preferable because it's more controllable. Here the videotape is started three seconds before it is needed, so is always rolling when it is switched in and can never appear to be frozen as it starts: the downside is that, once the VT has started rolling, the presenter has to introduce it for *precisely* three seconds more—not easy to do well, and certainly not at six o'clock in the morning.

Because of the complexity of these tasks, when the programme is on the air the atmosphere in the gallery is like that of an operating theatre, and the precision required is much the same. Like surgeons, television directors get accustomed to the task and go about it with concentration and determination rather than panic. On the other hand the adrenaline rises alarmingly when things go wrong, when cues are missed, when guests won't stop speaking, or when VTs don't come in on time.

That Monday, Jane Tomlins was the production assistant responsible for timing in the gallery attached to the main studio. A twenty-four-year-old blonde, she had all the poise and glamour normally associated with those who worked in front of the cameras. When told she worked at AM-TV, people invariably assumed she was one of the presenters—which Jane always took as a compliment, even though being a presenter couldn't be further from her mind. The personality traits needed to be a successful on-screen TV personality are often the exact opposite of those needed in the production department, and there is no envy of each other's job: presenters seldom want to do production, and the last thing members of the production team want is to go in front of the cameras. Jane was a production type, and she knew it.

Clipboard in hand, she took her place at the extreme left of the control desk. On her right was the director, in charge of the deployment of all the technical resources needed to create the programme; it was the director who called the camera shots, instructed the videotape operators and directed the rest of the gallery crew.

On the right of the director sat the vision mixer, controlling which camera or videotape was transmitted. Behind them all sat the executive producer, in overall charge of the programme.

On the studio floor, the presenter for the first hour of the show was Duncan Matthews, a strikingly handsome man in his mid-thirties with a tanned complexion and dark wavy hair. Jane could see him on the monitors, busily screwing his earpiece into place. She flipped the intercom switch. 'Can you hear me all right, Duncan?'

'Yes, fine.' Although Jane's voice travelled to Duncan by the 'private' line to the earpiece, Duncan's voice was relayed back to the gallery through the studio microphone clipped to his tie.

Jane switched her talkback to the floor manager's headset. 'Five minutes.'

The production team settled into place, running last-minute

checks on the equipment, making sure that their notes were in the correct running order, and checking that the whole studio and gallery was ready for off.

Down in the studio final adjustments were being made to seating positions and camera angles. Duncan wriggled into a more comfortable position. The last minutes before you're on are always the worst, he thought—once the programme's started it becomes easy, but the wait beforehand is exhausting.

'Two minutes, studio.'

The gallery monitor showing networked transmission was relaying the end of the ITN early morning news, followed by the national weather and the beginning of the adverts.

'One minute.' Jane thumbed through her papers in a final check of the running order. The clock in front of them ticked inexorably up to the hour.

'Thirty seconds. Ready to go studio. Good luck everyone,' said the director into her microphone. On her right the vision controller was looking intently at the monitors showing output from the four studio cameras: directly in front of him were three videotape monitors, all of them stopped on test cards showing that there were three seconds to go before the start of the VT proper. The first monitor held the legend 'Opening credits'.

'Ten seconds . . . '

'Nine . . . '

'Eight . . . '

'Seven . . . '

'Six . . . '

'Five . . . '

'Four . . . '

'Three . . . '

'Roll opening credits,' said the director, and the first VT sprang into life. The three-second clock faded to a blank screen.

'Two . . . '

'One . . . '

'Take control from network.'

As AM-TV began to supply the whole of the independent television network with programme output, the vision mixer switched output to the running videotape, and just as the second hand hit the top of the hour AM-TV's familiar opening credits appeared simultaneously on the first VT monitor, the programme output monitor, and network transmission monitor.

'Ten seconds to VT out,' said Jane.

'Ten seconds,' repeated the floor manager down in the studio. 'Studio silence.'

Duncan waited, staring fixedly at camera one. 'VT coming out in five,' said Jane in his ear, 'four, three, two, one . . . '— Duncan began to smile at the camera—' . . . *out.*'

'Camera one,' said the director in the gallery. The video controller hit a button on his section of the production desk, and Duncan's face appeared simultaneously on three of the gallery monitors.

'Good morning to you on this wet and windy October day,' said Duncan briskly, reading off the autocue which was scrolling up in front of him. 'In today's programme we'll be looking at why cabbages may not be the health food you once thought they were; and in the aftermath of the fatal shooting during Friday's bank raid in Manchester, we'll be asking whether it's now time for the police to be armed. But first we go to Luton Airport where . . .'

'Roll VT 2,' said the producer.

'Three seconds to VT,' said Jane into Duncan's earpiece.

' . . . travelling to the continent has been made easier overnight . . .'

'Two . . .'

' . . . thanks to a new way of checking in.'

'One . . .'

'Alan Humphries investigates.'

'Out.'

The vision mixer switched to the videotape, and the pre-recorded report appeared on three of the monitors. As the VT began to feed through the atmosphere in both studio and gallery relaxed.

'Two minutes, studio,' said Jane into her microphone, watching the monitors as the first guest settled himself down in the guest's chair: Tristram Powell, AM-TV's City correspondent.

-4-

A few miles away, Paul Ignatius Greatorex woke to the electronic bleep of his alarm clock, rolled over sleepily, turned on the TV to catch AM-TV's City report, and then blearily turned over again whilst deciding whether he was really trying to wake up or stay asleep. Waking up gradually won. He rolled out of bed, pulled on a blue silk dressing gown and sleepily went to the kitchen to make breakfast. Jane of course had been up long before him, and he thought briefly of her, working away, as the sound of Duncan's voice introducing another videotaped report drifted across from the TV in the bedroom. He put some bread in the toaster and yawned again.

Paul Greatorex's mother had had many social pretensions and not much IQ. She had of course married into the Greatorex family—an old and noble line of which her husband had been a very small scion indeed. This had not deterred her. Determined to inject a touch of elegance into her very ordinary middle-class '60s surroundings she had decided to give Paul an upper-class middle name: at least, that is the more charitable way of looking at things. The other is to assume that she named him during the three-day post-baby blues period.

Paul was baptised of course: C. of E., very socialite high church—the only time Paul's mother had been inside one since her wedding three years earlier. It was only *after* the christening when everything was fixed and—like the laws of the Medes and the Persians—immutable, that it suddenly dawned on her what she'd done. No more would there be subtle thoughts of Ignatius Loyola, no hints of assumed greatness, sensitivity or subtlety. There was a greater (or lesser, depending on how you looked at it) item of relevance that she had inadvertently bestowed upon her infant son. Paul Ignatius Greatorex—initials P. I. G.

Thus, literally from his cradle, her son's destiny was mapped out—his nickname; the way others would refer to him; and how he would see himself. Short of bequeathing him congenital syphilis, Paul's mother couldn't have done a better job in giving him a bad start in life. P. I. G. It was to haunt him. People really do tend to behave according to their name, whether it is descriptive or an attribute, and Paul was no different.

He lived up to his name—his nickname, rather—to the full: pig by name, and a swine by nature. Yet in the odd way in which real badness tends to spread only into certain areas of a person's life, Piggy Greatorex was a swine in business only: otherwise he was charming. It so often happens. The Kray Brothers, whose empire of crime terrified the East End for years, were renowned for their impeccable manners and their kindnesses to family and friends.

This odd dichotomy was present to the full in Paul Ignatius Greatorex: a charmer with a killer instinct. Educated at public school (where else would his mother send him?), he developed all the social graces, the speech, the mannerisms and the body language of a cultured man. But the ragging and the teasing and the bullying produced another side to his nature. He couldn't get away from his name, so he became it: a pig, capable of doing his best friend in, if he could profit from it. The rest of his personality developed normally; paradoxically, the more he honed his politeness and sweetness, the more it helped his alter ego. The trouble was that nobody really *believed* that he had a killer instinct—he was just too nice: and so Paul Greatorex turned into the archetypal conman—handsome, suave and sophisticated on the surface, but a self-interested cynical killer underneath. Not, you understand, a physical killer—that would be quite outside his mores. Paul was just a business killer. His morality was quite simple: I shall survive—to hell with anyone else.

By the time he reached the sixth form the taunts, the teasing and the physical bullying had stopped—but he was still referred to by all and sundry as 'Piggy' or 'The Pig', depending on whether you were talking to him or behind his back. Do what he might the name never left him, so when he left to go to university it was with a mind full of assumptions about himself. They were quite simple: he carried them around like personalised sweatshirts, in layers. The first layer read, 'Gee, I'm great, I'm a Wow in society.' The next said, 'Actually I'm not, everybody points at me, laughs at me and doesn't really like me.' The third sweatshirt read, 'But I don't care.' The fourth layer said, 'Yes I do, deeply.' The fifth quite simply said, ' . . . . the lot of them.' But the most interesting was the next, the deepest, the one closest to Paul's personality, which

said, 'I'm so frail, so vulnerable, that I'll do anything—*anything*—
to avoid revealing the depth of my frailty.' This last message was
so deep in him that it was known only to his subconscious. It was
too dangerous an idea even to let his conscious mind know about.

These concepts about himself were, at heart, what Paul
Ignatius Greatorex took with him from childhood into the world:
and all because of his mother and *that name*—a simple enough
thing, but with unexpectedly profound consequences.

With a personality like Paul's it was only natural that
he would start up a business before he'd left school. By the time
he'd left university (Oxford, of course) he'd got six of them, and
an income of £50,000 a year. There was only one occupation for
a man like Paul—the City: he homed in on it like a guided
missile, to the place where his killer instinct could be used to the
benefit of mankind—or at least, of his employers and himself.
He revelled in it. He rejoiced in it. He joined one of the leading
firms of stockbrokers. Four years later he had a salary of
£200,000 and was vying for a place on the board.

With a personality like his, whatever he wanted he got—
things just seemed to happen that way for him. He lived (of
course) in Docklands, in an elegant converted warehouse that
overlooked the Thames and from whose windows he could see
Tower Bridge in the distance. There was the obligatory red
Porsche in the basement car park—number plate *PIG 1*. (By this
time he didn't care about his name and even revelled in it.) He'd
acquired the plate from a gentleman farmer whom he'd
bankrupted in a series of slightly near-the-knuckle deals. *PIG 1*
had originally been attached to the farmer's modest saloon car,
which Paul then magnanimously bought off him for somewhat
less than it was worth. He promptly sold the car for a lot more
money, and kept the number-plate for himself.

It seemed only natural that he should acquire the most
glamorous of all his acquaintances as his companion. Jane
Tomlins suited him fine—stunning looks, and intelligence to
boot: great in bed and a good cook too. What more could he
want? Never mind that she was engaged, he soon saw her fiancé
off. Three months afterwards she'd moved in with him, and that
had been two years ago.

In short, the world was fine for Paul Ignatius Greatorex: a

thought which had not escaped him as he tidied their breakfast
things into the dishwasher. He had a surprise for Jane tonight, too.
He'd tell her when she rang him at the office after the programme.

*   *   *

Glass is an interesting substance, with odd properties, one of
which is its tendency to shatter under external stress. As it cools,
internal stresses are sealed into its structure, and outside forces
which by chance combine with these hidden fault lines can
produce sudden catastrophic failure.

Laboratory flasks are no exception to this rule. The one containing the broth from Peter Elliot's lung sample, like all other
laboratory glassware, had its own set of in-built stress areas.
Normally this would not have been a problem—except that the
flask was not intended to withstand much internal pressure and
this one was under a lot of it. The build-up of carbon dioxide
released by the bacteria had raised the internal pressure in the
flask considerably. So far it had withstood the pressure inside it,
but only just: it was teetering on the brink of failure.

At nine o'clock on Monday morning Sean McConnell, one
of the lab technicians, entered the lab, suitably attired in a full
protective suit. All the staff were accustomed to dealing with
very infectious samples and they always took proper precautions
like this. It was about ten minutes before Sean noticed there was
something wrong, but eventually it dawned on him that the
refrigerator's working lights were no longer on. I bet that's
ruined a few samples, he thought, pulling open the door to
investigate and rocking the fridge slightly in the process.

For the flask the extra nudge was the last straw. With an
unimportant-sounding 'phut' it disintegrated, its contents
foaming with the release of pressure, spraying a fine mist of
nutrient broth and bacteria over the inside of the refrigerator, into
the air and over Sean.

He swore, knowing just how long it would take him to clean
up the refrigerator and its entire contents. He wasn't worried for
himself, because the protective suit was impervious to bacterial
contamination—after all, that was why it was worn.

Bending down, he patiently began to clear up the mess of
pieces of glass and the nutrient broth which had spilled into

everything and, cursing his bad fortune on what was always the busiest day of the week, set about putting things back to normal.

High above him in the roof the fans cut in, sucking air from the laboratory and through the filters which removed any escaped bacteria. The system was designed to cope with exactly this sort of situation, wafting infectious agents away from the laboratory workers and out into the ducts, to be arrested by the filters.

Bob Harris' makeshift mending of filter number six was about to have an effect out of proportion to its significance. It's a pity that Bob hadn't learned the elementary laws of physics. Had he known them, he wouldn't have tried to mend the filter in the way he did. Unfortunately, just because he didn't know the laws didn't mean that they had somehow ceased to operate. One of them states that the greatest flow occurs at the point of least resistance: short-circuit the power supply, and the rest of the lights dim. Thus it was with the air filtering system. At the point where Bob Harris had performed his makeshift repair the join held for all of two seconds, then gave way, causing a half-centimetre gap to open up, rapidly widening as more air rushed through. Although the gap was small in comparison with the total surface area of all the filters, most of the air from the inside of the lab flowed straight through the hole without any restriction, and out into the car park beyond, where the director of the laboratory, Sir Richard Miles, was just locking up his Volvo estate.

-5-

Wednesday Morning, 9.30 a.m.

Although the offices at AM-TV are quiet when the programme is being transmitted, the place becomes a hive of activity once normal office hours start. There are programmes to plan, staff to be trained, videotaped reports to be edited, news items to follow up and specialist speakers to be organised for future programmes.

As usual, Wednesday's daily news briefing started at 9.30 a.m. Roland Keating, the news editor, was in charge as always. A likeable man in his mid-forties, with tufts of thinning fair hair on either side of his balding head, and a prominent nose, he had an easygoing, slightly pessimistic manner which belied the calculating brain within.

All newsroom journalists not already out on assignments were present at the meeting. Although major news items can break at any time, many occur in a fairly predictable way during the day—in the courts, in Parliament, in the City. Roland assigned the day's routine stories to reporters with particular specialist interests and then they came on to the other items that had come in to the news desk.

'*Sir Richard Miles, director of Southill Laboratory, found dead in car,*' read out Roland from his VDU. 'I wonder what that's about? Amanda, would you follow that up?'

Amanda Baker nodded. Aged twenty-two, and of medium build, she would have been quite pretty were it not for her habit of wearing thick spectacles which were quite unsuited to her face, and the tousled mane of shoulder-length mousy hair that always looked like the 'before' picture in the advert for conditioner for uncontrollable hair. She was one of the newer journalists, keen to prove herself, and with all the drive and idealism that those in their first job so often possess. Just routine work, she thought—a call to the police; establish where the body was found; were there any suspicious circumstances? and so on. Probably nothing much in it, except for his position as head of the laboratory. Not much of a story there.

'Wasn't Sir Richard the man involved in the cover-up at Southill a couple of years ago?' chipped in Hywel Davies. Unlike Amanda, whose face had never been seen on screen, Hywel was well-known. A stocky, dark-haired man of forty-five, he had a reputation for ferreting out information that others were reluctant to part with. He had a glittering track record—it was he who had managed to find out who had really planted the Piccadilly bomb. It was Hywel who had nosed out the insider dealing that led to the resignation of the Chairman of the CamCop Corporation and his subsequent jailing for seven years for fraud. Hywel had an impressive record and a nose for suspicious circumstances that was the envy of many a cub reporter like Amanda.

Originally he'd been with the BBC, but had been poached by AM-TV for what was reputed to be a quite extortionate sum. Still, everyone thought he was worth it: whenever he got onto a major story the viewing figures always rose. As a result the management at AM-TV was very happy to pay even the salary Hywel demanded.

What the directors didn't know—and what perhaps they were glad not to have known—was that the way that Hywel conducted his investigations was not always as straightforward as it appeared from his final filmed reports. To be blunt, Hywel had absolutely no qualms about who he interviewed, how he did it or what trouble he caused, so long as the results came. He never showed any of this on screen—just the results, when it seemed that he was all sweetness and light in encouraging the interviewee to talk.

Hywel always worked with the same camera, sound and editing team who were sworn to secrecy, and never *ever* showed his unedited interview tapes to anyone else. The only clue that Hywel might not be in the ordinary run of reporters was that his expense account was just a little large. But Hywel's reputation was so great and he obviously did such good work in ferreting out things that others quite wrongly wanted to try to cover up, that nobody felt they could question him about it.

The truth was that Hywel used his expense account, if necessary, to pay 'expenses' to those who 'chose' to help him— which is how he was able to get much of the more delicate information that had come his way.

He didn't have any conscience about all this—after all, he was in pursuit of those who were blatantly doing wrong, so greasing a few palms in order to make the mouth they were attached to talk seemed to be a very moral thing to do. Anyway, Hywel was delighted with the results, the news editor was delighted with the results, the board of AM-TV were delighted with the results, the viewing figures went up and Hywel's work was constantly being referred to in the papers and even—at times—in Parliament.

There was another side to Hywel too—an absolute hatred and mistrust of the Establishment and anything connected with it, especially those who used the Establishment to cover up their misdeeds.

He repeated the question. 'Wasn't Sir Richard the man in charge at Southill at the time of that affair a couple of years ago?'

'Come to think of it, yes, I think he was,' replied Roland.

'What affair?' asked Amanda, ears pricking up.

'Southill was probably involved in germ warfare research,' said Hywel. 'It's quite a secure establishment, and it's kitted out to do a lot of unpleasant bacteriological work—rather like Porton Down, but not quite so high-powered. Two years ago we received information that Southill was a front for other work that wasn't directly hospital . . .'

'That's all, no real facts,' said Roland blandly to Amanda, 'just suspicions. Hywel takes these things too seriously. It all blew over.'

'Worth remembering though,' said Hywel. 'No smoke without fire, you know. What's next on the agenda?'

They discussed the rest of the news leads. Roland detailed off assistants to chase up stories still in their infancy, and assigned reporters to more developed leads. The production desk would independently be responsible for sending technical crews—cameraman and sound-man—to accompany each reporter on his travels.

After the meeting Amanda returned to her desk and dialled the police station in Barnes, where Sir Richard's body had been found. A few minutes later she went back to Roland. 'I think there may be something in this Sir Richard Miles affair.'

'Why's that?'

'The police are treating it as suspicious. Apparently they've got the full forensic works down there.'

'Better send a reporter and a crew,' said Roland. He picked up the phone. 'Hywel? You may be right yet again. Sir Richard Miles—the police are treating his death as suspicious and they've got the forensic squad down there at the moment. I think this may be one for you. Marshall Street in Barnes.'

'OK,' said Hywel, 'tell my crew to meet me there.'

Half an hour later, waving their police accreditation passes, Hywel and his crew were allowed inside the police barriers cordoning off the area. While Hywel went off asking questions, his crew started taking general pictures of the scene—establishing shots, as they are called—to set the scene for the viewer.

Sir Richard's car stood on its own on the levelled building site, surrounded by blue and white tapes with '*POLICE—DON'T CROSS*' written on. Even from a distance the body of Sir Richard could be seen slumped in the driving seat, cosmetically covered with a cloth, whilst white-suited forensic officers carried out a detailed examination of the car and the surrounding area. It was a miserable morning and the white Volvo stood out forlornly against the bleak background of the rubble-strewn wasteland.

The cameraman, Justin, set up a couple more shots then turned round as Hywel came back with a uniformed policeman. 'This is Sergeant Bennett, the officer in charge. He'll give us an interview now. Can we do it here with the car in the background?'

'That should be fine,' said Justin and set up his tripod appropriately.

'Ever been interviewed for TV before?' asked Hywel disarmingly, putting the policeman at his ease.

'Me? No. Mind you, there's a first time for everything.'

'OK,' said Hywel. 'I'm sure you'll be fine. Don't talk to the camera, talk to me because it'll look better when we edit the tapes. All I want you to do is give me a brief account of what you've found. OK?'

He turned to Justin. 'Ready?'

'OK, when you are.'

Hywel turned full face to the camera and began his report.

'Behind me you can see the body of Sir Richard Miles slumped in the driving seat of his car. Sir Richard was the director at Southill, one of the top bacteriological laboratories in London.' He turned to the policeman. 'Sergeant Bennett. I believe you're treating this death as suspicious?'

'Yes,' said the policeman rather nervously, 'one of our squad cars was proceeding down Marshall Street when they noticed the presence of a suspicious vehicle.'

Why, thought Hywel, do policemen always talk as though they're reading a report to a court?

'When was this?'

'It was about five-thirty this morning when the patrol noticed the car.' That's better, thought Hywel: I'll use that instead of his first sentence.

'What made them suspicious?'

'It had its lights full on and the engine was going. When they passed it again twenty minutes later it hadn't moved and the headlights were still on, so they went to investigate.'

'What did they find?'

'Sir Richard was slumped over the driving column, obviously dead. The officers felt that the circumstances were suspicious enough to call in the forensic unit.'

Hywel turned round to look at the white-coated figures moving around in the distance and then turned back to face the camera. 'And you can see the forensic unit doing their job at this very moment. Sir Richard was due back home at 9 o'clock last night, but it was not until midnight that the alarm was raised, and it won't be until a postmortem is carried out this afternoon that we will know the precise cause of death. This is Hywel Davies, AM-TV, Barnes.'

Hywel turned round to Sergeant Bennett. 'Thank you very much indeed. You don't usually call in forensics so quickly do you?'

'No, but there were special circumstances in this case.'

'Really? What?'

Sergeant Bennett looked uncomfortable.

'Off the record, what do you think has happened?'

'We don't really know,' said the policeman, relaxing, relieved that the interview was over. 'It looks very suspicious. There's a lot of blood around.'

'You didn't say anything about blood before.'

'It's not for general release yet.'

'Where was the blood?'

'Spattered all over the dashboard.'

'Any sign of a wound?'

'No, that's what we don't understand. It might be someone else's blood, so there might have been a struggle.'

'Were there any signs of one?'

'Not that we're aware of. From the way Sir Richard was slumped in his seat it looks as though he just collapsed there. On the other hand it does look very suspicious with all that blood around.'

'Yes it does, doesn't it?' said Hywel smoothly, looking very concerned. 'Murder?'

'We can't be sure of anything until the postmortem.'

'When will you have any more information?'

'Not until we have the postmortem results. I don't think there's anything more I can usefully tell you.' Sergeant Bennett was uncomfortably aware that he'd probably said far too much already.

'Well, thank you again—you've been most helpful.' Sergeant Bennett went back towards the Volvo. Hywel turned round to his cameraman. 'You did catch that last bit, didn't you?'

Justin, busy dismantling the equipment, grinned up at him. 'You know us. We always keep the camera rolling after the interview's finished. That's when you get all the best information.'

'Fine,' said Hywel. 'Just checking.'

-6-

Wednesday, 2.00 p.m.

*L*eighton Buzzard Magistrates' Court is a bleak brick edifice with that Spartan, dusty, behind-the-times ambience of so many minor public buildings. Although the popular image of a courtroom is a place filled with bustle, high drama and lots of people, in reality most players act out their parts on a very empty stage indeed, watched over by no more than a relative or two, plus a single representative of the local press.

It was like that today. The eight people involved in the trial looked lost, out of proportion in the bare expanse of the courtroom. Hardly the stuff of films, but there was drama enough for one of the players, Detective Sergeant Peter Abrahams, who was being tried on a charge of aiding and abetting drunk driving and failing to stop at the scene of an accident. A small man with hangdog brown eyes and bushy black hair, he wasn't on trial for his life as much as for his livelihood, for, unlike most defendants, if he were found guilty he would not only be punished for the offence itself, but would almost certainly be dismissed from the force, and his life's efforts would disappear in an afternoon. He didn't relish the prospect. He enjoyed being a detective; and anyway, he had a young family to keep.

That he had got drunk was unquestioned. Whether he deserved to be punished for any offence at all was a completely different matter.

'All rise,' intoned the usher as the three magistrates entered. The magistrates bowed to the solicitors and the solicitors bowed to the magistrates. Then they all sat down again, eight little peas clustered at one end of a very large pod.

After the preliminaries and the pleas of not guilty, the Crown solicitor rose. 'May it please the Court: the Crown intends to show that Detective Sergeant Abrahams became drunk whilst on duty, and then travelled as a passenger in a car driven by Constable Andrew Illingworth. The car ran into the back of a van, but failed to stop at the scene of the accident. Constable Illingworth only reported the accident two hours later, and has already admitted a charge of driving while unfit through drink, failing to stop at the scene of an accident, and failing to report an accident.

'The Crown intends to show that as both policemen were still on duty, Detective Sergeant Abrahams, being the senior officer, was in command and is therefore guilty of aiding and abetting drunk driving.

'I will call the first witness . . .'

The sorry tale unfolded. Together with another four policemen Abrahams and Illingworth had driven to a routine meeting with officers of the police force in the adjoining county. They had finished the meeting earlier than expected, so on the way back they dropped in at a pub for a drink and a meal. Sergeant Abrahams and Constable Illingworth had a long-standing agreement whereby when they went to a pub, if one drank, the other drove. Sergeant Abrahams told the court that it was Constable Illingworth's turn to drive, that Illingworth knew this and therefore should not have had too much to drink. In the event however, both of them consumed alcohol with their meal, and then continued on their way home, with Constable Illingworth at the wheel. Sergeant Abrahams was in the passenger seat, and eventually fell asleep.

Halfway home Constable Illingworth ran into the back of a van on a motorway slip road, but didn't stop to exchange names with the other driver, and it was only after a full two hours had elapsed that he eventually reported the accident.

Illingworth was charged with driving while under the influence of alcohol, with failing to stop at the scene of an accident, and with careless driving. He had already pleaded guilty to all three charges and was awaiting sentence.

The court had now to consider Sergeant Abraham's involvement in the incident. He had been charged with aiding and abetting drunk driving, and with failing to stop at the scene of an accident.

Sergeant Abraham's GP, James McFarlane, was called to the witness box and recounted how Sergeant Abrahams had suffered severe concussion in the accident: he had no recollection of the accident itself and had shown typical signs of concussion for ten days afterwards. It was Dr McFarlane's opinion that Abrahams had been knocked out by the collision, had suffered severe concussion, and as a result could not have been responsible for his actions—or lack of them—immediately after the collision.

After conferring, the magistrates agreed that the charge of failing to stop at the scene of an accident should be dropped in view of the medical evidence.

So far so good, thought Peter—now comes the tricky bit. Under cross-examination he admitted that he *had* been drinking on duty—but in fairness, pointed out that they had all completed their tasks for the day, and were all in plain clothes. He accepted that he had drunk too much to drive a vehicle, but then it was Constable Illingworth's turn to drive, while he—Abrahams—had taken the passenger seat. He deeply regretted the fact that he had got drunk on duty, but strenuously denied that he was in charge of the car, not being the driver. And anyway, he was asleep.

Then the legal arguments began. The Crown pressed its case. Peter Abrahams, being the senior officer, was in law in charge of the car even though he was in the passenger seat and asleep at the time. As the senior officer he should have prevented his junior from taking control of the wheel, knowing him to be over the limit—even though Sergeant Abrahams swore that he didn't know that Constable Illingworth had drunk too much to drive.

The magistrates asked for legal guidance. The clerk to the justices looked up the precedents. 'Your Worships, in 1974 in *Carter* v. *Richardson*, it was held that the supervisor of a learner driver who was drunk was himself guilty of aiding and abetting drunken driving. Much the same thing was held to be true in 1969 in *Crampton* v. *Fish*.'

The defending solicitor, David Kennedy, rose. 'Your Worships, you have heard the evidence. Sergeant Abrahams has admitted that he became drunk on duty, but it does seem inappropriate to describe him as being on duty when he was in plain clothes, and he had already completed his duties for that day. Additionally, he didn't know that Constable Illingworth would go against their prearranged agreement, and have too much to drink. In any case, at the time of the accident Sergeant Abrahams was asleep. How can a man who is asleep be in charge of a motor vehicle? I invite the court to find the defendant not guilty.'

As the three magistrates retired to consider their verdict, Peter Abrahams went outside with his solicitor, nervously lighting a cigarette in the process.

'What do you think the verdict's going to be?' he asked.

'I really don't know. I don't like the look of the magistrate on the right. She always managed to look incredulous whenever there was something in your favour.'

'I still can't believe I'm being charged with this. I mean, I was asleep—I didn't even know there had been an accident until I woke up the next day. How could I possibly have been in control? They can't find me guilty. It wouldn't be fair.'

Dr McFarlane, who had stayed behind to hear the result, nodded in agreement. 'You really were an idiot to drink on duty—we all agree on that—but prosecuting you for being in charge of a vehicle when you're asleep does seem totally unjust.'

'I'm afraid that the law has nothing to do with justice,' replied the solicitor. 'It's just a game, like chess, but played with different rules. It's the system that's the problem. Parliament makes laws, which they *intend* to be just, but whenever the courts apply these laws they interpret them, and set precedents, and then these precedents have to be obeyed as if they were part of the

original law. It's quite possible to end up with the courts
interpreting the law in completely the opposite direction from the
intentions of those who devised the law in the first place. All you
need is a judge who interprets the law slightly oddly, then
subsequent magistrates are bound by his judgement: so a
potentially good law can get turned completely on its head.'

Dr McFarlane pricked up his ears. 'So how can we be
certain what the law says?'

'We can't always,' replied Kennedy. 'Especially where no
one's tested the law yet, and there aren't any precedents.'

'So there are areas where we don't even *know* that the law
says?'

Kennedy nodded his agreement.

'So *no one* knows what the law says on these occasions?'

'That's right.'

'But I thought that judges always said that "Ignorance of the
law is no excuse." '

'Yes.'

'So where the law hasn't been tested out, and no one knows
what the law is, you've still got obey it anyway?'

'You've got it. *And* you'll get punished if you get it wrong.'

Dr McFarlane cast his eyes to the ceiling, then slowly shook
his head, lost for words.

Peter sucked anxiously at his cigarette. The wait seemed
like an eternity. 'It still seems all wrong. I mean . . . if *I'm*
guilty, what about all those who make and sell alcohol? Aren't
they guilty of aiding and abetting drunk driving too? Why pick
on me?'

'It's not your fault. As I said, it's a game. It's nothing to do
with justice.' Peter wandered disconsolately towards the door,
looked out into the real world outside and shook his head,
blowing smoke out through his nostrils at the same time.

'What do you think the result will be?' whispered Dr
McFarlane in David Kennedy's ear.

'Not good. The precedents are all wrong. The court is
almost certain to abide by them.'

'But it would be a technical offence, wouldn't it? Won't they
give him an absolute discharge, or a token fine, seeing as there
was no malice involved? After all, it is a very fine point of law.'

'I hope so,' said Kennedy, 'but it doesn't always work that way.' He looked through the doorway, into the courtroom. 'We'd better go in. The magistrates are coming back.'

Peter threw his cigarette on the floor and ground his heel on it, then followed his solicitor back in.

'The defendant will rise,' intoned the clerk.

The senior of the three magistrates spoke. 'Peter Radcliffe Abrahams, we find you guilty of aiding and abetting drunk driving. You will be disqualified from driving for a year and be fined £300.'

And you'll lose your livelihood as well, thought David Kennedy. The police won't have you back, not now.

'All rise,' commanded the clerk.

As the magistrates retired Peter wandered out of the court-room in a daze, muttering, 'I'm asleep in a car and then I'm con-cussed. I don't know anything about the accident. I was asleep, and I wasn't even driving, yet they say I'm guilty of aiding and abetting a drunk driver. And black is white, and white is black, and white is black and black is white . . .' He kicked viciously at the cigarette end he'd squashed into the ground on the way in. As he walked out of the lobby area the reporter from the local newspaper pushed past him, mentally drafting her report.

He walked down the steps of the courtroom, dazzled by the unfamiliar sunlight outside, dazed by the unreal world he'd just left. After a judgement based on a fine point of law, not only had he been found guilty, but he'd also lost his job. Not only had he been fined, he'd also been stopped from driving, and was therefore prevented from getting most of the jobs open to ex-policemen, such as security work. Moreover, the press reports were about to make him an object of local ridicule, to boot.

Peter Abrahams' ignominy was complete.

*   *   *

The court heard several more cases that day. Among them was Nigel Bannister who, whilst drunk, had attacked a doctor's receptionist, breaking her nose and cheekbone and blacking her eye. As a result she'd been off work for three weeks. He was fined £90, and given a six-month suspended jail sentence. He walked out of the court a free man, dropped into the pub next

door, and promptly got drunk again. He would pay the fine
easily out of next week's wages.

-7-

Wednesday Afternoon

*I*t was 4.00 p.m. when the results of the postmortem were
released. Amanda came running back from the telephone into
Roland's office. Hywel was there also, having just finished
editing a completely separate item.

'I thought you'd like to see this,' said Amanda.

'What is it?' said Hywel, lifting his feet off the desk.

'The first postmortem results on Sir Richard.'

'What did they show?' asked Roland, looking up from a file
he was reading.

'They don't know,' said Amanda.

'What do you mean, *they don't know*?' expostulated Hywel,
suddenly very alert.

'Just that—they don't know what happened. No signs of
injury: and nothing else except that the lungs were filled with
fluid and looked infected. They said they thought it was
probably something like pneumonia—but evidently they're not
really sure what they're dealing with. They've still got to do
some tests on samples they've taken.'

'How did the blood get on the dashboard then?'

'They said either from the back of the throat or the lungs . . .'

Hywel turned round to Roland. 'Are you thinking what I'm
thinking?'

There was a pause.

'You're thinking there's a cover-up, aren't you?' said Roland,
slightly irritated. 'Not everything's a cover-up, you know.'

'Well, it had just crossed my mind. *"Director of high
powered bacteriological lab found dead of unknown cause."*
Doesn't sound right, somehow.'

'What *did* happen in the affair two years ago?' asked Amanda.

'There were reports that Southill was involved in genetic manipulation related to bacteriological warfare,' replied Hywel.

'Just a suspicion,' said Roland, ever cautious. 'Nothing was ever proved. It caused a stink in the surrounding area because it's densely populated, and nobody wanted a rogue virus let out into the community. Hywel made some enquiries, and afterwards a couple of MPs asked questions in Parliament, but no one would admit to anything. It was all covered by the Official Secrets Act, so we didn't get very far. If I remember correctly, we got the original information from a technician who'd just been dismissed, so it's possible that he was trying to set the management up for sacking him.'

'But what if he *was* right, and it's still continuing?' said Amanda. 'What if Southill is still connected with bacteriological warfare?'

'They'll never admit it voluntarily, that's for sure,' said Roland. He turned to Hywel. 'I think it's time to do a little investigating—don't you?'

*   *   *

The crew pulled up outside Sir Richard's house in Richmond. It was a prosperous-looking building, set back from the road, with a gravelled drive. A tearful woman of about fifty-two answered the door.

'Lady Miles?'

'Yes.'

'I'm sorry to trouble you at this time. I'm Hywel Davies.'

'I know.'

'I'd like to talk with you about your husband's death,' said Hywel, putting his foot inconspicuously against the side of the door, just in case.

'Why? What business is it of yours?'

'Your husband was a very important person,' said Hywel in his most sympathetic manner. 'He was a gifted researcher, wasn't he? It would be nice to say something about his life and work, don't you think? Could we come in and just do a short interview? It will only be a few moments, I promise you.'

'All right.' Her voice showed no enthusiasm. She ushered them into the sitting room.

'Can we film here?'

'If you want.'

They set up quickly. Justin did a couple of establishing shots of them talking together, then repositioned his camera to concentrate on Lady Miles alone.

'Can you tell us a little bit about your husband and the work he did?'

'Richard read medicine at Cambridge in the mid-fifties. He soon specialised in bacteriology, and started research almost as soon as he'd qualified.'

'He made quite a name for himself, didn't he? Can you tell us about it?'

'He was one of the first to work on vaccines against meningitis. Not really the sort of thing that hits the headlines: in the early days it was really more academic—establishing the structure of the meningitis bacterium. I worked with him in the early years—that's how I got to know him. Together we worked out how to produce a vaccine.'

'For which he was eventually knighted?'

'That's right. That was in 1982.'

'And after that he started working at Southill?'

'Yes, he went there in 1983, I think.'

'What sort of research was he doing there?'

'Mainly working for the hospital.'

'You say mainly. What else was he doing?'

'Well . . .'

'Government work?'

'A little.'

'Associated with Porton Down?'

'How did you . . .?' Then, composing herself, she stopped, and with an effort pulled herself together. 'I really can't talk any more about this. I think the interview has to end here.'

'Oh, please go on,' said Hywel, gently. 'I don't want to intrude. Just a few more things about your husband, if you will. What happened last night?'

'He was due home at nine o'clock. He'd been out to a presentation at the Royal Society of Medicine, and when he didn't get back by midnight I got a bit concerned and rang them, but they said he'd left at half past eight. So then I got really worried and rang the police. And then . . . they found him . . .'

'Yes, I understand,' said Hywel. 'I am so sorry.' He brightened up slightly. 'What was he working on just before his death?'

'Nothing special, just routine work for the hospital.'

'There weren't any accidents?'

'What do you mean, accidents?'

'Well, no accidents in the lab, no spillages, nothing like that?'

'Not that he mentioned. Why?'

'Well, the pathologists don't know why he died. I just wondered whether there had been an accident at the lab and that he might have got infected as a result of his work?'

Lady Miles looked taken aback. 'No, no, he didn't mention any accidents to me.'

'Was he still working with Porton Down?'

'I've told you that I'm not going to answer any questions about that,' she said angrily.

'But don't you think it's important?' said Hywel. 'After all, if he was still working in conjunction with Porton Down and if one of the organisms he was working with had got out it could be very dangerous—important for us all to know about, don't you think?'

'No, no,' she said, 'he's not working with Porton Down. Not now.'

'So he was working with Porton Down before?' replied Hywel, thinking gleefully, 'Got her!'

'Oh . . . yes . . . no . . . I really can't say. You really will have to go.' She looked weary and despondent. 'I'm sorry, I can't give you any more interviewing time.'

Hywel doggedly continued. 'But surely this is important? We have a man who is not supposed to be involved with bacteriological warfare, yet now you say that he was. Just what is going on in that lab, Lady Miles?'

She got up, furious. 'How dare you come into my house at a time like this and ask me questions of this nature? Get out.'

'I'm sorry, Lady Miles, I'm only doing my job. In any case the questions will still remain even if you won't answer them. Why don't you sit down and let us have the answers that we

need? If everything is all right then you have nothing to be afraid
of; and if anything is wrong then we *all* need to know about it—
including you. You don't want to know that the cause of your
husband's death has been subjected to a cover-up, do you?'

Lady Miles subsided into her chair. Normally she would
have ended the interview there and then, but the disorientation and
confusion engendered by the death of her husband had left her
drained and vulnerable. 'I don't know what he was working on.'

'But he was working with Porton Down?'

'Yes, but not recently. It finished about two years ago when
all those questions were asked.' The light dawned. 'It was you
who was asking all the questions too. I remember now. At the
time he *was* doing some work for Porton Down—but nothing
special, and nothing like you thought it was at the time. I'm not
allowed to give you any details, but it wasn't connected with
bacteriological warfare. That's all I can say, and all you need to
know. And he certainly wasn't working with Porton Down for
the last two years.'

'How can you be so sure?' said Hywel.

'Well, if he was, he never mentioned it, and he never kept
any secrets from me. We were very close.'

'But would he discuss it with you?'

'Oh yes, we discussed all his work. Don't forget I'm a
bacteriologist too.'

'So what was he working on just before he died?'

'I told you—routine hospital bacteriology, and some
research into AIDS, but then, so's everybody. Nothing more.'

'Lady Miles, thank you,' said Hywel, to end the interview
officially for the tapes. 'Listen, I'm sorry I had to ask you all
those questions, I really am—especially at a time like this—but
I'm sure you appreciate that our viewers have a right to know
these things, especially if there's a question of any risk to the
public.'

'Yes, yes, I suppose so,' said Lady Miles distantly, 'but will
you go now please?'

'Of course,' said Hywel. They went outside. Justin took a
few last shots outside the house, and then they packed up.

*   *   *

'Do you believe her?' said Hywel to Justin on the way back to the studios.

'I don't know. He might not have told her anything, especially after all the hoo-ha two years ago.'

'That was just what I was thinking,' said Hywel.

-8-

Thursday Morning, 7.45 a.m.

'. . . So it does seem as though we will have to wait another two weeks before we know the Government's intentions,' said Duncan to camera one.

He paused and then adopted an even more serious tone of voice. 'As you may have heard on the news, Sir Richard Miles, the director of the Southill Laboratory, was found dead yesterday under circumstances which the police are still treating as suspicious. Hywel Davies has been investigating.'

'Go to VT,' said the director in the gallery, and in the adjoining videotape room the edited version of Hywel's assorted interviews sped past the tape heads.

'Three and a half minutes to go,' said Jane. Three minutes is a long time, especially in broadcasting and it afforded a welcome respite from the pressures of the programme. Jane continued counting, watching the transmission at the same time. It opened with Hywel standing at the front gates of a hospital.

'Behind me is Southill Hospital. Until yesterday the head of the bacteriology department was Sir Richard Miles. Twenty-four hours ago he was found dead in his car.'

The scene changed to general shots of the car on the building site. 'He was found collapsed over the wheel with the engine running. Sergeant Bennett was the officer in charge at the scene.' The picture cut to Sergeant Bennett: there was a brief interview, which ended with Bennett saying, 'It does look very suspicious with all that blood around.'

'They might well be suspicious. Two years ago, Sir Richard was involved in controversy when there were suspicions that his laboratory was secretly engaged in covert research for the Ministry of Defence's bacteriological warfare division at Porton Down.' The picture shifted to archive footage of Sir Richard meeting ministers in Whitehall. 'Questions were asked in Parliament, but the government of the day wouldn't admit to anything further.'

'Now, however, his widow has confirmed that indeed the lab was working for the Ministry of Defence.'

The video changed to the inside of the Miles' house, with Hywel asking, 'But he was working with Porton Down?', and then cut to Lady Miles saying, 'Yes, but not recently. It finished about two years ago when all those questions were asked.' Then they'd edited in a picture of Hywel nodding, to enable them, quite fairly, to jump to her next important statement.

'He certainly wasn't working with Porton Down for the last two years.'

'How can you be so sure?'

'Well, if he was, he never mentioned it.' They'd cut away the rest of the sentence about not keeping secrets from one another, but only Hywel and his editor knew that. Jane never suspected a thing.

The scene changed to Hywel standing in the car park, in front of the laboratory.

'A postmortem report showed that Sir Richard died of some unknown lung infection, but no one in the police, pathology or forensic departments will tell us any more.

'The question is—did Sir Richard contract his fatal illness during his research work here? And if so, what is it? Is secret defence work currently being carried out at Southill? Are the workers there safe? And what about those who live in the surrounding area? Is there something about the work at Southill that we all ought to be told?'

'Counting out,' said Jane, 'Three . . .'

'This is Hywel Davies . . .'

' Two . . .'

' . . . AM-TV . . .'

' One . . .'

' . . . in south London.'

'Go Duncan,' said the director. Duncan looked up at camera one and paused slightly. 'Now on to brighter things,' he said. 'Autumn is traditionally the time of year when . . .'

*   *   *

'No, Lady Miles, Mr Davies did not make any allegations that your husband was still involved in work for the MOD,' said AM-TV's controller of news, Alan Fortescue.

There was an agitated noise down the line. 'No, I'm sorry. No, he did not say that. He did *not* say that your husband died as a result of bacteriological warfare work.'

A pause: more agitated noises.

'Well, I know he may have implied that, but implying it and saying it are not the same thing, are they? And we have a right to ask the questions, you know. I realise this is a difficult time for you, but your husband was involved in a potentially dangerous occupation and we now know that our worst fears about Southill two years ago were right—you confirmed it yourself yesterday— so I think we have a right to make enquiries, don't you?'

More noises on the end of the line.

'Lady Miles, I have looked at the whole of this report myself.' His tone became firm. 'We have not said anywhere that your husband was currently involved in bacteriological warfare research or genetic engineering. All we said– . . . No, do let me speak. All we have said is that he was once involved in covert work for Porton Down—you told us that yourself. We've just asked the question "What else might be going on? And what about the people who live nearby?" Lady Miles, if you want I will send you a videotape copy of the report so that you can see precisely what we *did* say. Yes . . . yes . . . Yes, Lady Miles, goodbye.'

He sat back in his chair and then rang through to his secretary. 'Sandra, will you get Roland and Hywel in here as soon as possible, please.'

They were both in the office within two minutes. Alan looked first at Hywel and then at Roland. 'Aren't we skating on thin ice here?' Roland shrugged. 'What if it turns out he's died from something completely natural?'

'Don't be silly,' said Hywel. 'If they could have announced it they would have. They're covering up. Something really odd has happened here. Either the guy's been killed by one of his own bacteria or else there's been some sort of foul play and he's been murdered. They wouldn't still be treating it as suspicious and flannel us with the postmortem report if they really thought he'd died of something very ordinary, now would they?'

Alan looked down. 'No, I suppose you're right, but I don't like the idea of going and shoving a microphone straight up his widow's left nostril. You might have told the cameraman not to zoom in so close.'

'It was a good shot,' said Hywel defiantly. 'It was a good report altogether. Anyway, there's something behind it. I know. I can feel it.'

Alan leaned back in his chair. 'All right then,' he said. 'Tell me what else you know.'

Hywel sat on the edge of his desk. 'Nothing,' he said. 'Except that no one is admitting to anything. That in itself makes me suspicious.'

'But it's still very thin, isn't it?' said the news controller. Roland nodded, looking even more worried than usual. No wonder he was going so thin on top, Alan thought.

'Why the secrecy, why the uncertainty?' said Hywel. 'Why can't they tell us what he died of? *Can* they tell us? Don't they know, or do they know, but they won't let on? I think there's a lot more to it. All we have to do is a bit more digging.'

There was a silence. Alan toyed with his pencil, then suddenly flung it down on the desk.

'All right. Let's see what you can do, but do go carefully. What if it turns out that he died of something terribly innocuous? That would explain why no one's saying anything—because there really is nothing to say.'

Roland spoke. 'I think we're quite justified, Alan. We've already had the wool pulled over our eyes about the Porton Down relationship. Nobody can blame us if at long last we ask questions about something that ought to have been out in the open years ago.'

*   *   *

That afternoon the Evening Standard carried a banner headline: 'GERM WARFARE LAB IN LONDON?' Its sales went up by 35,000 copies.

*   *   *

Hywel's report didn't just cause a stir, it caused a hurricane. At two o'clock the police called a press conference in order to release the final postmortem results. The room was packed, flashbulbs going off everywhere and at least four sets of news cameras were trained on the spokesman, a serious-faced anonymous-looking inspector.

They must clone policemen's voices, thought Hywel, as he listened to him reading a prepared statement with exactly the same pedantic voice and delivery that Sergeant Bennett had used the day before.

'The final pathologist's report on Sir Richard Miles reads as follows: "The lesions in the lungs and the results of the microscopical analysis of Sir Richard's lung tissue show that he died from Legionnaires' disease." He looked up. 'Accordingly the police are no longer treating this as a suspicious death. Thank you gentlemen.' He stood up.

'Why the blood on the steering wheel then?' asked one of the reporters.

The inspector looked down. 'I am afraid I have nothing more to say.' There was a clamour of further questions, but the inspector, tight-lipped, merely walked off the platform and out of the room. In the back of the hall Hywel looked around in amazement at Justin.

'I don't believe it,' he said. 'I just don't believe it. If it really were Legionnaires' disease they'd have known immediately they did the postmortem. And why the blood? You don't cough up blood in Legionnaires', do you? Why won't he take further questions? Let's do a report outside, on the steps of the police station.'

*   *   *

'. . . but this pathologist's report begs more questions than it answers. Why didn't the doctors know immediately that he'd died of Legionnaires'? Why the blood on the dashboard?' Still looking at the camera, he paused, for once lost for words. 'Oh, maybe I was wrong. Come on, Justin—let's pack it up.'

*   *   *

All the way back to the studio there was something nagging away at the back of Hywel's brain, nagging, nagging, nagging, though he couldn't put his finger on it. He went upstairs into Roland's office.

'So?'

'Legionnaires' disease.'

'Legionnaires'? Don't you get that from water coolers?'

'Something like that.'

'Why Legionnaires'?'

'That's what I thought.'

Roland paused. 'I once did an interview in hospital with someone with Legionnaires' disease . . .'

The bells in Hywel's brain suddenly stopped ringing. 'That's it,' he said. 'I *knew* there was something wrong. People with Legionnaires' don't just collapse like somebody with a heart attack. It's always in hospital when they finally go. Legionnaires' doesn't work like that, does it? Or does it? Who can we ask?'

Roland consulted his contacts file.

'Try Michael Williams. He's one of the pathologists at the Central Middlesex Hospital. He did something for us a couple of years ago when they had the outbreak of Legionnaires' at the BBC.'

'I'll ring him,' said Hywel.

'No,' said Roland, anxious to remain in control. '*I'll* ring him.' He looked at the card index again, then dialled the number. After a couple of minutes he got through. Hywel listened in on the extension. 'Dr Williams? Roland Keating from AM-TV. You remember that we did an item with you a couple of years ago . . .? Fine. I wonder whether you can give me a couple of minutes of your time. I'm sure you've heard about Sir Richard Miles . . . Yes, a sad business . . . The pathologist's report says he died of Legionnaires' disease and the police have closed their files on the whole incident, but there are some loose ends that we don't understand. Does it sound like Legionnaires' to you?'

'People with Legionnaires' don't die suddenly,' said Mike in his clear tenor voice.

'That's what we thought,' said Roland.

'With Legionnaires' you get ill slowly, and progressively become worse. There are often signs of a chest infection. Death occurs after a few days. No, they don't collapse with it.'

'*Could* Sir Richard have died of Legionnaires'?'

'I don't know. It doesn't sound right.'

'There was blood on the dashboard of his car. Would that fit in?'

'Yes, if he was coughing a lot just before he died.'

'I thought people only coughed up blood when they had TB?'

'Any lung infection will do it. You can even cough up blood with just a throat infection. No, that's no problem, especially if he had a paroxysmal fit of coughing.'

'A what?' said Roland.

'A paroxysmal fit of coughing. It means you keep on going and can't stop. If he had a paroxysmal fit of coughing he'd strip the delicate lining off the inside of the tubes that lead to the lungs. You could certainly get bleeding from that.'

'So *could* the whole thing have been Legionnaires'?'

'I can't see how. It doesn't really fit. As I've said, people with Legionnaires' get ill slowly and progressively. They don't suddenly go down like that. Unless of course he had a heart attack at the same time as starting the lung infection. Coincidences like that do happen, you know.'

'But surely they'd have spotted that at the postmortem?' asked Roland.

'Normally you can, but if the death has been instantaneous you can't always.'

'Any ideas what he was researching into?'

'Not really. Southill takes a lot of the samples that are too dangerous to handle in our own labs. They did a lot of the initial work on AIDS before we knew how to handle it. It's a high-powered place.'

'Could it be something that they've been handling there? What about some of the tropical diseases that we hear about? Gaza fever?'

'Do you mean *Lassa* fever?' said Dr Williams in a slightly mocking tone.

'Oh yes,' said Roland, grimacing. 'Yes, I do mean Lassa fever.' Hywel grinned.

'It's *possible* that he got infected at work,' Mike continued.

'What sort of infection?'

'Anything. Depends what they were handling at the time. AIDS; hepatitis; samples from people who've just come back from the tropics; and don't forget that our own bacteria and viruses can change. Something that is pretty innocuous one year can mutate and become a lot worse the next—flu for example.'

'But this wasn't flu,' said Roland.

'I didn't say it was,' said Dr Williams. 'I was just giving you an example. It's why we keep on having flu epidemics: the virus changes its structure from year to year, so although we get immune to this year's flu—and can't get it again—next year's flu virus has a slightly different structure to its outside viral coat, so our bodies don't recognise it, and down we go with flu again.

'The opposite can happen, too. At the turn of the century diseases like measles and scarlet fever were killers. Nowadays they're usually relatively innocuous.'

'Isn't that because we've got antibiotics?'

'No. Measles doesn't respond to any antibiotics, so the reason it's declined in severity is something to do with the measles virus itself.

'Some infections change to become more virulent. Some become less virulent. That's how we make vaccines —change a naturally occurring virus into an artificially weak one, then give it to the patient. The patient has an illness—say, German measles—but it's very mild: but when the real German measles comes along it's sufficiently like the weak form for the body to recognise it and destroy it.'

'How do you change a virus to make a vaccine?'

'Assuming there isn't a naturally occurring variant you can use—like cowpox and smallpox—the quickest way is to infect laboratory animals, then culture the virus from the one that lasted the longest, and reinoculate other animals, each time reculturing the virus from the animal that was least affected.'

'And to make it worse?'

'Do the opposite. Cultivate viruses from the animals that died first.'

'Is this where genetic manipulation comes in?'

'It can do. By using genetic manipulation to change the genes that make the virus particles themselves you can do much the same thing, but more quickly, and much more violently.'

'So could Sir Richard have died from a new, more virulent form of Legionnaires'?'

'It's possible. But I can't really say much about Sir Richard because I don't know enough detail about his case. If you really want me to comment I'd have to see the microscope slides, look at the cultures, read the postmortem report, see the body. I can't be categorical until I've looked at the evidence and obviously I'm not likely to see any of it.'

'No,' said Roland. Then a thought struck him.

'You wouldn't be prepared to come and talk about this on air would you, tomorrow?'

'I wouldn't be prepared to talk about the individual case of Sir Richard because that wouldn't be ethical, but I don't mind coming to talk about Legionnaires' disease in general, if you want.'

'That would be fine. I'll get one of our researchers to contact you later. She'll ask a few more questions and make arrangements to get you here. All right?'

'That's fine by me.'

'Thanks, Mike.' He put the phone down.

'Well?' said Hywel, looking at him with a disbelieving air.

'If it really is Legionnaires' disease,' said Roland, 'it's an extremely virulent variety, isn't it?'

-9-

Friday Morning

*T*he car came for Mike at a quarter past five the following morning. Even at that hour there was some traffic on the roads as outlying commuters tried to beat the rush hour, but the streets were mostly empty and they had an uninterrupted journey. It wasn't even beginning to get light when they turned in under the central archway in front of AM-TV.

The entrance arch seemed to be made out of scaffold poles; behind it was a small parking area, which wasn't particularly well lit, and the front entrance looked as though it had originally been a side door. In the half-light it looked like the back end of a hospital in the middle of the night. Mike had had enough experience of the latter to notice the similarity.

The car pulled up by the front door. Mike entered the building through the automatic sliding glass doors, to be stopped immediately by a porter.

'Good morning sir, you are . . .?'

'Mike Williams, Dr Mike Williams. I'm due on the programme at about twenty past.'

The porter consulted his printed list. 'Ah yes, sir, we'll have somebody for you in a moment.'

A fresh-faced young man in a sharp suit came across and introduced himself as Adrian Potter. He was AM-TV's official greeter, paid to do nothing more than make guests comfortable, calm nerves, feed them with whatever refreshments they wanted and guide them to the right places at the right times. They went together past the circular reception desk, unoccupied for the moment, and entered the bright main cavern of the administration block.

'Everybody's surprised how quiet it is,' said Adrian brightly. Mike was vaguely aware of him chattering away, but by now the adrenaline had taken over in a big way and he had that awful mixture of being overtired, overanxious and overexcited. They went through the main waiting area with framed pictures of all AM-TV's presenters and sat down in a pagoda-like structure at the far end.

'Coffee?' said Adrian.

'Uh . . . yes please,' said Mike, trying desperately to look nonchalant.

'The papers are here if you want to look at them. I'll get your coffee.'

Mike picked up a paper and stared at it in a blank sort of way, taking absolutely nothing in, conscious only of a tightening in his throat as though a golf ball was swinging there; that and the fact that his heart was pounding away even faster.

Adrian came back with the coffee. 'Milk and sugar?'

'Thanks.'

'You're going to talk about Legionnaires' disease, aren't you, and this chap who died, Sir Richard . . .?'

'Well, I'm going to be talking about Legionnaires' but I'm not going to be talking about Sir Richard, no.'

'The papers are full of it.'

Mike suddenly realised what he was reading. There were headlines everywhere. *'Bacteriologist Killed by Legionnaires' Disease,'* said the *Daily Telegraph. 'Legionnaires' Kills Scientist,'* said the *Daily Mail. 'Win a Million in our Fab Prize Bingo,'* shrieked the *Daily Mirror* and underneath *'Killer Bug Slays Germ Boffin,'* almost as an afterthought. He glanced through a few of the reports. They didn't add much to what he already knew. He noticed the names of one or two of his colleagues who had obviously been contacted for background information.

After a few moments Adrian interrupted his thoughts. 'Time to go to make-up.'

Five minutes later, following a light dusting of powder over the potentially shiny spots of forehead and cheeks, Mike was back in the pagoda, nervously fingering his tie, and taking a last look at the notes that he'd made.

'Six-ten. Time to go,' said Adrian, leading him down a corridor, across to a set of low padded doors—like an airlock, but designed to keep sound out. Mike walked through the second of the doors and entered the main studio. It was high and quite dim. He was in a corner of the studio, behind the scenery, in the middle of a small cluster of people. Everyone was talking in whispers; and floating over the top of the scenery Mike could hear the sound of Duncan talking with Tristram Powell about exchange rates.

'This is Dr Mike Williams,' whispered Adrian to one of the assistants near the door. 'I'll leave you now,' he said to Mike. 'Good luck.'

'Thanks.' The golf ball still wobbled precariously and made him want to clear his throat again, a desire which he managed to suppress. He was ushered sideways to where a long-haired youth with acne looked him up and down, selected a minute microphone on a clip, attached it to his tie and then proceeded to run the microphone lead down inside his shirt and out by his left hip. It's not unlike being frisked by the police, Mike thought, though this latter activity had never actually happened to him.

'There you are, Doc,' whispered the youth cheerfully. 'Grab this,' and handed him the connector at the other end of the microphone cable. It's like holding your own drip feed, thought Mike as he sat down on a sofa opposite a monitor that showed what was happening in the main studio. There were several other guests there, nervously waiting to go on. Why am I doing this, thought Mike. How did I let myself be conned into doing this? I don't have to—I only have to get up, turn left and walk out of the door . . .

It was an odd sensation watching Duncan's face on the monitor, yet hearing his voice, live, floating over the scenery. It all added to the air of unreality, the sense of dreaming the whole thing.

In the gallery Jane started counting out into Duncan's ear. 'VT coming in three, two . . .'

'. . . so, with this report from Newmarket, here's Anna O'Brien.'

'Out,' said Jane as the picture changed from the studio to the video report. 'Two minutes to go.'

Quietly and efficiently the floor manager came up to Mike. 'Would you come this way please, Doctor.' Mike noticed the head-set that kept her in touch with the gallery. He was ushered round the back of the set into an entirely different world. In contrast to the gloom and claustrophobia of the waiting area behind the set, the studio was large and bright. Two sides of it consisted of a permanent background set, with imitation brick walls and windows: there were firm seats in the left-hand area, whilst the 'soft area' with the sofas was on the wall facing him. The lighting gave the whole place a curiously bright, slightly yellow glow. It didn't seem particularly directional, yet it illuminated everything strongly and seemed to cast no shadows. The walls were much pinker than they looked on the monitor, he thought.

In the middle of the floor four cameras were being moved around noiselessly on rubber wheels. As he passed round them towards his seat he could hear the video report being relayed on TV monitors placed strategically round the studio. In the centre of the set Duncan was talking, apparently in agitated conversation with himself, and it took Mike a little time to realise that he was conversing with the director in the gallery.

The floor manager guided Mike to a wickerwork chair at the table, opposite Duncan. Duncan smiled briefly across at him, said 'Hi,' and continued talking into space. Mike looked around in a nervous sort of way and suddenly became aware of how warm it was. In front of him he could see a monitor relaying the taped report from Newmarket.

Crouched on the floor by his left side a sound technician was attaching the end of his drip-feed microphone cable to a permanent lead plugged into the floor. Mike sat back in the chair and realised that it was one of the most uncomfortable chairs he'd ever had the misfortune to sit on. He tried to cross his knees and nearly knocked the table in front of him flying. He sat forward.

'Can you lean back, Doctor?' said the floor manager as two of the cameras lined up on him. He swallowed.

'Thirty seconds, studio.'

In the gallery Jane could see Mike for the first time as the cameras lined up. He had a nice face, she thought—long, with fair hair, a jutting out chin and a twinkle in his blue eyes that made him look as though he was about to break out into laughter at any moment. A reassuring face: it looked good on a doctor.

Duncan turned to Mike. 'Hello,' he said, 'we'll be coming to you in about half a minute.'

'Just one thing,' said Mike. 'I'm here to talk about Legionnaires' disease. I don't want to talk about Sir Richard personally.'

'That's fine,' said Duncan.

'Quiet, studio,' said the floor manager.

'Three, two, one, *go*,' came Jane's voice into Duncan's ear. Duncan looked up at camera one. Mike suddenly realised he couldn't see the lens because in front of each camera was a two-way mirror reflecting the image of a black and white television screen—the autocue. It was an odd sensation watching what in the past he had thought had been spontaneous speech as Duncan read off his lines.

'. . . and that report was from Anna O'Brien in Newmarket.

'Legionnaires' disease has been in the news again, so on the medical spot this morning we've got Dr Mike Williams . . .'

Mike became uncomfortably aware that the camera on the left now had a red light on the end of it, and that the camera was pointing at *him*. He tried to look relaxed, which in the chair was impossible. Either he sat forward and looked wrong, or sat back and looked wrong. He managed a faint smile.

'Good morning, Mike,' said Duncan.

'Good morning,' said Mike, hoping the throat would keep going for the next three minutes.

'Tell me, why is it called Legionnaires' disease?'

'It was only discovered fairly recently: a number of people fell ill after a banquet for the American Legion in 1976 and some of them died. At first we thought it might be food poisoning, but when we couldn't find what was causing it, we called it Legionnaires' disease. We knew that it must be some form of infection, but it was a number of years before we found out exactly what it was.'

'Why did it take so long?'

'Two reasons; firstly it turned out that Legionnaires' disease isn't infectious from person to person—we get it by inhaling droplets of contaminated air. And secondly, the organism itself was very difficult to culture in the laboratory—at least in the ways we used at the time.'

'So where does the infection come from?'

'The bug that causes Legionnaires' disease is rather choosy about where it lives. Basically it's most at home in hot moist conditions, and many outbreaks have occurred when water coolers have got infected.'

'Why water coolers?'

'That's because the water is being cooled down from really high temperatures, but isn't quite cold enough to stop the bacteria multiplying.'

'What sort of water coolers are you talking about? The big things near power stations?'

'Oh, no—the air-conditioning ones, at the top of offices and tower blocks. Get infection in those and the wind blows the bacteria over the nearby streets.'

'What does Legionnaires' disease do?'

'It's a lung infection, so you'll feel a bit breathless and sometimes you may have a tickly cough; you'll have a temperature, you'll feel rotten and you'll have a headache.' He suddenly became acutely aware of the frog in his throat but managed to suppress a desire to clear it. 'Typically it's an illness that gets progressively worse if you don't do something about it.'

'It's a killer, isn't it?'

'It can be. Most people survive, but some don't, though if we can make the diagnosis quickly enough and treat the patient with the right sort of antibiotic then we can usually get them through it. The trick is to recognise it as early as possible.'

'Can you isolate the bacteria in the lab?'

'Not easily. Remember, it's very choosy about where it lives and breeds. It can be difficult even to establish that there are bacteria in the lungs, though blood tests can help us make the diagnosis.'

Up in the gallery the director spoke into her intercom. 'Thirty seconds, wind him up. Ask him how it can be prevented.'

'Finally, Dr Williams,' said Duncan, 'how can we stop people getting Legionnaires' disease?'

'Public health measures are the most important—controlling the temperature of cooling towers and water heaters to make sure that they're either hot or cold, but not in between. We can't immunise against Legionnaires' disease, but there are antibiotics that will attack it, and it's up to the doctor to be on the lookout for those cases of pneumonia that don't seem to be getting better.'

'But it *is* rare?'

'Oh yes,' said Mike. 'Rare as hen's teeth.'

'Thank you very much, Dr Mike Williams,' said Duncan and turned back to camera one.

'VT in five,' said Jane into his right ear.

'Now you've probably been for a Chinese meal many times, but Nepalese cooking is beginning to catch on. Gail Jenkins has been trying it out.'

'*Zero*,' said Jane as the VT came on. Everyone in the studio relaxed and there was subdued talking between various members of the floor team.

Duncan beamed at Mike. 'That was great,' he said. 'Thanks a lot,' and started talking into the air again. The sound engineer scrabbled underneath Mike's feet and disconnected his microphone lead. Somewhat dazed with the speed of it all, Mike walked back behind the set where the other sound engineer frisked him for his tie microphone. He went out through the sound lock back into the main reception area, where Adrian met him.

'Would you like some breakfast, Doctor?'

'I think I'll get the powder off my nose, if you don't mind, first,' said Mike, aware that his bladder was full again. Five minutes later he found to his relief that with the reduction in his level of tension the golf ball in his throat had finally disappeared.

Half an hour later, after a splendid breakfast in the canteen which overlooked Hawley Locks, Mike went out to the waiting car, and as they drove out underneath the scaffolding arch Mike thought how, for the people in the studio, the working day was half over—and yet for most of London it was only just time to get up. Looking back he caught a glimpse of the curious eight-foot-high egg cups decorating each arch of the AM-TV building's sawtooth roof.

*   *   *

Roland met with the rest of the reporters at their regular 9.30 a.m. meeting. 'The medical item was good,' he observed.

'Yes, Mike Williams is good on air,' said Amanda. 'Maybe we can use him more in the future.'

'It doesn't fit in with what happened to Sir Richard, does it?' mused Roland. He motioned towards Hywel who was sitting in one corner of the room looking out of the window at the canal below them. 'What do you think?'

Hywel squinted up at him. 'All the papers are asking the same questions. "Was Sir Richard working on germ warfare when he died?" "Could it really be Legionnaires'?" So it's not just us wondering.

'Is there a cover-up? I don't know. My gut reaction is that there's a lot more to it than we've been told.'

'What do you think we do now?' asked Roland.

'The MOD won't tell us anything. The same goes for Porton Down. I think I'll nose around Southill and see if I can find anybody who can give me any off-the-record information. It's probably the only way we'll get any further.'

As it happened, it wasn't.

*   *   *

Half an hour later Roland glanced at his VDU; hardened newsman though he was, what he saw there made his heart miss a beat. '*Lady Fiona Miles found dead on the doorstep of her Richmond house at eight o'clock this morning. Lady Miles was the wife of Sir Richard Miles, the director . . .*'

What *is* going on? he wondered. I hope she hasn't killed herself after Hywel's interview. He rang Hywel's office. No answer. He dialled his mobile and Hywel answered immediately.

'We know where to go,' said Hywel. 'We're on our way.'

They got to the house to find the usual knot of people rubbernecking outside. The main door was open and in front of it on the semicircular brick steps lay a body draped in a white sheet. The report Roland had read was completely correct: Hywel soon found that there was little to add. No, there were no suspicious signs; no, there was no sign of an intruder and despite the recent death of her husband her friends testified to the way that she had borne it all courageously and refused to let it get her down, so there was no thought of suicide either. Hywel had managed to find the milk roundsman who discovered the body and did a short interview with him, but there was little else to go on. Between them Justin and Hywel put together a short piece, but there was nothing more to do there so they packed up their equipment and headed on to Southill.

-10-

Friday Midday

'*H*ywel?'

'Yep.'

'Roland here. I thought you ought to know we've just had a report in. You know Dr Sherman—the man who did the postmortem on Sir Richard?'

'Yes . . .'

'He's dead too.'

'*Dead*?'

'Yes. This morning.'

'Where? What happened?'

'He was apparently in his lab, sitting at his desk dictating some reports when he told his secretary he wasn't feeling too good. She says that half an hour later he started coughing, couldn't stop, and kept on coughing until he collapsed and died.'

There was a silence at the other end of the line.

'They've got to be connected. It's just got to be the same thing—it would fit for all of them, wouldn't it? Sir Richard gets taken ill while he's driving, finds the nearest place to stop his car, coughs himself to death and while he's doing that, brings up a bit of blood-stained phlegm—which is where the blood on the dashboard came from. His wife, who's already been infected by contact with him, is taken ill in the house and is trying to go for help when she dies. It fits. It fits.'

'Well, if Sir Richard died of Legionnaires' then they all died of Legionnaires', but that's not how Dr Williams said people catch Legionnaires'. He said it didn't get passed on from person to person.'

'I know. Why don't you ring him again?'

Roland put the phone down and consulted his card index. He dialled the number. It took a couple of minutes to find his quarry. 'Dr Williams?'

'Yes.'

'Roland Keating at AM-TV. There've been some developments over Sir Richard. By the way—thanks for your contribution this morning. Everybody up here said how well it went.'

'Thanks. What's happened with Sir Richard?'

'You know his wife's died too?'

'Yes.'

'Well the pathologist who did the postmortem on Sir Richard has just collapsed and died in his lab as well.'

'Poor chap, who was he?'

'Ed Sherman, know him?'

'Vaguely. Why do you think it's important?'

'It looks as though he may have died from the same thing that killed the other two. His secretary said that he felt unwell about half an hour beforehand and then started coughing, couldn't stop and collapsed. Does that sound like anything to you?'

'Not really. I suppose a very bad pneumonia might just do

it, but I've never seen one like that myself.'

'If Sir Richard and his wife both had the same thing, it would explain everything, wouldn't it? The way Sir Richard was found almost on his route home, but not quite. His wife suddenly gets taken ill too, tries to get help, then collapses and dies.'

'But Legionnaires' disease doesn't get transmitted like that,' said Mike. 'And we know that Sir Richard died of Legionnaires' because we've got the microscopic and bacterial samples to prove it.'

'What if we work it the other way round? What if we assume that they've all died of the same thing, and in the same way—suddenly, in a fit of coughing. And that what you're seeing is a much more virulent form of Legionnaires' disease?'

'That would fit . . . If it's true of course. Legionnaires' normally doesn't behave like that, but I don't see in theory why it shouldn't. Some organisms can get very virulent under certain conditions.'

'We were discussing this the last time we talked.'

'I remember. Yes, it would explain it—a more virulent strain of the Legionnaires' bacillus.'

'How does a strain like this get created?' said Roland.

'There's three ways I can think of. The first is that it's a natural variant of the disease that just happens to have occurred. Secondly, you could create a bug like this artificially in a lab by infecting animals with Legionnaires' and cultivating samples from the ones that died most quickly, then reinfecting further animals, cultivating it from the ones that died most quickly and so on and so on.'

'And the third way?'

'Genetic manipulation.'

He paused. Visions of Porton Down flashed through both their minds.

'Are you thinking what I'm thinking?' asked Roland.

*   *   *

'It *must* be Porton Down,' said Hywel. 'It's got to be. It's too great a coincidence. Why else should Legionnaires' suddenly change its nature? They've got to have been fiddling with it.'

'We have no evidence,' said Roland.

'We can't yet prove it in a court of law, but we've got quite enough circumstantial evidence. Three people, all connected, die of a completely new version of an old disease and, surprise, surprise, one of them just happens to be the director of a laboratory that was linked with Porton Down until, at the very least, two years ago. Come off it, Roland, they've *got* to have been fiddling with the bug. Lady Miles admitted it anyway, didn't she? She said Sir Richard had been involved with Porton Down.'

'But only until two years ago.'

'She would say that, wouldn't she?'

'I tell you what we'll do. You go round to Dr Sherman's lab and interview his secretary, and anyone else you can find, and in the meantime I'll get some of our researchers working on the Porton Down end, and we'll see what we can come up with. Shall we meet back here in about two and a half hours?'

'OK.'

Roland went across to Amanda's desk and told her the situation. 'I'd like you to attack it from the government side. Ring Porton Down, the Ministry of Defence—any way you can think of that might give us a lead in. Treat it as if we are certain that there is a link between the two, because if they think we know already, they're more likely to admit what's going on.

'You could try the politicians too. How about the MPs for the constituencies which include Porton Down and Southill? Ask them what they think about it, now that they've had an accident—you know, that sort of thing. Push them. Make them talk.

'While you're at it, ring the press office of the Secretaries of State for Defence, the Environment and Health and see how much you can wheedle out of them. Telephone the general manager of Southill Hospital and get his angle on it. Say we know they're involved with Porton Down and can you have details. Don't take no for an answer. I'm meeting Hywel in two and a half hours so I want some information by then.'

*   *   *

By Friday evening they'd got their report together. There still wasn't much to go on. No one was saying anything, and the press officers at the Departments of Health and Defence had obviously been told to stonewall on any connection between Southill and Porton Down. Legionnaires' disease was what Sir Richard had died of, there was no risk to the population, and that was that: there would be no further comment until after the weekend. Press officers are civil servants, and government departments work a five-day week. Nothing can happen over a weekend. It's not allowed to.

Nevertheless Hywel found enough information to make up a report, tenuous though it was.

-11-

Saturday Morning

At the same time as the death of Lady Miles was beginning to send little shivers of panic down the spines of those who were thinking ahead a little, out in Bedfordshire a much happier event was taking place. The Jones family was on holiday. It was half-term and the four of them had decided to try canal boating.

It was a good week to go narrow-boating for the first time. Although it was autumn, the air was still warm and the weather was fine. None of them had been on a canal before, and they were all looking forward to it. They were not disappointed. A week on the canal, with life lived in the slow lane—the *very* slow lane—is enough to unstress even the most wound-up businessman. The holiday would prepare the whole family for the onset of winter.

Derek Jones was in his early forties, a solid, slightly stout fellow with thinning hair swept back, a round face with a sharp nose, and an easygoing manner. An engineer by training, he had transferred easily into the Civil Service, and after a short time at the Ministry of Defence he was now working as a specialist in the Patent Office, a job he enjoyed because of its constant freshness and interest. Each day he was amazed at the number of ways ingenious minds had found to solve problems that other people might—or might not—have.

Of course they had more than their fair share of cranks. Alternative versions of perpetual motion machines turned up in his in-tray at the rate of about one a week, despite the laws of physics which say conclusively that such a machine is impossible. It didn't stop people from trying.

On the other hand, there were many inventions that were far more interesting and much more ingenious. Derek always thought that the simplest ones were the best, like the zip, catseyes, and Velcro—very simple, very elegant, and very obvious after somebody else has invented it, yet fiendishly difficult to dream up oneself. For some reason the human mind doesn't seem to think laterally. Derek frequently reflected on the fact that the Aztecs and Mayans, with all their immense knowledge of astronomy and architecture, never got round to inventing the wheel.

His wife Anne, a dainty, fine-boned, dark-haired woman of thirty-eight, was his emotional support and stay. To outsiders they seemed, even when separated from each other, like the covers of a book which when wide apart are still working together, indissolubly joined. Before they'd had the children, Anne had been a primary school teacher, but when first Alison, and then later David had come along she had willingly given up her job and thrown herself into being full-time chief cook, bottle-washer and first-class mum; and in the annoying way that success breeds success, and maturity and relaxed satisfaction in parents encourages the development of maturity and relaxed satisfaction in others, their children were similarly easy-going. True, there was a certain amount of sibling rivalry, but basically the whole family were friends with each other—a rare thing in this day and age.

They lived in London, near Isleworth, but although in London the Grand Union Canal flowed almost past their door, they had decided to join it some forty miles north: narrow-boating through the back of the city is not always the most pleasurable way to start a canal holiday.

And so it was on that fine October morning that they drew up on the waterside car park of the Wyvern Shipping Company of Linslade, one of the many small hire companies to be found up and down the Grand Union as it meandered on its way from London to the Midlands. The company mainly hired out narrow-boats, brightly painted craft with dazzlingly elongated proportions, seven feet wide and up to seventy feet long.

The boat the Jones family had hired was *Willow*: a custom-built fifty-footer complete with bunk beds, kitchen, sitting area and even a shower and toilet. Really like a long caravan, thought David as he helped his father transfer their suitcases from the car. He was a twelve-year-old lad with a round face, a flat-top haircut that made him look like an inverted yard brush, and a cheeky grin showing off overlarge front teeth which seemed to owe more to rabbit than human origin.

The provisions they'd ordered had already been loaded, so all that was left to do before they set sail was to learn how to use the facilities inside the craft, and the rather delicate job of steering it—not easy unless you know the knack. The yard owner, Frank Yates, ran through the check list with Derek, showing him how to turn the central heating on (yes really, central heating in a boat—very necessary in autumn). 'Are you sure we've put everything you wanted on?' he asked.

'I hope so,' replied Derek. 'Food, drink, matches and a waterways map.'

'Television?' asked Frank.

It's strange how big things happen as a result of small decisions. 'No,' said Derek, 'we don't want a television. We're not even going to listen to the radio. We're really going to get away from it all for a week.'

'As you wish,' said Frank, 'but you'll be the only boat out that hasn't got one.'

Frank showed them how to operate the boat. Then he took them up the canal to Leighton Lock and showed them how to take a boat through.

It looks too easy, thought Derek. I have a sneaking suspicion that when I try it myself things won't go quite so smoothly.

Frank bade them goodbye, and then they were on their own, chugging into another world, leaving the twentieth century with its strains and stresses behind them.

-12-

Saturday Afternoon

*T*o the immense gratification of all at AM-TV, not only did Hywel and Roland's report get used on the news section of Saturday's programme, but it was also rebroadcast by ITN in their news bulletins for the remainder of that day. It caused a sensation. They still hadn't much to go on, but Hywel had strung the whole story together so cleverly that although he hadn't yet got any really hard evidence, it was obvious how well the hypothesis fitted; and as usual Hywel had couched it in such a fashion that no one could sue.

He found it easy enough to do. If he hadn't got direct evidence he would merely ask a question: 'But how do we know this is what *really* happened?' leaving the viewer to make up his or her mind. It's an old ploy: guilt by invitation. Sometimes it's accurate, sometimes not. If anyone challenged Hywel, he would immediately reply that he wasn't accusing anyone, he was just asking a question.

'Are Southill and Porton Down interconnected?' he asked. 'We know they were linked two years ago. Are they still linked? Do they have anything to do with the deaths of these three people? If not, how is it that Legionnaires' disease has suddenly changed into something much more lethal? And why is it that whenever we ask about these things nobody is prepared to comment?'

By Saturday evening there was hardly a person in the land who hadn't heard the story. It was the topic of conversation in pubs, in restaurants, in sitting rooms up and down the country. In Heston Martin Freeman abandoned his original ideas for next day's sermon and at short notice put together a tirade against bacteriological warfare, using as his text the passage from Genesis where God gives an injunction to mankind to go forth and subdue the earth. 'Subdue the earth,' said Martin the next day. 'Yes, but not annihilate it, not obliterate it, not twist it to our own selfish warlike uses.' It was a good sermon, apposite and delivered with fervour, and for once had the desired electrifying effect on his congregation.

*   *   *

That same Sunday, Mary Harper joined with her Greenpeace colleagues in demonstrating outside Porton Down. They had managed to get over two thousand people there at twelve hours' notice—not bad for such a hastily organised event. A smaller number congregated outside Southill Hospital; and a third group, this time organised by CND, marched from Trafalgar Square down Whitehall and presented a hastily organised petition against bacteriological warfare to Number 10 Downing Street.

That evening ITN showed extensive coverage of the demonstrations. Later that night the BBC postponed the planned programme in the *Everyman* series in favour of a hastily convened studio discussion on the rights and wrongs of germ warfare.

Next morning a MORI poll showed the government's standing had dropped ten points in two days, owing entirely to the furore about Southill and Porton Down.

-13-

Monday Afternoon

'Statement, the Secretary of State for Defence,' said the Speaker.

The House was packed, its noisy atmosphere even louder than usual. The Minister rose to the despatch box amid catcalls from the Opposition benches. 'Madam Speaker,' he began, 'reports in the media have implied that the recent deaths from Legionnaires' disease of Sir Richard and Lady Miles and Dr Edward Sherman are in some way connected with bacteriological research at the government establishment at Porton Down. I wish to reassure the House that there is no connection whatsoever between Porton Down–'

Hubbub.

'–and Southill. Furthermore Sir Richard Miles was not involved in any research work relating to Porton Down–'

Uproar. Cries of 'Shame' and 'Resign' came from all directions, and not just on the Opposition benches. The Minister tried to speak, but his voice was drowned out.

'Order. *Order*,' yelled the Speaker, to little avail. After a couple of minutes the noise abated somewhat. 'Order, order. Honourable Members really must let the Secretary of State complete his statement.'

'May I repeat, Madam Speaker, for those who may not have heard: there is no scientific or research connection whatsoever between Sir Richard Miles and the government research establishment at Porton Down.'

Uproar again.

'*Order*,' cried the Speaker. 'If the House does not return to order I shall have to suspend the sitting. *Order*! Statement from the Secretary of State for Health.'

Edwin Molyneux rose to the despatch box, a tall dignified man in his sixties. 'Madam Speaker, as far as we can tell at the moment, the deaths of Sir Richard and Lady Miles and Dr Sherman were all caused by the same strain of the Legionnaires' bacterium–'

Cries of 'Where did it come from?' emanated from the Opposition benches.

'I will tell Honourable Members where it came from,' said the Secretary of State, 'if they will just be patient.'

Not really the right words for the moment. Further uproar supervened.

'Order, order,' cried the Speaker. '*Order*!'

'As you know, Southill Laboratory is equipped to deal with the most virulent bacteria and viruses.'

'From Porton Down,' yelled a voice.

The Minister continued unperturbed. 'Samples from a patient who died of an unknown infection ten days ago were sent to Southill Laboratory. There was apparently an accident in the laboratory, due to a failure of one of the refrigerators. As a result bottles containing specimens from this patient shattered and it is possible that Sir Richard became contaminated from this source–'

Uproar again. Shouts of 'Rubbish', 'Cover-up', 'Whitewash' came from all corners of the chamber.

'I must tell Honourable Members once again, Madam Speaker, that the truth is often simpler than fiction.'

More uproar.

'We have isolated the cause of the three deaths and all personnel at Southill Laboratory are currently undergoing tests to ensure that none of them is carrying the bacterium. All the tests performed on them have so far been negative.'

He sat down. The Leader of the Opposition was on his feet immediately.

'Madam Speaker,' he said, trying to make himself heard above the din, 'whilst I understand how important it is for ministers on the Government side of the House to want to cover their tracks, nevertheless members on this side feel that they have been given a very inadequate explanation indeed. The Minister for Defence has told us that there is no connection at all between Porton Down and Southill, yet we know from the late Lady Fiona Miles that such a connection existed, at least until two years ago.'

'What is worse, the Secretary of State for Health seems to think that everything is under control, which we on this side of the House doubt. How does he know that those who have already died haven't already passed the disease on to others? Madam Speaker, in view of the gravity of the situation, may we call upon you to agree to an emergency debate on this subject?'

The Speaker rose. She was used to the Opposition's tactic of demanding special consideration for any subject that might even faintly embarrass the Government.

'I think, in view of the clear statements given by the Secretary of State for Defence and the Secretary of State for Health, that no good purpose would be served by debating this matter further at this moment.'

Total uproar. Members were standing, shouting, waving order papers, pointing fingers, making gestures towards ministers. Some members even crossed the floor of the House to argue with Government ministers directly. The Speaker called for order, but her voice was lost. After three minutes of this, in despair she shouted, 'The House is in uproar, the session is suspended,' and motioned to the Serjeant-at-Arms to clear the chamber.

In the suite of rooms controlling the televising of Parliament, the videotape machines kept rolling, recording the scenes that would make headlines on every news bulletin that evening.

Down on the floor of the House the Secretary of State for Defence turned to his colleague and shouted in his ear, 'What more can I do to persuade them? The more I say that there is no connection between Porton Down and Southill, the more they think I'm covering up. How do you convince someone in that state? Say nothing and you're held to be covering up. Say something and you're held to be lying. They only want to hear what *they* think is the truth, whether it *is* the truth or not.'

The Secretary of State for Health shrugged. 'Are you *sure* you're not covering up?' he replied.

*   *   *

Peter Abrahams was beginning to realise just how difficult life was going to become after his sentence. He lived in one of the villages near Luton, poorly supplied by public transport, so getting to work was going to be next to impossible—not that he had any work to go to. The day after his trial he had been informed curtly by the divisional inspector that his presence would no longer be required at the police station, permanently, and that he was to be discharged from the force with dishonour.

In the past Peter had imagined that after retiring from the police he might set himself up as a private detective, or as part of a security firm—but without a driving licence neither option was open to him. He also had connections in the motor trade—but without a licence that wasn't much good either. So he was left kicking his heels, wondering what on earth he could do for the next year to support his family, and ruminating on his solicitor's words which seemed to echo around in his head wherever he went: 'The law has nothing to do with justice. It's just a game— a game played with different rules.'

For the fourth time that day he picked up the paper and began scanning it for suitable jobs—ones that didn't need a driver's licence; ones that he could travel to on foot or by bicycle. He didn't find any.

*   *   *

If time was passing slowly for Peter Abrahams, it was doing exactly the reverse for Paul Greatorex, who had just started another week's frenetic activity on the broking floor, surrounded by screens, telephones and hubbub. Out of the corner of his eye, on the news screen he saw something about '*Uproar in Parliament. Sitting Suspended*', but took little notice of it as he was just completing a deal that had earned his firm nearly half a million in four hours. Not a bad day's work, he thought. Life was going just fine.

-14-

*T*he late Dr Sherman's house looked familiar. Hywel and his crew were halfway up the front drive before they realised it looked almost the same as the Miles' house where they had been four days earlier. Hywel rang the bell, and just as before it was answered by a woman who had obviously been crying.

'Mrs Sherman?' said Hywel.

Mrs Sherman pulled herself together. 'You're Hywel Davies, aren't you?' she said.

'That's right.'

'I thought you'd be round. You'd better come in.' As they went into the lounge Hywel realised with a shiver that this house had been built on exactly the same plan as the Miles' house.

'Do sit down,' said Mrs Sherman. 'I suppose you want to know about Ed.'

'Well, if you don't mind,' said Hywel. This is going to be easy, he thought. Normally I have to push hard to get to this stage.

'Do you mind if I just go and make myself look a bit more respectable?'

'Fine, we'll take a few general pictures while we're waiting, if that's all right.'

Justin took a few establishing shots in the room, plus pictures of Hywel nodding in an interested fashion, ready to be used as fill-in clips if they wanted to edit what Mrs Sherman said without causing her head to jump suddenly at the point the edit was made.

Mrs Sherman came back just as they were finishing. She looked different somehow—strangely determined. Probably nerving herself not to break down, thought Hywel. He was wrong—oh, so wrong.

The camera rolled again. 'Mrs Sherman,' said Hywel in his kindliest voice. 'Can you tell us a little bit about your husband?'

'He was a forensic pathologist,' said Mrs Sherman. 'He'd been doing that for the past fifteen years.'

'Was he in good health?'

'Oh yes,' she said. 'He was well the last time I saw him.' There was a pause. Then she looked straight at Hywel. 'And what right do you think you have to come here and barge into my private grief asking me silly questions like that?' she asked suddenly. It was so unexpected a change of behaviour that for once Hywel was wrong-footed. 'Ed was a good man and you want to intrude. Does it really matter what he did, how he did it? I've lost my husband, the only person who ever really mattered to me, and all you want to do is try to make a few seconds of television out of it to satisfy your ego and the voyeuristic minds of those who are watching.'

Hywel recovered his composure. 'Mrs Sherman,' he said coolly. 'I didn't force my way in here. You invited me in.'

'You didn't force your way in physically,' she replied. 'You just barged in emotionally. How would you feel if you'd just lost your wife and suddenly there was a whole group of people round you shoving microphones in your face asking "How do you feel about it?" Well, how would you feel about it, Mr Davies? How would you feel?

'You did exactly the same to Fiona Miles. Oh yes, I know exactly what went on there because she just happens to be one of my friends. You *used* her. You used her while she was in a state of shock to wheedle things out of her that really should have been kept secret. And you knew, you *knew* what you were doing. It didn't just happen, you did it deliberately. Do you really think it helps anyone to know that I'm grief-stricken because my husband died? Do you think it's edifying to poke your nose in? Do you think it helps anyone?

'I'd like you to get out, you and your crew, and I'd like you to get out *now*, please.'

'As you wish, Mrs Sherman. You did invite us in, you know, but we will go. Thank you for speaking to us.' They packed up. As Hywel went white-faced and silent down the drive he heard the front door slam behind him. For once in his life he'd been shaken.

'I don't think we'll get much out of that one,' he confided to Justin.

But he was wrong. Viewers next day saw Mrs Sherman saying, 'He'd been a forensic pathologist for fifteen years,' then the picture cut to Hywel nodding sympathetically. 'He was well the last time I saw him.'

Then the picture cut to Hywel talking to the camera. 'But that was to be the last morning he said goodbye to his wife, because four hours later . . .'

Roland however had somehow managed to see the whole of the original videotape and word of Hywel's come-uppance spread round AM-TV like wildfire.

*   *   *

Watching television separately that Monday evening, both Martin Freeman and Mary Harper felt a great sense of satisfaction at taking a stance for good, and being part of a movement that was daily growing bigger and stronger. They were proud to speak out against man's interference with nature, proud to stand up and be counted in opposition to man's warlike adaptation of science.

They were not alone. By now hardly one person in ten thousand believed what they were being told by Government ministers. The next day's headlines were epitomised by the Daily Mirror in a one-word banner headline: '*Resign*!' it shrieked. Even the fab prize bingo had been relegated to the bottom corner of the page. The more ministers denied a connection between Legionnaires' disease and the secret establishments, the less anybody believed them, for although he had still not managed to turn up any hard evidence, by now Hywel had got round to believing his own propaganda and where Hywel led, others followed.

Next morning there were over ten thousand people camped outside Porton Down. The name was on everybody's lips—except, that is, for one family in a canal boat without a television, out of contact, relaxing, blissfully unaware of the turmoil around them.

*   *   *

Unknown to Hywel, the Ministers of State, or most other people for that matter, there had been other deaths: but as those involved were not famous, nor obviously connected with the events at Southill, they hadn't been noticed. After all, each day in London there are many unexpected sudden deaths, most of which are put down to heart attacks.

So it happened that a small litany of deaths occurred, unremarked and unnoticed: the head doorman at the Royal Society of Medicine, a Polish emigré called Stanislaw Zwolinski, a sixty-two-year-old widower, found dead in bed by a neighbour. He'd been known to have a heart condition for some time: as it happened, he was also the last man to have spoken to Sir Richard Miles before he died, but no one was to know that. Rajesh Gupta, the owner of a corner shop in Richmond was dead, too. He'd been one of the last people to see Ed Sherman alive when he served him on his way to work. Two days later he too was found dead. In Rajesh's case the coroner had decided to have a postmortem performed, but as there was something of a backlog of cases it would have to wait a couple of days.

Then there was Gary Harding, a milk roundsman at both the Miles' and the Shermans' houses, though no one made the connection at the time. When he died on the Friday it was a big shock because he was only twenty-two. There had been an immediate postmortem, but on finding pretty obvious signs of pneumonia the pathologist wrote 'lobar pneumonia' as a preliminary finding, took a few routine bacterial swabs (none of which were of the right sort to pick up Legionnaires') and considered the matter closed.

Mrs Sherman had also talked with Yvonne Porter, the delivery girl who had handed her a large bunch of flowers, together with an apologetic note from Hywel. Yvonne too was to die two days later. Eight people in eight days. Not a lot really, but the same rule of doubling applied to humans and bacteria as with chessboards filled with grains of rice. The new strain of Legionella had an incubation time of two days, after which it killed with half an hour's notice. The victims only felt ill in that last thirty minutes, but were infectious long before that, and unlike the bacteria in the flask which only doubled each time, one person with Legionnaires' could infect tens or even hundreds of others.

But it didn't dawn on anybody what was about to happen, because no one was looking in the right direction. The media were seeking a Government scapegoat. The Opposition was seeking a Government scapegoat. Government backbenchers were warily eyeing their own majorities. Those in the know knew that it couldn't possibly have come from Porton Down because they weren't working on Legionnaires' disease at all. (They *were* working on anthrax and cholera, though, together with some genetic modifications of botulism, but no one— absolutely *no one*—was going to say anything about that.)

Public health officials weren't looking for person-to-person transmission because that had never happened in the past with Legionnaires', which had always come from cooling towers, so instead they went out scouring southwest London for infected cooling plants on the top of buildings, and nobody gave a thought to the possibility that within a week this new variety of Legionnaires' disease could spread in a different, and much more lethal, way.

The penny was just about to drop.

-15-

Tuesday Morning

*R*oland looked round at the reporters who had been able to come to the 9.30 news briefing. 'We'll have to cover the demonstration at Porton Down; and I gather there's another march and rally in Trafalgar Square at midday, so we'll need a team there. And we ought to send someone to the Ministry of Defence to see if we can get another interview with the Secretary of State.' He turned to Hywel. 'Do you think the Government will resign?'

'Not a chance,' said Hywel. 'It'll take a lot more than this to bring them down. Mind you, anything that heightens public awareness of what's going on is a good thing. It's all grist to the mill. At least it'll teach them not to go behind our backs so often. The more frequently we find out about things like this the better.'

Roland looked at his terminal. He paused, lost in thought.

'Something come in?' asked Hywel.

'Look at this,' said Roland. ' *"Legionnaires' disease confirmed in two more people. Public health officials are investigating."* '

'Anyone connected with what we're doing?' queried Amanda.

'Not that I can see,' said Roland. 'One lives in Battersea, one in north London. Nowhere near Sir Richard, nor any of the others.'

Hywel, for all his willingness to see conspiracy theory at any turn, was still no fool. 'It may not be where they live that counts, but where they work and who they are in contact with. Anyway, how many Legionnaires' deaths normally go unreported because nobody has any suspicions?'

'Amanda, get Dr Williams again for me, would you?' Roland stood by the VDU, lost in thought until Amanda signalled that he was on the line.

'Mike,' said Roland, 'something rather worrying's just happened. We've had reports that there are two more Legionnaires' deaths that don't seem to be connected with the previous three—at least, not as far as we can tell. How can we find out if there really is an epidemic starting? Who would know? Would anybody be looking, even?'

'Usually the hospital laboratories would be the first to find out,' said Mike. 'If we get a number of samples from different sources that come up with the same type of bacteria we'll inform the public health people, district medical officers, and so on. When it's something like meningitis they'll look for a common source or carrier, warn people accordingly, tell them to take whatever precautions are necessary and try and contain the whole thing.

'Tell you what—why don't I ring around and see what I can find out? Doctors in other labs will talk to me when they might not want to talk to the press. I'll ring you back.'

*   *   *

It was noon before he returned the call. 'Roland, I think you're right. I can't give you details of individual patients for ethical reasons, but I've rung round a number of my colleagues and there's been a sudden upsurge in people who've apparently died of pneumonia. They've started tests on eight of them for the Legionella bacterium—do you remember I said it needed special techniques to identify it? I've alerted all the labs to the fact that we ought to be looking for it, and looking very carefully. I'll keep you posted.'

'How long before we have the final results on the new postmortems?'

'Probably this afternoon or early this evening. Now that the pathology boys have been alerted they'll be looking that much harder. I'll ring you if I find anything more.'

*   *   *

At five o'clock that afternoon the producer of the next day's programme had the whole of the show planned, wrapped up and ready. Five minutes later she had to do the whole lot again.

*   *   *

'Roland? Mike Williams here. Prepare yourself for a bit of a shock. At the last count there were fifty-eight . . .'

'What . . .?'

'Fifty-eight. Fifty-eight deaths that could be Legionnaires'. None of them is definite. They're all awaiting confirmation, postmortem, bacteriological results: nothing's certain.'

Roland put his hand over the mouthpiece and turned to Amanda. 'Get Hywel, fast.'

'Can you give me any names?'

'You must be joking,' said Mike. 'It would be totally unethical.'

'All right, I understand. Let me plug you for a bit more information. Is there any evidence of how these people are connected—if they *are* connected—to Sir Richard and Lady Miles, or Dr Sherman?'

'I don't *think* so. At least I don't know of any. They didn't work in the lab. They don't live in the same area.'

'Do they *work* in the same area?'

'I don't know. I can only tell you about the bodies and the postmortems.' Mike paused. 'We don't actually know what we're looking for, do we?'

'What do you mean?'

'All this arose because Hywel kept on chasing the idea that Sir Richard was doing something unpleasant at Southill. Yes?'

'Right.'

'Now the usual way in which Legionnaires' disease spreads is through contamination of an air-conditioning plant on the top of a building, or else an inadequately heated hot-water supply to a shower. Right?'

'Right.'

'But don't you see?—they're incompatible. Either we're looking for something unpleasant that crawled out of Southill and spread to other people in the area, *or* we're looking for a completely separate source of contamination like a water cooler on the top of a West End office, which all the victims have gone past. It might have nothing to do with Southill at all.'

'How do we tell the difference?'

'We have to find whether what connects them all is a place, or a chain of people.'

Roland suddenly felt overwhelmed. 'But how do we track down where all these people have been? It could be anywhere in London. Where do we start? And if it is spreading quickly how are we going to find out fast enough to stop other people getting contaminated?'

'You could do it the other way round,' said Mike. 'Why not see if you could link the people who have died directly to the lab, or to someone who worked in the lab, or else to one of the people who has already died? If you can make that connection it points towards Southill being the source. If you can't, it indicates that there may be a common source elsewhere that we'll still have to identify.'

'But how will we know where to start if we haven't got the names?'

There was a pause on the end of the line.

Roland tried again. 'Listen, Mike, I know you have an ethical duty to your patients, but what about your ethical duty towards all the people who might get Legionnaires' and die if no one finds the source?'

'The public health people will be searching pretty soon.'

'Before they've got the full postmortem results?'

'Well . . . no.'

'And how many other people are going to get infected in the two days before we get the final results?'

There was a long pause on the other end of the line while Mike weighed up the ethical pros and cons. He knew that there are occasions when it was appropriate for a doctor to break confidence—largely when the well-being of another individual, especially a child, is at stake—but they are not many: and revealing confidential information inappropriately can result in the doctor who does it being struck off. He was in an awkward dilemma, and he knew it.

'OK,' he said, with a long sigh. 'I'll tell you what I'll do. I won't give you the names, but I will tell you where each of them died. If you contact the local police they'll be able to give you information about those sudden deaths where the coroner's been informed.'

'Right,' said Roland, 'fire away.'

Mike began to read off a string of locations. They were scattered all over London.

'Nobody from outside London?'

'Be reasonable. I haven't had the opportunity to contact more than a few laboratories. I haven't even tried any of the non-metropolitan hospitals. For all we know there might be someone up in Edinburgh with it.' Roland groaned inwardly at the thought.

'Mike, you've been great. Can I talk to you later on?'

'Yes,' said Mike and gave him his home number. Roland turned to Amanda and Hywel.

'I want every researcher that we can lay our hands on. Each of you take two or three of these locations. See if you can find who the dead are that are under suspicion for having Legionnaires'. Then interview the relatives. See if you can find any connections with Southill or the three who've died. Don't spend too long on any one case because for all we know it may be completely unrelated. We'll meet again at eight and see what we've got.'

'Is it really that important?' asked Amanda. 'After all we're way ahead of everybody else with this. Why don't we just wait twenty-four hours until the results are announced? We know we'll be able to go to the public health people and get a story out of them before anybody else gets near them.'

'And how many people will pick up the disease in the meantime?'

They met at eight.

*   *   *

'Let's go round the table. Amanda?'

'Well, I've got four names. I couldn't find any relatives for one of them; the family of another wouldn't talk to me at all; the third one's a teenager—worked as a delivery girl for a florist in the Richmond area. The fourth guy's an Indian; owned a corner shop.'

'Where?' said Roland.

'Richmond.'

Roland turned to the researcher on Amanda's right. 'Keith?'

'I did four people as well. I couldn't get anywhere with three of them. The last one was quite interesting—worked at the Royal Society of Medicine. Just for good measure I rang the Royal Society and found out a few things about him. Polish guy, widower, kept things very much to himself, didn't go out much, spent virtually his whole time at the RSM—and the day before and the day before that he was on a twelve-hour shift, because one of their other doormen was on holiday.'

'Where did he live?' asked Roland.

'East Ham.'

'Miles away. He won't be connected.'

Hywel sat in the corner, brows furrowed, a faraway look on his face. He knew something. He knew he knew it. The only trouble was, he didn't know what it was he knew. He kept on thinking.

Roland went through the reports of the other researchers. At least ten of the suspects had either lived or worked in the Richmond area. Except the doorman.

Roland rang Mike. 'What have you found?' asked Mike.

'We've got ten people at least who've got connections with the Richmond area, where the Miles family used to live. Nobody connected obviously with Southill. And there's one oddity, the head doorman at the Royal Society of Medicine. He doesn't fit into it at all—lives in East Ham, works just off Oxford Street, nowhere near Richmond, nowhere near Southill. Mind you we don't know that he's necessarily connected. He may not have had Legionnaires' at all.'

'He is,' said Mike, throwing all caution to the winds. 'He's one we're almost sure about.'

Hywel, who'd been sitting in the corner looking pensive, suddenly started back into life again, got up and walked briskly out of the room. A few minutes later he came back and slipped a videotape into the VCR in the corner of Roland's room. There was a pause, and then Lady Miles came on the screen.

'He'd been out to a presentation at the Royal Society of Medicine, and when he didn't get back by midnight, I got a bit concerned and rang them, but they said he'd left at half past eight . . .'

Hywel switched off with the remote control. There was a deathly silence.

'Mike,' said Roland, 'it's not coming from cooling towers.'

$$* \qquad * \qquad *$$

Ten minutes later newsmen, reporters, camera teams, researchers, assistant researchers, and deputy assistant locum researchers sped outwards from AM-TV like shrapnel from an exploding grenade. Every available reporter, camera team and newsman was pressed into action. Next day's producer, who three hours earlier had thought she'd finished, reckoned that she'd be lucky to get two hours' sleep before the end of the programme. Roland sent a car to bring Mike into the building, and ordered a lot of food and refreshments.

It was five in the morning before everything had been organised, edited, introduced, commented on and sewn together into a seamless whole. The producer had been wrong. She didn't get two hours' sleep: she didn't get any, but she didn't mind. Bleary-eyed, and with that odd distant feeling that comes from being awake for far too long she watched as, at 6 o'clock the next morning, the production team and the studio rolled into action with what was the most devastating news to hit Britain since the announcement of Hiroshima.

'Roll opening credits,' said the director in the gallery.

'Counting out, Duncan,' said Jane. 'Five, four, three, two, one, *go.*'

Duncan rose to the occasion. Presiding magisterially over videotapes, studio interviews and expert reports, he fused them together in one massive coherent argument, like a prosecuting counsel weaving a net of unassailable logic and inviting the jury to agree that there was only one possible verdict. They began with a brief announcement from the newsroom that, 'To date fifty-eight people have died unexpectedly in circumstances which may be connected with the current outbreak of Legionnaires' disease.' Then they continued in the main studio where Hywel explained in meticulous detail how they were sure that all these cases were connected, and connected with Southill.

But the climax had yet to come. Gently but firmly Duncan and Hywel took the viewers on a masterly journey in which they showed how everything fitted together. First they started with the videotapes of Sir Richard dead in his car, the interview with his wife and the damning admission that he had indeed been involved with Porton Down until, at the very least, two years earlier.

Then the new videotaped interviews began. The reporters had somehow managed to find all the people who really mattered: the parents of the girl who'd delivered the flowers to the Miles' and Shermans' homes, the shopkeeper's wife, the friends of the RSM doorman.

The interviews were astounding. Knowing how much depended upon finding the right answers, the researchers had impressed upon victims' relatives that this time they really *weren't* looking for an intrusive story, but that other people's lives were at stake; and as so often happens, when people know that other's lives depend upon their actions, they rose to the occasion.

The interviews were moving—much more so than the forced interventions that Hywel had perpetrated upon people in the past—and they were telling. Deft editing had removed all the irrelevant details and left just the connections between the victims, Sir Richard and the laboratory. The owner of the florist's shop told of the day and the time when his delivery girl went to the

Miles household, a weeping Indian widow spoke of Dr Sherman and how he so often popped in for a few items on his way home.

Then there was the most revealing of all—Stanislaw Zwolinski, the doorman at the Royal Society of Medicine. They cut back to the interview with Lady Miles telling of Sir Richard's appointment there shortly before his death. Then they showed tapes of interviews with fellow porters at the RSM telling how the dead man had spent most of his last forty-eight hours of life at the RSM itself.

Finally there was Mike Williams in a live interview with Duncan, explaining patiently how in the past Legionnaires' disease was known to be transmitted only from inanimate objects like cooling systems and showers; that a number of the deaths were definitely Legionnaires' disease and many more likely to prove so later (though, ethical to a fault, he delicately refrained from mentioning names or identifying with any certainty which cases had and which had not been diagnosed).

'Dr Williams,' said Duncan. 'If what you say is true, is there any way that we can fit together the deaths of these fifty-eight people according to our usual understanding of Legionnaires'?'

'No,' replied Mike, 'it doesn't fit together at all. There are at least two people who never went near Southill. There's only one way we can connect these things together.'

'And that is?' said Duncan.

'If we're dealing with a change in the nature of the bacteria that causes Legionnaires' disease, so that instead of needing an inanimate reservoir, like a cooling tower, the germ can now be passed on from person to person, like flu.'

They cut across to Hywel. 'If this is true, it makes everything simple,' he said, talking to camera. 'Sir Richard contracts the disease in the lab and passes it on to his wife. He also infects the doorman at the Royal Society of Medicine, then, whilst on his way home, collapses and dies in his car. Two days later his wife dies, but not before she's passed on the infection to the florist's delivery girl. Dr Sherman does a postmortem on Sir Richard and is infected directly from him. In turn he passes it on to Rajesh Gupta at his local shop, who, if you remember, is not a contact of anybody else connected with the whole of this case.'

They cut back to Mike. 'Dr Williams, assuming this is all true,' said Duncan, 'what do you think we can say about this new type of Legionnaires' disease?'

'It has an incubation period of about two days. People feel well at first, but then they get only half an hour's warning before they start coughing. They cough repeatedly and increasingly violently—what we call paroxysmal coughing—then suddenly the lungs fill up with fluid and blood and the patient drowns in his own sputum.'

'How much warning would the victim get?'

'About half an hour of feeling unwell,' said Mike, 'then five minutes while he coughed himself to death.'

'Is there anything else you can tell us?'

'Yes,' said Mike. 'We know that the delivery girl at the Miles household only spent about half a minute there because of the other calls she had to make, so it must be extremely infectious.'

In the gallery Jane shivered.

*   *   *

When the programme finished they had a celebration. Really they should have gone off to get some sleep, but they were all in that overstimulated, overexcited state that makes sleep impossible, even though they were so tired they ached. Each person's mind was whirring away, recalling bits of the programme.

The exhilaration of knowing they'd pulled it off merely added to the sense of euphoria. The controller of news was delighted, the directors were delighted, everyone was delighted. AM-TV had just made the biggest scoop of the past fifteen years. They had beaten everybody—newspapers, BBC News, Reuters, Associated Press, the Department of Health, the public health laboratory, the lot. Hywel, grinning from ear to ear, was almost dancing round the office in his delight and excitement. Even Roland (who had the somewhat undeserved reputation of scarcely being delighted at anything) was smiling. For once nobody was looking at the computer screens—which was a pity, because glaring in baleful green were the words *Legionnaires' death toll now stands at 159*.

-16-

Wednesday 2.30 p.m.

'*O*rder. Order. Statement, the Secretary of State for Health.'

Edwin Molyneux rose to the despatch box.

'Madam Speaker, Honourable Members may have seen reports in the press concerning a number of people who have died recently in London from Legionnaires' disease. After consultation with the Chief Medical Officer and his public health colleagues I have to tell the House that these reports are greatly exaggerated–'

Cries of 'Shame' and 'Cover-up'.

'–as there are to date only three cases that have been proved to be caused by the Legionnaires' bacillus–'

The chamber, not normally among the quietest places in the world, was especially rowdy that day. All around the packed House members were standing, shouting, and trying to get the Speaker's attention in order to be able to interrupt the Secretary of State with a pertinent and well-timed question. Molyneux tried to make his voice heard over the hubbub, but all that could be seen was his lips moving.

'It is true–' he started.

'Order. Order.'

'It is true–'

'*Order.*'

He dropped his voice half an octave and bellowed. 'It is true that more than the usual number of sudden deaths have been reported to the coroner, but the medical profession is being ultracautious at this time and it may well be that some deaths that would normally have passed without special comment have in fact been notified to the coroner. I am informed by my officials in the Public Health Department that they confidently expect most of the remaining cases which have been mentioned on certain TV programmes to turn out to be totally unrelated to Legionnaires' disease.'

The Leader of the Opposition was on his feet. 'Madam Speaker, would the Secretary of State tell us what precautions he has taken to stop further release of Legionnaires' disease from Southill Hospital, and can he assure the House and those living around Southill that they will no longer be subjected to dangerous bacteria manufactured by his Government?'

Molyneux rose from the green baize bench. 'Madam Speaker, there is no evidence that Southill Laboratory–' The rest of his words were lost. The Speaker was on her feet, gesticulating and trying to make her voice heard, but to no avail. Everyone seemed to be shouting at once. Cries of 'Resign' were hurled across the chamber.

'Honourable Members must allow the Secretary of State to finish answering the question,' said the Speaker eventually, and sat down again. The House simmered down a little. Molyneux tried again.

'I have the assurance of my Right Honourable friend, the Secretary of State for Defence, that no work connected with Porton Down is going on at Southill; nor has there been any connection with Porton Down for some considerable time. In any case members will know that Legionnaires' disease is spread not from person to person, but from cooling tanks. The tanks on the roof of the hospital at Southill have been tested and no trace of the Legionnaires' bacillus has been found.'

'What about inside?' yelled an opposition backbencher.

'I understand,' said the Secretary of State, looking in the direction of the question, 'that samples from a patient who is thought to have died of Legionnaires' disease have been handled in the laboratory, but as it is now known that Sir Richard had not been in the part of the laboratory that was dealing with those specimens, these are unlikely to be the source.' He sat down.

The Leader of the Opposition rose to put his supplementary question. 'I am glad to hear that the Secretary of State has at long last admitted that Legionnaires' bacillus has been handled in Southill Laboratory, but members will want to make their own minds up about the reasons they were there.'

Molyneux was on his feet in a fury. 'Madam Speaker, it is against the rules of this House for a member to call another member a liar and the Honourable Member has implied that.'

Shouts of 'Withdraw' came from the Government backbenchers.

The Speaker turned to the Leader of the Opposition. 'I agree. The Honourable Member will please withdraw that remark.'

'Madam Speaker,' said the Leader of the Opposition. 'I am quite sure that the Secretary of State has been told by his department and by the Secretary of State for Defence and his department that research into bacteriological warfare is not being carried on at Southill. He is only repeating what he has been told. I am not saying that he is a liar, just that he has been incorrectly briefed and in any case, whatever I say, members will want to make up their own minds as to where the real truth lies. I would certainly not wish to impute that the Secretary of State was a liar. Misguided and gullible perhaps, but not a liar.'

He sat down. At least eighty members rose as one, brandishing their order papers. This time it was the turn of John Gowland, a Government backbencher. 'If the Secretary of State is sure that the infection has not started at Southill Hospital can he please tell us what he is doing to find the source of the infection, and then minimise the danger to the public?'

Molyneux returned to the despatch box. 'The Chief Medical Officer and all Public Health Departments have guidelines laid down for identifying and tracing the source of infections like this. May I remind the House that only three cases are known so far–' the usual hubbub ensued '–and at this stage we do not feel that it is appropriate to overreact. Once the cause of death of other patients has been fully identified we may well be in a better position to judge where the site of the infection is. May I assure the House that the Department has the matter well under control.'

The Shadow Spokesman on Health rose to his feet. 'Madam Speaker, how can the Minister say that everything is under control? If—and I say *if*—even a substantial proportion of the fifty-eight cases mentioned by the media turn out to be due to Legionnaires' disease, then he has a major outbreak on his hands. May I remind the Secretary of State that Legionnaires' disease is not always fatal—the three confirmed and fifty-five unconfirmed deaths may just be the tip of the iceberg. How can he therefore say that the situation is under control?'

'The Honourable Member has obviously not been listening

to what I've been saying. Once we can establish exactly how
many people have died of Legionnaires' disease, and trace their
movements, we will be much better placed to discover the source
of the infection. May I remind the House that the source could
be anywhere in London, or even, for that matter, outside. The
whole situation has been blown up totally out of proportion, as so
often happens when those on the other side of this House
interfere in decision-making.'

Derisive hoots came from the Opposition. Molyneux had
lost control and he knew it.

'The Member for Stockport,' intoned the Speaker. Alison
Frayn rose. Despite her height—she was a small woman of
apparently insignificant stature—she was renowned for her razor-
sharp intellect. Although a loyal party member, she would never
stand for any cant and often spoke against her own party when its
opponents were, in her opinion, in the right. She was one of
those people who, when they stand up to talk, instantly command
respect and silence.

'Madam Speaker,' she said gently, and the House became
quiet, members straining their ears to hear her. 'Madam Speaker,
the Secretary of State accuses members on this side of the House
of blowing things up out of proportion, but may I remind him
that the hard work of tracking down these fifty-eight unfortunate
people was done not by his department, nor by any of the
Honourable and Right Honourable Members opposite, but by
completely independent investigators involved in the media,
without any help from his department, nor from any government
institution whatsoever. The media investigators, more than
anyone else, have thrown some semblance of light on the
situation. May I put to him the following scenario? What if he is
wrong? What if, as usual, the Department of Health has reacted
with all the alacrity of a hippopotamus?'

Laughter. Then with her eyes becoming steely and her voice
hard, she finished off. 'What if he's wrong? What if these fifty-
eight people really did die of Legionnaires' disease, changed so
that it is infectious from person to person like flu? It's all very
well for him to say that things are under control, but they are only
under control if none of them died of Legionnaires'. Will the
Secretary of State say whether he thinks things will still be under

control if *thirty* of the fifty-eight prove to have Legionnaires'?'

Molyneux wearily rose to the despatch box yet again. 'I can only repeat once again to the House the advice I've been given by my own expert medical officials. They feel that there is no need for panic. Everything is under control and the best and most effective way of sorting out where the infection comes from is to wait until we know more. That will be in two days' time.'

Alison Frayn knew that the best way to make anyone panic is for a government department to say there is no need to panic. It usually means they're covering something up; or can't be bothered to get round to doing anything about it; or else that the consequences of being wrong are so awful that they really cannot bring themselves to contemplate it. She remained on her feet, still talking persuasively, logically, quietly. 'What measures does the Secretary of State propose taking if Legionnaires' disease is now transmissible from person to person? Three days ago we had three people dead, now we have the possibility—and I emphasise the possibility— of fifty-eight. If we wait two more days, at this rate of growth by Friday we may have three thousand people dying from it. Madam Speaker, I really think that we should have an emergency debate on the whole subject.'

She sat down. The Speaker rose. 'I agree with the Member for Stockport. I think the House will need to have a debate, and I will therefore allocate Friday afternoon for that purpose.'

It is strange how small decisions can have huge effects on the lives of people. Stranger, too, was the fact that the Speaker's decision was ultimately to have no effect at all.

*   *   *

AM-TV's journalists hadn't been the only active ones. '*150 Dead in New Killer Plague*' screamed the *Evening Standard*'s headline. '*Uproar in Parliament. Emergency Debate on Friday*'. With total unanimity the leader writers declared that, as usual, the Department of Health was doing far too little, far too late.

By now the subject of Legionnaires' disease had grown to occupy the whole of every news bulletin. Pages of speculation were being prepared for next morning's dailies, and even headline writers at the *Sunday Sport* were thinking on the lines of

'Is Legionnaires' a Disease from Outer Space?'

As so often happens on these occasions, the nation became glued to the TV, gawping at the misery of the relatives of those one hundred and fifty people whose lives had been terminated prematurely.

Earlier that day it had been different: everyone had applauded the tact and subtlety with which Hywel and his colleagues had obtained their information, whilst at the same time giving as little offence as possible. They had had a goal, an object that was higher than the mere gathering of news or the titillation of a curious public. Without question they had succeeded.

What followed twelve hours later was not so edifying. Shorn of the need to prove anything and deprived of a scoop, most of the papers and news programmes descended to their old habits, shoving cameras into the faces of the bereaved and asking how they felt about the death of their husband. Or son. Or baby.

The nation watched fascinated, bewitched, lapping it up. The doommongers came to the fore again, extrapolating as usual on the minimum of facts. Whose fault was it—a judgement from God? Where would it end? How many would die before the outbreak was brought under control? It was all terribly exciting, like watching war footage from the other side of the world. Thrills by proxy: the viewers weren't truly involved at all. They sat watching in their front rooms, dissociated entirely from the misery and pain portrayed on the other side of the camera, yet able to defend their voyeurism on the grounds that it was all about 'News', 'Truth' and 'Reality'.

As the body count rose, paper vied with paper to provide ever-inflated estimates of the numbers of dead and infected, and speculated on what might have been the source, and why the organism might have changed.

While the other fifty-five million in the nation looked on and speculated, the families of the one hundred and fifty mourned, as if in a goldfish bowl, spied on by the rest, unable to move outside their houses for the journalists camped outside, afraid of the telephoto lenses of photographers perched on top of blocks of flats a quarter of a mile away.

The most poignant moment concerned a young mother whose

child of three had just died. 'Go away,' she screamed at the waiting newsmen. 'Can't you leave me alone? My baby's dead. Don't you care? Or are you more interested in making a story out of my misery?' She had pushed aside a cameraman, knocking him to the floor, and slamming the door behind her. 'But don't you think the public has a right to know about all this?' went through the minds of the journalists who saw the footage, which inevitably found its way into all the news bulletins. It went down well. Human story. Poignant, good for the ratings, what the viewer wants. And the viewers lapped it up: they too were just as guilty and involved as the reporters. After all, indirectly, they were paying them.

-17-

Thursday 6.00 a.m.

*I*f the previous day's programme had been the zenith of Hywel's career and of AM-TV's output, then the next morning's was certainly the nadir. After the exhilaration of the chase, with journalists playing medical officers of health and succeeding wildly beyond their expectations, Thursday morning's programme proved to be like a dose of cold water. All the officials were on— the Secretary of State for Health, the Chief Medical Officer, the Secretary of State for the Environment—all the bigwigs. It was as dull as ditchwater and as about as palatable.

Duncan did the best he could, but what with the politicians stonewalling and refusing to take anything but the most optimistic view of events, there wasn't much of practical value in the whole of the proceedings—with the exception, that is, of Mike Williams. In the past week he'd become part of the furniture at AM-TV and his quiet, measured and realistic response was a refreshing change from the dour unflappability of Government and Whitehall.

Wisely, the day's producer had decided (with Mike's permission) to pit him against Sir Bernard Hopkins, the Chief

Medical Officer. Sir Bernard, a small, insignificant man with
uneasy eyes and a bland manner, had as much drive about him as
a sloth in full flight.

There was one thing that Sir Bernard was, and always had
been, good at—saying no. With a lifetime's service (or was it
servitude) in Whitehall he had learned that the art of power is not
so much about exhibiting it oneself as about denying it to other
people. His family motto was probably *Veni, Vidi, Negavi* (I
came, I saw, I said you mustn't do it).

Delay being the deadliest form of denial, he was also a
master of the that tactic as well. In short, Sir Bernard represented
leaden bureaucracy and officialdom, all rolled into one
insignificant, self-satisfied paunch. How he managed at the same
time to *look* concerned, yet *be* totally impractical, was a mystery
to most people. He had obviously practised until he was perfect.

'No,' he said to Duncan's first question. (He had to start off
with the word 'No'. It wouldn't have been like him otherwise.)
'No, I don't see the need for any special investigation at this
stage. We have well-established routines for tracing infections
like this and it won't be long before we've found the answer.'

'How many more people are going to die before you find out?'

'None, probably,' said Sir Bernard huffily.

Duncan turned to Mike. 'Do you think that's realistic?'

'No, I don't,' said Mike firmly. 'Although Sir Bernard is
quite right to say that only three people so far have been
confirmed as having Legionnaires', results so far on the fifty-
eight other victims we investigated would fit with Legionnaires'
disease. I would expect *at least* two-thirds of the fifty-eight to
have died of it.'

'Oh come, come,' said Sir Bernard. 'You've no evidence.'

'Yes, I have,' said Mike calmly. 'I've spoken to a large
number of the people who did the postmortems. Have you?'

'No,' he said in an offhand manner. 'I've had the
preliminary reports on my desk and I'll be getting the full reports
later on today.'

'Well,' said Mike, 'the people I've spoken to are as sure as
they can be that they're dealing with Legionnaires' disease, and
when I said at least two-thirds of the fifty-eight have
Legionnaires' disease, I mean that. The true figure will probably

be at least fifty out of the fifty-eight.'

He went on the attack. Duncan leaned back and let him get on with it.

'And if fifty or more people really have died of Legionnaires', what will you have done to prevent it, Sir Bernard? By the time your department has got its act together the whole thing will be out of control, if indeed it ever was in control.'

Sir Bernard's colour rose. Duncan stepped in smartly.

'Dr Williams, you've just said that Sir Bernard's department hasn't done enough. So what would you do?'

From then on Sir Bernard wasn't in the running at all. He'd been totally outfaced and he knew it, and for the rest of the discussion Duncan concentrated on Mike.

'Normally Legionnaires' disease isn't passed on by person-to-person contact. This sort seems to be, and from what we've been able to find out, all the people who have got it have met one or more of the other victims: what's more, they've only needed a brief moment of contact to get the disease, so it must be highly infectious. By the end of last week we had three known deaths, yesterday we had fifty-eight—let's say fifty to be on the safe side—so . . .'

Sir Bernard started to expostulate.

'I don't care what you say, Sir Bernard, it will be at least fifty. There's no point in even arguing about it.' Off-screen the studio manager handed Duncan a typed piece of paper. He stared at it and then looked up at camera one, which fortunately wasn't selected because his face showed pure shock.

'Once it gets going it will spread quite quickly,' said Mike. 'It's like AIDS was, only very much faster, because the period of incubation is so much shorter.'

'All right,' said Sir Bernard, angrily. 'Answer the question. What would *you* do about it?'

'It's no use looking at this as though it's someone else's difficulty. It's everybody's problem—yours, mine, everyone who's watching. If it is as infectious as it appears to be then we need to quarantine off London. We must stop movement within the capital, encourage people to stay indoors and above all, discourage travel.'

Duncan butted in. 'But wouldn't that be intolerable—an invasion of public privacy?'

'I think,' said Mike, carefully, 'that the equation is quite simple. If we don't do something *now*, quickly, we may have on our hands the worst plague since the Black Death. Three people last week, fifty-eight the day before yesterday, one hundred and fifty yesterday. It's growing exponentially.'

The analogy of the chessboard and the Chinaman came into Mike's mind. He wondered whether to explain it, then thought of a different analogy. 'It's like throwing a snowball at the top of one of the mountains in the Alps—just a little snowball, just a simple, small action, but it causes a little more snow to roll down the slope, which disturbs even more snow, and before you know it you've got an avalanche big enough to bury a village.'

Duncan stared at him with an odd look in his eyes. 'I think you may be right, Dr Williams,' he said, turning to camera one. 'We've just had word from the police in Richmond. There are people dying all over the borough, just dropping dead in the street.' He looked at the piece of paper in his hand, which unusually for him, was shaking. He looked up again. 'We're going over to the newsroom for a special report.'

In the news studio a somewhat flustered newscaster began reading off the autocue, but was obviously receiving instructions in his earpiece at the same time because he stopped several times to correct himself or to add further information.

'Police in Richmond have reported that ten people have collapsed and died in the street this morning. They are–' he paused '–I'm sorry, I've now been told *twenty* people are known to have died. The police are urging people not to go into the area.

'Some victims died while driving their cars, and as a result there are a number of crashes blocking the road. We'll come back to you with more information just as soon as we have it.'

Duncan turned round to Mike. 'It looks as if you were right.'

'It does rather,' said Mike, grimly.

'What can we do to stop it?' asked Duncan. 'Can't we immunise people against it?'

'No,' said Mike. 'We don't have vaccines against Legionnaires' disease.'

'What about antibiotics?'

'Ordinary Legionnaires' disease is sensitive to an antibiotic we often use—erythromycin.'

'Is this commonly available?'

'Oh yes.'

'So could we give everybody antibiotics to prevent them getting the disease?'

'That might work, but the change in the bacteria that's made it infectious from person to person might also have changed its sensitivity to antibiotics. And in any case I doubt if there would be enough to go round. It takes some time to produce a batch of antibiotic, and unless the manufacturers have a lot in stock there won't be enough for everybody.'

'Is there anything that the Department of Health can do?' said Duncan, rather pointedly asking the question of Mike rather than of Sir Bernard.

'They should *insist* that everybody stays put wherever they are *now*. All right—some may die, because they remain in contact with someone who's already infected, but if they try to run away from the infection they'll just take it with them and accelerate its spread. It's vital that people stay where they are, in their homes, in isolation. That way we may stop the spread of the infection. I can only give this advice to people watching—stay put. If you've already got the disease you're going to die anyway. If you haven't got it, you're not going to get it easily if you don't go outside.'

'Sounds sensible to me,' said Duncan. He turned to Sir Bernard. 'Why didn't the Department give advice like this? You must admit it's practical, and it does seem as though it ought to work.'

'We didn't have any proof that it was needed,' said Sir Bernard lamely. 'We didn't know it was necessary until ten minutes ago.'

-18-

Thursday 9.30 a.m.

'What a clown,' said Keith just before the daily newsroom meeting took place. 'Only known about it for ten minutes. What an imbecile. Why can't government departments ever manage to

think ahead properly? It's like ice and snow in winter. We get it
every year, yet every year people seem to think it's a freak
occurrence, and use it to explain why the trains and roads have
been disrupted yet again.'

'Wrong sort of snow . . .' parodied Amanda.

'Wrong sort of Legionnaires' disease, more like,' echoed
Keith grimly.

'Are we all here?' said Roland coming into the office and
sitting down. 'Where's Hywel? We'd better start without him.
Amanda, I want you to ring the Departments of Health and
Environment to see whether they've got any plans for stopping
people moving out of Richmond. Oh . . . and the local police.
Keith, will you contact the RAC and the AA about the road
conditions in the Richmond area.'

Alan Fortescue popped his head round the door. 'Great
stuff, everyone,' he said. 'Keep going. This is the scoop of the
century and we're in the middle of it.'

'Thanks, Alan.' Roland looked down at his screen again.
' "Reports are coming in of a huge increase in traffic out of
London." ' He turned round. 'You tell people to do one thing so
they immediately do the opposite. That's human nature for you.
Streaming out of London, no thought for anybody else. What
happens if they're carrying the disease and they go off to Birmingham, or Manchester, or Newcastle or Glasgow? Why don't
they do what Mike suggested and just stay put? Cretinous lot.

'Where were we? Oh yes, I need somebody to go down to
Richmond. See if we can get some pictures of the crashed cars
and the bodies on the streets; and an interview with the police
officer who issued the warning to keep out of the area too. That
ought to make good viewing.'

The phone rang, and he motioned to Amanda to take it. 'We
ought to get a comment from the Secretary of State for Health. I
should think he'll have to resign over this. What if we send
Hywel to do that one, or would it be better to send him to
Richmond, do you think?'

Amanda looked up from the phone, her face white.
'Neither,' she said. 'You won't send him anywhere. He's dead.'

-19-

Thursday 9.45 a.m.

*O*ver in the East End of London Kevin Jensen kicked aimlessly at an empty Coke can, thinking vaguely of what he'd seen on the television that morning. Unemployed and pretty well unemployable, he was a nineteen-year-old misfit, the leader of a small gang of teenagers with similar ambitions—or lack of them. To the outsider their sole aim in life appeared to be hanging around at street corners and avoiding work of any nature whenever possible—not that Kevin could get work that easily. For a start he'd never been taught how to work, so the thought of applying himself rigorously to anything for more than half an hour—except for watching football— was totally alien to him.

Kevin lived in a council flat on the fourteenth floor of a tower block on the Commercial Road. The tower block was huge and grey: it had been white when it was built, but city dirt and the English climate have a salutary effect on most architects' intentions in concrete. Vaguely reminiscent of a hundred and twenty television sets stacked one on top of the other, the block of flats overwhelmed its occupants by the sheer disparity between them and it. As far as Kevin was concerned there could be no better metaphor for living in society than the relationship between himself and his home. It was the monolith, he was the ant-like acolyte doomed through sheer insignificance to a perpetual inability to change anything.

His inability was fuelled by three problems: money, power and learning—or, to be precise, his lack of each. He was the exact inverse of Paul Greatorex. He had no capital, so he couldn't start himself up in business, even if he wanted to. Power—he had none. No influence over anybody—no friends or acquaintances with any clout. In his short but eventful life he'd managed to alienate just about everyone who could have been a help in the future. This powerlessness was what drove him and the other gang members to each other. Here was at least one small area of life they could be king of for a bit.

Education? He'd spent all of his life trying to avoid it and now, having succeeded, he was at long last beginning to learn something—that avoiding education was perhaps not the best thing he could have done.

Sociologists would probably have attributed his lack of achievement at least in part to his having no father: more precisely, like everyone in the world he did have a father, but he just didn't know which of the rest of humanity it was. If his mother knew she wasn't letting on: she hadn't been well enough to go out to work since he'd been born and they'd both lived on state handouts ever since.

Life wasn't helped by her agoraphobia. Trapped on the fourteenth floor, she never went out from one year to another, staying indoors smoking and taking the tranquillisers which her GP gave her whenever she asked. He didn't see her often: he had many other people to attend to and dealing with agoraphobic single mothers takes time.

Probably what Kevin's mother needed most was a caring husband and a supportive family network. She had neither. What Kevin needed was somebody to teach him true self-reliance, application, concentration and determination. He didn't have an adequate role model for this either, so he continued week after week picking up his dole from Social Security, and, when he had to, going to job interviews for jobs that he didn't fancy at a rate of pay that he certainly didn't want, but thankfully requiring qualifications he largely didn't have anyway: so he needn't have worried—he never made the short lists.

In short, Kevin was one of those people who didn't fit into the society around him. At heart he would have liked to have done so—not that he'd let on about it to anyone—but he didn't quite know how to do it, and in any case didn't know where to get started.

As the Irish joke goes, 'If you want to get to Dublin, sir, I wouldn't start from here.' At the age of nineteen that roughly summed up Kevin Jensen's life, social standing and potential.

As he kicked the can along the street he thought for a moment about what he'd just seen on the television. He hadn't

got many powers of concentration and it was a very selective
power anyway. He could remember that the Hammers had just
lost two–nil, which displeased him intensely. He also
remembered something about a germ that had got out and was
causing people to be ill over in the West End, but with an
attention span of only three minutes he hadn't really been able to
take it in—not that he cared much anyway. It was another world.
It was happening to somebody else. It didn't involve him.
Losing two–nil did.

*   *   *

After the telephone call there was a stunned silence in
Roland's office. 'Why Hywel?' said Amanda, a tear trickling
unbidden down her left cheek. 'I know he was a brute sometimes,
but he was an honest brute. At least he always wanted to root out
the truth, whatever his methods. It seems such a waste.'

There was another silence. No one wanted to speak—eight
of them, lost in their thoughts.

'You realise of course that that makes us all contacts,' said
Roland. There was an uneasy stirring and a communal
uncrossing and recrossing of legs. They'd all realised it of
course, but most of them hadn't wanted to be faced with the truth
so directly, quite so soon. Better let it get into the subconscious
first and bubble up slowly from there.

There was another silence. No one wanted to say anything,
yet no one wanted to leave either. It was as if mutual together-
ness somehow made them stronger. Or perhaps it was because in
that room things were familiar, easier, whilst outside they didn't
know quite what they'd have to face.

'It's strange,' said Roland slowly. 'Up until now it's been
them and us. We've been observing what's happening to others.
Now it's us and us—we're part of it.' There was another silence.
'There was I, only a few moments ago, saying people were cretins
for moving out of London, when *I* was sending off everyone here
to make reports—and each of us here could be . . . ' He couldn't
bring himself to say it. 'It just hadn't occurred to me that we
might be . . . involved . . . It was always someone else.'

'That's why everyone's moving out,' said Amanda. 'They
don't think it could happen to them—unless they stay behind.'

There was another pause. Finally Roland spoke again.
'We'll have to put it on the news tomorrow.'

'What?'

'Hywel's death.'

'Oh . . . ' Amanda looked up. 'It's the first time I've ever
been part of the news,' she said. 'It's a strange feeling. Somehow
. . . vulnerable.' She pulled her jacket round her and shivered.

'I suppose we'd better do some form of tribute to him, hadn't
we?' said Keith. 'Interviews with one or two of you, friends
he's worked with, that sort of thing. And somebody ought to go
and interview his wife.'

Amanda turned round. 'You *can't* do that,' she said angrily.
'The man's just died.'

'It didn't stop Hywel doing it after accidents.'

Another pause. Another silence.

'No,' said Roland, 'somehow I don't think we'll interview
his wife. Maybe a tribute from the controller of news.' Roland's
heart was not in it, and it showed.

There was silence again. Each one's subconscious knew
something, but it wasn't letting on about its deadly secret to its
owner's conscious mind. At least—not in a rush. Deep down
they all knew what was going to happen, but it was too awful to
contemplate, so their minds had clammed up against it: so they
sat there paralysed, depressed.

In the distance they could hear the familiar sounds of that
morning's programme being retransmitted on monitors through
the building, as it always was.

Finally Roland, still in a daze, spoke again. 'I had a friend
once . . . She worked at the *Birmingham Post* at the time of the
Bradford stadium fire disaster. Do you remember, it happened
live, on TV. The day it happened, they were all in the office,
watching it on the monitors saying to themselves, "Great copy;
fantastic pictures; what a story."

'Then she went home, saw the whole thing again on the
television and broke down and cried. She said it was only when
she was at home that she could appreciate that it was happening
to people—real people, with feelings, pain and relatives—rather
than just being an abstract event, to be documented.'

Another silence.

It was finally broken by Mike. 'What are we going to do now?'

It was an interesting way of putting the question. Mike had meant, 'What are your plans for the next day's programme?' Everybody else in the room perceived it as, 'What are we—as individuals—going to do?' And then the awful truth began to rise from each one's subconscious.

'You mean who's going to be the next?' said Amanda.

'Actually I didn't, but there is that, too. No, I was thinking what we are going to do for tomorrow's programme. More to the point, do you want me, or can I go back to my lab?'

'Is it worth going back?' asked Roland. 'Is it worth doing anything? Is there going to be anything to go back to in a week?' And then it was no longer in the subconscious. 'What chances have we got? What chances has anybody got? We've now got a death toll of—' he looked down at the monitor '—about four hundred and fifty, according to the police. What's it going to be this evening, tomorrow or the next day?'

They shifted uneasily on their chairs.

'Let's face it, we're probably going to die. We've all been in contact with Hywel.'

'Not necessarily,' said Mike, still unflappable. 'It all depends when people become infectious.'

'That was what I was going to ask you,' said Roland. 'What are the chances for us, for anyone?'

'It's hard to say. Whenever there's an infection you need seed and soil. The seed is the virus and the soil is the person. If the seed isn't virulent or the soil isn't receptive then the infection won't spread much. On the other hand if the seed is particularly nasty and can nearly always get a hold, then you've got a big problem.

'And if you can make the soil less receptive for the seed you can reduce the chances of getting an infection.'

'All right,' said Roland, 'spell it out. Is there any way we can find out what this thing is going to do? What does it depend on in practical terms? How fast does it spread? For crying out loud Mike, can't you give us a bit of reassurance instead of just being cold about it all?' He was shouting now and he checked himself. 'I'm sorry. I didn't mean to shout. I'm just finding it a bit difficult to come to terms with, that's all.'

'You mean you're allowing your emotions to cloud your journalist's judgement?' said Mike with a wry, but kindly, smile.

'Something like that,' said Roland, subsiding.

'OK,' said Mike, 'let me tell you what I think will happen. The most infectious time for any disease is usually just around the time you start to feel unwell, and shortly afterwards. Let's take measles, for example. During this time the virus or bacteria is rapidly multiplying inside you. Then your body does one of two things—either it gets better and quietly learns how to kill off the viruses . . . or else it can't quite manage to do that and the viruses overwhelm the body.'

'And kill it?' said Amanda.

'And kill it,' said Mike. 'It doesn't happen often now with measles—it used to. The sailors who discovered Fiji brought measles with them, and many of the natives died off as a result because they'd never experienced measles in the past and their bodies didn't know how to cope.

'As I said, the time when you're most infectious is during the early phase of feeling ill, and shortly afterwards. If people were only infectious when they had the measles rash, measles would have gone a long time ago, because every time somebody had the rash we'd put them in an isolation unit, the viruses wouldn't be passed on, and nobody else could get the illness. But the problem is that people are infectious *before* they know they've got it, and they go round breathing it over others.

'The same thing will be happening with Legionnaires'. We know that this strain has an incubation period of about two days before symptoms occur. I wouldn't doubt that people who are coughing and spluttering as they do at the end are probably quite infectious, but they're probably infectious for some hours beforehand, before they realise they're ill.'

'A bit like AIDS,' said Amanda.

'*Exactly* like AIDS,' said Mike, 'only the cycle is quicker in Legionnaires'.'

'There's another variable. We don't know how many people are naturally resistant to the disease. But the bottom line is that all of this is hypothesis. I don't know for certain how much of this applies to the current strain of Legionnaires'. I'm only guessing, extrapolating from what we know about other diseases.'

'So what you're saying,' said Roland, 'is that what we ought to do is get hold of some of the antibiotics and hope that it will protect us in case we were in contact with Hywel at the time when he was infectious.'

'That's right. And the more that you can keep people away from one another the less chance there is of the disease being passed on. We don't know how long the organism is going to hang around in the air, but ordinary Legionnaires' is not a particularly strong organism—most germs aren't for that matter—and it's surprising how quickly sunlight will destroy them.'

It was Roland who finally voiced the last terrible thought that he could suppress no longer. 'That's for us here. What's going to happen to all the people outside? Are we really going to be able to stop it? What would happen if we gave everybody the antibiotics you were talking about? Could we stop it then?'

'Not a chance,' said Mike. 'There won't be enough to go round.'

'So what we're really up against is a plague like the Black Death—which killed four-fifths of Europe?'

'Yes,' said Mike, 'only I fancy this one's more infectious.'

There was another silence, broken only by the distant sound of the monitors. Then, over the background murmur came a sound which made the blood of every single one of them in that room run cold. From down the corridor came the sound of Alan Fortescue—having a paroxysm of coughing.

-20-

Thursday, Noon

*P*anic.

Sheer unadulterated panic. The hourly news bulletins—and later the quarter-hourly news flashes—conveyed the magnitude of the situation. All over London people were dying. It had

started around Richmond—those who had been in contact with
the first few victims and their contacts, and the people with
whom *they'd* been in contact . . . Many of these were in the
Richmond area, but there were others who had travelled further
afield: those who worked in Richmond and travelled home to the
other side of London; and those who worked outside and
travelled home to Richmond. And in the places they'd travelled
to they had infected not one or two, but hundreds and thousands
of their own contacts. Two days earlier, just one infectious
person travelling on the tube would infect most of those he
passed on the way—and it was these new contacts who were now
dying by the thousand.

The effect was of a set of dominoes going down, spreading
outwards from Richmond, but here and there jumping a few
miles or tens of miles to a new focus of infection. Around each
centre of infection further waves of infection fanned out. A
single person might infect one hundred, two hundred or a
thousand before he died. Two days later, when his contacts in
turn became ill, they too infected several hundred people each.
Like a wave far out on the ocean which gets bigger and bigger as
the sea bed rises, until it curls over to crash and thunder on to a
beach, so the wave of infection rose and crashed down on the
city. At 9.00 a.m. there had been some two hundred people dead.
By eleven o'clock it was nearer two thousand. At noon it was
eight thousand. The rise was terrifying, remorseless and
exponential. Like the grains of rice on a chess board, nemesis
occurred in the last three or four multiplications. So it was with
the plague. It had started off slowly, but now it was out of
control, thundering along, carving a swathe through the city.

The fall of the Roman Empire took several hundred years.
Britain fell to the plague in about as many hours. It soon became
clear that nothing was going to stop it. No one was prepared to
stay in London, when there was a possibility that he might not
already have been infected, and by running away might save his
life. Unfortunately although a large number thought that they
were safe, many were already infected, and as they went along on
train, on bus, or on foot they infected their neighbours, who in
turn would die in two days' time. Mike had been right. If people
had only stayed put the outcome could have been quite different,

but—with a few notable exceptions—most wanted to save their own skins, and considered that first, and everybody else second. As a result they died in their thousands and tens of thousands and hundreds of thousands—collapsing in the streets, in the trains, in their cars, and lying where they had fallen.

In the first hours of the exodus only a small percentage became ill and died, so there were relatively few bodies in the centre of the city: but by the time the tide of refugees reached the outskirts the death rate had multiplied a thousandfold and bodies littered the streets.

By noon the traffic across Vauxhall Bridge resembled the rush hour on the evening of a Bank Holiday. An hour and a half later it was three times worse. Not only did all those working in London want to get out and get home, but those who normally lived in the centre wanted to get out as well. They streamed across its bridges over the Thames. They crammed into cars. They packed into trains. They walked, they went on bicycles, they pushed prams with their belongings in.

Very soon it became every man for himself. All courtesies were lost in the Gadarene-like rush to get away. The first sign of breakdown had come shortly after Mike's announcement that erythromycin might just stave off the infection. Within half an hour there wasn't a tablet, a capsule or a syrup left in any pharmacy within a radius of forty miles. The medication wasn't available without a prescription, but that didn't stop most people. Some, by persuading their GPs to write an urgent prescription, acquired the drugs legally. They were the minority. The majority just walked into the pharmacies and stole them, usually by threatening violence with whatever convenient blunt object happened to be available.

Crisis brings out the best and worst in people. The best is glorious and noble. The worst is far more pitiable and horrible than we care to acknowledge in a civilised society. Self-preservation made animals out of many. Not only would people steal for the drugs, they bribed, cajoled, bullied, assaulted for them. Women were prepared to give sexual favours just to get their hands on a few tablets. Parents took for themselves the medicines their children had been prescribed for their earache.

Yet amongst this there was also the best: parents who

stopped taking their own medicines to give them to their children; husbands who gave it to their wives; wives who gave it to their husbands. Older people who'd been prescribed erythromycin for chest infections took it round to the young family next door.

But as Mike had predicted, there wasn't enough to go round. Soon stocks ran out and the wholesalers had little to fall back on—it would take weeks to manufacture a new batch.

Then came the looting. Hatton Garden suffered it first, but no area was completely immune. There was very little resistance. Many people had left their shops and businesses unlocked in the hope of making a quicker getaway, and often the looters didn't even have to break in. They went for anything and everything—jewellery, watches, computers, clothes, video recorders. But even the looting had to stop, because it took time: and there's only a limit to what one person can carry. A man or woman running for their life wants to stay light, so after a time much of the produce that had been purloined was cast aside to litter the pavements while its 'owner' struggled to keep up with the onrushing crowd.

By three o'clock the death toll had risen to eighty thousand. Not all of these had died from Legionnaires': some had been trampled underfoot in the rush, knocked down at street corners, or hit by cars. Increasingly and ominously there were accidents and pile-ups as drivers died at the wheel from the disease that had been incubating within them. They had started their journey feeling well, only to die before they could complete it.

The victims got little warning. They would start to shiver and feel unwell: then they began to cough. Their faces would go pink from the effort of coughing, then more dusky and purple, until with blue lips, swollen tongue and protruding eyes they collapsed lifeless.

When the victim was a driver no one dared open the door and steer the car out of the way, in case he too became infected, so the vehicle would remain where it was, blocking the street. The cars behind couldn't turn round because of the traffic jammed behind them, so they would try to push the blocking car, with its dead occupant, out of the way. Sometimes they were successful, more often they were not. Sometimes they damaged their own cars in the process, causing a bigger blockage. Then the frightened and anxious motorists behind *them* would in turn try to get past, mounting the pavement, using their cars as battering rams, doing *anything* to get through.

Soon, at practically every crossroads there was a pile of cars blocking the entire road: from time to time a crash would rupture the fuel tank of a car, which turned instantly into a funeral pyre for its dead occupant, setting all the adjacent vehicles on fire.

The biggest jams occurred on the major roads round the outside of the city—the North and South Circular, Westway, the A1, A5 and of course the M25. Soon all the important junctions and roundabouts were blocked, with cars piling up behind desperately trying to get out. By four o'clock there was a solid ring of cars round London with quarter-mile traffic jams behind even the most insignificant junctions. Meanwhile the centre of the city had become a ghost town, the streets empty apart from the occasional car with its dead occupant, and by five o'clock, as darkness started to fall, the only people left in central London were the immobile, the elderly, and sometimes the very young.

*   *   *

Ensconced in his vicarage, Martin had watched the whole of the previous week's events unfold in its macabre detail. At first he'd been angry—angry that as a result of man's selfishness and stupidity, genetic and bacteriological warfare had rebounded on the nation. It had to come, he thought. They've been hankering for war for so long and now they've got their just deserts.

Serve him right, he thought on hearing of the death of Sir Richard, though he immediately corrected himself, as a good Christian, and offered up a prayer for Sir Richard's soul and family, even if he had been stupid enough to get involved in germ warfare. Nevertheless Martin was sufficiently imbued with the spirit of peace and gentleness about which he had always preached to make him realise that he shouldn't really be thinking in these terms. He shouldn't bear malice against others, whatever they had done, so he tried, with little success, to abandon his position of 'I told you so' and instead attempted to sympathise with them as victims of the system and of society.

Then, like the journalists at AM-TV, it suddenly began to dawn on him that it was no longer happening to people out there, but that he was part of what was happening and that he was likely to be a victim along with everybody else, and at that point his anger against society turned to rage. How dare the scientists manipulate and mutilate God's creation in this way? Why hadn't they listened? Enough voices had been raised saying, 'You're going to destroy the earth, you're going to destroy mankind.' Why hadn't somebody done something? Why hadn't they seen the danger until too late?

Then, on the television and on the radio, he heard about the victims, the panic, and the exodus. Outside the vicarage he saw the traffic building up to the point of total stagnation, whereupon the occupants of the cars left them where they were, stuck in the middle of the street, and continued on foot.

Shortly afterwards waves of pedestrians came—hundreds, rushing past, cursing and shoving, trampling weaker ones under foot. He could have gone out to help the ones who'd fallen, or become injured, or even the dying, but he'd realised the wisdom of Mike's injunction to stay put in case he himself had already been contaminated. It was also a good excuse for ensuring he didn't acquire the disease either, so he watched from the upstairs window of the vicarage, and as the light faded, he saw just how brutal men could be when self-interest drove them on.

In the past he had preached against those who abused their power, used money as a tool and economics as a weapon. What he had preached about was what he saw now, but here the power was that of ordinary people, of health and strength used against those who were feeble and frail. He saw an old lady desperately trying to keep up with her middle-aged son, but she couldn't, so he left her and went on ahead, leaving her stumbling along frail and frightened. He saw people being robbed at knife point, forced to hand over money and, more importantly, the antibiotics. He could have done something—gone outside to remonstrate perhaps, or to help the old, the frail and the little children, but he decided there wasn't any point in trying to stem the flow or stop the tide. He wouldn't be able to do anything; no one would listen to him; he'd just get caught up in the rush and besides, he might pick up the infection. So he stayed in the vicarage, looking out of the window, and watching the television reports as they came in.

But he also became aware of another voice within him. Like

those at AM-TV, he too found that his subconscious mind was asking a lot of questions, the sort which he really couldn't tolerate consciously, and a growing unease gripped him as he watched and listened while evil and selfishness poured itself out on the city, an evil that came not from outside, not from invasion from a foreign army nor from organised crime or planned vandalism—but evil that came from within.

As the light faded he didn't put the light on—he didn't want others to know he was there. Instead he stayed unobserved at the high windows, fascinated and appalled. The phone rang several times, and the doorbell went twice, but he didn't answer them. Even if it were a request for help he knew that he wouldn't go out. He wasn't prepared to die, not just yet.

He rationalised it, of course. He thought of Mike and how important it was to stay put and show an example—not that anybody could see him staying put, but it was a good excuse. He mustn't go and comfort the dying or the bereaved, the panic-stricken or the frightened, because that would mean exposing himself to the possibility of contamination and if all priests did likewise, he thought, there would be no on-going church to minister to people afterwards. So he stayed at his window as the sun went down and the bicycles and the motorcycles crawled past, winding their way between the stationary cars; pedestrians swarmed past and little babies were pushed in their prams and toddlers were pulled behind their parents. More than once he saw children who'd lost their parents wandering around, crying and panic-stricken. Some of them were knocked over and injured by pedestrians or cyclists, but he didn't venture out. He just stayed put, watching the shouting, heaving, pushing mass.

Then there were the people who started coughing. Whenever it started, the other refugees would immediately clear an area around them. Nobody would touch them, nobody would go near them. The others recoiled in horror, watching while they collapsed, dying alone and friendless. Soon there were bodies all over the road and the pavement.

And as the sun finally died and the last glimmerings of twilight faded, the little voice inside his head turned into a roar that he could no longer ignore. As the voice became louder and louder he could shut it out no longer, and as the hands of the

clock showed 6.13 the thought finally hit his conscious mind in
much the same way as an Atlantic wave crests and plunges on to
the rocks in full fury. 'O God, if you're good and kind and
loving and an all-powerful God, how can you possibly let this all
happen and stand by without doing anything to stop it? You're
either not good or you're not God.'

And at 6.13 that Thursday evening as the framework of
civilisation in London disintegrated in front of his eyes, so
Martin Freeman's theological civilisation disintegrated too, and
he was left with the shell of what once had been. At first he
couldn't comprehend the awfulness of the truth that had hit him
and he stayed at the window, staring out, seeing nothing, aware
only of a numbness in his mind.

He was there for two hours, motionless, vacant. Then he
crawled on to his bed, curled into a ball and sobbed his heart
out—not for what he'd seen so much as for what he'd lost. The
events of the world outside were like a dream compared to the
awfulness of the reality within himself. Martin Freeman had lost
his faith, his reason for living and—like Peter Abrahams—his
profession.

-21-

Thursday Afternoon

At the time when the exodus from London was just beginning,
Willow and its occupants were travelling south along the Grand
Union Canal. True to what Derek had said, they had got away
from it all. Without newspapers, or others to talk to—and above
all, without watching television or listening to the radio—they
moved into the last two days of their holiday totally oblivious to
what was going on in the world about them.

The morning had been spent traversing the one-and-three-
quarter-mile Blisworth Tunnel, the longest navigable canal tunnel
in Britain. Immediately on the south side of the tunnel they came

upon Stoke Bruerne, a charming late eighteenth-century village built round the canal, and now housing, among other things, several restaurants and a waterways museum.

In the season, Stoke Bruerne is a tourist trap, but in late October much of it was closed up. They didn't intend to stop, as they had already explored the village two days previously when going in the other direction, so they steered *Willow* between the lines of moored boats, and straight into the top lock of the Stoke Bruerne flight without speaking to anyone—nor seeing anyone for that matter.

Below the locks at Stoke Bruerne the canal winds round the contours of the gently rolling countryside as though it were in another world. This is one of the most deserted parts of the canal—rolling farmland for miles on either side, with the occasional small village in the distance.

That afternoon they chugged slowly past Grafton Regis, with its church set on a hill to the west, superbly picturesque. The whole world looked interesting, vibrant, inviting.

It was a tremendous autumn. The hedgerows by the towpath were full of berries, and the russets and browns of the dying leaves shone and glowed in the brilliant amber sunlight, contrasting dramatically with the clear blue sky that can be such a feature of autumn. They were all enthralled. Derek used up half a roll of film in that three-mile section alone. At one point they disturbed a heron which took off gracefully to land on the towpath about a quarter of a mile away and as *Willow* puttered up to it again the same thing happened. Ducks and coots swam behind the boat, conditioned by the events of the summer to realise that boats, especially ones with children on, usually meant a good supply of easy food.

So, completely ignorant of the momentous events occurring some fifty-five miles to the south, they passed Yardley Gobion, mooring for the night just below bridge 62, out in the middle of nowhere. That evening, having eaten a large meal of steak, peas and fried potatoes, they went out on to the towpath to look at the stars, and the moon, rising in the east. Even though they were in the depths of the countryside they could still hear the faint murmur of traffic in the distance; but the quiet rustle of the wind in the dying grass was much more noticeable. It was a peaceful, natural, restful sound.

But it was cold out on deck; and after a while they all went inside, shut the curtains, turned up the central heating and played Monopoly. It was a relaxing holiday. They were at peace with the world and at peace within themselves. Getting back to nature was the best thing they could have done.

-22-

Thursday Evening, 6.13 p.m.

At 6.13 that evening Paul Greatorex was standing at the semicircular window in the bedroom of his Dockland flat, looking west up the Thames to Tower Bridge as the last of the twilight reflected off the water. Behind him Jane was lying between the black satin sheets of the bed, wearing a particularly glamorous and somewhat revealing nightdress, her long blonde hair spread across the pillow.

But there the illusion of glamour ended. It was matted hair, and Jane was sweating like the proverbial pig. She also exuded that peculiar smell that people create when they've been in bed for a day or so. Jane had flu which had started just after the Wednesday morning programme. Later that day Paul had also come back early from the City with aching limbs, a thudding headache and a temperature of 104 and they both retired to bed, living off paracetamol and Perrier water, and feeling by the size of their headaches that for them the end of the world was just about to happen.

At first Jane had worried that they might be going down with this strange new disease that she'd heard Mike and Hywel talking about, but as she'd been ill for more than half an hour, and wasn't coughing (at least not much), she came to the conclusion that maybe she'd just got good old flu after all.

Paul had never had flu before. It was a revelation to him. Previously he'd thought that you were a bit of a cissy if you didn't manage to get to work even if you did have flu. Now he realised that his level of experience had been all wrong. Those who said they'd had a dose of flu, but had worked through it, had only had a heavy cold. When you really do have flu, he thought, there is nothing that you can do with it other than take to your bed.

So they had lain there, drowsy and half-delirious, as the sun went round the room twice, the light slanting in from the windows on the east in the morning and coming in through the semicircular window in the evening, as the sun set behind Tower Bridge.

By Thursday evening they had felt a little better so Paul was able to get up and stand at the window without actually falling over. Then he went to the kitchen to make a drink of hot fruit cordial for them both, together with a little toast and honey. It was all they could do to eat it. As the sun finally sank in the west they drifted off to sleep again, fitful sleep, full of dreams and disturbances.

-23-

Friday, 6.00 a.m.

Next morning, Jane woke early. She was accustomed to getting up at 4.00 a.m. in order to be at work in time to carry out the final checks before the programme went out, but in any case, as she'd been asleep for most of the past two days she was slept out. She got up quietly so as not to disturb Paul, went to the kitchen and made a cup of tea and some more toast. That was probably enough expenditure of energy for the next hour, she thought, so she curled up on the sofa and idly flicked the television on. Might as well look at the old show, she thought, selecting Channel Three. The opening credits were rolling and she could feel herself counting automatically, twenty seconds, fifteen seconds. Strange how difficult it is to get out of the habit of doing things like that, even when it's totally inappropriate, she thought. She felt on edge, then realised that the sights and sounds she was experiencing were always accompanied by tension in the gallery, where the smoothness of the programme depended, among other things, on the quality of her timing.

Then she saw something which made her heart beat even faster. There was something wrong—terribly wrong. For a start they were only using one camera. Secondly, they hadn't got a camera operator either: Duncan's head wasn't properly framed within the shot—he had moved slightly and the camera hadn't followed him. And the continuity—well, what little there was, was dreadful. There were long pauses between the introduction to a VT and the videotape itself; and when the videotapes did come on they were obviously raw, as photographed, without any editing whatsoever, with all sorts of blanks, false starts, out-of-focus shots and odd flashes and stripes across the screen.

In consternation, she turned the sound up. At least that was working all right. But the whole programme looked as though it had been produced by a bunch of amateurs—had she been involved, she would have expected the producer, the director and herself to be dismissed instantly for producing such an appalling technical mess.

Jane stared at the screen in horrid fascination. Duncan was speaking. 'Today London stands empty and deserted. Hardly anyone is left. The outbreak of Legionnaires' disease which started in Richmond has spread throughout the whole capital. It's impossible to estimate the number of dead—reports put it at between 100,000 and 200,000. The rest of the inhabitants of the city have fled, leaving hardly anybody behind. In fact this whole programme is being produced by just five volunteers who've chosen to remain here at AM-TV—which is why it's so rough and ready.

'Yesterday eight million people streamed out of London in one continuous movement, resulting in massive traffic jams. Now all the major routes out of London are blocked, with cars stuck behind the hundreds of accidents that have occurred. The M25 has ground to a complete halt, the M1 is blocked as far as Junction 12 and all other motorways out of the capital are similarly impassable.'

The scene changed to a hastily put together videotape. It was obviously Richmond—Jane could see the bridge over the Thames—and the camera slowly panned round the streets which were littered with bodies. The devastation was indescribable.

Another change of scene followed, to the roundabout at the junction between the North Circular road and the M1. All the traffic was at a standstill, with cars at all angles. In some the occupants were slumped forward over the driving wheel and there had been a couple of vehicles that had caught fire and burned out. In one car Jane saw to her horror that the two adults at the front were dead, whilst in the back a baby of about six months old was strapped in a child's seat, screaming. No one went to rescue it. No one had dared.

The scene changed again, with jerks and flickers, to the centre of the City. 'As you can see the centre of London is relatively clear of traffic and bodies because everyone has moved outwards: the big traffic jams have occurred further from the centre.

'Quite who has fallen victim to the plague we can't say for sure. Here at AM-TV we've lost one of our best-known reporters, Hywel Davies, and the medical pathologist who's been helping us, Dr Mike Williams, but like most businesses we don't know if those who didn't turn up this morning are still alive or whether they have just fled in the panic.'

Duncan screwed up his face, paused for a few moments and then recovered himself. 'We don't know the whereabouts of the Royal Family, nor is there much news from the Government. We understand that the secure bunkers that were to be used to house members of the Government in the case of a nuclear attack have been opened up, but at least one report says that the plague has swept through them also.

'All airports have been closed. In an attempt to isolate the disease to Britain no flights from Britain are being allowed to land at any other airport, but we understand that this action is already too late, as outbreaks of the disease are known to have occurred in Paris, Hamburg, Moscow, Berlin, New York and San Francisco, presumably carried by air travellers who left London several days ago.

'Outbreaks have been reported in all major cities in the British Isles. In Birmingham ten thousand people are known to have died so far. The pattern of events in all these cities has been exactly the same—a central nucleus of infection which spread rapidly outwards: in all cases the inhabitants ignored official

warnings to stay put, and fled to the countryside. Exactly the
same problems as those we have experienced in London have
occurred in all these cities—all major roads have become
impassable as a result of accidents and traffic jams, and ordinary
travel is impossible.' He screwed his eyes up, swayed slightly
and recovered again.

'There has been some looting, but not much, as people have
been more interested in getting away from the city . . .' He swayed
again and Jane noticed how pale and drawn he looked. Duncan
began coughing paroxysmally, collapsed forwards, and disappeared
from view. After a few seconds more the screen went blank.

Jane stared at the television, transfixed. Death—real death,
not the film variety—was almost unknown to her, and to see one
of her business friends collapse and die on the screen left her
wide-eyed with horror. As if in a dream she flipped over to the
other channels. Nothing. BBC 1 was showing the test card; the
other channels were either blank or filled with 'snow'.

She switched the television off and turned on the radio.
None of the network radio channels were transmitting, nor any of
the independent local radio stations in London. She could pick
up some foreign stations—one in French, one in German; and
Radio Moscow was still there. And she could also pick up,
faintly, some of the local radio stations from more distant towns.
Radio Kent was still working and so was BBC Three Counties
Radio, broadcasting from Bedfordshire.

She left the radio on and went to the window, still totally
unable to take in what she'd heard. Outside dawn was breaking.
To the west she could see London, looking much as usual—the
street lights were on, though there weren't many lights in the
houses and flats. It all looks so normal, she thought, finding it
hard to believe that what she'd heard on television could actually
have happened to the city spread out in front of her.

She looked down, but could see no one moving in the street,
though her attention was caught by something flapping on the
opposite corner. In the dim light it looked like a piece of fabric
wafted around in the breeze, but she couldn't make out any
details. She looked up again at the city panorama in front of her
and realised that one or two of the lights were not lights at all, but
fires. About two miles away, a block of flats was starting to burn

and there was another one over towards the city—but the flames
didn't seem to be spreading to surrounding buildings.

As it got lighter she looked down again at the fluttering piece
of fabric at the street corner and realised with a start that there
was a body collapsed on the pavement, half obscured by the end
wall of the building: the fluttering was a piece of clothing, a
skirt blown about by the wind. Shaking, both from the effects of
the flu and the shock of what she'd just seen and heard, she
turned away from the window and sat down again, listening to
the voice on the radio.

-24-

The woman she'd been listening to, Chris Wilson, had earlier
driven into Three Counties Radio's main office in Luton from her
lodgings in Flitwick, some fifteen miles to the northwest. Aged
twenty-eight, Chris was a slender woman of medium height with
an oval, slightly spotty face, and mousy-coloured hair cut short
round her head. Although she always tried to give the impression
to others that she didn't quite know what she was doing, behind
her green eyes was a very sharp mind indeed, quick-witted and
well-organised.

Bearing in mind her normal punctuality, today was off to a
bad start. The previous day had turned itself into a nightmare for
her, for completely different reasons to those of the rest of the
world. Chris was prone to the occasional migraine, especially at
the time of her period, and the day before, as she launched into
the last half-hour of her morning show she had began to
experience the premonitory signs—the flickering lights in the
eyes, the blank spots in her field of vision.

Gamely she'd managed to get to the end of her show before
the real headache struck, and then it was a matter of quickly
making what preparations she had to for the following day's
programme, and getting home as fast as possible. From bitter
experience she had found that the best way to clear her headaches

was to take her medicines as soon as possible, then go to bed for twenty-four hours and sleep it off.

Gratefully, when the alarm went at 4.15 a.m. she found that the appalling headache had cleared, so she would be able to do her morning show as usual.

But things were still not going well for her. Normally her daily 5.00 a.m. run into Luton was quick and easy, unhampered by traffic; but this morning it was different: there were many more vehicles on the road. They weren't travelling in any particular direction—some were going into Luton, and some coming out—but it was enough to make Chris slightly pinched for time, so that instead of arriving with a comfortable forty minutes to spare before her show was due to go out, it was quarter to six by the time she turned her battered Renault into the car park and switched off the lights.

As if being late wasn't enough, she was irritated for another reason. Normally she would listen to the early morning news on her car radio as she came into work, but two days earlier the radio had been stolen, so that morning she was unable to catch up with the events in London.

Late and uninformed—and hence doubly irritated—Chris let herself in through the glass front door of the Three Counties Radio offices and went upstairs to the main reception area. 'Morning, Tim,' she shouted to the newsreader allocated to the early morning shift.

There was no answer.

'Tim?'

There was no one there. He's probably in the news cubicle, she thought, looking in through the window. Wrong again.

Maybe he's in the loo, or stuck in the traffic, she thought, ripping the latest news bulletins out of the fax. I'll have to read the news myself if he's not here in time—as if I haven't enough to do already with being late.

Gathering up the CDs and tapes she'd thrown together the previous day for her coming three-hour programme, and chewing absentmindedly on an apple—her only gesture towards breakfast—she went down to the studios on the floor below, and settled herself down at the U-shaped broadcasting console.

Even though there was no one in the building, throughout the night the station was still on the air, rebroadcasting the night service supply—a mixture of items both from other local radio stations, and Radio Two—so after putting down her cue-sheets and tapes Chris switched on the speakers to monitor the current output of the station, ready to cut in at the right moment with the start of her show.

Silence.

Suddenly alert, Chris put her apple down and studied the board to see why there was no programme output. The red panel in the centre had a light inside the 'Night Service' button showing that the desk was definitely accepting feed—which at this hour should have meant Radio Two—but the monitors were still silent and the dials measuring programme volume registered zero. Quickly she checked the desk again, but everything was in place and in order. It couldn't be just a failure of the studio loudspeakers—there was no signal coming down the night service line either.

Putting on her headphones, Chris switched them to monitor the output from Radio Two directly.

Nothing.

She tried Radio One: still nothing. Radios Three, Four and Five—the same. No output was being sent from London on network radio. Picking up the studio telephone by her left knee she dialled Broadcasting House. No reply. Maybe they'd had a power cut, she thought. She knew of course of the very beginnings of the problem with the outbreak of Legionnaires' disease in west London, but she hadn't heard the news since nine o'clock the previous morning.

There were only three minutes to go before the beginning of her own programme, so putting aside the problem of what might have happened down at the London end, she started her pre-programme checks, lining up the first two CDs, and making sure all her carts had the right jingles in them.

She linked up to the newsroom, hoping that Tim had got in by now. Maybe he'd been somewhere else in the building when she'd poked her head through the door.

'Studio 1A to news, are you ready?'

Silence.

'Tim, are you there?'

No answer.

Half a minute to go. She'd have to read the news herself. Still chewing at the apple in her right hand, she used the other awkwardly to smooth out the faxes so that she could practise what she was supposed to be reading. She finished reading the sheets—none of which was very recent, judging by the times printed on them—then nonchalantly lobbed the remains of the apple into the bin in the corner.

Ten seconds to go.

In front of her were the faders which controlled the volume of the microphone, tape recorders, cassettes and CDs. Pushing the cartridge with the station ID jingle into the first cartridge slot, she waited until the second hand on the wall clock was exactly at the hour, then pulled the fader open to set the cartridge off. The familiar music fed into her headphones, and thankfully she noticed the needles on the level gauges quivering into life as the signal was sent to the transmitter and broadcast over the three counties. At least there was nothing wrong with the equipment at her end.

Somewhat relieved, now that everything was going as normal again, Chris opened the second cartridge fader to obtain the introductory music for her own show together with the standard prerecorded voice-over. 'This is BBC Three Counties Radio serving Beds, Herts and Bucks. It's *Breakfast in Beds*, with Chris Wilson.'

She pulled her own microphone fader open. 'Good morning. I'm Chris Wilson, and I'm looking forward to the pleasure of your company for the next three hours, here on BBC Three Counties Radio.

'First a quick look at the news headlines.' She began reading from the newsroom brief: 'The outbreak of Legionnaires' disease in west London . . .'

When she'd finished the bulletin she started the first CD, shut down her own microphone, then turned to one of the two floor-mounted tape recorders on her right and loaded it with the reel containing the first of the interviews that had been pre-recorded and edited for her by other members of the Three Counties Radio staff.

As the CD ended she opened her own fader again and read

from the introductory transcript accompanying the tape. 'Now if you think you have problems getting up in the morning—and who doesn't—perhaps you ought to use the method that Henry McKilroy of Limbury has been using for years—green peppers. Josh Whiting went to talk to him and asked him what it was all about.'

She started the tape recorder playing. The report would last three minutes and twenty-three seconds—it said so on the accompanying script—so she could relax for a moment and gather her thoughts together.

The absence of feed from London was still bothering her, as was the lack of up-to-date news on the situation in London, so leaving the tape to play on its own she turned to the television. Although it might be thought odd to have a television in a radio studio, it is useful for a presenter to be able to glance at Ceefax headlines showing changes in scores of test matches, the weather, the FT index and so on. It also acts as a messaging device during phone-ins.

She switched it on, hoping to get *Breakfast Time* on BBC 1. Nothing. There must be a power failure at Broadcasting House, she thought. Then she thought again. No. The *radio* feeds come from Broadcasting House, but the *television* signal comes from Television Centre in Shepherds Bush. Anything that happened to one was unlikely to affect the other . . . little crawling fingers started to going up the back of her neck . . . unless it were very, very big.

She switched to ITV. That at least was showing something—AM-TV. She caught the same broadcast that Jane had been watching out in Docklands. The situation had obviously deteriorated considerably since the bulletin Chris had just read out had been prepared.

With a sense of rising panic she watched Duncan relating the events that had hit the capital the previous day, the death of Hywel, the lack of government, the traffic jams. No wonder I had problems getting into work, Chris thought. Then Duncan screwed his eyes up and began coughing . . .

She kept watching, transfixed, while Duncan collapsed in front of her and the screen went blank. She remained motionless, stunned, for a further thirty seconds, then with a start realised that her recorded tape was about to run out.

Too dumbfounded to say anything she switched another CD on without any intervening introduction, and sat back in her chair, heart pounding, wondering what to do.

Using the office intercom she rang up to the production room. 'Anybody up there yet?' No reply. She rang reception. No response. Using the studio telephone she dialled the home of the station manager. No reply there, either. The fingers crawling up and down her spine increased in intensity. The suddenness of it all was the most startling. She had known that the plague had hit London—who didn't—but when she had gone to bed the day before, she'd never dreamt, never even considered, that it would get out of hand so quickly.

Abandoning all her previous plans for the show she faded the CD out and opened her own microphone. 'I'm sure if you've been following the news,' she said to anyone in the three counties who was still alive and listening, 'you'll know that an epidemic of Legionnaires' disease has hit London. I can now give you an update on our previous news summary. There has been panic in London. Between 100,000 and 200,000 people have died and there is a mass exodus from the capital. The roads are jammed with traffic, and there have been many accidents. I can't give you any further news from the capital because the lines to Broadcasting House are all out of action, but if you can give further information about your area please ring me at BBC Three Counties Radio to tell us what's happening.'

She gave the number out. Within ten seconds the lights on her telephone board started flashing. After putting another CD on she answered the first call. 'BBC Three Counties Radio, Chris Wilson speaking.'

'Hello, my name's Ruby Coates.'

'Where are you calling from Ruby?'

'Harpenden.'

'Ruby, we'll come to you as soon as the music's finished. Just hang on.'

She went to the second line and did the same, and the third and the fourth.

The CD finished. Chris opened her microphone again. 'We've had several calls about what's happening over the epidemic. Ruby's rung in from Harpenden.' She switched the telephone in. 'Hello, Ruby.'

'Hello, Chris.'

'What's been happening near you?'

'There was a stream of cars going past until the early morning. Most of it seemed to be coming from the London direction. About two o'clock the traffic seemed to stop and after that there were lots of people walking, mainly going north.'

'Is there still traffic in the streets then?'

'Yes, but it's not moving. There's a hold-up somewhere. A lot of drivers have been honking their horns, but it doesn't seem to make any difference. No one's moved for ages.'

'Ruby, thanks for your call. We'll go to Wayne in Milton Keynes. Hello, Wayne.'

'Hi, Chris.'

'What's the situation with you?'

'Much the same as with your previous caller. There's been a lot of traffic and a lot of people walking . . .'

After four calls all saying much the same thing she put on another CD, and sat back in her chair to think. A sense of loneliness started to grip her. Surely there must be *somebody* in the production office by now. She rang through again. No answer. She was still the only person in the entire building.

She switched into the land line connecting the studio to AA Roadwatch in Stanmore. They, more than anyone else, should be able to tell her the current state of the roads and where the various traffic jams were. No one answered.

She tried the Luton police. This time her call was answered almost immediately, and she asked if she could speak to somebody on air about the current situation: she was put through to Inspector Bob Thorpe.

'What's the current situation in Luton?' asked Chris when the CD finished.

'There's a stream of refugees coming up from London. As you know there are massive traffic jams all round the outskirts of the capital. Not only are the people from London moving out, but those living in the surrounding towns are scared of the people coming from the city because they're afraid they'll bring the infection with them. We have reports of battles developing between villagers and refugees, and a number have already been killed and injured. People from the towns and villages north of London are also starting to move, and of course *they're* also moving away from the city; so there's a progressive movement of the whole of the population sweeping up northwards.'

'How long's this been going on? I must admit there was a lot more traffic than I'd normally expect when I came into the studio this morning.'

'It hit Harpenden and St Albans at about midnight,' said the Inspector. 'Luton started moving around four o'clock and since the announcement on AM-TV there's been a huge upsurge. People seem just to have dropped everything, got in their cars and driven off.'

'What are the roads like locally?'

'The M1 is blocked up to junction 12, but there's no problem beyond it—at least, not at the moment—though traffic is very heavy indeed.'

'Why aren't there blockages, then? Apparently London's jammed solid.'

'It's a bit different here. In London everybody was trying to get across and out of the city. All the traffic was trying to converge onto a few major roads, so there was a lot of congestion and many accidents. Once traffic's got on to the main roads it isn't quite so bad, because everyone is going in the same direction—though a number of drivers have died in their cars and the major roads are getting progressively more difficult to use.

'Junction 12 on the M1 is blocked on the exit side, but the slip road joining the motorway is clear, so if drivers want to travel north, that junction's still open. We do ask that everybody goes slowly and takes care, without panicking, because that way we'll keep the traffic moving. If drivers try to go too fast they'll only cause accidents, and then they'll never get to their destination.'

'Thank you Inspector,' said Chris. The lights on her telephone monitor were still flashing. She opened the first line. 'Hello, this is BBC Three Counties Radio. Where are you calling from?'

'From central London,' said a frail voice on the line.

'And what's your name?' said Chris.

'Winifred. I'm a pensioner and I live in a flat on my own. I can't get out—I've had a stroke, and my normal helper hasn't come this morning—but I can see from my window what's been going on.' And Winifred went on to describe much the sort of scene that Jane could see from her Docklands flat.

Jane, listening in her own flat, felt more and more lonely as the enormity of the situation began to sink in, with the realisation that in the silent London that she could see before her were hundreds of people on their own, isolated, their friends, relatives and helpers either fleeing or dead. Each victim was imprisoned in his own building, unable to get out, unable to find food . . .

She shuddered, and began to sweat and shake, though that was partly due to the flu. It was like a dream, a huge, ghastly nightmare. A sense of unreality took over. This wasn't happening to her. She was watching it, but it wasn't happening. De-realisation, the text books call it: when the mind, unable to cope with the strangeness of a situation, makes the observer feel she is somehow outside it all, looking in.

*　　　*　　　*

By five to nine Chris was convinced that nobody was going to come into the station that morning. Normally she would have handed over to Pam Jackson in cubicle 1B, on the opposite side of the main studio, but for once Pam's cheery face had not materialised (she usually started off her programme by making gestures at Chris through the intervening sound-proof windows, trying to make her burst out laughing on air).

Nine o'clock came and went, and Chris continued with her impromptu show, dashing upstairs to the library to get a few more CDs, because she was now running way over her expected time slot.

Once again she asked listeners to telephone in with information, to find out what had been happening in the intervening few hours. At first the calls were numerous, but after a time they became less frequent and by ten-thirty only the occasional call came in response to her requests. Between eleven o'clock and eleven twenty she asked three times for listeners to ring in with news without getting a single response, so at twenty-five past eleven she asked people to ring if they were still listening to the programme, never mind if they could give information or not.

There was no response.

At 11.42 Chris opened her fader, gave a brief summary of the situation as she knew it and then signed off for what she knew would be the very last time. Hoping against hope, she switched in the feed from Radio Two, but there was nothing there.

Switching the light off, she left the studios and went out into the downstairs foyer. She stood there for a moment, wondering what she'd find, then opened the glass door and walked through, letting it swing to behind her.

Outside it was a bright, clear October day. The sun was shining and there was blue sky overhead.

It was also totally silent. No traffic. No people. No footsteps. No aeroplanes in the sky. No traffic on the inner bypass, which ran only twenty yards away from the Three Counties Radio building. Chris listened for a good minute, but heard nothing, except the brief rustle of a dead leaf, blown past her feet by the light breeze.

Walking away from the front of the building, she stopped at the bypass and looked up and down. She'd never known the centre of Luton be so still. There was not a car, not a person in sight. She listened for a good five minutes, trying to take it all in, then retracing her steps to the car park, got into her Renault, and started it up. In the stillness the noise of the engine sounded overwhelmingly, embarrassingly loud. Pulling out of the gate, she headed on to the empty expanse of the inner bypass.

The streets were eerily empty, the first few roundabouts totally free of traffic, but near the fourth junction a knot of traffic blocked the road. The crashed cars were mostly empty, but some contained drivers who appeared to be sleeping at the wheel, and one had obviously careered into a lamppost. There were also some bodies on the pavement. Chris shuddered at the sight. Wisely deciding against investigating further, and trying hard not to look at the corpses, Chris turned her car around and attempted to get beyond the obstruction using the side roads. It proved harder than she expected. The first detour looked hopeful at first. All was going fine until she rounded the last bend—and came upon another solid knot of traffic blocking the road.

Turning round again she retraced her path until she spotted a back street on her left and went up it. Yet again she found the

way ahead was blocked. Slowly and painstakingly she tried
again and again until finally, after half an hour, she threaded a
way through. By a combination of going up one-way streets the
wrong way, mounting the pavement and in one case actually
physically pushing a car out of the way (she didn't really mind
putting a few more dints in her already rusty and marked car)
eventually she got back on to the Bedford Road, on the other
side of the original pile-up. Although there were more bodies
here, the roadway itself was virtually clear. She soon passed the
outskirts of the town and began to descend towards Barton,
taking avoiding action from time to time in order to skirt around
a wrecked car or a dead body lying in the roadway.

In all directions the countryside was deserted—no cars, no
people, no activity. The occasional cow stared at her in bovine
disbelief, but other than that and the birds, there was no evidence
of life anywhere.

By twelve-thirty she was back in Flitwick. Letting herself into
her flat, she put some food on to cook, then, suddenly exhausted,
she sat on the edge of her bed and wondered what on earth to do
next. Pills, she suddenly thought: I forgot the pills for my acne,
and went to the bathroom to take her daily dose of erythromycin.

-25-

At about the same time, Derek was steering *Willow* through
Cosgrove Lock. They entered the more populous part of the Grand
Union Canal as it begins to traverse Milton Keynes. They had not
met many other boats: but as it was autumn, this was to be
expected. There had been some pleasure craft out that first
weekend, but the numbers had dwindled significantly with the
beginning of the working week and today being a Friday, they
didn't expect to meet many others.

In this they were not disappointed: they didn't meet anyone.
However, this didn't concern them overmuch. It had been a
splendid week for boating, with clear blue skies and warm

autumnal sun, if chilly at night. The countryside was charming
to look at, and they had no desire for alternative company as
there was too much both to do and to look at.

Although canals are very quiet—especially when sitting at
the front end of a narrow-boat lapping along at four miles an
hour—standing at the tiller is quite noisy as the diesel engine
thunders away beneath the helmsman's feet, so as they passed
through Wolverton, underneath the railway arches alongside the
vast brick-walled cutting adjoining the railway station, they
hadn't noticed the extra noise of the traffic, the horns and the
shouts as the inhabitants headed north as fast as they could, in
turn hotly pursued by those coming from London.

After Wolverton the canal becomes rural again until it passes
Great Linford on a slight embankment. Great Linford is as
picturesque a village as you would care to imagine, with a wide
village green, a church and a squire's house all laid out as if it
were something out of an early American film which, although
made in Hollywood, was trying to evoke 'a real English village'.

As they progressed along the embankment they could see the
brightly coloured narrow-boats moored in a long line in front of
them. There was no one to be seen. The whole scene was a
vision of perfect rustic charm and quietness, unbroken by the
twentieth century: it could have come straight out of 1810. On
they went, viewing Milton Keynes by the back door, underneath
the vast square bridges that had been built to take the dual-
carriage main roads, past the private marina at Pennylands, past
the back of the many estates built in the seventies and eighties
until they came upon the strange lock at Fenny Stratford.

Fenny Stratford is another of those staging posts on the canal
that looks as though it's been kept in a time warp ever since it
was built. There wasn't anybody around, but they could just
imagine a boatman or an innkeeper, dressed in Regency attire,
rounding the corner of the typical utilitarian Georgian and early
Victorian architecture.

After Fenny Stratford the canal went out into the wilds
again, and as the afternoon drew on they climbed through Stoke
Hammond, a high seven-foot lock with its lock-keeper's cottage,
miles from anywhere. And as the sun began to set they reached
the picturesque Soulbury Three with the Three Locks Inn on the

westward side. They had planned to stop there for food, but the
place seemed deserted, so they went a further half mile and
moored for their last night on the river.

*   *   *

Earlier that day Martin had woken with a start from an
afternoon sleep, with a feeling of anxiety in his stomach, damp
hands and feet, and a fine, cold sweat on his forehead. He felt
dreadful. He was in a full-blown anxiety state, with all somatic
features present—bounding pulse, tense muscles, nausea and an
overwhelming sense of exhaustion.

He was still stuck in the vicarage, not daring to move. There
was quite a store of food in the larder, so rather than risk
becoming infected he decided to stay put. He too had seen
Duncan's final broadcast, and then watched from the upstairs
bedroom window for a good part of the morning without seeing
anyone pass by. In the distance he could see several plumes of
smoke, presumably from buildings that had caught fire, but apart
from that and the odd bird or dog that passed by, there was no
sign of activity all day.

When not looking out of the window, he tried the television
and later the radio. Like Jane he had discovered that now all the
terrestrial channels were dead, so after watching the last twenty
minutes of AM-TV he turned his attention to the radio. Like
Jane he had heard the nearby local radio stations, but one by one
they started to go off the air, and by noon he was unable to pick
up any broadcasts in English.

He tuned the radio to a French station and tried to make
sense of what he heard, but his pidgin French didn't allow him to
make much of what he heard other than the words which sounded
right—*maladie terrible* and *beaucoup de morts*. Leaving the
radio tuned to Radio Paris, he switched off and went back to sit at
his window, where he fell into a troubled sleep.

When he switched the radio on again three hours later, Radio
Paris was no longer transmitting and that same spine-tingling,
crawling feeling down the back of his neck that had affected
Chris transferred itself to Martin. Not just Britain but Europe as
well, and probably the rest of the world too. O God, what a
mess. (Not that he believed in God any more, he hastened to tell

himself. Purely a figure of speech.)

If Mike Williams was right, reasoned Martin, then all that a plague like this needs to spread throughout the world is for people to run away when they think they are well but actually harbouring the virus. They run to a far country and pass the infection on to others, who in turn run away and infect others . . . He had no doubt that the speed of air travel would ensure that this plague passed round the world far faster than ever the Black Death did, which could only travel as fast as its carrier, the rat, migrated.

Another thought formed itself in his subconscious, but checked itself as being too unwholesome for Martin to contemplate in his already emotionally battered state, so it sat there, hammering away for several hours, until finally it welled up into Martin's weary consciousness. *What if I'm the only one left*, he thought, and the panic, shame and exhaustion that he had experienced over the last twenty-four hours redoubled its intensity. A shattering, screaming, numbing fear overwhelmed him. Memories of being lost as a child and finding no friendly face in the crowd, no one to call Mummy or Daddy, no idea which way is home—primitive, fearful responses welled up into his brain, but instead of the childlike feeling that somehow Mummy and Daddy would return to make things better, he now knew that nobody would come. Nor had he a God that he could rely on. Daddy God had died the day before.

Somewhat of a loner at the best of times, within the past twenty-four hours Martin had been deprived at a stroke, not only of all potential human company, but also of the company of the God he once thought he had as his Friend and Guide. He felt utterly isolated and alone.

He'd already tried the phone. Most of his relatives were in London or adjoining towns and in desperation that morning he had tried ringing them. The phones had worked all right, but there was no answer, except for a cousin who'd left his answerphone on. Martin had left a message, but the call had not been returned despite the promise on the recorded message that its owner would 'return your call as soon as possible'.

*   *   *

Shortly before sunset the electric light flickered, faded, and finally went out. The refrigerator shuddered to a halt and the central heating went off. There was gas in the pipes all right—Martin checked that with his gas stove—but all the timers and the pumps worked off electricity, so the system as a whole was useless. So were the clocks, the television, the video, the doorbell, the immersion heater and his electric blanket. It was going to be a cold night and a dark one too.

He found some matches, heated some food on the stove, then wrapped himself in as many blankets as he could find and sat in the chair looking out of his upstairs window as the daylight faded, until it was totally black outside, blacker than he'd ever imagined it could be. In the distance the fires had largely burned themselves out, and the brightest were now only dim pin-pricks of light.

There were no street lights: there was no one in the street—at least, not left alive. The houses opposite were completely blacked out and there was no familiar orange glow over the horizon, as is normal in London.

Like most of those who've lived their whole lives in the city, Martin had never known what real blackness was like. With no artificial street lights illuminating the horizon, and with no light to guide his footsteps, inside the vicarage the night was as thick and impenetrable as if he had his face swathed in layers of black felt.

Looking up, Martin could see the stars. He'd never really noticed them before: previously in London only the very brightest had been visible, as the rest were obscured by the sodium lights, but tonight he could see everything. He couldn't believe how many there were, how brightly they shone and how vast the sky above seemed to be. He was suddenly aware that he was looking out at a vista that extended millions upon millions upon millions of miles away, gleaming points of fire that arched over his head, no longer looking like white paint sparsely splashed on a backdrop, but instead, in three dimensions, blazing out above him—and in colour, too! One or two were fiery red—others were a cool blue.

Arching above him he could see what at first he took to be a long band of wispy cloud, but when it seemed to stay in much the same place for over an hour he decided to investigate further. Fumbling in the dark, he went to the study to get his binoculars, then went back to the window and trained them on the cloud. It wasn't a cloud at all, but bank upon bank of stars: he was looking at the Milky Way.

The dimensions of space are enormous. Martin knew that light travels at 186,000 miles per *second*, and that the light from even the nearest star takes three and a half *years* to get to us, so that the light he was now looking at had started on its way long long before he was born. He began to feel even smaller. He couldn't contemplate the idea of a universe that big. Whereas two hours ago he'd conceived of himself as a tiny speck, the only one left on the vastness of a hostile, dark and empty earth, now he thought of himself as the only one of his kind in the entire universe. The universe was empty, alien, black and cold— *especially* cold now that the central heating was no longer working. He shivered involuntarily. The vastness of it all turned the whole thing into a gigantic conundrum. Imagining the size and scale of the universe was bad enough—but he just couldn't conceive of a god that was big enough to be bigger than the universe. The loneliness within him increased.

He kept looking at the amazing sight for an hour or so. Then something very strange happened, so strange that at first he didn't understand what was happening. He had an eerie feeling that all was not well because the scene in front of him started to become more visible. Then he could pick out the house in front. It wasn't as clear as he remembered it, but after a time he could make out most of the details on its front and face. It seemed to be illuminated in a curious whitish light, like that from one of the security lights that is so often put high up on the corners of industrial buildings, washing the ground around in luminance bright enough to spot movement and overall shape, but not clear enough to see any great detail, nor make out any colours.

The light became clearer and brighter until he could make out much of the detail in the street—the huddled bodies lying where they had fallen, the doorways opposite, the tree on the corner. He saw movement, too—a dog deprived of its normal source of food returning to its wild state and going out hunting. It was eerie, watching the scene, not knowing what was happening, nor why.

Maybe it was a searchlight. If so, why wasn't it moving?

And where was it coming from? Perhaps it was on board an airship, with people, *real people*, on board, trying to find out if there was anyone else alive in the city. The light seemed to be coming from the other side of the house so, slipping out of his blankets he went to peer out of the spare-room window . . . and found himself looking at the moon, rising slowly in the east, just past the full.

The disappointment was immense; but at least he'd lost the scared eerie feeling. No wonder primitive man became so superstitious. At least this was rational. He'd never realised moonlight could be so strong. A buried memory came to him: ' . . . the sun to give light by day, and the moon to give light by night . . . '

Genesis.

Strange how he'd always ignored the last part. He'd just forgotten about it: it had been of no relevance or importance. It had somehow ceased to exist. Instead, he'd concentrated on the first half: 'The sun to rule the day.' That was important: from the sun came everything we needed for life—light, warmth, power, and, via plants, food. The sun was definitely important: but in his mind, until this moment, the moon might as well have not existed.

Yes, he thought, moonlight is bright. I suppose I've just not been in a position to notice it before.

-26-

Saturday Morning

Just after dawn the following day, *Willow* left its mooring and started southwards on the last leg of its journey back to Linslade. As it was the beginning of the weekend the family had expected to see a few early fishermen and boatmen, but none materialised. Had they been regular visitors to the canal they would have known immediately that something was wrong, but as this was

their first trip, the oddness of the situation didn't percolate
through to them.

Once again they found themselves in a very rural area, and
so there was no absence of people to be remarked upon—it was
always isolated along this stretch. In fact, the only sign of the
twentieth century was the railway with its electric pylons, to the
west. It is not unusual for railways to have no traffic on for long
periods, and as they didn't see any trains they assumed it was just
luck.

The last lock of the journey beckoned as they rounded a
right-hand bend—Leighton Lock at Linslade, the first lock they'd
come down at the beginning of their holiday. Beyond this was
Linslade, and civilisation—pretty bungalows whose gardens
came down to the water's edge.

For the Jones family it was back to the twentieth century—
civilisation at last. It seemed a very quiet civilisation, for all
that—no children out playing, no one tending the gardens or
hanging out the washing, and as *Willow* putt-putt-putted up the
last two hundred yards of canal to the boatyard it all looked
peaceful and restful.

They moored the narrow-boat fore and aft against the quay:
and then, Derek cut the motor for the last time. It seemed
suddenly very quiet after the racket from the big diesel engine in
the stern. David, as usual always the first to rush off to do
anything, jumped ashore and ran up the winding stone pathway to
the office in the middle of the bungalow, to announce their arrival.

Derek and Anne had started to unload their luggage onto the
quayside when there was a scream from the direction of the
house. Derek shot out of the inside of the boat just in time to see
David, obviously upset, running back from the house. 'What's
the matter?' Derek shouted.

Out of breath and with tears in his eyes David looked up at
him.

'Dad, there's a man on the floor in there and he's not moving
and I think he's dead,' he gasped all in one breathless rush.

'David, you stay here with Mummy and I'll go and have a
look. No, Alison, you stay here as well.' Derek ran up the path
and into the office. Just as David had said, there was a body on
the floor—the owner of the yard who, just a week before, had

been showing them how to use the boat. Derek looked around.
There were no signs of any struggle—the office looked neat and
tidy. It was unlikely that there'd been a burglary, so perhaps he'd
had a stroke or a heart attack or something. On the other hand he
looked as though he'd been dead some time. Strange, thought
Derek, why hasn't anyone found him yet? Maybe he lives on his
own, and no one's missed him so far.

He went through the office door into the main part of the
house.

'Hello, anyone there?'

No reply. He turned to go through the hall into the
kitchen—and saw another body, crumpled on the floor. One
unexpected body could be an accident or a sudden death, two
together are anything but. Quickly, and touching nothing, he
backed away out through the office and then out of the bungalow
altogether. He thought of using the telephone in the office to ring
for the police but decided against it—fingerprints and all that,
amazing what you learn from films. He went back to the boat.
Three pairs of anxious eyes followed him from the stern. 'What's
happened, Daddy?' asked Alison.

'I don't know.' Derek looked visibly shaken. 'David's
absolutely right. The owner's dead on the floor in the office and
there's another body in the bungalow. There's no obvious sign
of theft or violence so I really don't know what's happened.'

'You'll have to tell the police,' said Anne.

'I thought of that. I didn't want to ring from the house just
in case I put fingerprints all over the telephone or disturbed any
evidence. We'd better go to the nearest phone box and ring.'

'Don't leave us here,' Alison gibbered, hugging herself.

'No, of course not,' said Derek. 'We'll put the cases back in
the boat, and then go for help.'

By this time David was starting to look quite ill with the
shock of his discovery. He thought to himself in a disjointed
way, I've seen so many people 'killed' on TV or in films but the
real thing is quite different. Films are not like real life after all;
and he sat in the back seat of the car shaking and shivering.

The others climbed in and Anne put her arm round him as
Derek drove the car out of the yard. The first fifty yards was a
quiet, hedge-lined lane which turned at a right angle into a

residential road. They drove round the corner—and saw in front of them four more bodies on the pavement. Anne put a hand to her mouth and gave out a stifled gasp. Alison started crying.

'What on earth–'

Derek stopped the car, switched off the engine and turned round to face the rest of the family, face white as a sheet. 'What on earth is going on?'

They all looked up the street, mouths agape, stunned. For all that Paul, Jane and Martin had had their world turned upside down, at least they had had some inkling of what was happening. Derek and his family had had no warning at all. From a happy holidaying group on the canal they had come back to civilisation and found, instead of normality, a nightmare.

'Could there have been some sort of leak of chemical?' asked Anne.

'A war?' said David.

His hand shaking, Derek switched on the engine again. They went out of the road and down into the town, staring at the bodies on the pavement and the occasional crashed car. It was like a nightmare and they were alone in it. Derek was aware of that odd dream-like feeling of unreality coming upon him.

'Do you think it's safe to be around here?' asked Anne. 'What if it is a poison?'

'Well, we've all been exposed to it by now if it is. If it was a poison it's either gone or it left no smell.'

'What are we going to do?'

'I'm going to find a phone box and ring the police.'

They found one at the bottom of the road. Derek pulled the car over. Anne could see him dialling, but there seemed to be no answer and Derek didn't speak. He put the phone down and dialled again. Again no reply. He tried three more numbers. No answer. He gave up and came back to the car, bent down and spoke through the open window.

'There's nothing from the police. I tried ringing the office in London—there's always someone on duty there, but there was no reply from them. I can't get either of our next-door neighbours and I can't raise either your mother or mine.' Anne went white and bit her lip.

Derek straightened up. 'I've got an idea. I'll be back in a

moment.' He crossed the road in the direction of the newsagents at the bottom of the street. Halfway there he could see the placards outside. '*Plague Latest*' they read. The door was open, but there was no one inside. A few unsold papers lay on the counter: he picked up *The Times* and an *Independent*, left the money on the counter, then went back to the car.

'There's your answer,' he said, handing Anne the papers. For three or four minutes they read in silence, trying to take in the enormity of what had happened in their absence. Eventually Anne spoke. 'There's no point in trying to get back home,' she said, ever the practical one. 'That's where the centre of the infection is.'

'We don't know that things are any better up north, either,' replied Derek. 'In fact, come to think of it, we don't even know whether anybody else is alive. We don't know how infectious this thing is or whether the infection hangs around in the air long after the people have died.'

'Well, I vote that we get out of here and try and find somewhere where there are fewer bodies. At least that will reduce the chances of our getting infected,' said Alison.

'Good idea. Where do you suggest?'

There was silence for a few moments.

'Could we find a hotel somewhere in an area that hasn't been affected?' asked Anne.

'Where? And even if we find somewhere like that, how do we know the people there won't be incubating it?' replied Derek, angrily.

'No need to get shirty.'

'I'm sorry—I'm just . . . I'm just scared . . . for us all. But if we make a wrong move now, we die. It's quite simple.'

'Why don't we go back on the boat?' said David.

'Don't interrupt, David,' said Anne. 'We're trying to be serious. What about going west, towards Oxford . . .'

'I'm serious. Why don't we go back on the boat?'

'Or we could go east, towards Cambridge . . .'

'*Why don't we go back on the boat*?' chorused Alison and David together.

'What?'

'We didn't catch the plague because we were away from

everyone else on the canal. All we have to do is go back there
and wait for a bit. We'll have somewhere to sleep, we've still
got some food left, we've got water, heating and a toilet. And
we'll be out of the way of anyone left who's infectious.'

'David, you're brilliant.'

'That's what I was trying to tell you, Dad.'

*   *   *

There was a time when Kevin thought that he was the Leader
of the Pack and, were it not for his slight disadvantage of birth,
was fully capable of being a future Prime Minister/Field
Marshal/Governor of the Bank of England. To a degree he was
right. He did have leadership ability in a somewhat primitive
form, and he also had a certain amount of brains which he could
have used to capitalise on that ability. What he didn't have was
knowledge. IQ without a knowledge base is almost worthless,
like a super-computer with no program to load. In the past Kevin
had been one of those who, whatever anybody else had tried to
get him to do, had always invented good reasons as to why their
plan was wrong. He would always have been able to do things
much better, whether it was run the class, the school, or the
country. The Leader of the Pack would be able to do it, of that
he was sure.

So much for the theory. The reality—when it came—
showed up considerable flaws in his otherwise immaculate self-
perception. To put it politely, when the evacuation started Kevin
didn't know which way to move and spent a lot of time dithering.
He thought of running away, and started to go east, but the ties of
loyalty to his agoraphobic mother proved too great and for a time
at least he went back to the flat. Then in a relatively unconcerned
way (because he hadn't actually perceived himself to be at risk)
he went out on to the street to watch the world pass by, which in
the course of the next three hours it did. 'Fools rush in where
angels fear to tread,' they say. Had Kevin known it he was
putting himself in the most recklessly dangerous position
possible, but the thought never occurred to him. Illness happened
to other people—so did AIDS, heroin addiction and famine. At
least, so far.

As it happened he was virtually immune to the disease

because of the antibiotic he was taking for his zits, but he didn't know that and no one else—not even Mike Williams—could have said for certain that he was safe. He was just plain lucky that when he went down to observe the exodus, the airborne germs that he inhaled did no harm at all to him, whilst another member of his gang standing next to him, watching, contracted the infection that two days later was to kill him.

Kevin's mother wasn't as lucky as her son. Normally an agoraphobic might have been expected to survive a plague spread by personal contact, except that Julia Forrester, her good friend and neighbour from the floor above, dropped in to ask how she was. What neither of them knew was that the good friend and neighbour was excreting bacteria in all directions. Little kindnesses sometimes rebound awkwardly, and little things sometimes have strange effects unrelated either to their value or their apparent significance—like small holes in air filters.

As evening fell and the greater part of the exodus had finished Kevin went back upstairs, walking up the fourteen flights because the lift had been vandalised. Some said it was members of his own gang that did it, but he knew better. After all why should he make life more difficult for himself and his mother (on those occasions when she did actually manage to get out), by wrecking his own lift? That at least was obvious to Kevin, even if wasn't obvious to everybody else.

And so he stayed with his mother for the next two days while they both wondered what to do. He had thought of leaving; then thought perhaps he'd better stay with his mother. After that he thought 'What if I get the disease?' and then 'What if she gets the disease?' 'What would we do for food now there's no one in the city to sell it to us and, what's more, no Social Security to give us the money to buy it? Anyway, if we do go *where* will we go? We haven't anywhere to go to.'

It was during this time, while he was contemplating the pros and cons of moving and working himself up to an instantaneous decision (that took him two days) that his mother started coughing. Kevin was in the toilet at the time and only heard her dimly through the keyhole. When he came out five minutes later she was dead on the floor of the sitting room.

From being the braggart Leader of the Pack Kevin made a

very swift descent into being a little boy of five. The degree of
loneliness he felt was unbearable. The insecurity was
unbelievable. The first thing he tried was artificial resuscitation
like he'd seen on the television. (It was a good job he was on the
antibiotic because the mouth-to-mouth contact would certainly
have given him Legionnaires' had he not been taking the
medicine.) But no one had shown him how to perform
resuscitation properly. It looked so easy on the films and the
heroine always came round smiling for the final reel, but his
mother didn't smile; she just stared straight out with sightless
eyes, a little trickle of blood-stained saliva dribbling from the
corner of her mouth. Her face went purple, and so did her lips
and tongue.

Kevin tried bashing on her chest, but no one had shown him
how to do it properly and he didn't know how hard to do it nor how
often, nor when to do the mouth-to-mouth breathing. (He couldn't
have learned it from the films either, because good mouth-to-mouth
resuscitation is brutal. If you don't break a rib when you're doing
it, you probably aren't doing it properly.) Had he known, he should
have opened his mother's mouth, cleared any foreign material out
of the back of the throat, lifted the chin forward and up to bring the
tongue out of the way, put his mouth round his mother's, holding
her nose shut, and breathed deeply out, watching for his mother's
chest rising at the same time. Then having done that once he should
have pumped the chest three times: *breathe*, punch, punch, punch,
breathe, punch, punch, punch, *breathe*; but Kevin didn't know any
of this. In a blind panic he pushed on her chest and tried to blow
into his mother's mouth, but either the air all came out of the nose
or it made a funny gurgling noise in the throat as the sputum and
vomit was driven back into her lungs.

He was desperate to bring his mum round and his tears and
her phlegm and saliva all mingled over both their faces as, in a
panic, he tried desperately for a full ten minutes to do
something—*anything*—that would help. But he had not got the
knowledge and the whole procedure was doomed from the start.

Finally, realising his impotence in the face of what seemed
to him implacable nature, he gave up and flung himself onto the
bed, the tears still pouring down his face. After a time the sobs
came less often and he fell asleep.

When he woke it was completely dark. He got up and as he moved his face he felt a curious sensation like pie crust breaking. He realised that his face was still covered with the secretions acquired during his abortive resuscitation effort and went to the bathroom to wash it off. There was no hot water but the cold tap worked and he used that.

It was pitch dark in the flat and getting colder by the minute. He was hungry and would have liked some hot food, but the electricity was off and they didn't have gas. Wondering what to do he went into the lounge and in the blackness tripped over the inert body of his mother, crashing full-length to the ground and splitting his lip in the process. Cursing he got to his feet. He could hardly see his hand in front of his face and couldn't see to find out how much damage he'd done to himself. He staggered back to the bathroom, tried to wash the cut and then pressed a towel against it for a few minutes hoping that this would stop the bleeding. Groping around he eventually made his way to the kitchen, without tripping over his mother, and tried to find something to eat.

There were a few tins in the larder, a bit of cheese in the fridge and some bread and jam. He got out the tin opener. In the darkness it was difficult to see what he was opening. He thought he'd have baked beans on toast, but after he'd opened the first tin, which turned out to be pears, and the second, which was peaches and the third, which was soup, he began to become a little dispirited. At last he opened the tin that contained baked beans—and then he realised that he had no way of heating them, nor of making toast. In the end he ate the baked beans cold, which wasn't too unpalatable, and afterwards some of the cheese and bread; then by touch he managed to find a spoon with which to eat the peaches.

After a time he became aware that he could see more inside the flat than previously. At first he assumed that it was his eyes becoming accustomed to the darkness, but when he went to the window he realised, as had Martin the day before, just how powerful moonlight was. Looking out over the city he saw the pale white light of the moon glinting off the roofs of the houses and the sides of the tower blocks. No street lights. No noise. None of the familiar, convivial bustle that he knew so well and that he had made his home in.

In a live city Kevin had been streetwise. In a dead city he was like a fish out of water. With rising panic he suddenly realised the enormity of his situation. His total supply of food consisted of three quarters of a loaf of sliced bread, an uneaten half of a tin of peaches, another tin (opened) of pear halves, a cold tin of soup, some bacon and half a pound of uncooked sausages. Not a lot to keep body and soul together for the rest of his life. And what sort of a life was it going to be? Up to now it had been a pretty dead-end one for him, but his future prospects looked even bleaker. His mother—his only relative—was dead. Living as a streetwise kid in a dead city had little appeal for him; nor did living as a city dweller in the countryside (dead or otherwise). Within the space of two days his whole way of life had been destroyed. As with Martin—but for different reasons— Kevin had had the bottom knocked out of his world.

-27-

Jane and Paul had taken stock in a completely different way. Though emotionally stunned, their training had made them both immensely pragmatic and swift to seize whatever opportunity presented itself. So, logically, they assessed the situation from first principles.

They knew their knowledge would, at best, be imperfect, that there were many imponderables, and that they could only fill in a proportion of the blanks. Still, it was better than nothing and at least allowed them to plan a more or less relevant strategy.

'All right,' said Paul. 'What do we know? Let's take it from the top.'

'We know that the plague has been caused by Legionnaires' bacillus,' said Jane. 'It has an incubation period of two days, then there's about half an hour when you feel unwell: then you cough yourself to death over a period of about five minutes.'

'Do we know how it's transmitted?'

'Yes,' said Jane slowly, thinking hard. 'I remember Dr

Williams saying it was passed on through one person coughing
bacteria into the air and another person inhaling them.'

'Presumably that's why neither of us got the disease—being
cooped up here with the flu meant that we were never exposed to
it. Do we know whether it's infectious from corpses?'

Jane thought again. 'Yes, we do, and yes, it is. The third
person to die . . .' she hesitated, then the words came in a rush,
'was the doctor who did the postmortem on Sir Richard. As far
as we're aware he wasn't in contact with anybody else.'

'Yes,' said Paul, 'but at a postmortem you cut the body open,
don't you? So maybe he was contaminated by the germs from
the lungs directly, which sprayed into the air by his face, rather
than just because he was in the vicinity of the body. My guess is
that provided we don't touch the bodies they're unlikely to be a
danger–'

'Yes, yes,' said Jane, interjecting hurriedly. 'Yes, now I
remember. Mike said that Legionnaires' disease was an *airborne*
infection. Well, of course it is,' she said, looking cross with
herself. 'Don't you remember? Originally people with
Legionnaires' disease got it from water coolers that had become
contaminated. It was droplets in the air, wasn't it?'

'That's right. So you do learn something from watching
three and a half hours of TV a day,' said Paul, grinning. Jane
kicked him under the table.

'Don't be so wretchedly flippant,' she said. 'This is serious.'

'All of life's serious,' said Paul, 'but it didn't stop me being
optimistic before all this lot happened, did it? So what's the
difference now? You either ride it or you go under. There'll be
an answer—I know there will. Nothing's hopeless. It never is.'

'I wish I shared your optimism,' said Jane. 'Now—where
were we?'

'We've just decided that the bodies are probably not a risk to
us, especially if we don't touch them. Mind you I don't know
what would happen if we were downwind of a decomposing one.
I wonder if the bacteria die off once the person has died?'

'They don't—at least, not at first. Otherwise how would the
pathologist have got it? Mind you, he'd be cutting into the body,
wouldn't he? If it's being spread by airborne contamination and
the victim's not breathing, then he won't be puffing out the

germs. If we don't go too close to people who've died we're probably going to be all right. And Mike did say that exposure to sunlight soon kills bacteria.'

They both looked out of the window. It was sunny.

'What about everyone else? How far has the plague got to?'

'We know it's gone abroad because all the foreign radio stations have gone off the air.'

'No, I didn't mean that. I meant what about Britain? How far has it got there?'

'It looks as if most people have left the capital; they'll have taken the disease with them.'

'Yes, but has the flow of refugees been halted anywhere?'

'It doesn't matter. Duncan said in the last broadcast that each of the big cities in England had experienced the same effect—infection in the centre spreading outwards, with refugees also going outwards. There'll have been a migration of refugees away from London meeting migrations of people coming out of the main cities like Birmingham and Manchester. I think we can assume that there won't be many people left by now, because the thing's so infectious.'

'No,' said Paul, 'we can't assume that. What we don't know is how many people are immune to it. And didn't Mike say something about certain drugs protecting against it?'

'He said they might, but it was only an idea off the top of his head. We don't know whether it's true or not. Apparently ordinary Legionnaires' disease responds to certain antibiotics, but we don't know whether the mutant form is susceptible or not.'

'So we can surmise that it's spread throughout Britain and that a lot of the population has migrated northwards, but we don't know how many people have finally succumbed to it. So let's do some investigations. Let's ring up a few people.'

'Who do you suggest? We haven't got any relatives north of Watford Gap.'

'Well, why don't we ring up some police stations?'

'How do you find their numbers?'

'Oh, ring Directory Enquiri . . . Ah . . .'

'We could look up the contact files at AM-TV.'

'Not on your life. Neither of us is leaving this building until we're sure that's it's safe to do so.'

'Well, why don't we try ringing up numbers in places like Glasgow and see if we can find somebody who answers?'

So they tried. Surprisingly, the telephone still worked, but although they dialled the codes and then enough numbers afterwards to get a ringing tone, no one answered.

'We don't know whether we've just been unlucky and dialled numbers where there's nobody there, or whether everybody really is dead. What about the radio?'

The big radio was mains-powered, but Jane had a portable radio in her Walkman. They tried with that for a time, but could raise nothing.

'There *must* be survivors,' said Paul, thinking out loud. 'People like us who have escaped just because they've not been in contact with it. People on scattered farms—on boats, trawlers, liners even, people who for one reason or another don't meet anybody: recluses, those living on their own with no visitors; remote monasteries; people like us who've been ill and haven't had visitors. What about all those who've already had Legionnaires' disease? Aren't they going to be immune just like adults are to measles and mumps? There's got to be people out there who haven't had the disease. All we've got to do is find them.'

'Wait a minute,' said Jane. 'How do we know that it will be safe to meet them? How do we know they're not incubating the disease?'

Paul thought for a minute. 'It's like a grass fire, isn't it? The fire starts in one spot, and goes outwards, but sometimes the fire doesn't quite get to a small area of grass. Once it's passed by it may burn out the whole field, but then because there's nothing else to catch fire the fire dies out so . . . although those areas of grass could potentially catch fire, they won't because there will never be any fire to set them alight. And if that's true, by analogy we're going to be perfectly safe because the disease will have burnt itself out by expanding so quickly into the population.'

'But what about those diseases that keep going year in year out, like measles?'

'Don't you see, it's because they're not lethal that they can keep going. I remember Mike saying that many of the people in Fiji died when sailors brought measles to them for the first time. It's because it's so instantly lethal that Legionnaires' disease will kill itself off, like a fire that burns itself out. If it were less lethal it might continue smouldering away, but because it's so virulent it's likely to spread throughout the world and then die out. So we shouldn't have a problem once the initial wave of infection has passed.'

'In other words,' said Jane, 'the longer we leave it the safer we are from getting infected from other live people, but the more chance we may have of being downwind of germs coming from decomposing bodies . . .'

'Assuming that those decomposing bodies are actually infectious.'

'Yes.'

'What about the other problems? Like living and eating and keeping warm?'

'We can't stay here, that's for sure,' said Jane. 'It's unlikely that the electricity is going to come back on for some time, if ever. We've still got gas so we can cook, but we don't know how long that's going to stay on.'

'And the only way that we can get food would be by stealing it. That would keep us going for a bit and if there aren't many others left alive in London it'll keep us going for a *very* long time.'

'But it wouldn't be a particularly healthy diet. All the refrigeration plants will have gone off. I know it's quite cold outside, being autumn, but sooner or later the stored meat and vegetables will go off. I should think produce inside the supermarkets has already started to fester. We might find some in their cold rooms, but that won't be for long either, and there won't be any fresh fruit or vegetables, so we'd be restricted to living out of tins. We could do that for some time, I suppose.'

'But how could we exist if we went to the country?' asked Paul. 'Do *you* know anything about farming?'

'No, but we expect to find other people alive, and just because *we* don't know anything about growing food doesn't mean that *they* won't. You said yourself that the people who are most likely to survive were those in rural areas. By the same token they're more likely to be involved in agriculture.'

'All the same, I don't think we ought to assume too much. We're obviously going to have to leave here—where for I don't know—but when we go we'd better make sure that we've got the right sort of equipment with us—and that includes knowledge.'

'So?'

'So we make sure we've got a book on growing vegetables and fruit, at the very least.'

'What else do we need to take?'

'I was thinking about that,' said Paul. 'Lots of warm clothes obviously, but tools are going to be important. There's nothing like having tins of food around you and no tin-opener to make you feel you're starving in the midst of plenty.'

'I remember reading somewhere that one of the most difficult things to make yourself is a needle, so we need to make sure that we've got all sorts of things like that—needles, pins, cotton, knives, scissors.'

'I suppose if there really are very few people left then we won't need to worry too much about acquiring them. We can just break in and steal them. After all, the original owners won't be coming back to claim them, will they?'

'That's a point. The next thing is—how do you break in . . .?'

'Club hammer and a chisel,' they both said at the same time.

'Yes,' said Paul, grinning, 'and a wrecking bar. What about medicines: your contraceptive pills for example?'

'I don't think I'll be needing those for a bit.'

'You got a new supply from the doctor's?' said Paul.

'No,' said Jane. 'I'm pregnant.'

*   *   *

Over in west London Martin was making similar preparations, but in a much less organised way. He was still numb after the events of the last two days. He'd lost his hope and his reason for living, his livelihood, his calling and his peace of mind, all at once. In many ways there is nothing more poignant than a minister who has lost his faith. It's sad when this happens to a layman—traumatic even—but when your faith is your profession, then losing it devastates every particle of your life and lifestyle. For many, religion is something to do as a spare-time activity. For others it is their whole reason for living, and Martin had been one of these.

To say that losing his faith unbalanced him would be putting it lightly. It destroyed him. From knowing that there was a real purpose to his life, and after life another life more permanent, more exciting and more rewarding, he had changed overnight to believing there was nothing outside this life at all, nothing to live for, nothing to come afterwards, and no source of strength or guidance for the present. In the past he had spent much of his time urging others to think not of this life, but beyond it to what was yet to come; to consider what they could do for others in this life, and in doing so ignore themselves; but now he was forced to turn round and view this life as all that there is. Suddenly it all seemed terribly pointless.

On the other hand, in the absence of God, he could create his own set of morals, and his own set of ethics. So what? It seemed pointless even trying. Once he'd wanted to. In theological college he'd often thought that our ideas of God were outmoded and should be superseded by better things, things learned since the Bible was written. He'd been at the forefront of those who had wanted to go on from where the New Testament left off, refining and improving Christian belief until it became really pure, and fully loving and truly modern. In his heart he'd longed for the freedom to be able to discard some of the more tiresome dictates of the Christian faith and of Jesus of Nazareth: the injunctions against divorced people remarrying—such a problem in the twentieth century, so unjust, so imperfect; the episode of Christ driving the money-changers out of the temple with a whip—so un-Christlike, so unbecoming for a man of peace. He longed to remove that as well.

Yet when it came to it and he'd lost all idea and semblance of God he found that he didn't really want to rewrite anything. It all seemed terribly . . . pointless; numbing; inappropriate.

Strangely he found he couldn't cry about it; nor about the complete waste of the fourteen years he'd spent training for and carrying out his pastoral duties. He didn't feel angry or despondent. In fact he didn't really feel anything; just numb and unresponsive. It seemed pointless his being alive: dying seemed pointless as well. He would be just as well off to have been one of the victims of the plague, he thought in a rather emotionless way, as he wandered round the dim and cold vicarage, wondering if there was any point in doing anything at all. He couldn't read; he couldn't think; he couldn't concentrate on anything. Even eating seemed too much trouble.

Had he but known it Martin was going straight into a reactive depression, somewhat akin to the effects of a bereavement. In fact he *had* been bereaved. For him God had just died. He'd lost the reason for his livelihood. He hadn't lost his livelihood itself—if there was anyone out there still alive he could still be paid to act as the official functionary of the Anglican Church. Even as an atheist he could still celebrate the Eucharist and officiate at services—how odd, he thought, that as an atheist he could still act as official mediator between man and God, whereas under Church regulations, a devout lay member of the Church wouldn't be allowed to act in the same manner. At other times Martin would have given a wry smile at this incongruity, but now it gave him no emotion of any sort, neither pain nor pleasure. It was just a thought suspended in space. A logical paradox without real meaning, containing no emotion.

After four days of his gloomy vicarage Martin could stand it no longer. Anywhere is better than here, he thought—but probably not much. He too knew about the complete blockage of all the roads, and reasoned that taking a car was not going to be a very good idea. He'd a bike in the garage so he took it out, oiled it, and packed a few things in a rucksack: some tins of food and a bottle of water. At the last minute he remembered that to get food out of a can one needs a tin-opener. As he passed through the hall into the kitchen to get it, he looked at himself in the mirror and suddenly realised he was still wearing his dog collar. Tearing it off he threw it in the corner of the room and replaced it with an ordinary shirt and a large green and white sweater. Then, carefully locking the vicarage door and putting the key in his pocket—he didn't know quite why he did this, but he couldn't have left the place open—he got onto his bike and headed north. It seemed as good a direction as any.

-28-

*K*evin had decided to escape from London as well. He made no real plans: nothing in his life and education had prepared him for anything like this. He'd never been taught to think ahead and so he lived for the present minute. This is supposed to be a Good and Christian Thing to Do—but only for those who, given their head, would otherwise live entirely in tomorrow.

For Kevin it was quite different. He had no idea about tomorrow except in a vaguely auspicious way, so when he left the flat for the last time he took a quite different selection of things—the girlie magazine he'd bought the week before, and all the money he could find, which wasn't much—£17.33 to be precise. He didn't consciously decide to take a waterproof, but as his anorak was the only outer clothing he had, and it was cold, he put it on. He felt guilty leaving his mum on the floor like that, but there was nothing he could do and nowhere he could put her, so he put his hand on her head for a moment, and then with tears running down his face walked somewhat aimlessly out of the door, glad that none of his gang were there to see him.

He went down the echoing stairs that smelled of damp and urine, out of the entrance to the tower block and onto the deserted street. A light wind blew little flurries of litter about. There weren't many bodies—but here and there a heap marked the last resting place of some poor anonymous unfortunate. For the first five minutes Kevin was fascinated by the corpses as he came across them. There were all sorts: large men, little children, babies in their prams, teenagers in bright clothes, old people in dark coats, all lying crumpled where they had fallen like so many molehills. Although there weren't that many bodies in the first few streets he came to, death—*real* death—was a novelty to him. Shorn of the emotional implications, compared to the death of his mother, real dead bodies looked much as he'd seen them on the films—except they somehow looked more human and yet less human. In the cinema dead bodies looked pink and healthy, except that convention and 'realism' forbade them to breathe. In reality the faces of the corpses were pale, except where the blood had drained to the lowest part, and that part of the skin became a livid, blotchy purple; the faces which had turned on their side had an appearance akin to red wine in a brandy glass, with a definite line below which the blood had settled.

The faces didn't look like faces in the films either. They were crumpled, squashed, abnormal in their stillness and the way their features had been pushed into odd shapes by gravity. Meryl Streep never looked like *that* when 'dead'.

After a time he became accustomed to the presence of the bodies and stopped staring at them, only recognising their existence when he had to alter his intended path to step round them. He moved more briskly now, not to get away from them but because he had suddenly developed an idea—a new purpose in life. Reaching the Commercial Road, he turned west, towards the City.

About two hundred yards from Aldgate he knew there was a shop full of motorbikes. He and his gang had often hung around in front of its windows, staring at the gleaming contents. Pride of place in the shop was a black Harley-Davidson, the *crème de la crème* of the motorcycle world.

Harley-Davidsons are to motorbikes what Beluga is to caviare. They caused Kevin to drool almost as much, too—not that he'd ever tasted the latter. He reached the shop and crossed over the road, automatically looking right to check for oncoming traffic before thinking to himself how unnecessary that action had just been.

He stuck his head against the plate-glass window and peered in. There it was, at the back, on a stand. For the first time he realised that he could have come better prepared. How was he to get in? This being the East End there were metal grilles everywhere. He looked round for something to break in with. Fifty yards up the road was a building site so he went there to find a couple of bricks. He came back, looked round furtively, just in case, then threw them through the plate-glass window. There was a satisfying smashing sound as the glass cascaded down, but the bars behind the glass still remained, locked and set firm. He threw a second brick through the door but there was a metal grille behind this as well, and he couldn't get through. Nor could he manage to get a hand through far enough to open the door from the other side. It was while extricating his arm from the door grille that he cut himself on a jagged piece of glass. He swore, wrapped his handkerchief round the wound and walked back to the centre of the road to look at the shop again and plan his next attack.

His gaze wandered skywards, to the first-floor windows—

and then he was running towards the building site to find a ladder. Propping it against the front of the shop, he ran up it, heaved a brick through the window, reached in, opened the sash and lifted it up. He looked round again—pure reflex again—then stepped through the open window into the owner's living room, out through the door on the other side and down the back stairs into the shop.

There was his prize, the bike, standing sleek and black on a small podium. All he had to do was to work out how to get it out of the shop, past the bars and the broken glass. It proved much easier than he thought. At the back of the shop was a pair of double doors. They were locked, but the key was still in place. He swung them open and found himself in the yard at the back, which in turn led into a back street, through another set of padlocked gates.

Kevin went back into the shop. All he needed now was the key. It must be there somewhere, he thought—that is, unless the owner had taken it with him when he ran away. *Had* he run away? Where was he? Upstairs, dead in the bedroom? As he went back into the showroom he noticed a small office with a desk. Sure enough, inside one of the drawers were the keys to all the motorbikes, together with another bunch which looked as though they ought to fit padlocks and doors. He went back to the padlock on the yard gate. The third key fitted. Now for the bike. This one was easy: the key fob proudly said 'Harley-Davidson' on the leather.

Petrol. Was there any in it? He switched on and tried to kick-start the motor. Nothing happened. He tried again and it burst into life. Wheeling it off its podium carefully, because it was heavy, and desperate not to mar his new acquisition, Kevin gingerly rode it out into the back yard and up and down the lane. He looked at the petrol gauge. Empty. There was a petrol station just up the road, so he roared up to it and stopped the bike outside the pump. A free fill, he thought. Great. At this rate the world is going to be my oyster. He picked up the pump handle, put the nozzle in the bike's tank and pressed the trigger.

Nothing happened. It took him a little time to realise why. Petrol pumps need motors to work and motors need electricity. He was starving in the midst of plenty—two feet underneath where he was standing was a five-thousand-gallon tank of petrol that he couldn't get at. He took the petrol line out of the filler tube of the tank, replaced the cap and roared back up the road to the shop.

What could he do? Maybe the owner had some petrol on the premises to fill up the bikes when they came off the delivery lorry. He found it almost immediately: a red plastic can, nearly full. He also found a length of plastic piping and an idea struck him, so he carefully coiled the tube and packed it in one of the side panniers of the bike. Then he filled up the tank from the can and packed the empty can in the pannier as well.

The shop also sold all sorts of motorcycle gear and ten minutes later Kevin was kitted out—leathers, helmet, gloves, boots. He chose the best. Surprisingly for Kevin, with some foresight he also chose a couple of other items—a road map, and an instruction manual on servicing the bike, together with the approved spanners and repair kits.

Then, with a last look round to make sure there was nothing else that he should acquire as a new, proud Harley-Davidson owner, he pulled the visor down over his face, revved the engine and sped off up the Commercial Road to Aldgate, and north up to Shoreditch.

He couldn't get up much speed because of the need to avoid the bodies that littered the roads, and in any case he had not really got the hang of the machine yet. He'd driven bikes before but only as a learner, and at first he found it heavy and difficult to control. However, after a few miles he got the feel of it and from then on life was pure delight as he roared through the echoing emptiness of the streets with their clusters of bodies littering his way. After a time he got quite expert and started using the corpses much as a skier uses slalom posts, spending an entertaining ten minutes weaving his way towards Highgate.

Just short of the North Circular road he hit the traffic. It wasn't moving of course; it hadn't moved for four days. When he came upon the back of the traffic jam all he could see in the distance was a jumbled line of car roofs, three-, four- and sometimes five-abreast, of all shapes, sizes and colours, blocking the road, often encroaching on the pavement, and forming a totally impassable mass—that is, if you were in a car.

But Kevin wasn't in a car. By dint of manoeuvring up pavements, down pedestrian-only alleyways, across green spaces, along pedestrian precincts and in one case, down steps, Kevin managed to navigate to the other side of the North Circular. It took time and patience, but he did it.

The worst of the jams were behind him when the engine of the bike spluttered, picked up, spluttered again and finally died. He looked down at the petrol gauge: empty again. He put the bike up on its support, unloaded the coil of plastic tubing and the petrol can and inspected the nearest cars until he found what he wanted—one with no lock on the petrol cap. He fed one end of the plastic hose down through the filler into the tank, sucked on the pipe until petrol came into his mouth, then syphoned off a gallon of petrol into the can, which he used to fill up the bike. He repeated the procedure until the bike's tank was full, and, for good measure, so was the petrol can. Having replaced the tubing in the pannier he headed north, up towards the A1.

*   *   *

Martin, meanwhile, had been making a similar journey on his push-bike, though much more slowly and with much more effort. Like Kevin, he first had to get used to the sight of bodies littering the ground. Unlike Kevin, however, he had already seen dead bodies for real: going to the morgue had been part of his training for the priesthood, and since then he had attended many a death, so for him the corpses didn't have the same macabre fascination. What hit Martin more was the sheer scale of the destruction that had taken place. Kevin had not yet grown up enough to be able to see the corpses as anything but objects, but for Martin behind every single one was a tale to be told—a husband, a wife, a son, a daughter: each of them with a family, relatives, friends, a personal history, a set of expectations, a list of achievements, a list of failures—and all now history, not even *remembered* history, because there was no one left to remember it.

When faced with disaster and tragedy on a grand scale the mind has a very good way of detaching itself from reality and not allowing any more emotional distress through. So it was with Martin, who, more than any of the others, was shocked by the turmoil within and around him, so his mind closed down even earlier than the others; he pedalled on, face to the wind, the cold air stinging his cheeks, oblivious to the huddled mounds on the road; oblivious to everything. He didn't really notice the silent traffic jams around the North Circular or the cars with their drivers dead at the wheel. On he went, pedalling furiously, blindly, automatically, as the afternoon drew to a close.

*   *   *

After news of Jane's pregnancy had finally sunk in, Paul experienced a mixture of feelings. Part of him was proud to be an expectant father. It wasn't what they'd planned; had life been continuing as normal he might have suggested that Jane had an abortion, because having a family was definitely not priority number one for at least three or four more years. It wouldn't have been convenient to have a child, not with their game-plan for life at its current position. Had Jane announced her impending motherhood two weeks earlier Paul would have treated it as an encumbrance, an irritation, an inconvenience, especially as it was unplanned, but with their world turned topsy-turvy, and with no more corporate ladders to climb for either of them, her pregnancy was not now undesirable. In fact he was actually quite proud of it. And if, as seemed possible, there was a need to repopulate the British Isles—or even the planet—he was proud that he, Paul Ignatius Greatorex, had been first off the mark.

On the other hand, one aspect of the situation was very disquieting—what about antenatal care? What was going to happen about the delivery? Would they find medical help available soon? And what would he do about it if there were none . . . ? Paul put the idea out of his mind immediately. It was a problem that could remain unsolved for at least six months. They would face it later rather than earlier. So they did the practical and sensible thing which was to get on with the packing of *PIG 1*, his beloved red Porsche, nestling in the garage two floors beneath them.

To be honest, a Porsche is not the best thing in which to migrate with a family, especially as with every minute that passed the migration began to look more like a safari. If he had been logical he would have taken a van or at the very least an estate car, but he couldn't bear to part with *PIG 1*—the thought

of leaving it behind was just too much. Eventually they finished
packing, and casting a last look round the flat, locked it up,
opened the garage door and set off towards the A12 and
Chelmsford.

They hadn't reckoned on the bodies. From the flat the road
outside had seemed completely clear—the one body in view
being on the pavement—but as they rounded the corner they
found that most of the streets had corpses on the roadway.
Negotiating a path between them proved difficult, much more so
for Paul than for Kevin and Martin who were both on two-wheel
machines. The dead were scattered randomly—mainly on the
pavement, but from time to time Paul had to do an awkward job
of negotiating a passage between them. Once or twice he felt the
back wheels bump as he miscalculated an angle and rode the car
over an inert arm or leg.

He cursed softly as it happened again. Jane looked at him.
'You don't need to worry,' she said. 'They can't feel it now.'

'I wasn't worried about *them*,' said Paul, without a trace of
feeling. 'We don't know if the bodies are still infectious: I don't
want to risk squirting bacteria over the car, or us.' Jane
shuddered, and rather pointedly looked out of the nearside
passenger window. At times, Paul could be a bit too practical.

Approaching the North Circular they came upon the traffic
jams. Paul got out of the car and looked about him at the vehicles,
spread everywhere, motionless and ghost-like in the pale autumnal
sun. Turning the car round, he aimed towards the North Circular at
a point three miles on, going anticlockwise. Again on the
approach roads they came upon a chaotic jumble of vehicles. They
tried once more, another three miles further round: it was still the
same. Wherever they tried there were solid jams for a quarter of a
mile on the inside of the North Circular. Paul might as well have
tried to drive *PIG 1* across the English Channel. He backed off yet
again, stopped the Porsche and switched off the engine. After the
roar of the engine the silence was profound.

'There *must* be a way,' he said to no one in particular, his
brain calculating furiously. 'What we need is somewhere where
everybody *didn't* go, somewhere terribly unpopular.'

'If I were trying to escape,' said Jane slowly, thinking aloud,
'I'd aim for the major roads. I wouldn't go the scenic route.'

'So *we'll* stick as close to the Thames as we can,' said Paul. 'Which way, east or west?'

'West,' said Jane decisively. 'The further west you go the narrower the Thames becomes and the more bridges there are. Once you're east of Tower Bridge there's no chance of nipping backwards and forwards across the river to get round a blockage.'

By now it was three o'clock. Paul turned the Porsche round and they slowly headed back towards the centre of London. The nearer they got the fewer bodies they found, until in the very centre there was hardly a corpse in sight: nor were there many vehicles. They roared up Victoria Embankment at seventy miles an hour, then turned right at Big Ben to go round the west side of Parliament Square. The Houses of Parliament looked strangely normal: the wind moving the flag of St George on the top of the tower gave the building a semblance of life. Only the body of a policeman collapsed in front of his kiosk showed that things were not quite as they seemed.

Continuing along the north bank of the Thames, the car passed the Tate Gallery, and travelled along the Chelsea Embankment until at the Albert Bridge the road was blocked by a series of pile-ups. Blessing Jane for her perspicacity, Paul crossed the Thames on the Chelsea Bridge, continued west, then recrossed the Thames to rejoin the Embankment road on the far side of the jam.

Shortly after, they left the Thames to cut across due west, but ominously the traffic began to get thicker as they approached the Hammersmith flyover. By snaking up and down back roads they managed to avoid the bulk of the traffic, but at Hammersmith they finally got stuck. There were cars *everywhere*, many with their doors open just as their occupants had left them, to continue on foot. They had come up on a main roundabout from a side street, so at least they weren't behind a quarter-mile queue, but at the roundabout the cars were nose to tail and further progress looked impossible.

It was Jane who spotted it: it seemed so simple afterwards. 'Why don't we try and move the cars closer together? Most of them are unlocked. If we move some of them forwards and others back we should be able to make a space for ourselves to cross.'

And that was how they did it. Cars in a traffic jam never really stop bumper to bumper; they always leave a couple of feet

spare, and by rolling twenty or thirty cars in each line of traffic
forwards or backwards, those extra feet became joined into one
large space.

'This is no sort of work for a woman in my condition,' Jane
grinned, but set to with a will anyway, though the effort, her
post-flu state and the pregnancy forced her to give up before the
job was completed. Paul finished it off. Eventually there was
enough room to put *PIG 1* gently and gingerly through the lanes
of traffic and out the other side.

The major roads on the far side were thick with cars, so they
continued as they had been doing on the inside of the North
Circular, using the back roads, and backtracking on themselves
where necessary, in order to avoid the blockages. It wasn't easy,
and they had to go back the way they had come many times
before they found a clear path through: like Hampton Court
maze, but played for real.

Originally they had thought of going west, but eventually
they had no choice—the blockages forced them to go more or
less north.

'I really don't think I can stand any more,' said Jane as they
got back into the car for what seemed the fiftieth time, having
shunted their way across yet another road. By then it was half
past four and starting to get really cold.

'We'd have had to stop in any case,' replied Paul. 'It's not
going to be daylight for long and we won't be able to see a thing
once night comes down.' They too were relearning the art of
living in a world with a day unprolonged by street lights. 'Let's
look for somewhere to stop. Where shall we try?'

'How about a nice hotel with crisp white sheets and a waiter
to bring us breakfast in bed?' said Jane, shutting her eyes, a
blissful smile on her face.

'We could always break into a house,' said Paul. They
looked at each other and looked away again. Not yet. It didn't
seem right—at least, not for the moment. Anyway the owner
might come back.

Paul stopped at the next hotel they came across. The first
room they went to was the kitchen. It was all electric.

'No point in staying here,' he said, returning to the car. It
took four more tries before they found an inn that not only used

gas for cooking but also had a room with a gas fire—in this case
the lounge bar.

The hotel was deserted, the guest rooms cold and damp: no
one had been near them in the past four days, so despite the
inviting look of the freshly laundered linen on the beds they went
downstairs again, unpacked their sleeping bags and turned on the
gas fire in the lounge bar. Then they went into the kitchen to get
some food; but not before Paul had taken a can of lager from
behind the bar. 'Fruit juice for you,' he said, with a smile.
'Ladies in your condition are not supposed to drink alcohol.'

In the gathering gloom they rummaged through the contents
of the kitchen. There was some bread which was going stale, but
they toasted it. Jane opened a catering pack of soup, and one of
lasagne. There was some cheese and a tin of peaches, so they
made themselves a passable meal; but there was no meat and no
milk—the fridge had failed days before.

Afterwards they thumbed idly through the books and papers
that were scattered around on the tables in the bar, until the
unaccustomed heat and the food made them drowsy. They got into
their sleeping bags in front of the gas fire well before nine o'clock.

The sudden resolution of his anxieties had made Paul relaxed
and he felt considerably more romantically inclined than in the past
four days, now that his flu was abating and the worry about getting
safely out of the city had gone. And he was an expectant father,
too. He felt proud and close to Jane, and put his arm across her.

'How about . . .' he began, turning to look at her. She was
asleep, her blonde hair falling haphazardly across the pillow. He
thought of waking her up, then thought again. Not worth it. He
was too tired.

-29-

At the same time as Paul and Jane were finding their hotel, Martin
was still plodding north on his bike. At about five o'clock he
suddenly became aware that it was getting colder, and the light was

changing as the day grew old. The sky was still quite light, but it
was dark in the streets as the buildings on either side cut out much
of the remaining daylight. Martin couldn't remember anything
about the last four miles—just an unending line of bodies in the
road round which he had had to negotiate. He too realised that the
exigencies of nature would make sure that he couldn't travel
beyond half past five. Like Paul and Jane he couldn't bear the
thought of breaking into a private house, but he also had an ulterior
motive behind choosing a hotel. Like Paul and Jane he needed
several attempts before he found a hotel with a gas cooker rather
than a microwave. Like Paul and Jane he spurned the neat guest
rooms because of the cold and made a bed for himself downstairs
in front of the gas fire, then cooked himself a meal with those
remnants of the larder that were still fit to eat. But unlike them,
after the meal he'd gone to the bar, opened up a whisky bottle and
proceeded to get systematically and energetically blind drunk.

*   *   *

The next morning Martin woke with a hangover of colossal
proportions. He staggered from his sleeping bag, grateful at least
to be warm, but his head was banging as though a maniac with a
pile-driver had been let loose between his ears. Not being
accustomed to overdosing on alcohol he had no quick or obvious
remedy to hand, but decided as he made himself some breakfast
that he really ought to do something to alleviate his symptoms.
He'd read somewhere that hangovers are partially due to
dehydration, so he went to the sink and drank half a pint of water.
He also remembered the 'hair of the dog' technique, which also
works, but isn't quite as helpful, as it continues the alcoholic
process. He went back to the whisky bottle and had another good
swig. Then he gathered his things together: after a moment's
pause he went back to retrieve the whisky bottle as well. Then he
set off once again, rather unsteadily, on his bicycle.

*   *   *

Paul and Jane had woken while it was still dark, from a
peaceful and relaxed sleep, grateful to be in a warm room. They
too made breakfast—it was a bit more difficult than their evening
meal because there was no milk, and no bacon.

About half an hour after sunrise they repacked *PIG 1*. It promised to be another bright day with the wind blowing from the south and a hint of rain in the air. Outside, they became aware of an odd sweet smell. There was nothing obvious that it could be coming from—it was an ordinary street with ordinary houses on either side and no sign of a factory.

They both worked it out, at roughly the same instant— rotting flesh, the smell of decomposing bodies, borne on the breeze from central London. Jane wrinkled her nose in disgust and then discovered that morning sickness is greatly stimulated by ordinary things that themselves cause nausea.

'I think we'd better get out of this place just as fast as we can,' murmured Paul. 'We don't know how safe the bodies are, now they're decomposing. We *must* get away.'

They set off, but the journey was not as easy as they had hoped. They continued on their northward direction, moving roughly parallel with the Edgware Road, but found progress annoyingly slow. The sky became overcast and a few drops of rain fell, threatening a shower.

As they rounded the corner of one suburban road, dotted as usual with corpses, Jane started.

'What's that?'

'What's what?'

'In front of us. I thought I saw something moving. Green-coloured—in the distance.'

Paul peered through the rain-smeared windscreen. The road was straight, with houses set back on the right and a line of pollarded plane trees on the left. The fluttering started again. They both peered through the windscreen, trying to make it out, but it disappeared. It took them some time to negotiate a way past the bodies to get up the road to where whatever was fluttering had been.

There was nothing there. Ahead of them the road bent slightly to the right, and the ground was clear of corpses, so they managed to get up a little speed and into third gear. As they rounded the corner they came full upon Martin, wavering around in the middle of the road, his sinusoidal path the result of both an attempt to avoid a new patch of bodies and his hangover, which didn't allow him as much manual dexterity and balance as he might otherwise have possessed. Paul slammed on the brakes and they missed Martin's back wheel by about a foot and a half. Martin stopped, got off and looked round. He wasn't actually drunk, but the headache wasn't much better and he was feeling terrible.

'Er, hello,' he said, thickly.

Jane wound the window down. 'I'm awfully sorry. We nearly knocked you down,' she said. 'Are you all right? We didn't expect . . . '

'That's all right,' said Martin, looking down at them.

Paul broke the silence. 'Are you . . . *well*?'

'Yes thanks, fine,' said Martin, wishing the man with the pile-driver would stop for a minute. This meeting, which might go down in the annals of history as being on a par with Stanley and Livingstone, was being thoroughly marred by the excesses of the previous evening. 'I escaped because I locked myself away in my house.'

'Same here,' said Jane. 'We both had flu.'

They both got out of the car. Paul moved round to Martin. 'Paul Greatorex,' he said, offering his hand.

'Oh . . . er . . . Martin Freeman.'

'And this is Jane Tomlins.'

'You're the first person we've met,' said Jane. 'Alive, that is.'

'Same here.'

'Do you live nearby?' asked Paul.

Martin wasn't too anxious to admit to his previous identity and profession. 'West London.'

'We used to live in Docklands,' said Paul. 'Are you going anywhere—anywhere specific, I mean?'

'No,' said Martin. 'Just trying to get away from London. See if there's anywhere that the plague hasn't got to.'

'We're the same,' said Jane. 'We just want to get away to somewhere safe.'

'Look,' said Paul, eyeing the clouds, Martin, and his bike, and noticing that he wasn't carrying very much, 'would you like to come along with us—in the car I mean? It'll take you an age to get out of London on that contraption and if you're not intending to go anywhere particular we'd be better sticking together, especially if there really isn't anybody else around.'

'Are you sure you can fit me in?' said Martin, eyeing the two-seater.

'Not really, but we'll manage.'

Martin leaned forward. 'I'd like that very much. Thank you. Are you sure you don't mind?'

Jane wrinkled her face in disgust at the smell of Martin's breath. He flushed red. 'Oh I'm sorry,' he said. 'I probably smell a bit. I'm afraid I got very drunk last night. I don't usually do it, but'—he waved an arm round—'I'm just finding it a bit . . . too much. I don't normally drink,' he said. 'At least, I don't normally get drunk . . . ' He tailed off into a miserable silence.

'That's OK,' said Jane. 'It's understandable really. After all you've been entirely on your own, haven't you? At least we've had each other. I think I'd have got drunk if I thought I was the only person left in the world.'

'You're sure you don't mind me coming with you?'

'Of course not.'

Human beings are strange, thought Martin later, reliving their first meeting. Three people, with any number of cars to choose from, and instead they crush themselves into a two-seater that isn't particularly well endowed with baggage space either. But then they still thought of everything belonging to someone else. Stealing someone else's car, when its owner might well come back to claim it, didn't seem to be appropriate. And while they could justify feeding themselves at a wayside inn, they couldn't yet contemplate breaking into a house, nor stealing a car.

Paul loaded Martin's rucksack into the back of the Porsche while Martin carefully leaned his bike against the nearest tree and chained it there, out of habit. His head was thumping a little less now, and the black despair of the past few days had lifted a little now that he knew he was not the only one left on the entire planet. The rain was coming down more heavily now as they squashed themselves into the front seats of the car and started off again.

For the next five minutes they introduced themselves and told each other their experiences of the past week.

Finally Paul asked Martin what he did for a living. There was an embarrassed silence. 'I . . . er . . . I'm . . . I used to be a priest,' he said.

'Oh,' said Jane, thinking of the alcohol.

'Yes,' said Martin. 'It seems a bit pointless now, doesn't it?'

'Never did see much use in the church myself. Still, now

you've got a congregation of two,' said Paul, and promptly
changed the subject. At least we'll be able to do the baptism
properly, he thought.

*   *   *

Eventually Kevin made it to Cambridge. He too had found
the main trunk roads jammed solid, impassable to cars, but just
about navigable on the slimmer bike. In the country, however,
the minor roads were almost always clear, although it was
common to find crashes at junctions, with little knots of traffic
stacked up behind them. Getting round these on the bike was not
too difficult, so Kevin made very much better time than did Paul.

Cambridge proved to be like a smaller version of London—
the centre streets empty, but cars and trucks piled up along all the
major roads out of the city, and severe blockages at all the big
junctions. Kevin hadn't yet seen anyone alive, though the
animals in the fields seemed to be all right, and on a number of
occasions he'd had to outrun packs of dogs roaming the streets.

After Cambridge he headed west for Bedford on the back
roads. Again, the cross-country roads were quite clear but
crossing the A10 and the A1 took him some time.

Bedford was like Cambridge—not a soul to be seen, but
cluttered with vehicles. He got lost approaching the town. His
map-reading wasn't up to much—another piece of expertise he'd
somehow failed to acquire in his short and uneventful life. He'd
intended to go north to Kimbolton, and although he got himself
onto the A6, he was actually going in the opposite direction to
the one he thought he was going in, so when he left the A6 and
bore right to go what he thought was north, he was in fact
heading due south, back towards London again.

-30-

*A*fter four extra days on *Willow* the Jones family's tempers
were getting a little more than just strained. Following David's

inspired piece of lateral thinking they had driven back to the quay, turned the boat round, and gone back the way they had come until they were well out in the country, far away from houses and roads. There they moored, and waited.

They soon found that living in the confines of a narrow-boat, doing nothing, is quite different from idly cruising. There was nothing to do: they had the same scenery to watch; there was no radio to listen to, of course; they'd read all the books they'd brought with them, and played Monopoly fifteen times already. It would have been nice to have had a change of scenery, but wisely, Derek had decided to stay put; moving around would just increase their chances of coming into contact with infection.

After four days their hand was forced: just before midday, the boat's water tank ran dry, so they would have to return. In any case, they had only enough food for one more day. In the meantime, however, they had read the papers from cover to cover, so they knew considerably more about the plague. Waiting there in the boat, Derek and Anne carried out much the same assessment of the situation as had Paul and Jane, and came to much the same conclusions. That was the easy part. Coming to conclusions was one thing—staking your life on the results was another.

'Do you really think we'll be safe?' asked Anne as they ascended Leighton Lock again.

'How can we be sure?' replied Derek, shrugging his shoulders. 'We should be all right if we don't meet anyone with the plague.'

'But couldn't we get it from germs hanging around in the air?'

'Then why didn't we get it on holiday? The wind must have blown it towards us—especially when we went through Milton Keynes. And we didn't go down with it after going through Linslade, did we? So the air's not likely to be infectious any longer, or one or other of us would have got it by now.'

They moored at the quay again and quickly unloaded their belongings, anxious to get into the car and away from the bodies in the house. Derek drove the Peugeot down the entrance road and into Linslade. Nothing had changed. They had wanted to go south, to see if they could possibly get towards London, but the roads were blocked: then they tried to go out on the westerly route, but that was blocked, too.

'Why don't we just head east, like I suggested originally?' said Anne. 'If the infection's been spread by people coming out of London, then we're more likely to find somewhere where the infection *hasn't* been carried if we look off the beaten track. Let's aim towards Norfolk and see what we find there. Maybe we can try to go home later on.'

'That sounds sensible,' said Derek finally. There was a murmur of approval from the children. He started up the car and headed slowly out of the town, towards Woburn. In the back, the children were subdued, overwhelmed with the number of bodies they passed.

'What happens if we're the only ones alive?' said Alison eventually.

'I'm sure we won't be,' replied Derek. 'After all we *are* alive. We just happened to be out in the wilds when the infection struck. There'll be lots of others. Don't worry, you'll see.'

'How can you be so sure, Dad?' said David. 'We might be just dead lucky . . . if you see what I mean,' he said sheepishly, wincing over the unintentional pun. Alison gave a little gasp.

'He's right you know. Look!' She pointed out beyond the bonnet of the car. There, two hundred yards in front of them, was a small girl dressed in a grubby white sweater, a red and green check skirt and bright pink socks. She'd come out of a garden and turned to look at them. Then she started running towards them, hesitated, stopped, put her finger in her mouth, looked hesitantly at them and ran back towards her garden again. Ten seconds later she put her head round the garden gate again, and eyed them suspiciously.

Anne got out of the car and walked up the road. Derek started the car and drove after her. By the time they drew level with the garden gate she had retreated to stand at the front corner of the semidetached house. Anne could see her more clearly now. A pretty girl with slightly pointed features, mousy hair and a fringe beneath which was a pair of frightened brown eyes.

'Hello,' said Anne. 'I'm Anne. What's your name?' The little girl looked at her hesitantly. She must have been about six or seven.

'I'm Sarah. Sarah Jane Whittaker.' She said it proudly and then deflated again.

'Are your mummy and daddy here?' asked Anne. Sarah looked behind her.

'They're in the house, in there. They're asleep. They've been asleep a long time.'

'Come and show me,' said Anne, holding out her hand.

Alison gave a gasp. 'No, Mum, what if she's . . .'

The little girl came a few steps towards her and then stopped. 'Mummy said I mustn't talk to strangers.'

'I know,' said Anne, 'but this is a bit different, isn't it?' By now the rest of the family had got out of the car and Alison and David had come up behind their mother.

'It's quite all right,' said David with a bubbly smile. 'We're very nice really.'

'Your mummy was right to say you shouldn't talk to strangers,' said Anne patiently. 'Why don't you bring me to see your mummy and daddy and then I won't be a stranger any more? How about that?'

'All right,' said Sarah, hesitantly and led the way round the back of the house. Anne was aware of her heart thumping inside her chest as she went to the back door, which stood open. She turned round to Alison and David.

'Stay back with your father. Don't come in the house.' They went into the kitchen, through into the hall and turned into the lounge. There on the couch was the body of a woman in her mid-thirties.

'This is my mummy,' said Sarah.

'Where's Daddy?'

'He's in the bedroom.' Sarah took Anne's hand and led her upstairs.

What am I doing? thought Anne. If they're infectious . . . if this house is infectious . . . I'm killing my family as well . . . But I can't leave Sarah here. Through the open door of the bedroom she could see the body lying in a heap at the corner of the bed.

'When did you talk to them last?'

'A long time ago. We were just going to have tea.'

Anne realised that there'd been food on the kitchen table.

'Have you got any brothers and sisters?'

'No. Just me.'

'What about other people? Have you got a granny or a

grandpa? Do any of your family live nearby?'

'No,' said Sarah, suddenly adopting all the seriousness and poise that only a seven-year-old can. 'Granny lives up in Northampton and Nanny lives in Cardiff. Granny comes to see us every two months, but Nanny only comes at Christmas. Would you like to see my room?'

'Yes,' said Anne as Sarah pulled her into her bedroom. It was a bright room with a white bed and pretty floral wallpaper. The family wasn't particularly well off, but they'd taken a great deal of care with Sarah's room and there was a line of dolls on a shelf above the bed. In one corner the dresser stood with its drawers hanging open, the dishevelled contents showing where Sarah had tried to find something to wear that morning.

'There are lots of other people asleep in the village, aren't there?' said Anne carefully.

'Yes,' said Sarah.

'Have you seen anybody awake?' The brown eyes looked at her warily.

'Only you.'

'Sarah,' said Anne cautiously. 'Your mummy and daddy have been asleep a long time, haven't they?'

Sarah looked up and the brown eyes were full of tears.

'Sarah . . . I don't think they're going to wake up again. I think they're dead.'

The next five minutes was a time that Anne would prefer to forget. Sarah screamed and struggled and cried, then tried to run away from Anne and cling to her parents' bodies.

'I don't think I would go too near them,' said Anne, 'or else you might fall asleep like them too,' and Sarah, caught between wanting to cuddle her mother and scared by her stillness, hovered outside the lounge.

'Come to me,' said Anne. Sarah ran back up the stairs, buried her head on Anne's shoulder and wailed. After a time the sobs died away, and then Sarah was shaking, and sobbing great heaving gasps. Anne waited patiently for her to calm down.

'How would you like to come with us?' she said gently.

'I'd like that very much,' said Sarah.

'Have you got a case?' said Anne.

'You mean to put clothes in like when we go on holiday?

Yes,' she said, pointing to the top of the wardrobe. 'On there.'

'We would have to go very quickly,' said Anne. 'Let's pack a few clothes for you. Where are your things?' They collected together a selection of clothes and shoes.

'What about some toys and dollies?' Together they filled a plastic bag with Sarah's favourite treasures and went downstairs. On the way out of the kitchen Anne saw the table laid for tea. There was the remains of a sliced loaf, a tub of margarine and a jar of jam, all of which had been quite liberally spread over the table and the plates as well as presumably over the bread. Sarah had obviously not gone too hungry in the past four days.

'Wait a minute,' said Sarah and reached up to the work surface. 'That's my medicine. Mummy said I had to make sure that I finished it all up.'

'When did she say that?' said Anne, picking up the bottle of pink medicine and looking at it. *Erythromycin sulphate*, it said. *One teaspoonful four times a day.*

'I don't quite know,' said Sarah, 'about four days ago I think. Everyone started talking about something that made you ill and Mummy said that I'd be all right because I was already taking medicine for my sore ear.' Anne put the bottle in the plastic bag and they went out to the car.

'We've got a new passenger,' she said. 'Sarah, this is Alison and David.'

'What's your name?' said Sarah looking at Derek.

'You can call me Uncle Derek.'

'Uncle Derek and Auntie Anne,' said Sarah. She turned round to look at the house again and began to cry. Anne picked her up.

'We'd better leave a note,' said Derek, 'just in case anybody comes . . .' He went back to the kitchen, found a piece of paper and a pencil and wrote a note. 'We've found Sarah alive and well but on her own. At the moment there's no one else in the town left alive so we've taken her with us. Normally we live at 55, Tennyson Road, Isleworth.'

He wrote down the telephone number for good measure and then put at the bottom: 'Don't be afraid. Sarah's in good hands. If you've found this note, please write on it where you can be found so that we can bring Sarah back to you. We'll try and come back in a week or two.'

He wedged the note prominently against the bottle of tomato ketchup and then went out, closing the door behind him. When he got back to the car he found Anne looking again at the bottle of medicine. Sarah meanwhile had strapped herself in the back between David and Alison and had recovered some of her previous composure.

'All right?' he whispered to Anne.

'Yes,' said Anne thoughtfully, looking at the bottle.

'What's that?'

'Medicine. An antibiotic I think. It looks rather like the stuff David used to have when he had all those ear infections.'

'What's so special about it?'

'Oh, it's just something Sarah said. "When mummy told me about the infection she said I'd be all right as I was on the medicine for my sore ear." I think we should make sure that she finishes it off, don't you—just in case?'

'Wasn't there something in the paper about erythromycin?'

'That's right, there'd been a lot of robberies to get it. And here are Sarah's parents making sure that she took her own supply,' said Anne looking at the bottle. 'And they can't have used any for themselves because the bottle's still a third full.' She turned round to Sarah. 'Have you had your dose this morning?'

'Yes,' said Sarah. 'I did as mummy told me,' and her eyes filled with tears again.

'That's a nice dolly,' said Alison, trying to change the subject, and looking at the rag doll that Sarah had brought in her plastic bag. 'What's her name?'

The tears receded a little from the brown eyes. 'Spaggy,' said Sarah.

'Spaggy?' said Alison. 'Why Spaggy?'

'Because I thought she looked like a lot of spaghetti,' said Sarah seriously.

Alison and David roared until the tears ran down their cheeks, looking at this thing that really did look like a bunch of spaghetti. And their tears and Sarah's tears all merged until they were all crying and laughing and laughing and crying together. Sarah had become one of the family.

*   *   *

Crammed into *PIG 1*, Paul, Jane and Martin had had a difficult journey. It's not easy to make progress through the countryside entirely on byroads. They can be quick enough in towns and cities—often quicker than the main roads—but in the country the geography and geology mitigate against an easy journey. Before the plague Paul had never been conscious of this—he just went wherever he wanted, and the main roads and motorways had taken him over rivers and across ranges of hills with no trouble at all. But navigating solely along secondary roads he became acutely aware of the way in which the major roads had the upper hand when it came to river crossings. The smaller roads didn't cross streams—after all, in the old days bridges were expensive, and the minor roads, which had developed from old cart tracks, tended to stay on the same side of the river. Only the more major roads had bridges. Even small streams prevented his going in the direction he wanted, and necessitated detours: and the detours often ended up on a more major—and hence more clogged—road.

At first they advanced extremely slowly, but as they got further and further away from London the major roads parted company like the outspread fingers of a hand; the proportion of byroads increased, and although they frequently had to skirt around little knots of traffic, they generally made good progress. At about three o'clock they came to the outskirts of Hitchin, where they planned to join the A1, hoping it might be less clogged now that they were some forty miles north of the capital.

They went up the approach road—and when they got to the top Paul reversed *PIG 1* straight back down again. The A1 was a mass of metal as far as the eye could see, the watery afternoon sun glinting brown off row upon row of car roofs.

So they went west instead, towards Stotfold. The road was clear, but they saw no one alive. Before they realised it they came to the A6 at Clophill with the setting sun straight in front of them. Strangely, the roundabout at the A6, next to the Flying Horse pub, was completely clear, so they turned north towards Bedford only to find that round the corner a large pantechnicon

had run into a large group of cars, blocking the carriageway. It
was impassable.

They returned to the Flying Horse roundabout and turned
east again.

'We'd better find somewhere to stay for the night,' said Jane.
The next roundabout was signposted 'Ampthill' and the brown
National Heritage sign said 'Georgian market town'.

'Shall we try it?'

'Suits me,' said Martin.

Paul turned right and gunned the car towards the town centre
along a see-sawing country road lined with houses.

'Strange . . .' said Jane.

'Strange what?'

'No cars.'

'And no bodies either,' said Paul, glad to get into fourth gear
for more than ten seconds at a time; but almost immediately he
had to slow down again as they approached the centre of the
town. The road led into a winding street, at the end of which was
an old building with a distinctive clock tower. In front of this
was a pair of miniroundabouts leading into the town square—and
in the middle of the square was a light brown Peugeot 309 with
what appeared to be five very live occupants.

Part II

Ampthill: Dunstable Street from Market Square

*A*mpthill is an ancient market town in the centre of Bedfordshire. It was appropriate that the eight refugees from the plague had ended up in its Market Square: five centuries earlier King Henry VIII had gone there for roughly the same reason—to escape 'the great sweat and pestilence' that regularly afflicted London during the hot summers.

It had been at Ampthill Castle, long since demolished, that Henry had kept Catherine of Aragon whilst awaiting her divorce at the court in Dunstable: Anne Boleyn was among the visitors to Ampthill in those days, shooting deer with Henry in the Great Park.

For all its momentous involvement in history, Ampthill seems not to have noticed. The castle has long gone, its stones finding their way into many of the old houses lining its streets. But despite this fall from glory, Ampthill is still a good place to live. Medieval man had known where to build; not for him the vagaries of the town planner placing houses on a greenfield site without regard for wind or shelter. Medieval man had taken a great deal more notice of the natural lie of the land when deciding where to build his houses, so Ampthill is in a sheltered spot: the town nestles snugly against the south side of a hill and has a good water supply from its wells. Only a mile to the south the stream which becomes the River Flit is just powerful enough to have worked the first mill—appropriately called Doolittle Mill, because the power of the river was so small that it couldn't turn the millwheel all that quickly.

Until the 1950s the town was little more than a few houses spread around a crossroads. It was really only a village—but call it a village and its inhabitants would get extremely annoyed: Ampthill is the smallest town in England and has a Charter to prove it.

Most of the houses in the centre were built in Elizabethan times, but were then given Georgian facades. To travel outwards from the central Market Square is like walking through the history of architecture in the last five hundred years—first the

Elizabethan, faced with Georgian, at the centre; shortly
afterwards the true Georgian, then the Victorian, Edwardian,
1930s Mock Tudor, and finally the estates of the '60s.

At the heart of the town is the old Market Square—really
little more than a widening of the road leading eastwards. To the
western side of this square lies the clock tower, on the site of the
old Moot Hall. As the guidebooks say, 'Ampthill is a charming
town, relatively unspoilt by the march of progress.' There's a
church—surprisingly, not in the centre but on the most eastern
aspect, yet even so, only two hundred yards from the town centre.
In front of the church, to one side of the road, is a tiny 'town'
square with, on its west side, a huge red-brick Georgian house,
Dynevor House—originally built for the Recorder of the City of
London. Facing Dynevor House across the square is another
Georgian house, with the old Feoffee Almshouses next to it,
themselves nestling on the south side of the churchyard.

The church itself is pretty, but not spectacular. It was there
in Henry's time: it would be nice to think of him attending Mass
there, but he probably used the chapel in the old castle instead.

Ampthill, small as it is, seems to be the centre of the whole
known universe: situated midway between the ancient
universities of Oxford and Cambridge, convenient for the M1
going either north or south, and very near to the railway joining
London, Bedford and Leicester. It's virtually the centre of
England.

Most people have heard about it, if only because of its odd
spelling; most people seem at some time or other to have passed
through it, often without stopping, saying on the way 'Oh look,
how charming' (remember the guidebook?). Everybody has
heard of it, few people have lived there (except for its population
of about eight thousand, which isn't much for a town) and it
really is a Nice Place to Live.

So thought the eight of them: which is at least one of the
reasons why they stopped. The other reasons were perhaps more
direct and compelling. The first was that the light was fading and
they had to find somewhere to stay the night. The second, and
extremely important, was that there were no bodies. There were
no people either, or at least none that they could see, and

strangely there were no crashed cars, even at the particularly awkward blind crossroads in the centre of the town. For some reason the whole population seemed to have fled before the plague could get to them.

*   *   *

Derek and his family had arrived first, having travelled east from Leighton Buzzard. They might well have gone past, but the afternoon was getting on and they needed to find somewhere safe to stay the night. The signs had said 'Ampthill, Georgian Town' which sounded interesting and—particularly because the body count seemed to be low—worth exploring. They had come up the Woburn Road and into the Market Square just as the clock on the tower showed twenty past two—which gave them a start until they realised that it had stopped several days before, at the time the local electricity supply had failed. Entering the Market Square they parked opposite the chemist's. The sun was setting behind the clock tower leaving most of the square in shadow, but still casting a warm ochre glow in front of them, down Church Street.

The place looked warm and welcoming but bare. Towns devoid of people have a curious sepulchral feeling about them— an intense sense of emptiness, like a skull. In this case however, the atmosphere felt quite different—not so much empty as expectant. Perhaps it was the size of the buildings—human-sized, not overwhelming as so many modern buildings are. The buildings were human in detail too—made from bricks of all different colours, with the glorious patina of hundreds of seasons of climate embedded in them.

'I wonder what happened to all the people?' said Anne as she got out of the car and stretched herself.

'It's like Hamlyn after the Pied Piper,' replied Derek. He raised his voice. 'Anyone there?' The sound echoed round the square, and then there was silence. He was about to suggest that they investigate the White Hart Hotel, opposite the clock tower, when they heard a growling noise in the distance—the roar of a car engine, coming nearer.

'Dad, listen!' said David.

'I know, I can hear it.' They stood there, not moving,

willing it to come closer. It was obviously a very powerful
engine. The sound became louder and louder until with a crackle
of its exhaust a red Porsche swept grandly into the square and
came to rest neatly behind their Peugeot. The Jones family stared
at it open-mouthed, the more so as it disgorged not two, but three
occupants. Martin and Jane climbed stiffly out of the passenger
seat, Martin dusting himself off in a shy sort of way before going
forward to meet Derek and his family.

'Before we get any nearer,' called out Paul, extricating
himself from the low driver's seat, 'can we just check—are you
all well?'

'As far as I know,' shouted back Derek. 'We've been
completely out of it, on the canal. We didn't know anything had
happened until we came back. What about you?'

'We should be all right,' said Paul. 'We've all been isolated
from it too.' He stepped forward and offered his hand. 'Paul
Greatorex.'

'Derek Jones.' They introduced each other.

'Where have you come from?' asked Derek.

'London. And you?'

'We live in London, but during the last week we were on the
Grand Union Canal. Have you come across anyone else who's
still alive?'

'No,' said Jane. 'Mind you, we didn't start out as a
threesome. We found Martin on the way.'

'Same here,' said Anne. 'We found Sarah in Leighton
Buzzard. Her parents were dead in the house.'

Martin looked alarmed. 'I thought you said that you were
free of infection?'

'I think we'll be safe,' said Anne. 'Her mother had told her
to keep taking her antibiotics, and I expect that was what saved
her.' Martin still eyed Sarah cautiously and kept his distance.

Derek looked up at the ever-darkening sky. By now the sun
had set and the warm hues of the square were beginning to be
replaced by a grey-brown gloom. 'I think we ought to find
somewhere to shelter and make food, don't you? Let's try across
the road.' Diagonally opposite the clock tower over the crossroads was the White Hart Hotel, a classic flat-fronted Georgian
building with sash windows. Paul and Derek went across to

investigate. It was clean and tidy, with no sign of looting. To their delight there was a gas stove on the back wall of the kitchen and gas fires in the bedrooms.

They returned to the cars and unloaded their kit. Paul found a candle which he stuck in the top of an empty wine bottle, and they quickly prepared a meal from what they found in the kitchen. As usual there was no milk, and no fresh meat: mainly they used food out of tins and catering packs. But it kept body and soul together for another few hours, and all of them were happier knowing that others had survived, and that they really *weren't* the only ones left in the whole of the universe, as each had begun the day fearing.

Sarah still looked shell-shocked, but she obviously enjoyed the company of Alison and David and when it was time for bed the three of them shared a room with the gas fire turned down low. After the children had gone to bed the five adults sat in the bar clustered around the one candle. Each of them had collected a few free drinks, except for Martin, who in view of the excesses of the night before contented himself with half a pint of lager which he managed to make last the whole evening.

The first half-hour was spent telling their individual stories. Derek and Anne, of course, knew little of the events of the previous week, and listened silently and solemnly as Jane, Paul and Martin related their tales. After each had concluded his or her own personal history the talk quite naturally turned to speculation about the future.

'I wonder how many other people are left alive?' said Jane.

'Quite a few, I should think,' replied Derek.

'You're only guessing,' said Anne, gloomily. 'For all you know we're the only ones left in the whole of Britain. But what a coincidence that we should meet like this.'

'I don't believe in coincidences that much,' said Derek. 'They're strange things, you know. We only think they're coincidences because we select them out. We meet up like this so we say it's a coincidence, but if we'd met someone completely different we wouldn't have known what we were missing. It's all a matter of statistics.'

'I don't follow,' said Paul. 'Isn't it remarkable that we all happen to be in the same place at the same time?'

'Not really. After all there was that woman in New York who won the New York State Lottery twice! The chances of doing it once are bad enough—twice is almost infinitesimal. But what you *don't* realise is that it's only because she won it that we talk about it.

'There are probably hundreds, thousands, tens of thousands of people left in Britain. For all we know we've passed within half a mile of hundreds of people today. We could have met up with any of them—but because we meet up with you we think it's a coincidence. It's not. We're bound to meet *someone* sooner or later. The real coincidence would have been if we'd known each other beforehand, and by chance met up in Ampthill.'

'I still think it's a coincidence,' said Jane, totally lost. 'I really don't follow you.'

'Let's do a calculation,' said Derek, grabbing an old menu card and a stump of pencil from the bar. 'How far have we come in the past two days?'

'We've done about sixty miles,' said Paul.

'And we've done about fifteen. And how many people have we met?'

'One each. Plus each other.'

'All right—let's forget about the two cars meeting and concentrate on the numbers of people we met on the way. How far can you see on either side when you're on the road—to be sure you're not missing somebody, I mean?'

'In the city you can only see the people in your own street and down side streets. I suppose it's just possible that somebody might hear you from a couple of streets away and run towards you, but you'd probably be past them before they could get to you.'

'So let's assume you've done thirty-five miles inside London and that you can only see at most fifty yards on either side. OK?'

'Right,' said Paul, not knowing where all this was leading.

'So actually you've only checked for people in an area thirty-five miles long by a hundred yards wide. That's about . . . two square miles. In the country you can see further—but not that much, because the further you go the less detail you see, and you can't be sure that there isn't somebody behind a hedge, or in a cottage or in a wood. So let's assume you can see about a hundred yards clearly on each side—say a hundred and fifty yards each way for good measure. So during the country journey you've combed an area twenty-five miles by three hundred yards, which is about four square miles. We've only covered about ten miles, so we've only combed about two square miles ourselves. Add that lot together and what do you get? Eight square miles. And in those eight square miles we've managed to find two people.'

'Go on,' said Paul, fascinated.

'Don't forget that the part of England we've been searching is the part that's been most hit by the plague, and the part that's been evacuated more than any other, so of any area of Britain this is likely to be the least populated. Right? In those eight square miles we've found two people, one per four square miles. How many square miles in the whole of Britain?' There was silence.

Paul's stockbroking mind went into top gear. 'It's about six hundred miles north to south and about a hundred and seventy-five miles east to west on average, isn't it? That's one hundred thousand square miles.'

'And at a minimum of one per four square miles . . .'

'. . . is 25,000 people.'

'Not a lot left out of fifty-six million,' said Martin.

'It's better than nothing,' said Anne.

'Now do you see what I mean when I say that our meeting is not that much of a coincidence? If we hadn't met up with each other we could just as easily have met up with any of the other twenty-five odd thousand who are probably knocking around somewhere. If you'd gone west instead of north you might have met up with a completely different set of people.'

'I suppose so,' said Paul. 'I think you're right.'

'Twenty-five thousand people's not a lot,' said Jane, 'even if it's a lot more hopeful than we thought this morning.'

'It must be an absolute minimum,' said Derek. 'We're basing our calculations on what we found in the most depopulated area. There are probably whole communities in isolated villages who haven't been touched by it.'

Anne chipped in. 'It happened in the Black Death. Remember Oberammergau? The only reason they hold the Passion Play now is because they made a vow to God that they would perform one in perpetuity if the village was spared. Nobody in the village got the plague. It bypassed them completely.'

'I don't believe in all that religious guff,' said Paul sardonically.

Martin winced inwardly, then wondered why, as broadly speaking he was now on Paul's side.

'I don't believe for one minute it was their oath that stopped them getting the plague,' continued Paul.

'No,' said Derek, 'neither do I, but it still bypassed them.'

'Maybe nobody carrying the plague went north,' observed Jane.

'No, that's not right for the Black Death,' said Anne, 'that was carried by rats, not people.'

'All right, maybe the rats went south,' said Paul. 'Same thing.'

'We haven't included antibiotics in our calculations, either,' said Jane. 'Oberammergau never had any of those.'

'We don't actually know that the antibiotics have anything to do with it,' said Derek.

Martin recoiled. 'I jolly well hope they do,' he spluttered, 'otherwise if Sarah gets it . . .'

Anne glared at him.

Derek looked at Jane. 'Yes, of course, I'd forgotten that,' he murmured absent-mindedly, quietly thinking to himself that Jane must be one of the most beautiful people he'd ever set eyes on. There was just something about her face, something special . . . Anne never looked like that, he thought. Maybe it was the candlelight.

He suddenly realised he wasn't concentrating, and brought his attention back to the conversation, hoping that Anne hadn't seen him looking at Jane. He needn't have worried—she hadn't.

'So what sort of people *are* going to survive?' asked Anne.

'Anybody who's isolated,' replied Jane, 'not in contact with people who are carrying it. Sailors for a start; people on oil rigs; anybody in an isolated community, especially if they haven't got an airport.'

'The Western Isles,' said Paul.

'The Orkneys,' suggested Jane.

'Might be,' said Paul, 'but they've got an airport.'

'Prisons?' queried Anne.

'No,' said Derek, 'the warders would carry it in, wouldn't they?' There was a silence, each wondering what it must have been like for prisoners who hadn't got the disease when the warders died, leaving them locked in the cells. It was Anne who broke the silence.

'I wonder how effective the antibiotics really are? It might make a lot of difference to the number who survive.'

'For all we know the antibiotics only work if you're already on them when you're first in contact with the disease,' said Paul. 'And what about those who actually took Mike Williams' advice and stayed away from other people—like Martin did.'

Martin flushed inwardly, knowing that it was not wisdom, but cowardice that had saved him.

'We know that most of London fled but we don't know how many others sat tight.'

'We haven't started to consider other countries, either,' said Anne. 'For all we know it hasn't spread to them at all.'

'I think we do know,' said Paul. 'There aren't any foreign radio stations still transmitting, are there?'

They fell silent again, each tight-lipped, lost in thought. So much gone without trace; such a loss in a short time. So difficult to comprehend the magnitude of the disaster. They sat there, silent, trying yet again to come to terms with it all. The candle outlined their faces in its soft glow as the flame burned further down towards the neck of the bottle. Suddenly it flickered and nearly went out as a draft of cold air came into the room.

'Hello,' said Chris Wilson, standing in the doorway tapping gently with her knuckles.

-32-

' . . . So when I got back from the radio station there didn't seem to be anybody around. The people around here just upped and went—which is why there are so few bodies. Most of them must have got onto the M1 at Junction 13, but by the time I got there the motorway was blocked and I couldn't get onto it. I travelled to a couple of the villages, though I didn't find anybody

around. Then the petrol in the car ran out. I couldn't get any
more because the electricity was off so the pumps were out of
action.'

'How did you get up here then?' asked Anne.

'Bike. I thought I might have a better chance of finding
somebody alive around dusk because they'd have a light on: a
candle, a torch or a car headlight.'

'Good thinking,' said Paul. 'But you didn't find anyone?'

'Not until just now.'

'Do you know the area well?' asked Jane.

'Passably. I've only lived here for six months. Doing a
local radio show helps. You get to know the things that are
happening and where they tend to happen.'

'Such as?'

'The night spots in Bedford and Luton, Milton Keynes Bowl,
Cranfield Aerodrome, the Agricultural Research Establishment at
Silsoe: and the Luton Town football ground of course.'

'Aerodrome,' said Paul pricking up his ears. 'Where?'

'Cranfield, five miles up the road. Why?'

'We can't easily search for survivors in the car because all
the major roads are blocked, but an aircraft could cover an
enormous area.'

'Good idea,' said Chris. 'Only I don't know anybody with a
pilot's licence.'

'I do,' said Paul. 'Me. I'm going to have another drink.
Anyone else want one?' They all refilled their glasses, except
Martin.

As she looked round the faces at the table, Jane thought that
at long last she detected a tiny sense of optimism. Maybe there
was hope after all. And it was nice to have the company of two
more women.

'The only problem I have,' said Paul, 'is I've never tried
being a burglar and I'm no engineer. I know how to start a plane,
but I don't know how to get it going without a key.'

'I can probably fix that,' said Derek. 'I'll bring the tool kit
from the car.'

'What about trailing a banner behind the plane?' suggested
Anne. 'You know, like the adverts in the sky in the thirties.'

'Good idea,' said Paul. 'When you're up in the air you don't always see people on the ground, but they can always see you.'

'What can we use for a sign?' asked Jane.

'How about sheets from the hotel, tied together with string? I'm sure we could get enough. And if we got some paint and wrote "Go to Ampthill" then anyone who saw us would know where we came from.'

'Have you got any paint?'

'No, but we know a man who has,' chorused Jane and Paul together and suddenly they all fell about laughing.

'There's a "Do It Yourself" shop about fifty yards up the street and I've got my jemmy,' said Paul with a mischievous smile.

Martin recoiled. He'd been very subdued the whole evening and hadn't taken much part in the conversation. 'But you can't do that, that's . . . that's burglary.'

'What do you think we're doing here?' said Paul. 'What about last night? You didn't pay for the food you ate, did you? What about that bottle of whisky?'

Martin went red. 'No, but that's not quite the same. The food was going off and the place was open and it is meant to be a *public* house.'

'Yes, but not so public that you don't pay for it. Listen—if the owners of the shop come back we can pay them for whatever we take. All right? But it's a small price to pay for contacting anybody else in the area.' Sensing Martin might be a good victim, Paul laid it on with a trowel. 'I'll go and get my wrecking bar from the boot.'

Martin started again and gave in.

'What about fuel for the plane?' asked Derek.

'Most light planes run quite happily on ordinary four-star petrol. All we've got to do is find some.'

'You can't go to any of the garages,' said Chris ruefully.

'No, but you can syphon it out of a car's petrol tank,' suggested Paul.

'I've got a better idea,' said Derek. 'If we can find a hose and a stirrup pump we can pump it out of the garage storage tanks themselves. We'd only have to take the lock off the inlet pipe that they use when they fill up from a tanker.'

'Where would we get a stirrup pump?' asked Jane.

'A motor repair shop?' suggested Derek, hesitantly.

'Would they carry one on a fire engine?' asked Chris.

'Brilliant. Yes, they do.'

'Then there's a fire station about half a mile from here, down Oliver Street.'

'We'll take a look in the morning.'

'Something else we ought to do,' said Chris. 'You probably didn't realise it, but Ampthill has a bypass, so anybody travelling on the east–west route won't pass through it. I think we ought to put notices on the bypass saying that we're here.'

'What about people travelling north–south?' asked Jane.

'They'll come straight through the centre,' said Chris, turning round and pointing up Bedford Street.

'Then we ought to have another sign at the crossroads. Who knows, we might find somebody swept round the corner and shot off again before we had a chance to get out and show them that we're here.'

As they continued to talk, Jane looked again round the faces illuminated by the flickering candle, and suddenly felt very positive indeed.

*   *   *

They were ready at first light. In his usual bullying fashion, Paul had insisted on taking Martin with him to the 'Do It Yourself' shop in Dunstable Street. It was locked. Paul pushed the wrecking bar between the double doors and pulled sharply. There was a splintering crash and the right-hand door jerked open. He went inside. Martin surreptitiously glanced up and down the street to make sure no one was looking before he followed. Between them they gathered up a tin of black emulsion paint, some brushes and several reels of plastic twine.

By the time they got back to the hotel Anne and Jane had managed to locate the hotel's store of bed linen and had selected eight sheets which they proceeded to tie firmly together with the twine. Then the three children painted 'Go to Ampthill' on one side. They had been intending to do both sides, but they found that the black paint seeped through, so just one side it had to be. They made similar signs to go on the bypass. 'Won't you need a post to mount them on?' asked Anne.

'No,' said Derek, 'we'll wrap it against the sign that points

to Ampthill. It will probably give more protection against the
wind than if we tried to put up a lightweight sign ourselves.'

'Who's coming to Cranfield then?' asked Paul. 'Derek—I
may need you to start the engine. Chris—you know where the
aerodrome is and also a bit about the countryside and where
people are likely to be. You'd better come along as well.'

Derek turned to Anne. 'You'll be all right here with the
children, won't you?' he said and then hesitated, seeing her face:
'Won't you?'

'Oh yes,' replied Anne, not meaning it, and wondering what
would happen if someone slightly less than friendly were the next
to turn up—like the owner of the hotel, for example.

Then reason regained control. 'No,' she said, 'we'll be fine.
We'll stay here and make tea and form a reception committee for
the hordes of people that you'll bring in.'

Martin gave a slight cough.

'I'd forgotten you,' said Derek.

'I'll stay behind,' said Martin.

'Think you can handle a gun?' asked Paul. Martin jumped
and flushed as he realised that Paul was winding him up yet
again. He muttered something under his breath about being a
pacifist, which Paul didn't quite catch. If it did come to a fight,
thought Paul, he'd prefer Martin to be with the opposition . . .

Five minutes later, Derek, Paul and Chris set off for Cranfield
in the Peugeot, complete with a wrecking bar, cold chisel and
hammer, and two five-gallon petrol cans. Most precious of all,
Derek had purloined a stirrup pump and a length of inch-wide hose
from one of the fire tenders and, as they had discussed the night
before, they went to one of the petrol stations in Bedford Street,
knocked the lock off one of the storage tank filler caps, let the tube
down and used the stirrup pump to fill up the jerry-cans with petrol.

Cranfield lay about seven miles away. It was an awkward
cross-country journey, but as it lay almost exclusively along
minor roads they met little in the way of obstructions. There was
one difficult moment when they came across two interlocked
vehicles that almost obliterated a T-junction, but there was just
enough room for the car to squeeze past and soon they swung
into the aerodrome.

Like many airfields, Cranfield had the typical sprawl of old hangars next to the control tower. The light aircraft were parked on the far side of the field. They drove over and surveyed the available aircraft.

'I want a Jodel or a Piper Cherokee if there is one,' said Paul. 'The Jodel's what I learned on. Both of them are easy to fly, there's not much to go wrong, and I know all about them. I don't fancy being two thousand feet up in a strange plane if its engine starts playing up.'

They soon found a Jodel, tied down to the ground to prevent damage from high winds. Paul opened the cockpit which, as usual, was unlocked.

'It's very simple, Derek. There's no electrical system worth speaking about, and no starter motor. You just switch on, swing the propeller and that's it. The engine drives a small generator which supplies all the electrical equipment on the plane, like the radio, but there's no battery, so all we have to do is bypass the ignition switch. How do we do that?'

'Easy enough,' said Derek. 'It's the exact opposite of a car engine. With a car engine you've got to *make* a circuit. An aero-engine uses magnetos so you've got to *break* the circuit in order for the magnetos to produce a spark.' He reached underneath the instrument panel, found the key switch, traced the wires behind it and cut one of them with a pair of pliers.

'That should do it—unless it's got a steering lock.'

Paul gave him a sideways glance.

'Only joking.'

The filler cap was in front of the cockpit, on the nose. Derek went to the car and pulled out the jerry-cans. 'How do I know when it's full?' he said. 'Where's the gauge?'

'In front of you,' said Paul pointing to a cork on a long wire. 'There's a float on the other end of that in the petrol tank. When you pour in the petrol the float rises, takes the wire up and the cork shows you how full it is.'

'A bit primitive, isn't it?'

'Yes, but it works.'

'Gives a new meaning to the phrase "Fly by wire", I suppose.' He filled the tank.

'Aren't you going to get in?' said Paul to Chris, who suddenly looked somewhat green. 'Haven't you flown before?'

'Oh yes,' said Chris, 'but in a proper aircraft, not one that looks as though it's likely to collapse and let me out at any moment.'

'Safe as houses,' said Paul clapping her on the shoulder and with the other hand pulling on one of the wings so that the whole aircraft rocked alarmingly. Another victim, he thought.

'Get in—you'll enjoy it.' Chris crawled awkwardly into the seat on the right-hand side of the cockpit.

'Put the headphones on, otherwise you won't be able to hear me above the engine.'

Derek attached one end of the banner to the tail strut, rolled it up and knotted it together with a highwayman's hitch, passing the end of the string back to Chris. 'When you're airborne, tug this. It'll allow the sign to unravel.'

Derek swung the propeller. The engine caught at the second attempt and the headphones crackled into life.

'Can you hear me all right?' asked Paul.

'Loud and clear.'

'Did you bring the map?'

'Oh, I never thought,' said Chris. Paul leaned out of the cockpit and shouted to Derek to bring the car's road map.

'OK. Here we go, ready for takeoff.'

'Good luck,' said Derek. Paul closed the canopy, waved to Derek and revved the engine, then switched the transmit button of the radio. 'Golf Bravo India Zulu Yankee to control tower . . .'

Chris looked at him.

'Sorry,' said Paul, flushing. 'Habit.'

He revved the engine and they began to taxi. The plane turned into the wind and began to accelerate over the grass, parallel to the main runway. Chris had never experienced the sensation of travelling across grass at sixty miles an hour before and she found the bumpiness of it somewhat alarming. She was just hoping there were no such things as rabbit holes on airfields when suddenly the bumping stopped and they were airborne. The ground dropped away beneath them, and then seemed to lift on their left as Paul banked.

They circled the airfield: Paul waved to Derek as Chris pulled the release cord of the highwayman's hitch. The banner streamed out behind them, its end flapping in the wind. She looked back anxiously at it, wondering whether it would stand the strain, but the aircraft was only travelling at about sixty and at that speed the turbulence on the row of sheets was really quite small.

'Which way shall we go?' Paul shouted into his microphone.

'Let's try north first,' said Chris, 'and then west, towards Northampton.'

Although the air temperature was low, the sky was clear and the sun beat fiercely down on them through the perspex of the cockpit window. Paul flew at about a thousand feet—high enough for a good view of the countryside, but low enough to spot people; and low enough too for anyone on the ground to read the banner streaming behind them.

Chris had never flown in a light aircraft before. She thought how unreal everything looked: the dark fields all planted out with winter wheat; the red and gold of the autumn leaves on the trees; the curious way the sun reflected off lakes and ponds like a mirror; and the foreshortening which made even steep hills look strangely flat. It felt as though they were just above a large model rather than a long way above the real thing.

Their first port of call was Bedford, over to the northeast. They could see the River Ouse as it meandered beneath them, glinting yellow in the sunlight. They flew over the town bridge and across the main square, staring down intently. Everything was still. Beneath them they could see the traffic jams and the bodies in the streets, as well as the occasional blackened shell where a house had burned out. For a quarter of an hour they flew backwards and forwards over the town, trying to make sure that any survivors could get a good look at the message they were carrying, but they didn't see anyone there to respond.

Then they set course towards Kimbolton. North of Bedford, the land rolls gently, isolated villages dotting the landscape.

'Much more the sort of territory that we'd expect to see survivors,' shouted Paul above the din. Whenever he saw a village near their flight path he diverted so as to pass more or less directly over it.

As they passed over Kimbolton Castle, now a boarding school, Chris suddenly yelled, 'Look, down there, on your left—in the school grounds.' There were two figures, waving frantically at the aeroplane. As they watched, a third figure ran out of the main entrance, stopped, stared, and began waving too.

Paul banked into a steep turn, circled the school and made a second pass, more slowly, to make sure that the people on the ground could see the message splayed out behind them. The tiny clump of figures below them waved and jumped up and down. Paul waggled his wings and set off west towards Northampton.

They saw several more people as they passed over isolated farms and villages. Each time Paul made a second pass to show them that they had been seen, and to give them a good chance to read the banner.

Northampton was like Bedford, only worse. The wide anonymous ring roads were cluttered with cars, and there was no sign of human life. They traversed the city, but then Paul pointed to the cork on the petrol indicator in front of the cockpit window.

'We'd better be getting back,' he shouted. 'I don't want to risk running out of fuel. We ought to give ourselves a lot of leeway.'

Chris nodded, and Paul swung the plane round in an arc towards Milton Keynes, and almost immediately passed over the M1, which was jammed solid as far as they could see. No one would be travelling on it for a very long time, thought Chris, unhappily.

As they came to Milton Keynes Paul nudged Chris and pointed down. Below them the sun was shining orange off a long thread of water with boats moored at the bank—the Grand Union Canal, along which Derek and his family had passed a few days before.

Nothing moved below them except for the occasional farm animal. They swung over central Milton Keynes and then returned to the airfield, the cork now showing that they had only a quarter of a tank left. As the airfield came into view Paul turned into the wind, landed uneventfully on the tarmac and taxied to where Derek and the car were waiting.

'How did you get on?' he shouted to them.

'Brilliant,' said Chris. 'We must have seen at least twenty people.'

Derek's face fell. It was not as many as he had hoped for.

They made four journeys in all. By three o'clock they were

tired, but satisfied; landing for the last time they returned the plane to its original site and tied it down again. Chris removed the banner from the rear skid and then they set off back to Ampthill.

As they were parking in the square Anne came out of the hotel. Derek took one look at her and his heart sank.

'What's the matter?'

'How did you get on?' said Anne, ignoring the question.

'Fine,' said Paul. 'We've seen about fifty people, and there must be be more whom we couldn't see, but who could see us. I think Derek must be right over the number of people who've survived. It's looking a lot better than we thought. Correction–,' he said, ruefully. 'It's looking a lot better than *I* thought. It just shows I ought to trust your husband's judgement more. I'm starving and I'm cold too. How about a nice cup of tea?'

'That's just the problem,' said Anne. 'The gas has gone off.'

-33-

'It had to happen sooner or later,' said Derek as they held a council of war in the bar of the White Hart.

'Why's it lasted so long?' asked Martin. 'Are gas workers immune, d'you think? The electricity went off quickly enough.'

'Nothing like that,' said Derek. 'Electricity has to be created at the time we use it. If the generators aren't supplied with coal or gas we don't get any electricity, whereas all our gas just flows out from the wellheads in the North Sea. It's just taken longer for the automatic systems to find faults big enough to shut the gas supply down, that's all.'

'What are we going to do now?' asked Anne, still looking shaken. 'We can't go on for long without heat and some way to cook.'

Jane shivered. Even inside the hotel it was getting cold, with a raw, damp autumnal chill that penetrated every layer of clothing.

'We'll just have to do what they did last century,' said Derek. 'Use open fires and cook on ranges.'

'That's not going to be easy,' said Paul. 'Not many houses nowadays have open fires, and even fewer have ranges. We could always cook outside if we had to, I suppose.'

'Not necessarily,' said Jane. 'What about those people who've got solid-fuel cookers, like Agas? They're popular enough.' She glanced outside; the afternoon light was starting to fade and it was getting gloomy inside the bar. 'One thing's for sure, it won't be sensible to stay in the hotel any longer. We'd just freeze: there aren't any open fires here.'

'Let's look at some of the big old houses in the town,' said Derek. 'They would have been built with fireplaces and chimneys, and you don't usually modernise a really old house. The owners usually like to keep it more or less as it is.'

'I think we're going to need our cold chisel again,' said Paul, winking at Martin, who turned pink again.

'I'm not sure . . .' began Martin, ' . . . I'm really not sure that we ought to go and burgle somebody's house. I mean . . .'

'Rot,' said Paul. 'You mean it's all right to go and live in a hotel and steal their food and their drink, but it's not all right to borrow someone's house for a bit? It's a matter of self-preservation. We've got to eat; and we've got to stay warm.' Martin subsided, pinker than ever for having lost yet again.

'Are you joining me on my burglary spree?' Paul asked Derek.

'Might as well.'

'Come on then.' He turned round. 'You'll be all right, Martin. It's not a hanging offence any more.'

They went out into the square. Opposite them the children's poster was displayed prominently on the old pump. 'We're here. We've survived,' it read. 'Come and join us.'

'Left or right?' said Paul.

Anne shrugged. 'It probably doesn't matter much. Try right.'

They walked east, up Church Street, surveying the houses on either side. Eventually they came almost to the edge of the town and turned to face Church Square. In front was the church, and forming the left-hand side of the square was the large and elegant Georgian front of Dynevor House, facing into the square, its side forming part of Church Street.

'Why not start with the best and work down?' said Paul,
looking at Martin who flushed again—but his teeth were
chattering and the thought of a night without heat convinced him
that Paul was right. Paul knocked hard on the front door, for
form's sake. The knock had an empty echo. Strange how you
can so often tell whether a house has any occupants by the
quality of noise the knocker makes, thought Derek.

There was no reply. Paul studied the front door. 'It seems a
shame to wreck it,' he said. 'Besides, it's probably got six bolts
on the other side. Let's try round the back.' They retraced their
steps along Church Street passing the end of the house, and came
to a side gate in the garden wall: it was unlocked. The house had
been built at the bottom of a slight incline, and behind it the
garden rose progressively.

In front of them was a long patio with, on the left, an
ornamental pond containing golden carp and on their right the
back of the house, flat, like the front. There was a back door, and
further along a pair of French windows.

'This is more like it,' said Paul. 'All good burglars know
that everybody fortifies their front door like Fort Knox, and
leaves the back door protected only by a tiny lock.' He looked in
through one of the panes of glass in the door, and tried the
handle, but it was locked. He tried to force the end of the wrecking bar between the door and the jamb, but the fit was too tight.

'This looks more promising,' he said, moving to the French
window, and fitting the end of the wrecking bar into the gap
between its two halves. He looked up at Martin. 'Do you want
to help?' Then he swung his weight on the crowbar and with a
bursting, tearing crash the wood gave and the left-hand French
window sprang open.

Paul put his head inside. 'Anybody here?' he yelled.

No reply.

'If so, we've come to borrow your home.'

They trooped in. The room looked like a morning room or a
small lounge—not big, but with a pleasant view across the
garden. To their relief it had an open grate.

Derek went into the hall beyond. It was gloomy in the dusk,
and instinctively he reached out to find the light switch. 'Stupid

me,' he said under his breath when nothing happened. Old habits die hard.

The hall was immense with an elegant Georgian light-fitting in the middle and a large and important-looking staircase, cantilevered out from the stairwell at the back. Very grand, thought Paul, following on behind Derek. Wouldn't mind it myself. Now—where's the kitchen?

Much as he'd expected, the room next to the main door was a cloakroom, but next to it was the kitchen. Two seconds later there was a whoop of joy. 'Got it in one,' said Paul. 'Look.'

They rushed in. There in front of them was a brand-new Aga.

'Wouldn't it be just our luck if it was gas-fired,' muttered Chris under her breath. But it wasn't. Paul found the detachable handle that fitted into the filler plug in the left-hand hotplate, lifted it and looked inside.

'It's gone out. It's been working until very recently: you can feel—it's quite warm. It shouldn't be too difficult to relight. I wonder where they keep the coke?'

'In the cellar most probably,' said Derek. They went back into the hall, which was getting gloomier by the minute as the light failed.

'There's no point in us all trying to do the same things at the same time,' said Paul. 'Jane, and Anne, why don't you go back to the hotel with the children and bring all the things that we left there, including the candles and the food. While you're at it—' he turned to Alison, 'can you make another couple of notices to show where we are now? Put something in the town square next to the one you've just made, and then put another notice on the main road outside this house.

'Chris, can you get a fire going in the room that we came into first? Derek, would you go and see what else is in the rest of the house? I'll go and look in the cellars for some fuel.'

The entrance to the cellar was, as he expected, underneath the main stairs. There was a warren of rooms underneath, one of which was full of coke, coal and wood.

Chris looked slightly ill at ease. Eventually she turned round to Paul. 'I've never made a fire in a grate. We've always had central heating or gas fires.'

'Weren't you ever a Guide?' said Paul, superciliously. Chris shook her head.

Martin stepped forward. 'I'll show you how to do it. Victorian vicarages are renowned for their open fires. I've had a lot of practice.'

The fire in the morning room was soon blazing away. Derek set about repairing the damage that Paul had done to the window so that at least they could keep the heat inside the room. Paul had only burst a small amount of wood around the lock and it was quite easy to reseat it and close the door firmly.

By the time Anne, Jane and the children had transported their belongings the hundred and fifty yards from the hotel to Dynevor House, Paul had the Aga burning, but it was going to be another six hours before it would be hot enough to cook with.

'In the meantime we could always put a kettle half into the fire in the morning room,' said Anne brightly, 'and we can also heat up tinned food that way.'

Anne and Jane braved the fire in the morning room, making tea and heating up some baked beans, half blistering their knuckles and their faces in the process. But it was food, it was hot, they were warm and the soreness in their faces and hands was a small price to pay. At Derek's suggestion they'd put a candle in the study window—the one on the far side of the hall which overlooked both the square and the road—to show any newcomers where they might be found.

'We probably can't afford to do this too often,' said Derek, 'or we'll run out of candles, but we may well get people coming today or tomorrow and it would be awful if they went straight past the door.'

They didn't have long to wait. They were in the morning room finishing off their meal when there was a loud banging on the door. Derek was greeted by a man in full motorcycle leathers, with a sleek and somewhat hot Harley-Davidson parked in front of the house.

Kevin had arrived.

34

*A*s it happened, Kevin had seen neither the plane nor the notices on the bypass. The plane had long since landed by the time he came down the road from Bedford, misguidedly thinking he was travelling towards Northampton, so it was with some surprise that on coming into the centre of Ampthill he had seen a notice, 'Survivors this way'. Not being one to pass up the chance of company, Kevin had obeyed. It was to prove a source of great amusement to Paul that despite all his hard work canvassing the area with the plane, the first person to find them had chanced upon them by pure serendipity.

That first evening they bedded down wherever they could find a warm spot in the house—which meant either the kitchen or the morning room.

The next morning they explored the upper part of the house. There was a large main bedroom, with many other smaller bedrooms at each end of the house. But the biggest surprise was that the grandest reception room was upstairs. A vast room running the length of the first floor and overlooking Church Square, it had a high vaulted ceiling, an elaborate plasterwork dado and an ornate carved fireplace at one end. The ceiling was deep blue, with elegant white shuttering around the windows and antique furniture to match, with a grand piano at one end.

Anne found the room first, and just gasped. Derek, following behind her, stared at it in silence.

'You're dying to tell me why it's upstairs, I can feel it,' he said, knowing Anne's knowledge of history.

'It's quite simple. At the time the house was built it was the custom for the gentry to entertain on the first floor—the ground floor was for the servants, which is why the rooms there are much smaller and gloomier. All the important rooms were upstairs— they even used to receive guests in their bedrooms during the morning, which is why the main bedroom is so vast, too.'

'It also explains the layout of the rest of the house,' reflected Derek. 'Because this room is two stories high, the two end wings can't communicate with each other, which is why the first and second floor bedrooms have to have a set of stairs each.'

'If only walls could talk,' sighed Anne. 'Just imagine what it must have been like when it was first built—ladies sweeping up the grand staircase in all their finery . . .'

'Makes you feel underdressed, doesn't it?' said Derek, looking at his trousers, now less than well creased after the rigours of the past few days.

'We ought to make Dynevor our permanent base, you know.'

'I was just thinking that. It's near the centre, it's big, and because there's an open fire in almost every room we can heat it easily. Most important, we can cook food on the solid fuel stove.'

'Let's see what the others think.'

*   *   *

Kevin was the first of many. They didn't all come at once: some had obviously taken time to gather their belongings together; others had been anxious about leaving their homes in case they met others who were still incubating Legionnaires'. Those from the south got there first, because the ones from the north of the county had to find a way of crossing the River Ouse. Although there were bridges at Bedford, the whole area was clogged with cars. Some refugees had tried going directly through the town; others tried to go round it, but the Ouse made that difficult. It was a wide river, and there were jams at all the major crossing points: the refugees had to go a long way upstream before there were enough bridges to allow crossings to be made on the more minor, unclogged, roads. But eventually, they made it and over the next week a steady trickle of refugees knocked on the door of Dynevor House.

The tales the refugees told were many and varied, but they all bore an uncanny resemblance to Derek's predictions. Some had escaped the plague because they were in isolated communities; others, because they were already taking erythromycin at the time the plague struck. Many of the survivors had escaped the infection simply by staying indoors, avoiding all contact with

Church Square, with Dynevor House on the left

others, and as she helped process each new wave of refugees, Jane couldn't help thinking what a pity it was that more people hadn't taken Mike Williams' advice and stayed put. Then she thought of Mike, and the announcement of his death, and suddenly felt empty and alone. He'd been so good, so kind, so open, and so wise. People like him were going to be missed.

Among the first group of refugees was Peter Abrahams, the ex-policeman, who had watched his family die around him, but had himself emerged unscathed—a previous dose of Legionnaires' disease when he was fourteen had, unknown to him, immunised him.

There was Mary Harper, who had been demonstrating with the Women's Peace Movement outside Porton Down the day the plague struck. Sensibly she didn't try to get back into London—instead she had realised the wisdom of self-quarantine, so she bought a week's supply of food, then stayed out of the way in her car until the full fury of the plague had passed. After that she decided to head cross-country towards Suffolk, as she had had relatives there, but then saw the plane and its message when she stopped to let Howler perform one of nature's necessities.

The refugees came from all walks of life. Some were old, some young; there were some couples; and even some families; and many who had recently been widowed. There were many trades and occupations—but no doctor. Jane had particular reason to hope for one. Still, she thought, it's only the first week. Maybe we'll find one later—or a midwife: either would do.

During that first week Chris, Paul and Derek had gone around the town to see what facilities there were. In particular they looked for houses with open fires and solid-fuel cooking and found a surprisingly good selection spread over the square mile of the town. Unless they got a sudden huge influx, Paul thought, it should be easy to provide all the refugees with a place they could call home, and where at least they could keep themselves warm through the coming winter.

The children had adapted well to the changes of the past few days, though Alison seemed to have lost weight. Perhaps it was worry, thought Derek. Sarah certainly seemed to have taken to her new family, though there were many tearful moments. David was revelling in it—as far as he was concerned it was like a gigantic Scout camp, with foraging for food and fuel, the absence of electric light, and the inability to take baths easily.

At the end of the first week they all met for a council of war, in the entrance hall at Dynevor, the only warm room big enough to hold the whole community. They squeezed in, sitting on the floor or on the stairs, and hanging over the bannisters of the upstairs gallery.

Derek began the proceedings. 'I want to start with a summary of what we know. As far as we know the plague has passed from London to the whole of the British Isles and on to the continent. None of us has been able to pick up any transmissions on any of the normal broadcast frequencies so it looks as though the ordinary radio stations have ceased to function. On the other hand, that doesn't mean everyone has died: there may be radio hams trying to get in contact with us, so if anyone finds a house with amateur radio equipment then let us know.

'We're pretty sure a lot of people will have escaped the plague by one means or another. At a rough guess we think there must be at least twenty thousand people on mainland Britain alone, but there may be more, particularly in the more remote areas.

'We have a number of problems to face over the next weeks. Although we're all right for food at the moment—because we've been able to raid the hotel and the houses that we're occupying—these stocks aren't going to last for long. Obviously, we'll be able to get large supplies of tins from the local shops, but that's not going to last for ever, either, and we've got to make sure that we use whatever food we have very wisely indeed.

'We've also got to make sure that we learn how to grow our own food, and that's not going to be easy because as far as I am aware none of us has had experience of growing food commercially. I know a number of you are keen gardeners, but from what I understand trying to grow produce on a commercial scale is quite different; what the amateur gardener thinks is a good crop may well be the sort that a commercial gardener would throw away because it wasn't up to standard: so we've got to realise that producing food may not be as easy as we might think.

'Fresh food is obviously our immediate problem. The

countryside round here grows mostly vegetables, so we are going to be all right this winter. On the other hand, meat, and particularly milk, is going to be difficult to get.

'In the short term, heating isn't a problem. There's a big storage depot at Elstow, five miles north of here. Chris has reconnoitred it and says that there's a coal yard there with supplies that will last us for a very long time.

'Similarly, we'll be OK for petrol, but only in the short term. We can go round mining for it in petrol stations—but eventually they'll run dry, and obviously we're not going to be able to get more once it runs out. So we'll have to be careful over how we use it.

'There's no electricity, but Paul found one diesel and one petrol generator in the council yard, so if we really need electricity for something—say, powering an amateur radio transmitter—we could produce it. However, we don't want to use fuel unnecessarily, so it's not a good idea to use the generators unless we have no option.

'There's no gas either. Presumably that shut off automatically once those who were controlling it left their posts or died. Strangely, we seem to be all right for water. There's a water tower at Pulloxhill, five miles away: we're not sure whether the water is coming from there or whether we're just lucky and we're downhill from the natural supply. If it is coming from Pulloxhill then eventually it's going to run out, because something has to pump the water up from its source to the top of the tower. However, this is an old town and it would have had a water supply of its own long before anybody thought of water towers. A number of the houses have wells in their gardens, and we may need to start using them.

'Why stay here if the water supply fails, you may ask? In fact, why stay here at all? Well, it's sheltered, it's convenient, and it's got a large number of old houses that are just right for living in under the sort of conditions we now face. There are hardly any bodies around, and the roads are clear, probably because the population was able to run away before the plague caught up with them. I'm sure that there are many other villages and towns that we could live in, but as we've got to live somewhere, here seems to be as good as anywhere.

'Ampthill also has the advantage of being surrounded by rich farmland, and that's going to be important for the future. We don't want to have to go a long way to be able to produce our food.'

He sat down.

'Thank you, Derek,' said Paul, who was chairing the proceedings. 'Anyone got any questions?'

'What about sewage?' asked Peter.

'We're on a hill, so gravity does it all for us,' replied Derek. 'There's a sewage works about a mile from here, but of course it's not working any more and we think that anything discharged into the drains just goes straight into the river Flit.'

'Not very good for the environment,' observed Mary, ever the ecologist.

'There's nothing we can do about it. We can't start operating the sewage works without electricity and a lot more know-how. In any case, the amount will be small by comparison with what the animals in the fields produce.'

'I want us now to think about the future,' said Paul, standing up. 'We need to make plans—good ones. We won't have much leeway, and if we get it wrong there won't be anyone to rescue us. If we use our resources wisely we'll probably do well: but if we use them *up* . . .'—he looked round at the faces in the room— '. . . I don't think I need to elaborate further.

'Planning is the key. We've got to make sure that we do things at the right time. It's no use discovering in April that we ought to have planted seeds in March. There's just no margin for error: each year will be make or break.'

'We're just going to have to get used to living in the Dark Ages again,' said Peter, sitting on the stairs.

'No,' said Derek, getting to his feet. 'With respect, I don't think so. Yes, I agree with you in some ways. We'll have to do without central heating, piped gas and for the moment most electricity—but we won't lose the knowledge that we've got. Knowledge doesn't degrade. We won't go back to thinking that the sun moves round the earth. We'll know about the internal combustion engine; we won't have any doubts about how babies are created.'

Too right, thought Jane.

'So long as we can ensure that skills and knowledge are kept
intact we should manage well. You're right, Peter, but only up to
a point—in some ways it *will* be like living in the Middle Ages,
but in others it will be completely different: rather like living in
a developing country before the plague struck—the knowledge is
there but not the infrastructure to support it.'

Paul took over. 'In the future we'll be living in a mixture of
low-tech and hi-tech. Life will certainly have to get simpler,
though—and I'm sure we'll have to get more concerned about
the more basic aspects of living, like food.'

And medicine, thought Jane, consciously feeling her abdomen.

'In the past, if the harvest failed, we just imported food from
somewhere where the harvest *didn't* fail. We won't have that
luxury in the future. We have to get it right, first time, every
time. We'll have to grow lots of different types of crops, if only
to reduce the chances that all of them will fail at the same time.

'As far as the next year's crop is concerned, we're in luck.
The winter wheat has already been sown, so all we've got to do is
harvest it when it comes up—between now and then all I've got
to do is work out how to drive a combine harvester as well as fly
a plane.' There was a ripple of laughter. 'But quite seriously,
has anybody got any experience of farming? Anybody we've
missed so far?'

Silence.

Then a hand went up. 'I used to work on a farm,' said
Trevor Smith, a heavily built red-faced man in his mid-thirties:
'But I was just a general handyman—I don't know much about
farming itself. I just did what I was told.'

'Well, that's a start. At least I don't have to learn to drive a
combine, after all.

'The other thing is, has anybody got any experience of
medicine or of nursing?'

Deafening silence. Jane felt her stomach again.

'We've also got to think about teaching: and not just the
children. As Derek said, knowledge is the difference between us
and the Middle Ages. We need to make sure that our knowledge,
our experience and our skills are not lost.

'So we need to teach the adults *and* the children. Has anyone had experience of teaching?'

A couple of hands were put up, including, of course, Anne's. Paul turned to her. 'Anne, could you get together with the other teachers to draw up some plans? It will have to be very practical from now on, I should think, to make sure that skills are passed on properly. Is that all right?' Another murmur of assent.

'Is there anything else that you think we ought to consider? Anything we've missed?'

Mary Harper spoke from the back of the room. 'Can I just say on behalf of all of us—thank you very much, particularly to you, Paul, and you, Derek, for what you've done so far.'

Derek rose. 'That's very kind of you. We didn't actually do very much. It rather organised itself.'

'I still think you did it well. Maybe we ought to elect you as official leaders?'

Derek grinned. 'Thanks for the compliment, but we'd already thought about a ruling body and really it doesn't seem appropriate. There are only a hundred and twenty of us and I'm sure that we can make any decisions all together. If our community gets bigger we may need to think about some form of council, but for the moment it's best if we rule by consensus. Does that seem fair?' Another murmur of assent.

Chris got to her feet. 'We haven't yet taken an inventory of the skills we've got. Derek, you're quite right in what you said about sharing our expertise and teaching each other the skills we have, and I think we ought to start straight away. It would be silly if we tried to do something which really needed a particular skill if someone here already possesses it without our realising.' Again there was a murmur of agreement.

'In which case please will each of you write down the various skills you've got—not just your job, but any other skills you've acquired—hobbies you've had, that sort of thing. Put down everything, however insignificant, even if you can't think of a use for it now. For all we know, in the future it may be important that we have someone who knows how to pilot a boat, or build radios.'

They set to work.

35

*T*hat evening the six of them—Paul, Jane, Derek, Anne, Martin and Chris—went through the inventory. After about half an hour's hard work, made harder because it was all done by the light of a single candle, Chris threw down her pen and paper, leaned back in her chair and gave a cackle.

'You know it would be funny if it wasn't so serious,' she said. 'Do you realise that of the six of us here only two of us have got qualifications that are even remotely usable? That's Derek and Anne. As for Paul, Jane and myself, well, we're instantly redundant. Two people in broadcasting, and one used to staring at TV screens on the broking floor. Not a lot of use for a future existence in a world with no electricity, eh?'

Paul grinned. 'I hadn't thought of it like that. Our ability to plan is a qualification in itself, though. Planning is a speciality all of its own.'

'I agree,' said Derek. 'It's a bit like the difference between wisdom and knowledge.'

'Sounds like a good line for you, Vicar,' said Paul, looking at Martin who flushed yet again, but he couldn't think of a rejoinder, so he remained silent.

'It's all very well having knowledge about a subject,' continued Derek, 'but the wisdom to know how to use that knowledge is over and above the knowledge of the subject itself. You've only got to look at the medical experiments that were done in the concentration camps to get the point. The doctors had the knowledge, but they didn't use their knowledge very wisely, did they?'

'Hey,' said Paul. 'This conversation is getting serious, deep and out of hand. I vote that this meeting returns to what it was originally doing.'

'All right,' said Derek, 'what have we got?'

Anne read out the list. 'Eighteen children, twenty-two pensioners, the rest between the ages of sixteen and sixty-five. Two engineers, one long-distance lorry driver, four secretaries, three people who've been involved in the building trade, a motor mechanic, four teachers, *five* shopkeepers, *four* salesmen, *three* farmworkers, *two* computer programmers–'

'–and a partridge in a pear tree,' interjected Chris.

Derek grinned. Things seemed funnier now—like the humour of war, a necessity, a foil to the big problems that were looming.

'The rest are a motley assortment of people who've worked in factories, on assembly lines, pushing paper round in desk jobs, that sort of thing. Really quite a good cross-section of skills and trades, I suppose.'

'But no doctors or nurses,' said Jane.

'No, and although we've got three farmworkers I don't think from the look of them that they know too much about farming: they just got on with what they were told to do. They can do basic things like drive tractors, but I don't know whether they can operate the more complex machinery.'

'Nothing remotely allied to medicine?' Jane persisted.

'No drug reps, no pharmaceutical chemists, no vets, nothing. It may be bad luck or they may all have died off. After all, doctors and nurses are going to be the first ones exposed to any illness when they get called to see the first victims, aren't they?'

'Paul, I'm sure you're right about planning,' said Anne. 'The more I think about it the more important it seems. We *must* make sure we can produce what we need before we run out of our current stocks.'

'Look,' said Paul, 'in principle it's very simple. We've got to make sure that we use our resources efficiently. In particular, that means not using vehicles when we don't need to. It also means using only one vehicle rather than a whole host of them, so I suggest that we look round for one or two big lorries that we can use to cart things around. It makes much more sense to take a lorry with us when we raid a shop or a supermarket, so that we clean them out completely, and in sequence, rather than getting only what we want for one day.'

'Agreed,' said Anne, 'but why in sequence?'

'What's the point of going back to the same shop twice? Or going round a set of shops, trying to find if any one of them still has any peach halves? If you clear the shops out systematically then you *know* they'll be empty and there's no point in going back to look for anything. Far more efficient. We can always

use one of the shops here to store what we've collected but don't
yet need: then it can be the first port of call for anybody trying to
find a specific item.

'The next thing we want to do is ensure that we have proper
supplies of fuel. Coal will come from the depot at Elstow for the
moment, but we also need to find other coal yards, maybe further
afield. I suspect that in a few years' time—'

Anne and Jane looked at each other as if to say, 'This isn't
going on for ever, is it?' and then realised that it *was* going on for
ever.

'—in a few years' time we'll have to get our petrol from
some distance away. Again, let's do it efficiently. Why don't we
find a petrol bowser that we can take to individual service
stations, fill up with petrol, drain the tanks completely and then
we know that service station needn't be visited again? We can
leave the bowser somewhere nearby—preferably not too near in
case there's a fire. That way we'll all be able to get petrol when
we need it. It also means we can keep a check on who's using
the stuff, and make sure that no one uses too much.

'Then there's education—and not just for the children.
People like Chris need retraining, to learn crafts that are more
relevant to the way we're living. And the children will need to
be taught the same sort of thing, for later on.'

'Like how to break into supermarkets without getting glass
all over the place,' suggested Chris helpfully. Martin winced.

'Quite. And farming and fishing and how to grind wheat to
make flour.'

'I hope you don't mean that the children won't be learning
about anything else that isn't just practical?' asked Anne.

'I never said that at all. Derek was quite right when he said
that we wouldn't go back to the Dark Ages because we'd always
have knowledge. It's very important that we pass that knowledge
down, even if we can't do any more research for decades or even
centuries. Before the plague people were talking about
information overload: that we'd actually got too much.'

'Medicine for example,' interjected Derek. 'I remember our
GP saying how difficult it was for him to keep abreast of new
discoveries and how even specialists couldn't keep up with the
research in their own fields.'

Chris leaned forward. 'There's a lot of knowledge around, if only we look after it and keep it safe. Maybe our two librarians can help with that?'

'Where is all this information?' asked Jane.

'All over the place,' said Derek. 'Public libraries; and for the more specialised stuff, colleges, universities and research institutes. Each will have its own collection of books and papers.'

'There's the Agricultural Research Institute at Silsoe for a start,' said Chris, 'and the Engineering Institute at Cranfield. Medically there'll be libraries at Bedford Hospital and the Luton and Dunstable, Milton Keynes and the Lister at Stevenage. Our librarians should know just where to acquire the more esoteric bits of information—that is, if we need them.'

'A couple of manuals on farming wouldn't go amiss at the moment,' said Paul, wryly.

'Book knowledge isn't everything,' said Anne.

'That's why I want to make sure that we keep the *skills* that everybody has and pass them on to the children. You know the proverb—"A picture is worth a thousand words". Having practical experience is the same, in comparison with pure book learning.

'Look, I know we said we didn't want any form of leadership, but I do think we need someone to plan ahead, otherwise nobody will do it and we'll all get in a mess.'

'I agree,' said Derek, 'and I'm sure, Paul, that you ought to be the one to do it. Why don't you go away and write down a few of the things you've just said and we can all meet to see if we agree?'

'All right,' said Paul. 'I'll tell you the first thing I want to do. I want to break into the council offices and get some maps: then we can mark on them which shops we've raided for food, and also those places where we can find special types of goods that we might need.'

'I can put something on your list immediately,' said Chris.

'What's that?'

'There's an oil supply company not three miles from here. I passed it this morning. It's at Houghton Conquest.'

36

*T*he next few weeks saw a steady trickle of refugees coming to Ampthill. Invariably each one was asked the same two questions: Are you a farmer? Are you a doctor? Always there had been a shake of the head, and as the weeks drew on the community began to feel acutely vulnerable: they only needed someone to fall and break a leg, or to forget to plant a crop at the appropriate time, to cause almost insurmountable difficulties.

By now the original survivors were well established within the town. The community had decided that Derek and Anne should occupy Dynevor House on a permanent basis. This would allow them to welcome any newcomers—because all the signs still pointed to Dynevor—and also gave Derek a home that was suitable for his recently expanded family.

The routine for welcoming visitors was always the same: after the initial pleasantries and a good hot meal—for some of the survivors hadn't eaten properly for weeks—Anne quizzed them on where they had come from and what they had seen on the way; whether they knew of any other survivors or communities; and, most importantly, what their own skills were. Then Derek showed them round the town, and allocated them a house with open fires, and sometimes even inside cooking facilities.

Paul and Jane hadn't wanted to live in Dynevor House—it was too big for them, and anyway, they didn't want the fuss of greeting all the new arrivals—so after some thought they ensconced themselves in Gates House, an elegant Victorian mansion on Church Street, just right for a local dignitary—which was why Paul chose it. It was a symmetrical square-fronted building set back from Church Street, with a small formal garden in front with low box hedges and pea shingle paths, but its most distinctive feature was the high wrought-iron railings and gates at the front, giving onto the street—hence the name. Truly a palace, thought Paul when he looked round it: much more aloof than Dynevor; much more classy; just right for an up-and-coming local squire and his newly expanding family.

Chris had no such pretensions. She took up residence in

Foulislea Cottage on Church Street, almost opposite Dynevor House. Built in the reign of Elizabeth I, it was one of the oldest houses in the town—white-fronted, full of character, but small and easy to keep warm. It was comfortable and homely, and it suited her down to the ground.

Peter Abrahams, shell-shocked by the loss of his wife and young family, didn't really care where he lived, except that he desperately wanted company: he just couldn't bear to be alone. So he occupied one of the almshouses across the square from Dynevor—that way he could be at the centre of all the activity in the community. From the first Anne had sensed his need and taken him under her motherly wing: most of the time she cooked for him—his house hadn't got a range—and he often joined the family, plus whoever new had turned up that day, for food. There was no sense of his being a scrounger—he was a willing helper with whatever task presented itself that day, anxious above all else to keep busy, to avoid the perils of silence and the thoughts that come in inactivity.

Martin's reaction had been similar but different: like Peter he had been severely traumatised, but unlike Peter, he wanted to get as far away from everyone as possible. Between the church and Dynevor House was a gravelled path, Holly Walk, at the end of which was a drive lined with laburnum and rhododendrons which led to an isolated house on the top of a small hill, mainly surrounded by trees. Martin went to it like a homing pigeon. Originally Georgian, it had had Victorian additions at both ends, neither of which respected the original roof- or window-lines, and an odd squashed entrance portico that owed more to ancient Egypt than Victorian society, so architecturally the house was something of a mish-mash: it wasn't a beautiful house in the classical sense, but it was a serene and interesting building for all that, set in secluded grounds overlooking the surrounding countryside, and had the quintessential attribute for Martin of being out of the way. As it was situated at the end of a long lane, no one, but *no one*, went past.

Mary Harper had taken up residence in a modern bungalow nestling in the shelter of the greensand ridge on the road between Ampthill and Maulden. She wanted to develop the land around it as a smallholding, for which it was ideal, as it had a couple of outhouses and a good-sized area of ground attached. There was even a large black pig and a tame goat, left by the previous owners of the house. Mary had visions of a really green future: living in peace and harmony off the land, giving to it what she got from it. Of all the survivors, she was the most positive—now she could get down to demonstrating that green living really worked.

Howler liked his new surroundings as well, particularly as, in the absence of vegetarian dog food—which could no longer be acquired locally—his mistress had relented and had decided that it wouldn't hurt to use the cans of dog food from the shelves of the local supermarkets: in fact, it was quite a green idea—the animals had already died, so they might as well not have died in vain. So Howler gratefully changed his diet from vegetarian back to his natural carnivorous state.

After some time Mary decided to keep chickens, and after settling herself in, her first job was to construct them a shelter: in her typically efficient and intense fashion she converted one of the barns, found some straw for the floor and went round the local farms collecting a flock together.

All went well, and after the first three weeks she concluded that she had some very contented free-range chickens indeed, who showed how happy they were by laying well. Life, to Mary, had at long last begun to be natural, and quite, quite idyllic. Just as it should be, she thought.

*   *   *

October faded into November and the bright blue skies and russet hedges slowly changed; the countryside became much more drab, and the climate more wintry, with high bitter winds, rain storms and unsettled weather: it mirrored the emotional uncertainty that all of them were beginning to feel. It had been all very well living off the produce in the shops and supermarkets, but the shelves were starting to empty, and the problems of continual self-sufficiency were becoming apparent.

Despite the uncertainty, the various members of the community set to, and were happy enough going about their allotted jobs. To date there had been no major hitches. Paul had

got his technique with the cold chisel and crowbar down to a fine
art, and could get inside most houses or shops in about half a
minute with little to show in the way of damage. So much for
security, he thought, as he jemmied himself into yet another
office or shop. What one man can make, another can break.

Having announced to the world that she was expecting, Jane
had settled down with Paul in Gates House, and prepared for her
new life as mother and squire's wife. She didn't often go on
Paul's raiding expeditions and spent most of her time happily
helping Anne with the food over at Dynevor, when she wasn't
resting.

Peter made the most of his new-found freedom to drive a car.
He still had a large part of his ban still to run, but who was to
know? More important, who cared? With no one to enforce it,
the very idea of law and order seemed irrelevant, and the
revocation of his licence even more inappropriate. For him,
driving was the one positive thing that had come out of the
plague, and he revelled in it. It was something to do to occupy
the time: he made himself indispensable as driver, carrier and
general factotum.

Martin remained in his isolated house as much as he could.
It was a good house to live in—there were wood-burning stoves
in every room, and an extensive library, which he enjoyed, when
his depression allowed him to concentrate for more than five
minutes at a time, which wasn't often. He spent a listless first
few weeks pottering around in a haphazard sort of way, feeling
lost and supremely purposeless. After he'd been in the house a
few weeks he discovered that it was 'The Old Rectory'—rather
appropriate really since it had long since ceased to house anyone
officially connected with the church. It was well suited to the job
of housing an ex-man of the cloth.

The isolation allowed Martin to get the solitude that he
wanted—even in a world that was vastly depopulated—but
increasingly he became reclusive as his depression, loneliness
and spiritual isolation deepened. Although there were one or two
communicant members of the Anglican Church amongst the
community, he made no effort to continue his previous work as a
priest, and for the moment no one pressed the matter further.
News of Martin's loss of faith had gradually passed round the

community. All felt genuinely sorry for him—except for Paul, who seemed to take an especial delight in needling him in a manner that was just *too* much to be a joke. Anne in particular became increasingly exasperated with Paul's approach, and longed to help Martin: what he needed, she thought, was a cuddle—but any attempt by her or Derek to show positive affection was met with indifference, even hostility. Martin just didn't want to know. He hated himself, and the more he hated himself, the more he drank.

For all his reclusiveness, however, Martin joined in with the work of the community as it was needed—not that there was much at this time of year, especially as the wheat had already been planted.

The first problem had been to acquire milk and meat. Paul's organised reconnoitring had come up with several herds of cattle, though many of the cows had not been milked for two weeks, so the supply had largely dried up, but they managed to get one or two of them going again, milking by hand into a bucket. Much to his surprise, Martin took to milking. What for some might have become a mindlessly repetitive job was a source of great comfort to him. The rhythmic plucking at the teats and the squirt of the milk into the pail were soporific and restful—like listening to a regular heartbeat with its memories of the earliest days in the womb, when that was the only noise that could be perceived.

About the only part of milking he didn't like was carting the milk around in pails. Lifting a single pail in his right hand caused such a continuing strain that it threatened to put his back out, so he tried constructing a yoke, as he'd seen in paintings of milkmaids—a simple beam of wood, carved to fit round his neck, carrying a pail at each end. To his surprise, lifting twice the weight of milk like this was easy, because the yoke stopped him lifting awkwardly.

But acquiring milk requires a lot more than finding a cow. It has to be a cow that's been deprived of its calf. First get your calf. This is where the farmworkers came into their own. To ensure a continuing supply of milk they had acquired a bull from one of the farms and had put it to the cows. No one knew how long it would take before the cows were in season, nor

Dunstable Street

how long the gestation period was, but the sooner the cows were exposed to the bull the more quickly would they be in calf.

They'd also had to work out how to kill and butcher animals—not work for the squeamish. Mary of course, would have nothing to do with it, but for most of the community a meat-less diet was proving a trial, and they had to decide what to do.

In the end, the slaughtering was left to the farmworkers, who had never done this sort of thing before. At least they had had some experience of handling animals. But how would they kill them? With no power there could be no electrical stunning: and they didn't have a captive bolt. In the end they went back to the methods of a century before—poleaxing: the animal was tied to a ring in the wall and then one of the farmworkers hit it on the back of the neck with a heavy block of wood, breaking its neck and killing it instantly and humanely.

They had to butcher it immediately, hauling it up on its hind legs, slitting the abdomen and removing the organs—gut, heart and lungs, before cutting the carcass up into manageable pieces which could be butchered further into usable chunks. After six weeks on a restricted diet of mainly canned food, everyone appreciated having fresh meat again—except Mary, of course; and many others felt squeamish about it at first. But eventually, butchering cattle and sheep became an event that aroused no special comment. After all, they had to eat.

On a different front, Derek's training in engineering had come to the fore, and he began again to put into practice some of the techniques he had learned at college, then not used again. Without power to turn lathes or perform electrical welding he was at a bit of a disadvantage: but the portable generators proved handy for those occasions when either of these was really necessary.

It was very much a make-do-and-mend existence. Unlike a year previously, the community never threw anything away when it didn't work, because they knew they couldn't get a replacement. Instead, they attempted to mend it. Mary was delighted! Derek found it very satisfying, too: there is something about using your own skills to create and mend that is deeply satisfying: far nicer than merely ordering a new part and dropping the original in the dustbin, as had been the practice before.

Sarah had adapted to her surrogate parents very quickly, and said little or nothing about her family in Leighton Buzzard. Every fortnight Derek went back to Sarah's old house, but the message on the table had remained unanswered, becoming covered in an ever thicker layer of dust. On his last visit he had added a message saying that they could be contacted at Ampthill. After that he never went back.

-37-

*A*lison, outwardly, was enjoying the lessons she was being given—they had set up school in the spacious upstairs reception room at Dynevor—but was looking distinctly less than well. Anne was dimly aware that she had been up to the toilet a number of times each night. Despite losing weight she was very hungry, and perpetually thirsty too.

One cold and dismal November afternoon Derek returned from tinkering with the engine on one of the lorries to be met at the door by a distraught Anne.

'What's the matter?' he said, startled.

'It's Alison. She's delirious. She's been like it most of the afternoon.'

He rushed upstairs. 'How are you feeling?' said Anne to the inert form of her daughter laid out on the bed. Alison mumbled something and drifted off again.

'Wake up, Alison,' said Derek. 'Just for a minute, talk to me. What's the matter?'

Mumble, mumble.

'Does anything hurt?'

No reply.

'Speak to me, Alison. Does anything hurt?'

'No.'

The voice drifted away. Derek bent over her.

'Has she been eating anything odd?'

'Nothing special.'

'Her breath smells—as though she's been eating pear drops

or something. You don't think she could have found some drugs . . .?'

'You must be joking,' said Anne. 'Alison?'

Derek leaned over her again. 'Have you got a headache?' No response. 'Has she got a temperature?'

'She doesn't feel hot. I wonder if there's a thermometer in the bathroom.' Taking the candle from the bedroom, she found a thermometer at the back of one of the shelves.

'I can never read one of these things,' said Derek peering at it in the dim light. 'I know you have to shake it down first, though.' He put it underneath Alison's armpit. After a minute or two Anne took it out.

'It's not even up to normal.' She turned round to Derek, her last hope gone that it might be something easy, like flu. 'Derek, what are we going to do?'

Derek stood there panic-stricken, trying to force himself to think calmly and rationally. Suddenly he felt totally alone, the same sort of loneliness that Martin had felt. There was no one to turn to *at all*—no one to advise or even give reassurance for now, never mind the future. No one even to tell him where to start looking for the answer.

'I'll go to the Health Centre,' he said finally. 'There may be some books there that can help.'

Turning up his collar against the wind which was now howling in from the east, biting and cold, he went up Church Street to Gates House. Paul dropped what he was doing, grabbed the cold chisel, the jemmy and one of their carefully husbanded flashlights and came with him. They hurried through the Market Square in the darkness, then into Dunstable Street. The night was pitch-black with dark clouds overhead, obscuring the moon. Most of the houses were silent and dark, but the occasional one had candlelight flickering in the window.

They didn't have to break in to the Health Centre—the main door had been left open. At least inside the front door they were out of the wind. It was a warren of a place, damp and cold. It took a few minutes before they got their bearings, but eventually they found the main waiting room. Paul swung the flashlight round.

'Let's try behind here,' he said, opening a door marked 'Staff Only'. On the left there were carousels of patients' records and on the opposite wall tables and desks, but no books. There was a computer in the room behind the reception hatch, and on the floor by it a body that had once been dressed in rather shapeless brown trousers. Paul turned away. It was the first body he'd seen in Ampthill itself and it gave him a start. The town had somehow seemed unaffected by the plague and he didn't like to be reminded of how near it had come.

Retracing their steps they went back into the main waiting room and tried a door leading to one of the doctors' surgeries.

'There we are,' said Paul, training the flashlight on the bookshelf at the far end. 'What do we want to know?'

Derek grabbed a textbook of medicine and opened it. Thirty seconds later he shut it again. It was incomprehensible.

'What *is* onychogryphosis?' he asked.

'Not a clue,' said Paul. Derek thumbed through the books with a rising sense of panic.

'I can't make head nor tail of this. I don't even know where to start. What are we going to do? What are we going to do about Alison?'

'Steady on,' said Paul. 'Don't panic. If you panic you'll just add to your problems. Let's just sit down for a minute and think. What do we know about her? We know that she's fourteen and that she's in a sort of coma. She hasn't got a temperature; she's losing weight; she's eating and drinking a lot; and often has to get up to the toilet in the night.

'What we need isn't a book of detailed medicine. We want an idiot's guide to home nursing, and you won't find one of those in a Health Centre.'

'But you will find one—'

'—in a library,' they both said together.

'Where is it?'

'Saunders Piece.'

Out of the Health Centre they went, back into the cold and the wind. As they ran along Queen's Road the clouds scudding across the sky parted to show the moon, then closed up again. The tiny library was locked, but it remained so for only five more seconds once Paul had applied a little brute force and a cold chisel to the hasp of the padlock. They charged in.

'Here's the catalogue,' said Paul, thumbing through it, his

hands numb with cold. 'M . . . managerial, mandrakes, Manhattan, maximum security gaols, Memphis . . . too far . . . Mediterranean, *medicine*, got it. Dewey No. 610.'

'This'll do,' said Derek, pulling out a book on Home Nursing. 'Symptoms, symptoms . . .' he murmured, flicking through the pages. 'Coma . . . here we are. "*A patient who is unconscious may be seriously ill and you should send for a doctor or ambulance immediately*." Great. I'll telephone straight away. "*Causes . . . Head injury . . .*" '

'She hasn't injured herself, has she . . .?'

' "*Diabetic coma . . . weight loss, drinking large quantities of fluid and passing a lot of urine*." That's it! "*In diabetic coma you may get ketosis, which gives a smell like pear drops. This is because the normal way of producing energy in the body has been disrupted . . .*" That's it, it's diabetes! She smelled just like that.'

'What about treatment?' asked Paul, but there was nothing in the book apart from instructing the reader to send for the doctor: urgent hospital treatment would be needed.

'At least we know what the diagnosis is,' said Paul. 'We should be able to find out about treatment from the books in the Health Centre.'

Out into the bitter wind they went yet again, back to the Health Centre. This time it was easier.

'Diabetes,' said Derek, looking it up in the textbook of medicine. 'More problems—there are two sorts. Diabetes insipidus and diabetes mellitus.'

They looked up diabetes insipidus first. Something told Derek that this wasn't what it was at all. His subconscious was right. "*Diabetes insipidus is caused by failure of the production of antidiuretic hormones by the posterior pituitary. It is an uncommon disease . . .*" That won't be it. It's got to be the other one. "*Diabetes mellitus is a disorder of sugar metabolism, and is called 'mellitus' because the urine is sweet to taste as a result of the extra sugar it contains. There are two forms . . .*" Oh, why does everything in medicine seem to subdivide? "*Type I (juvenile diabetes) is caused by total failure of insulin production in the islets of Langerhans in the pancreas. Type II, otherwise known as maturity onset diabetes . . .*" It's not Type II, it must be Type I. *"Diabetic coma . . . polydypsia . . ."* What on earth's that?'

Paul scanned the shelves with his flashlight and stopped at a large purple volume labelled *Dorland's Illustrated Dictionary of Medicine*. There was a pause while he looked it up. 'It means drinking a lot. *Poly*, Greek; means "much"; *dypsia*, drinking. You obviously had a wasted education, not knowing Greek.'

'Polyuria?'

'By the same token, probably too much urine,' queried Paul, looking it up. 'Yes, I was right.'

' *"Loss of weight, drowsiness . . . coma. A sweet smell to the breath indicates ketosis."* What would that be?'

' *"Ketosis . . . production of ketone bodies, particularly in diabetes."* '

'So we've got the right diagnosis. Treatment . . . *"Admission to hospital is mandatory . . . drip . . . regular injections of soluble insulin depending on the level of the blood sugar."* How are we going to measure the blood sugar?'

'I once had a friend with diabetes. He used some special plastic sticks with chemicals impregnated at the tip. When he wanted to check his blood-sugar level he pricked his finger, smeared some blood on the end of one of the sticks, washed it off, then looked at the colour change that had taken place.'

'What were the sticks called?'

'Gluco . . . something.'

Derek picked up the formulary from the doctor's desk and looked in the index.

'Glucagon?'

'No.'

'Glucophage? Glucoplex? Glucostix?'

'That's it.'

'Here it is. *"Glucostix: Plastic reagent strip for visual or machine reading of blood-sugar level."* '

'Anything else we need?'

'Syringes and needles?'

'Here we are,' said Paul, opening up one of the drawers in the mobile equipment trolley. 'Anything else?'

'Don't think so.'

'Chemist?'

'Chemist.' Derek picked up the medical textbook and the formulary and they hurried out into the night. By now the wind had veered to the north, a real gale, biting cold, whipping into their faces. They leaned into it as they went back towards the centre of the town. In the distance a door was banging in the breeze, and drops of rain started to prick their faces.

The chemist's shop was in the centre of the Market Square, near the White Hart Hotel where they had stayed the first few nights. Another job for the jemmy, thought Paul. A few seconds later they went inside, glad to get out of the howling gale.

Inside, the shop was freezing cold. It had not been heated for over a month, and the clammy coldness settled all around them. Derek shivered. After a short search, they found the pharmacy tucked in a corner at the far end of the shop, a pitch-black windowless room. Around the walls medicines were laid out neatly in alphabetical order on shelves, but try as they might, they couldn't find anything labelled 'Insulin'.

'S for soluble insulin?' queried Paul. It wasn't under the S's. They looked in all the cupboards. One, made of metal and stronger than the others, was locked. Paul jemmied it open. It was full of vials of morphine, pethidine and heroin.

'Phew,' said Derek. 'That would have been worth something once.' He shut it again. 'I don't really know what we're looking for.'

'Little ampoules, tiny glass jars with rubber tops,' said Paul. 'My friend used to keep them in his fridge . . . I'm a clot. Where is it?' It was under one of the worktops. They opened it—Derek expected to see a light come on and half a second later realised that without electricity it wouldn't.

'How about these?' said Paul, handing Derek a carton of tiny bottles. Derek took four of the vials and replaced the rest.

'What about the Glucostix?'

'On the shelf up there.'

'Thanks for your help, Paul—you've been great.'

'You did all the diagnosis. I just told you where to look for the information.'

They hurried out of the shop and back into the gale outside. In the distance the door was still banging, louder and more insistently now that the wind was rising even more. Pulling his coat collar tightly round the front of his neck, Derek headed back to Dynevor, going in by the garden entrance, if only to gain shelter more quickly. He rushed upstairs, clutching the medical textbook under his arm, the vials in his pocket.

'How is she?'

'Worse,' said Anne who was sitting on the bed holding Alison's hand. He could see her dark hair on the pillow and her gaunt face turned on one side.

'Alison.'

No response.

'She hasn't talked to me for three-quarters of an hour.'

Using one of the needles as a lancet, Derek pricked Alison's thumb, smeared the blood over the end of a reagent strip, waited a minute, washed it off, then compared its colour with the chart on the side of the bottle. It had gone off scale, greater than thirty-five. Derek looked in his textbook. *'Normal blood sugar varies between 3.0 and 5.5,'* it said. *'Levels above twenty-five are potentially dangerous . . .'* It gave a dose regime, which unfortunately included setting up an intravenous drip. He had no idea how to do this, and now wasn't the time to learn. Putting a needle on the end of one of the syringes, he drew up some of the contents of the insulin vial, and tried desperately to calculate how many units of insulin he ought to be giving, according to the rules laid down in the textbook.

'It's to be given intravenously,' he said. 'What does that mean?'

'Into a vein,' said Anne. 'Don't you remember when I had the children . . .'

'Where?'

'In the back of the hand.' Derek searched Alison's hand, but he couldn't see any veins. She had lost too much body fluid in her urine for them to remain distended. They were losing time and Derek knew it.

'I think I'll just give it into a muscle. It'll probably be safe and if we don't do something she's going to die.' He pulled up the arm of her nightdress and rammed the needle up to its hilt in the muscle at the top, then squeezed the plunger. As he pulled the needle out a tiny speck of blood formed as the only sign of what he'd done.

'What do we do now?' said Anne.

'Monitor the blood sugar every hour,' said Derek, reading from the book.

-38-

*T*hey toiled through the night: every hour, as measured by the chiming of the grandfather clock in the hall, Derek took a sample of blood and tested it for sugar; then he consulted the textbook to work out how much more insulin to give. They sat there, lit by a solitary candle flickering wildly in the draught, holding Alison's hand, willing her to live, while outside the storm raged and the rain battered against the windows.

It shouldn't have worked but it did: by rights Derek should have killed his daughter. What he didn't know was that an overdose of insulin can kill more easily than an underdose, and that rehydration with a drip is normally essential to recovery. But he was lucky—by some fluke the doses of insulin he gave never took Alison's blood sugar below the lower level of normal, and Alison, being young and strong, tolerated the dehydration.

At 5.30 a.m. she regained consciousness and mumbled something, then lapsed back into unconsciousness again. It had only been a mumble, and neither Derek nor Anne could make out what she was trying to say, but it was an improvement.

At eight o'clock she mumbled something else, and kept mumbling. Anne knew that they shouldn't give fluids to an unconscious patient—that much she'd remembered from her basic teacher's First Aid training—but now that Alison was semiconscious they felt safe in giving her something to drink. Once she could swallow without gagging or choking, they poured fluid into her—water, tea—Derek remembered just in time to leave it unsweetened—diluted fruit juice: anything and everything that she would take, the two of them gave her. She'd been incontinent several times in the early part of the coma, but as the insulin took effect the high level of sugar in the blood dropped; and as the extra was no longer escaping through the kidneys into the urine dragging along with it vast quantities of water, the amount of urine dropped as the water that they gave stayed in.

By midday, when the gale had died down to an almost unnoticed whisper, Alison was sitting up in bed feeling as though she'd been trampled on, but awake, alert, and looking very much better: more so than her parents who as well as being worried sick had also spent an entire night without sleep.

It was only after that, when the real work was over, that Anne could cope no longer, and rushed out of the room, downstairs to her own bedroom. Then the tears came. She cried and cried, sobbing on the bed for what might have been, could have been and—but for her husband and Paul—nearly had been.

In the twenty-four hours that followed Derek learned a lot about management of the diabetic patient. He read about controlling the blood-sugar level with insulin and of the different types of insulin—short- medium- and long-acting: of the need for regular controlled intake of food; of calories and dietary equivalents and how a diet high in fibre reduces the absorbence of sugar from the gut, so allowing a smaller dose of insulin to be used. Only then did he realise the danger of too low a blood sugar—hypoglycaemia—and how diabetics have to keep a barley sugar or a sugar lump in their pocket in case their dose of insulin proves too much, or else they've given themselves insulin, but for some reason have been unable to eat. When that happens the blood-sugar level suddenly drops, and the brain can't cope. Although muscles have their own stores of glucose for an emergency, the brain hasn't, and if starved of glucose can die, and very quickly indeed. The book said that new diabetics ought to be given the experience of a hypo to know what it felt like, so if they felt one coming on they could suck a sugar lump before it was too late. Derek hadn't got the nerve to try this yet—and in any case, he didn't know how to reverse it if it got out of hand.

He found out anyway, just two days later—either he'd miscalculated on a dose, or else it was given just too far before breakfast. Alison suddenly went light-headed and started acting most peculiarly. For once Anne was quicker than Derek. She stirred some sugar into a mug of milk (using a quarter of their precious milk supply for the whole week) and got it into Alison before she finally lost consciousness.

Before she finally went 'out' Alison behaved like a rabid animal, shouting, screaming, throwing herself around, banging into furniture, thrashing around like a mad thing, but then the sugar took effect, and she quietened; and then sense returned. The first thing she knew was the anxious face of her mother leaning over her, and she said in her normal voice, 'It's all right Mummy. I'm OK now. That was a hypo, wasn't it?'

'Yes,' said Anne sitting down on her kitchen chair with a bump and looking pale. 'Yes, it was.' Anne started to tremble but managed to hide it from the children; however, Sarah, who had been observing all of this, became very frightened and ran to her.

'It's all right Sarah,' said Anne. 'It's over. It hasn't done any damage and we'll make sure it doesn't happen again.' *I hope*, she added under her breath. It was all too much.

Alison's blood sugar returned to normal quickly and very soon they were able to monitor her using a different diagnostic stick on her urine. Alison was very grateful about this as her thumbs and fingers were beginning to resemble pin-cushions. However, it took her a lot longer to get fully back to normal and to regain her previous weight, for her cheeks to fill out and for her to regain her previous good looks.

Puppy love was even rearing its head—fifteen-year-old Darren Rogers, the son of one of the teachers, had taken quite a shine to her and visited her every day throughout her illness. He couldn't bring her flowers—there weren't any left at that time of year—but he kept her company, lifting her spirits and willing her back to health.

*   *   *

A week later Derek and his family were all sitting down to their evening meal when there was a knock on the front door of Dynevor House. Derek opened it to find Chris at the head of a group of five people: Darren's parents, Jane, and a short dapper man of about seventy, with white hair and a white moustache. Derek vaguely remembered him as a retired ex-army man called Major Thornton who always insisted on being referred to by his rank.

'Can we come in?' said Chris, looking strangely serious.

'Of course,' said Derek wiping the remains of the soup from

his lips, and wondering what all this was about. He showed them into the morning room with its warm fire. 'Sit down, do.'

'We came to ask you,' said Chris, looking round nervously at the assembled company, 'if you would . . .' For once she was lost for words. Susan Rogers took over.

'We wondered if you would become our doctor–'

'That is, if we did all your other work for you,' broke in her husband, Alan. 'Get your fuel, help with the motors, tend the fields and so on. If you didn't have any other work you could start learning how to do it. We all know what you did for Alison. Darren told us.'

'That was just luck,' said Derek, thinking of the hypoglycaemia. 'Anyway, Paul helped a lot in working it all out. Why not ask him? He's younger and he's not got a trade that we can use in the community.'

'No,' said the Major firmly. 'We all think that you'd make a good doctor. You're the right sort of person. You weigh things up. You don't go head over heels at things quite like Paul does. You're older and more mature than Paul; anyway, your scientific background means that you'll probably find medicine easier to grasp.'

'But how could I possibly learn?' asked Derek. 'Medicine isn't something that you get out of books. You learn it by experience—by watching others do it. I mean—do you realise what you're asking me to do? Before the plague medical students spent two or three years just learning how the body worked before they even saw a patient: then three years following in the footsteps of other doctors; and even then they hadn't finished. They'd have another three years' training at least before they could be a GP. How could I possibly do any of that without having someone to teach me?'

'We wouldn't expect you to be anything more than a barefoot doctor, Derek,' replied Chris. 'We know the problems just as much as you do. But you know we haven't got anybody in the community who can look after us if we're sick. We only need somebody to break a leg or get pneumonia–'

'And what about childbirth?' interjected Jane. 'In six months' time somebody will have to know what to do, because my baby won't wait.'

'We must have someone who can start learning about medicine,' said Chris, 'and we think it ought to be you. We'd *like* it to be you. What we're saying is that we will support you, and encourage you and make life as easy for you as we possibly can while you're trying to learn.'

'Do you mean just the five of you, or have you discussed it with the others?'

'It's just the five of us at the moment, but I'm sure that if we put this to the whole community everyone will agree.'

Derek sat in his chair staring at the floor, thinking, and then bent to put another log on the fire which sparkled and spat. The faces in the dark room suddenly became brighter by its stirring. There was a long pause. From the kitchen came the sound of Anne and the children having their evening meal.

'We need it for the children's sake too,' said Susan. 'Not just Alison—all of them.'

'Do you realise what you're asking?' said Derek, suddenly straightening up and looking at them in an agitated manner. 'You're asking me to take the responsibility for looking after your lives, for giving you drugs, for helping you through childbirth, or maybe even operating on you—when I haven't got anyone to teach me? If I make mistakes there won't be anyone to show me what I'm doing wrong. And what happens when the drugs run out? There isn't an infinite supply in the pharmacy.'

'Yes, but medicine's more than just drugs,' said Jane. 'It was practised for years before any of the pharmaceutical companies came along. People two hundred years ago grew their own, they used herbs–'

'–and it didn't always work,' said Derek, pointedly. But he didn't mean it, and he knew it. Secretly he was thrilled to have been asked, but he was also terrified by the thought of what he was letting himself in for.

'I'll think about it. I'm not going to say anything on the spur of the moment. No one in the past has ever had to do this—learn medicine without any tutors. It was always one person handing his knowledge down to the next person; and that next person would also learn other things as well, and then he'd pass on what he knew to the next generation. It was always handed down person to person, never book to person.'

'You were the one who said that knowledge wouldn't die, and that we should continue to use the knowledge already preserved in books; and that we wouldn't go back to the Dark Ages.'

'Yes,' said Derek, 'but I was thinking more about theoretical knowledge—factual stuff like how big Jupiter is, or the structure of DNA. Applied knowledge is quite different. Knowledge like that is hard to get from a book because it's all about watching people do things and seeing how they go about it, learning the rules of thumb that often aren't written down because nobody has ever tried to work out quite what they are: knacks—ways of doing things—tips and wrinkles. It's very hard to learn those without having a tutor. I could certainly do the book work—but only up to a point, because there's nobody there to tell me if I've misunderstood something.'

He laughed. 'It's a bit like a Dutch chap I heard about. He'd learned English—only he learned it entirely from a textbook and never heard any of it spoken. When he went to England he could read and write perfect English, but when he tried to speak it no one could understand a word he said. I might turn out like that.' He was worried now, worried that he was going to have to say yes, but that he wouldn't be able to cope

Jane put her hand on his arm. 'Derek,' she said, 'we're quite prepared to risk that. We know you'll do your best. You're that sort of person and we won't hold it against you if you get things wrong and make mistakes,'—she turned to the group—'will we?'

They all shook their heads. 'We're not asking you to be perfect; we don't expect you to be perfect. As you've just said the conditions aren't right, but so long as you can provide a little bit of help when we need it we'd . . .'

'. . . we'd be grateful,' said the Major. '*Very* grateful.'

Derek stared at the fire, his thoughts in a turmoil. Finally he looked up at them. 'I'm going to think about it, with Anne. I don't mind trying, provided you don't blame me if things go wrong. I'll do my best, but I must insist that no matter what happens you won't blame me—*ever*. Before the plague doctors were always being accused of negligence. It must have been hard, having to deal with people's lives, knowing also that they might be sued if they made the wrong decision.'

He laughed, slightly uneasily. 'I'm sure you're not going to sue me—after all we haven't got any courts any more—but I don't want to find that you all send me to Coventry because I make a bad mistake. All right—I know I'm looking on the gloomy side, but when it comes to peoples' lives they and their families get very tetchy. I mean . . . I can't even promise that I'll be anything other than useless and you'll have been doing all my work in vain.'

'Derek,' said Chris. 'We know you'll try your best. All that we ask—*all* that we ask—is that you try. We promise we won't hold you responsible if things go wrong.'

'Very well, I'll think about it,' said Derek, 'but it's got to be approved by everybody in the community—not just the five of you—and it's got to be on the terms that I've just stated. I don't want to end up as the only person in the community who's held responsible for other people.'

'Thank you, Derek,' said Chris. 'Those terms suit us fine. You think about it, and let us know: we'll talk to the others. And don't forget—we think you'd make a smashing doctor.'

*   *   *

That evening any refugee who chanced to come to Dynevor House by the garden entrance and look through the window would have seen Derek and Anne in animated conversation, with Derek pacing up and down in the morning room. It didn't stop until the small hours of the morning, by which time the fire had died down and the candle had guttered out.

-39-

*T*wo days later Derek and Paul were in the morning room at Dynevor House, planning, when there was a knock at the front door. Derek opened it to find a solidly built man of about forty dressed in a green tweed suit and wellingtons, standing on the step. The man looked up in surprise.

'Oh. I was expecting Mr Courtauld. Is he in?'

'Er . . . No. I'm Derek Jones.'

'You a friend of his, then?'

'No. Come in, I'll explain.'

The stranger looked about him as he came through the door. 'So Henry's not here?' he said.

'No.'

'Then who are you?'

'Derek Jones. And this is Paul Greatorex. You are . . . ?'

'Neil Rawsthorne.' He held out a hand. 'May I ask what you're doing here?'

Derek explained.

'Oh I see,' said Neil. 'When the plague came I just waited. It's out of the way where I live, so I thought I'd be on the safe side and stay put for a few weeks. This is the first time I've ventured out. To be honest, I didn't expect to see anyone alive at all.'

'So you knew the chap who lived here?' asked Paul.

'Old Henry? Of course I know Henry. One of the pillars of Ampthill society. Known him for years.' He suddenly fell silent. 'I don't suppose you know what's happened to him?'

'No,' replied Derek. 'The whole place was locked up when we got here. No bodies, though,' he added brightly.

'He's probably made a run for it. I wonder if he's still alive . . . '

Paul poked the fire. There was silence for a moment.

'Where did you say you live?'

'Haynes West End. It's about three miles from here.'

'What do you do?' asked Derek.

'I've got a farm there.'

-40-

The next meeting of the community was considerably more optimistic than the first one. News that they at last had someone who knew about farming was greeted with enthusiasm and relief, especially by Derek. He'd tried to maintain an optimistic

attitude, so he hadn't let on to the others what he really felt—
which was that without decent farming skills they were doomed.
It was all very well playing amateur gardeners and planting a few
vegetables, but growing food in sufficient quantities to feed a
community for the next twelve months, year after year, was quite
a different proposition altogether. One slip, one poor season, or
one growing season lost through inexperience, and they were
finished. Quite frankly, until Neil came along, Derek had never
once thought they'd make it.

Now things were different. With Neil to rely on he felt they
could relax; now they would be sure the crops would grow,
because Neil would always know how and when to plant,
fertilise, weed and harvest.

He was wrong. He was soon to find that there was a lot
more risk in farming than he'd previously believed.

'Neil, I think we might as well turn the meeting over to you,'
said Paul. Neil stood up, his back to the ornate fireplace in the
upstairs drawing room at Dynevor House. It was a good place to
be at that moment, because outside it was blowing a gale, and
Neil was nearest the blazing fire.

'Thank you, Paul,' he said. 'As you know our greatest need
is for a continual supply of food, all the year round, starting from
now and going on for . . . who knows, for ever. Certainly for a
long time. We won't be able to rely on any outside help at all.

'That means several things—we'll only be able to eat
produce as it comes into season—no more Cape apples, or
Egyptian potatoes to help us out in the winter or spring. We
can't freeze any of our produce, so we'll have to use most of
what we grow at the time it comes into season. Some things we
can store, like potatoes and wheat, some we can cook and store,
like fruit, but green vegetables and many fruits will have to be
eaten soon after they're harvested.

'Presumably this means we won't have any green vegetables
until the spring?' asked Paul.

'Oh no,' said Neil, 'the Brussels will be ready soon. You'll
enjoy that—picking sprouts in the frost . . . But you won't have
peas or beans for a long time, so you're right there.'

'Is there a good variety of crops planted round here?' asked Anne.

'In the main. Lots of vegetables of different types, and quite a lot of wheat. For the moment we'll have to make the best of what's already been planted, but next year . . . ' —Anne winced at yet another reminder that their changed circumstances were likely to be permanent— '. . . next year we'll plan an even wider variety.'

'What about your own farm?' asked Jane. 'What have you got there?'

Neil gave a wry smile. 'Not much use to us now, I'm afraid. I don't have any livestock at all, and many of the fields have been sown with oilseed rape. That's no use to us now, so I'm going to move down into the town and farm the countryside immediately around.'

'What about equipment, seed and fertilisers?' asked Paul.

Neil counted off his fingers.

'Seed—we can just keep some back to sow the next season—though that'll cause problems for the future, because obviously seed like this won't already have been treated to remove diseases or weeds.   Equipment—that's not a problem, either—there's enough on the farms around us. All we need is fuel to drive them—I can show you how to do the rest.

'Fertiliser's not so easy. I've got some of my own stocks, but we usually buy in what we need just as we're about to use it—and even if we find the supplier's warehouse, sooner or later stocks are going to run out.'

Mary's moment had come. 'But if we carry out mixed farming we shouldn't need fertilisers or weedkillers, should we? We can use animal dung and rotate the crops.'

'We'll have to, eventually. But I hope you realise what it means. Weeds grow as fast as crops do—and sometimes faster. If I spray weedkiller on my wheat I can stop the weeds growing and let the wheat get all the soil and the sunlight. I can do the same thing if I use a harrow to grub up the weeds between the lines of corn shoots, but it's nothing like as accurate and we'll pull up a lot of wheat in the process. Using purely mechanical methods like harrowing reduces the crop yield.'

'By how much?' asked Paul, expecting a percentage in single figures.

'About thirty per cent.'

'You mean that we'll lose *a third* of our crops if we don't use weedkillers?' he gasped. 'That's an awful lot.'

'We'll have to do it like that eventually,' replied Neil. 'But because so many fields have already been sown with wheat, the percentage yield this year isn't important—provided that the crop doesn't fail altogether. If we only get half the wheat off a field it doesn't matter—we'll just have to harvest from twice as many fields. *Next* year is when it's going to count. We won't be able to sow anything like the same number of fields that we have now, so I'd like to try to keep what weedkiller we have in reserve for then.'

Mary looked annoyed. 'I'd like to see us go back to organic farming as soon as possible. It's much healthier.'

'I'm glad you think so,' replied Neil, 'but I fancy you'll change your mind when you try hoeing the weeds out of two acres of beetroot by hand. It's back-breaking work, you know. Nothing like gardening.'

'But at least we'll be able to use animal manure, won't we?' she persisted.

'Obviously—but you'd be surprised at how little manure you get compared to what the fields need. Even with a full complement of cattle, you can't expect adequately to fertilise more than a sixth of your acreage in any one year. In the past, most farmers using animal manure also used chemical fertilisers on all their fields as well. Otherwise the productivity of the fields drops away very quickly.'

'What are your overall plans, Neil?' asked Anne.

'I want to try to use the fields nearby. That way we don't waste fuel and time getting around. And also, it's easier to use the manure from the animals if they're near the fields with the crops. In the past the area around here has mainly been used for arable farming, so we'll need to bring in quite a few sheep, cattle and pigs, plus a good-sized flock of hens.'

'We've already done that,' said Paul.

'I know you have, but I think we need about three times as many as you've brought so far.'

'What about milking equipment?' asked Derek. 'Won't that be too big to transport? Have we got a dairy farm nearby?'

'You've forgotten something,' said Neil. 'It's all powered by electricity. Unless you want to use up petrol and oil for the generators it's back to milking by hand.

'Oh—and one more thing. We'll need to round up as many horses as we can. There'll be no point in waiting until the petrol's run out—they may all be dead by then. And the quicker we get on with using them, the more we can eke out our fuel supplies.'

'Good idea,' murmured Derek to himself.

'What about clothes?' asked Anne. 'Don't we need to grow flax, and rear sheep for their wool?'

'I don't think we need to do that yet, surely,' interjected Paul. 'There's so much clothing in the shops. We'll be able to use that source for ages.'

'I agree with Paul,' said Neil. 'Later, maybe—but not yet. Food is the thing we have to concentrate on—to make sure that as far as possible we've got an all-year-round supply.'

Finally Paul asked the question everyone else hadn't dared to ask. 'Neil—what do you think are our chances?' He expected a positive answer.

Neil shrugged. 'It all depends on the weather,' was the laconic reply.

'Surely you can be more definite,' said Mary.

Neil shook his head. 'There are too many variables—all produce needs the right combination of weather, which is why we can grow some things in England and not others. It's not just whether we get enough sun, it's whether we get the rain, and how much, and when; and whether the frosts come early or late. A late frost will kill off all your strawberries; if there's no rain the fruit won't fill out; and if there's no sun the wheat won't ripen.

'There's not just one harvest in a year, there are lots, as each type of crop ripens—but it's only seldom that every crop in a year does well. One year the potatoes fail—another the wheat harvest isn't so good.'

Neil looked downcast. Paul suddenly remembered the old adage about there being no such thing as a happy farmer, except to his bank manager, and suddenly felt a little better. Farmers always seemed to look on the glum side, he thought. I suppose it's being so vulnerable to outside events that does it, he decided.

'We should be all right—at least I *hope* we'll be all right, though without fertilisers and weedkillers we aren't half going to be working hard.'

'We'll have to conserve our fuel, too, or else we'll be doing everything by hand—including cutting the wheat,' added Paul. 'So we really will have to be careful how we use our stocks from now.'

-41-

*K*evin, meanwhile, was causing problems. He had taken Paul's request for everyone to reduce their consumption of fuel as a direct abuse of Freedom and the Rights of Man—for no other reason than sheer bloodymindedness he took himself off almost on a daily basis, and, dressed in all his leather finery, drove the Harley-Davidson around at high speed for hour upon hour. Although the roads running radially from London were blocked, most of the transverse roads were not. Kevin found himself a ten-mile run east to Shefford and Stotfold that was virtually clear, and he burned up and down this stretch of road regularly for the next three or four weeks.

His activities had three unfortunate effects. Firstly, it wasted a lot of petrol; secondly, it alienated him from the rest of the community, who could see their precious stocks of fuel being used up in the most frivolous manner possible. Lastly, unbeknown to Kevin, his activities attracted the attention of a small community which had started up in the Stotfold area. This group was much smaller than the one at Ampthill, and much less well-organised, living in a much more aggressively consuming fashion and in a much more random and somewhat destructive way.

The members of the community—gang might be a better word—were not unlike Kevin in many ways, but Kevin had had the advantage of being protected by the rest of the Ampthill community from his previous hand-to-mouth existence and was at least beginning to understand the importance of planning for the future.

This was quite different to what had happened to him before. In his previous existence Kevin had been cocooned in the wrong sort of way. Even if he didn't work, there had always been a handout from Social Security. Although Kevin was particularly streetwise his wisdom encompassed only a small area, mainly concerned with interpersonal power struggles and who was King of the Castle, rather than the more important matters of earning the wherewithal to keep oneself alive.

In short, Kevin had been mollycoddled in all the wrong directions. As he'd never had a job, Nanny State gave him money. If he had bothered to find employment Nanny State would have taken away part of what he earned—in what he would have seen as a punishment for working. If he didn't work he got all sorts of expensive things—like medicines—free. If he started working he had to pay for them. No wonder he and his gang had grown up with the idea that you're a fool if you work. They had been the victims of a giant conditioning experiment, in which they functioned just like Pavlov's dogs.

Pavlov was a Russian scientist who had discovered that by associating unrelated ideas he could cause an animal to react completely inappropriately. By presenting a dog with food, he made it salivate: he also rang a bell at the same time. Eventually the dog came to associate the ringing of the bell with food, and when, eventually Pavlov just rang the bell (but gave no food) the dog salivated in anticipation. Pavlov named this a conditioned reflex.

Kevin didn't know about Pavlov, but he had been conditioned all the same. *His* conditioning had been quite unerring and totally debilitating. Kevin had been conditioned to believe that you were entitled to anything you needed; if he were hungry the State shouldn't allow it and would make sure he could eat; if he were ill the State would give him medicines; if he were homeless the State would provide him with a house. He and his friends had come to depend on this conditioning, totally passively. Moreover the State had convinced him that any attempt to fend for himself would immediately be responded to with antagonism and antipathy—the instant removal of benefits, and immediate taxation. In short, Kevin quite unwittingly had been taught with some considerable ferocity a total and complete lie about the world—that he had a *right* to everything he needed, and indeed anything he wanted—and a duty to no one. He really believed

that there was such a thing as a free lunch, and had never worked
out that somewhere along the line somebody else had to pay for it.

Since the plague he'd unlearned a little of this. He'd
grudgingly done a little work in the fields, but had had to be
coerced into it. His house—he'd taken an old farm building
almost on the brow of the hill on the north side of Ampthill—was
the despair of everyone who went near it because he just didn't
know how to keep the place organised, tidy or clean.

He'd chosen it because it had barns at the back, in which he
stored the Harley-Davidson. That at least did get attention—it
was cleaned and polished and oiled, and serviced lovingly and
carefully. It was the pride of his life and around it the whole of
the rest of his existence circled. In some ways it was a surrogate
for his mother whose presence and comfort he missed sorely—
though he wouldn't have dreamed of admitting this to any of his
former cronies.

Against this background of disorganised consumerism,
Kevin had had the influence of Paul. Paul hated Kevin, and
Kevin hated Paul. They were complete opposites: Paul planned
carefully for the future—Kevin couldn't see further than the next
evening. Paul had gained qualifications, and learned to use his
knowledge, which gained him respect in the eyes of others.
Kevin had no qualifications, and, apart from his street-wisdom,
no reason to earn anyone's respect. In one way they *were* the
same—they were both receiving the fruits of their labours:
Kevin had had little fruit because he had little labour. Paul had at
least earned the money to pay for his Porsche, even if his hourly
rate was just a little inflated.

Despite not liking Paul, Kevin envied him his success, his
leadership, the respect he enjoyed, but couldn't see that this
respect was earned: Kevin wanted to know why he couldn't have
some of it, as well. Why shouldn't he, Kevin, be leader? There
wasn't that much difference in their ages. They were both young
and strong. Just because Paul had a toffee-nosed accent he
seemed to think he was entitled to rule everyone. Well, thought
Kevin, we'll see about that. He won't rule *me*. And there are no
police to stop me any more, either. I'll show him. And so he
burned up and down the Stotfold road on a daily basis, using up
precious fuel in an idiotic attempt to establish his pre-eminence.

The small group at Stotfold were much like Kevin, except that there had been no others to counterbalance them. They too had a view of life which was all about taking rather than giving, of rights rather than duties, of demands rather than responsibilities. As far as they were concerned the demise of most of the people in the world meant that they could have a field day looting—which they did in a conspicuously consumerist fashion, breaking into any shop or house they fancied, using whatever was there and moving on. There was none of Paul's care in ensuring that they used everything they could from a particular site before moving on. They got what they wanted and then left the place in a shambles.

The leader of the group, a large heavily-built, bearded man of about thirty, who would have fitted neatly into any Hell's Angels Chapter, was called Lewis Pritchard. Or rather, that was the name on his birth certificate. Anybody who called him Lewis usually didn't want to do it again after Pritchard had finished with him. He preferred to be called simply 'The Boss'. Those near to him he sometimes allowed to call him Lew.

And so it was that one bright December morning when Kevin was doing his usual eighty-mile-an-hour burn-up down the bypass that the noise and activity attracted, not for the first time, the attention of Lew and his friends. Lew also was a biker. Unfortunately he didn't possess a Harley-Davidson, nor had he managed to locate one in the time since he and his friends had escaped the plague through a simple process of stealing a large bottle of erythromycin tablets from his local chemist.

Lew was envious of Kevin—or, rather, coveted the bike— and he didn't see any reason why what Kevin had shouldn't be his (Lew had an abiding belief that all property was theft, but particularly that other people's property was theft from him). Gradually, acquiring the Harley-Davidson became an obsession with Lew, so much so that, while he and his gang were descending upon the innocent and undefended shops of Stotfold like a swarm of locusts, they also spent a lot of time in trying to work out where this strange man and his bulleting machine came from.

*   *   *

As Chris and the others had expected, the community agreed
wholeheartedly with their plan for Derek to learn medicine: they
would all support Derek while he was learning and would
continue to support him afterwards when he started putting his
knowledge into practice. Derek was overwhelmed by the
sincerity of their belief in him—that he really could become their
medical adviser; but he was intensely apprehensive, even
though, as he had insisted, the community had formally agreed
that under no circumstances would he be held responsible for his
mistakes; they also understood that his medical resources were
going to be limited because of the lack of equipment, drugs, and
above all specialist expertise.

Derek set to work willingly, and genuinely enjoyed studying
for his new-found profession. Sensibly, rather than diving into it
head first he sat back and planned. Surprisingly to many, he
didn't start by studying the textbooks in the Health Centre.
Instead, he went to the library and found as much as he could of a
general nature relating to home nursing. With this he developed
an overview of medicine, and only when he had obtained that did
he go into each area more deeply. Thus his knowledge was
always based on a solid foundation of what he had previously
learned, rather than specialist knowledge that was suspended in
space, isolated from everything else.

He learned simple things first—how to stitch up cuts; what
to do about infections; and, particularly with Jane as his first
subject, the delicate matter of antenatal care and midwifery.
He'd been present at the birth of both of his children, but
remembered little of it—seeing the new baby's head starting to
appear; how the midwife had put her hand over the head to stop
it being pushed out too quickly; how she'd then checked the
neck for the cord; and how she'd finally asked Anne to push
with a contraction, in order to deliver the rest of the baby.

Jane felt confident with the care that Derek was giving her.
She knew that he was on a very steep learning curve—as she
was, never having been pregnant before—but Derek had an
encouraging manner about him that instilled confidence, (even
when inside himself he felt anything but) and as the baby grew

inside her and she started to change shape, she began looking forward to the day when both her efforts and Derek's new-found skills would come to fruition.

*   *   *

Meanwhile, Martin was causing concern to the rest of the community. Although he joined in the communal work completely, it was always with a total lack of interest; obvious to all, yet belied by the fact that he always did his work with a hundred per cent effectiveness. The pile of empty whisky bottles outside his house kept growing at an alarming rate and he was soon forced to travel further and further afield as the stocks of the pubs, hotels and off-licences from which he got his supplies became gradually more and more depleted.

He drank on his own—which is always the worst way. He drank to anaesthetise himself from the world; and sitting in the Old Rectory, surrounded by reminders of the life that once had been both for the house, and for its original incumbent, he thought and thought and became more and more morose.

In the second week of December, he also received a deputation. At 11 o'clock one morning three of the more dyed-in-the-wool Anglicans led by Major Thornton came to Martin to ask him whether he would consider conducting a service at Christmas: in particular a service of carols and a Christmas morning Eucharist. They had picked 11 o'clock to ask him because by then Martin should have slept off the excesses of the previous night's drinking, but would not have had time to get too drunk that day. They were right—Martin was usually at his best at about that time, but everything was relative. Would he consider taking the service?

'No,' he said immediately.

'But it *would* help,' said their leader, Major Thornton. This was his second deputation, having been part of the group that had approached Derek. As a result of his military experience, he was accustomed to getting his own way, though he invariably expressed his wishes in a precise and firm—but gentle—manner.

'I do hope you'll reconsider,' he said. 'It is your duty, you know. After all, you're the only ordained minister we have and we can't celebrate the Eucharist without you.'

'I'm sure you can,' said Martin, irascibly. 'The apostles didn't have a five-year course at an Anglican theological college before they started their churches.'

Major Thornton looked shocked. As he came from the Anglican High Church tradition this was something he found rather difficult.

'Besides,' said Martin, 'I don't believe in God any more.'

'Once a priest, always a priest,' said the Major. 'Just because you have a temporary personal crisis doesn't mean that you aren't fit to celebrate the Eucharist. Before the plague I should think a good proportion of priests had doubts at some time or other, but that didn't stop them doing their duty.'

'I don't think of it as my duty any more,' said Martin. 'I'm not a priest. No one pays me for being a priest. I don't have any duties or responsibilities in that direction at all. I don't believe any more.'

The Major wouldn't give ground. Backing down was not his style. 'You'll always be a priest and have duties as a priest, because you were ordained one. Even if you became a practising Buddhist you would still have been ordained a priest and entitled to celebrate the Eucharist.

'We aren't asking much—just that you conduct two services, that's all. There are some of us who would like to make our communion and Christmas seems an appropriate time to do it. It's only two services.'

Martin looked uninterested.

'Can't you do it mechanically, by rote?' asked the Major, irritatedly, his white moustache bristling. 'Does it have to be felt or believed? Can't you do it just because other people here would like you to?'

There was silence for a moment.

'I'd be doing something that was a lie,' he said eventually.

'That's not important for the ones who are receiving the communion because they believe that God is there, even if you don't.'

'Yes,' said Martin. '*I* know that—but I don't want to do it because I don't want to take part in anything which isn't true. Now if you don't mind I'd like to be on my own.'

The Major left, for once the loser.

But Martin did do the services. Why he changed his mind he didn't know—cowardice, love, consideration, harking back to the old order, the Christmas spirit, habit. He didn't know why he changed his mind. With thoughts and emotions that were all jumbled up—not helped by the whisky—he went round to the house down the lane that before the plague had been the Rectory proper and found a cassock and a clerical collar: then he checked in the church vestry to see that the vestments were still there. Finally—and why, he just didn't know—he went to the Major and told him that he would conduct the services, after all, reluctantly, and without feeling.

-42-

After a week of discreet observation, the Boss and his four colleagues discovered where Kevin lived, and where he kept the bike. Kevin's house was at the edge of the town, so it had been easy to spy on his comings and goings without being seen, and as the community wasn't expecting trouble, they weren't on the lookout for it.

So it was that, on the afternoon of Christmas Eve, when Kevin had finished his daily run to Stotfold, polished his bike and put it away in the shed, two leather-clad figures observed him carefully from the bushes at the top of the hill. They waited, expecting him to go out, but as it happened, he stayed in: while in Stotfold he'd wandered into a newsagent's and found on its shelves a copy of a girlie magazine that he hadn't seen before, so he took it home. He hadn't planned to go to the carol service anyway: he'd not been inside a church since he was baptised and in any case even if he wanted to go he wouldn't know what to do; but more importantly his anti-establishment feelings very definitely extended to the Church and all it stood for; so that evening he stayed at home.

The Market Square

*   *   *

The community had decked the church out for Christmas as
best they could, bearing in mind that it had been totally unheated for
more than two months, and that there was no electricity to light it,
nor to power the organ. To those who'd been accustomed to the
closeted warmth and cosiness of a traditional candlelit carol service,
that year's service came as a great contrast. In the past after a
candlelit service they could switch the lights on again, go home
through streets that were lit and watch television in houses that were
warm throughout. It was quite different when candles were the
only source of light available, and the houses to which they went
back were, except for the rooms with fires in, cold and damp.

The organ couldn't be used, being electrically powered, but
there was a piano in the church which Anne played for the carols.
Everyone in the community came—apart from Kevin—and as
Martin looked round the packed church he reflected ruefully that
before, when he believed, he attracted few newcomers, yet now
when he didn't, everybody wanted to come. The irony of the
situation was not lost on him. Why are they here? he thought.
Not to hear me, though some of them seem to think I've got to be
present in order to have a proper service. What about the rest of
them? Is it because it's Christmas, and it's reminiscent of the old
times? Perhaps.

Certainly some had come for purely nostalgic purposes, but
there were others whose outlook on the world was beginning to
change. Stripped of the infrastructure of civilisation, their
sudden change to a hand-to-mouth existence had made them
more aware of the vagaries of life, and the tenuous links that
human beings have with the planet. No longer could they depend
on food from elsewhere if the harvest failed here. No longer
would there be rice in plenty in the shops, bananas, pineapples,
oranges. If the harvest failed, just once, that might be it. Now
there was only a thin line marking the difference between living
on the earth and not managing to fend for themselves.

In much the same way that people cross themselves, wear St
Christopher medals, or read horoscopes, some had actually
started to pray, on the basis that it wouldn't do any harm, and it
might just make a difference to whether the crops grew or not.

When their hold on life gets tenuous people cling to whatever assistance they can—even, as a last resort, to God.

For them the service was quite different from what they had expected. As they heard the story unfolding from the Bible about the incredible, unbelievable idea that God could actually send his son to live on earth, not a few were moved and in a curious way, the fact that Martin now no longer believed a word of it made no difference whatsoever. He was the channel through which the message itself was flowing. Odd though the Major's beliefs had been—that only Martin could celebrate the Eucharist because only Martin was ordained—in another way he was curiously right. What happened in the church that night didn't depend at all on the quality of the priest, but instead upon the message that he was reciting from the Bible.

But there was one person for whom the service was an utter disaster. For most of the time Sarah had been sitting halfway up the aisle, with Derek, David and Alison. Halfway through 'Away in a Manger' the sadness and loss that she had suffered silently since the death of her parents broke through like a river in flood. She left the pew where she was standing and rushed up the aisle in floods of tears to bury herself in Anne's arms. Anne was playing the piano, so the rest of the hymn was unaccompanied, except by the sound of Sarah's wails.

'I want my mummy,' she said to Anne over and over again. 'I want my mummy and my daddy'; and Anne hugged her and cuddled her and rocked her while the congregation sang, unaccompanied,

> *Be near me Lord Jesus, I ask Thee to stay*
> *Close by me for ever, And love me I pray.*

And Sarah's little sobs were the trigger for many others in the community who had not really got round to mourning the people that they had lost, whom they would never talk to again; the ones far away whom they had not been able to contact because the telephones had broken down so quickly; the ones they had left behind, dead; and the ones whose fate they did not know.

By the time the hymn finished there were not many dry eyes

left, and Martin, sensing this, found his previous training and professionalism coming to the fore. He responded by leading an extempore prayer for those who had gone, committing them to the care of God (in whom, as it happened, he didn't currently believe).

That point in the service was when the mood changed. Just as between a death and a burial there's a curious sense of incompleteness, of unfinished business that somehow becomes completed and ruled off with the interment, so Martin's prayer ended a two-month wait in the hearts and minds of those present. At long last their relatives and friends were mentally laid to rest, even if physically their remains were still decomposing on the streets of London. They had all said goodbye, and they knew it; and just as a funeral is followed by a wake so, released of their emotional burdens at last, the congregation was able to express itself more fluently and with greater feeling in the hymns, readings and prayers that followed until with the final hymn 'O come all ye faithful' the whole church vibrated with noise, and despite the lack of heating the whole atmosphere was warm and cosy instead of the cold and gloom they had felt on the way in.

When the service ended they wished each other a Happy Christmas, and went outside to find that the clouds which had previously covered the sky had moved away and in the crisp night air the stars shone on them more brightly than they had remembered from Christmases before.

Martin was the last one out of the church, and as he shut the door he looked up at the stars and marvelled yet again at how bright they were. Then he recalled that dreadful night after the plague when he'd realised for the first time just how black the world could become without light. 'And the light shined upon us,' he thought, quoting the words from John's Gospel on the coming of Jesus, words that he'd just read to the congregation. When those who had written the gospels talked about Jesus being the Light of the World they were making a very important contrast. Martin remembered the physical darkness that had descended upon the world, and the emotional darkness that had descended upon his soul, and reflected as he went out of the churchyard on the great contrast between light and dark: yet so few in England could really appreciate it once civilisation had brought sodium lighting.

He stopped in the square outside Dynevor House and looked upwards, amazed by the sheer number and intensity of the stars that he could see. Over to his left was Orion, with the fiery red Betelgeuse at its right shoulder; Sirius, the dog star, the brightest in the whole sky, was peeping over the tops of the houses, looking for all the world like an aircraft searchlight, so bright was it. He turned to look to the northeast and saw just above the horizon the moon, past the full, beginning to rise between the church and the almshouses.

'The sun to rule the day and the moon to rule the night,' he thought again, then jumped as he felt a hand on his right elbow.

'Did I startle you?' said Derek.

'A bit,' said Martin. 'Sorry—I was just thinking.'

'Would you like to come and share the rest of the evening with us?' asked Derek, beckoning towards the doorway of Dynevor House. More than anyone else in the community, Derek was the closest to Martin—not that anyone could get very close to him at that time—but Derek felt a special sympathy for the predicament of the man ten years his junior who was finding life such an emotional struggle.

Martin hesitated, thought no, and said, 'Yes.' Yes, he would like to come out from being a recluse for a little bit. The darkness inside his soul had receded a little as the result of the service, the stars and the moon; and a little seed of a thought had popped into his subconscious and was starting to grow, whispering, telling him things that he didn't understand, giving him a vague glimmer of hope.

'Yes, I'd like that, thank you Derek,' he heard himself saying as he followed him across the square.

Derek had a houseful. As well as the three children—by now Sarah had recovered her former self, having exorcised her own ghost too—there were many guests, and Anne was bustling about making everyone welcome. The first person Martin bumped into was Major Thornton, and as Derek pressed a glass of mulled wine into his hand the Major took him on one side and said in a voice not unaffected by emotion, 'I just wanted to say how grateful we all are to you for that service. It meant a lot to us you know—the more so because we know you didn't really want to do it'—and in a totally unexpected display of emotion for the Major, he gripped Martin warmly by the arm for a few seconds and then, as if this display was too much for him, made his excuses and disappeared off in the direction of the dining room.

There was something about that Christmas Eve that no one would ever forget. It wasn't an opulent Christmas—certainly not by the standards of the past—but it was a warm and gentle and pleasant time and Dynevor House, which had reverberated to many hundreds of Christmases, seemed to give off its own quiet welcoming warmth. In the mellowness of the candles and the crackling of logs on the fires, and the warmth of the wine and the closeness of the company, Martin started at long last to feel that he had some place among humanity and some small right to be alive. And all the while at the back of his mind that microscopic little thought which had popped into existence kept growing and growing, doubling, like rice on a chessboard.

*   *   *

He'd been there for about a quarter of an hour, standing chatting in the dining room in what was for him a remarkably casual and unconcerned way when there came a frantic knocking on the door. Derek detached himself from the rest of the company and hurried down the passage into the main hall, to be greeted by a breathless and somewhat disturbed gaggle of people. Fearing some sort of accident, he asked what was the matter.

'Can you come to the Market Square straight away?' said a voice which Derek eventually identified as belonging to Alan Rogers. Alan could see Martin in the passageway behind Derek's shoulder. 'And you, Vicar, I think you ought to come as well.'

Although Martin reacted internally to the sound of the word 'Vicar', he didn't show it, particularly in view of the expression on Alan's face. Some disaster must have happened—a death maybe. He would just have to shrug off his own problems and do what he could, he supposed. Derek grabbed his coat, Martin did the same, and they both ran out of the house and up Church Street. They were joined by Paul and Chris who had also been fetched, bewildered, from their respective houses.

'What's the matter? What's this all . . . What's this all about?' said Derek between gasps of breath, the icy air hitting his lungs.

'It's Kevin.' Derek's heart did a somersault as he thought of
the damage that Kevin could do to himself at the speeds at which
he was accustomed to travelling on the bike.

'What's he done to himself? What's happened?'

'Oh, he's not hurt *himself*. It's what he's just about to do
that's the problem.'

Rushing into the Market Square, they stopped short. A ring of
people was standing around the old pump, a stone obelisk set at the
corner of the Market Place. Someone had set up a burning torch
on a pole and by its light Derek could see Kevin standing, waving
something in his hand. Every time anyone from the crowd tried to
get near him he brandished it at them and they retreated.

Had Kevin gone mad, suddenly turned psychotic? thought
Derek. Then he realised that Kevin was not the only one in the
centre of the circle. There was another man that Derek had never
seen before, bent double, his hands tied behind his back, and a
noose round his neck which was attached to the stone pump three
feet off the ground, so that in order to avoid strangling himself he
had to bend double: but then he got cramp, whereupon he'd fall
forward and get strangled or try to straighten up and get throttled.
The figure was in constant motion, torn between spasm and
cramp of the muscles and a desire to keep his airway clear. He
had obviously been like that for some time and Kevin was
allowing him to suffer, whilst brandishing what Derek could now
see was a large leather belt.

'Keep away, I said,' Kevin shouted at the crowd; then
seeing the group of them arrive, 'and you keep away as well,
Derek. This one's mine.'

Kevin put his face three inches away from the other man's.
'So you're the Boss, are you?' he said, spitting the words in his
face. 'Well, you've picked on the wrong person to try to steal
from. Whose bike is it?' There was no answer from Lew as he
struggled to maintain an airway, his face contorted with fear and
pain. Kevin went round to Lew's rear, undid Lew's trousers and
pulled them down to his knees. He did the same with his
underpants and then returned and put his face an inch away from
Lew's. 'Whose bike is it?'

No answer. Kevin stood up and swung the belt against the
man's bare buttocks, buckle end first. There was a thwack and a

scream that died off as Lew half jerked in the air then found that
the noose round his neck brought him down again, and he was
back to the old routine of trying to avoid being strangled or
getting cramp.

Kevin put his face against Lew's and asked the question
again. 'Whose bike is it?'

Again no answer. Kevin hit him again, harder, drawing blood.
'Stop him, Derek,' said a voice.

'You get away, Derek,' said Kevin. 'This is none of your
business. This jerk here tried to steal my bike.'

'For goodness sake, Kevin,' said Derek, 'you can't do this.
It's inhuman.'

'You leave me alone. It's none of your business. It's my
bike and this is between him and me.'

Someone in the crowd tried to push forward to get to Kevin,
but Kevin whipped the belt across at him, just missing his face.
The figure drew back hastily. Kevin brought his face down again
level with Lew's. 'Whose bike is it?'

'Yours,' said Lew, his face purple and half-choked.

'And you're not going to touch it again, are you?' said
Kevin.

No answer. The strap flailed mercilessly and drew blood
again. Lew screamed and collapsed, hanging limp by his neck.

'You've killed him,' said Paul.

'No, I haven't,' said Kevin as Lew recovered, and clambered
desperately to the half-crouching position again. 'I'm just
teaching him a lesson.'

'It's barbaric,' said Chris. 'Stop it. Taking revenge on
somebody isn't human. It isn't civilised.'

'Who's going to stop me?' asked Kevin. 'More to the
point—who's going to stop him if I don't?'

There was a silence.

'None of you is able to stop him stealing my bike.'

'It wasn't even yours to start with,' said Derek.

'That's not the point. The original owner's dead. He
doesn't *want* it any more. He doesn't *need* it any more. I wanted
it, I found it, I look after it and it's *mine*. If you're going to take
a bike,' he said, turning round to Lew, 'go and take it from a bike
shop and *don't take it from me*. Got it?' He raised his arm again.

Lew nodded and spluttered all at the same time.

'Right,' said Kevin, 'and just to help you remember I'm going to give you a little more of this. Shall we say six . . . ? No . . . seven, for good measure.'

Kevin struck out at the writhing figure of Lew seven more times. When he'd finished he calmly buckled the belt on himself, untied Lew's hands from behind his back, then with a vicious kick to his shins, removed his legs from under him and marched off, the crowd parting to let him through.

Lew fell forward suspended by his neck. With his hands at long last free he clutched at the noose, struggling desperately to untie the knot as soon as possible. Derek and Martin rushed forward to help him. Aching, humiliated, half strangled and frightened out of his wits, Lew's face was a picture of rage.

'I'll kill the . . . .'

'No, you won't,' said Derek. 'Just go away.' Sensing a need, the rest of the crowd formed a barrier between Lew and the departing figure of Kevin.

'Just go away,' Derek repeated firmly. 'Leave him to us. We'll deal with him.' Lew struggled to pull his trousers back on.

'How did you get here?' asked Paul.

'On my bike,' he spat back.

'Where is it?'

'Over there, at the bottom of the hill.' He indicated Bedford Street.

'Well, we'll escort you to it and then, for your own sake, go away.' The crowd processed up Bedford Street, past Kevin's house and down to the bottom of the hill where on the far side Lew's bike lay hidden behind a hedge. His two companions had long since vanished.

'Now go,' said Paul. 'I'm sorry for what he did to you but for heaven's sake just go. We'll deal with him in the morning.'

Lew strode up to the bike, pulled it to the vertical and swung a leg over, wincing as his buttocks hit the seat. He started the engine, twisted in the saddle and uttered a few choice phrases then gunned the bike out towards Bedford.

The group struggled wearily back up the steep hill, their minds a jumble of thoughts. They paused on the far side as they came level with the entrance to Kevin's house.

'Shall we . . .?' said Paul.

'No,' said Derek. 'Not now. Tomorrow. Tomorrow afternoon. It's Christmas Eve, remember?'

-43-

Christmas morning was less of an ordeal than Martin had expected it to be. The cloudless night had allowed the earth to radiate off what little heat it had gathered during the previous day and by the time dawn came there was a thick layer of rime on the ground which sparkled in the clear sunlight. It wasn't snow—it seldom snows in Britain at Christmas whatever the Christmas cards like to imagine—but it was the next best thing. In any case, none of the inhabitants of the town really wanted to see the arrival of snow any more. Snow is wonderful when you can go inside to warm rooms and central heating, but trying to keep warm and dry in unheated rooms is not so funny.

Unlike the night before, when the windows had seemed as black as the walls and they could barely make out the roof in the dim candlelight, by nine o'clock that morning the sun was shining through the stained glass of the east window of the church, casting long coloured beams into the body of the congregation and making the whole building come alive. It reflected off the rime as well, giving that curious upwardly directed light on the ceilings that is so typical of light off snow. That Christmas morning the whole church was alive with light, brilliantly illuminating the blue of the chancel roof and glistening off the gilded wings of the carved angels set timelessly at each roof buttress.

Only twenty people had turned up for communion—nothing like as many as the previous night, but then it was a different type of service and a different sort of occasion.

This time, when the members of the congregation left the church they were welcomed by brilliant sunshine reflecting off the walls of Dynevor House on their right, soaking it in an orange-red light that made the bricks vibrate with colour and

warmth, contrasting spectacularly with the intense blue of the
sky. But it was cold, intensely cold, and their breath came in
clouds in front of them as they walked, stamping their feet
vigorously to keep themselves warm.

Christmas Day was less of a holiday than it had been in the
past. There were jobs to be done, cows to be milked, fodder to be
got, fuel to be brought in, eggs to be collected. It was also the day
when they had to meet to do something about Kevin. In the Middle
Ages, Christmas Day was often a day of meetings: and thus it was
in the new Middle Ages that followed the plague. The community,
now numbering some two hundred and fifty, had grown too big to
meet at Dynevor House, even in the upstairs reception room. It
didn't seem quite right to use the church or the chapter house, so
instead they decided to meet in the magistrates' court down
Woburn Street. This was quite a different building to the one in
which Peter Abrahams had so recently played his ill-fated role.
Unlike the Leighton Buzzard court this was a new building, in
typical sixties design, with neat light-oak panelling which still gave
an atmosphere of formality and authority, but without the
gloominess and dinginess of the Leighton Buzzard building.

Peter was not sure that he wanted to go into another court of
law so soon, but he put his memories behind him and attended, as
did all the rest. All the community came, except for a small
number who stayed behind to look after the children. Much to
everyone's surprise, Kevin came also. Although the court was
barely half a mile from his house, he had insisted on coming on
the Harley-Davidson, to everyone's disgust, both for his refusal
to take exercise and his profligacy in the use of petrol.

Paul took upon himself the chairmanship of the meeting, an
action to which there were no objectors. 'I really think we ought
to start laying down a few rules,' he began. 'What Kevin did last
night was quite illegal and improper. We can't have people in the
community taking the law into their own hands: nor can we
tolerate those who are not prepared to fit in. Kevin hasn't pulled
his weight in the communal work and despite our pleas to use fuel
carefully has quite deliberately used his bike purely for sport in a
most profligate fashion, and I think,' he said, turning to Kevin and
staring him straight in the eye, 'I think this has to stop.'

There was a general murmur of approval. Kevin stood up.

'All right then. I wonder whether you'd say the same thing if you'd had something of yours nicked? If it had been your Porsche that the raiders had gone for, would you've stood for it? What would you have done to them? Said, Here you are, take it, it's yours? Neah. You'd have got just as angry. You'd probably have got a gun and threatened them with that, and everyone would have said "Good on yer".

'You said what I did was illegal. Well, where *is* the law . . . eh? We haven't got a government, we haven't got any police any more, thank goodness; no judges, no magistrates,'—Peter offered a silent prayer of thanks—'so where is this law that I'm supposed to have broken? It's the law of the jungle here now, innit? You take what you want, and if anybody tries to take it off you, you grab it back and defend yourself.

'In any case, Paul Greatorex, you're a right one to talk about taking things. You've been breaking into one shop after another . . .'

'Yes,' rejoined Paul, 'I have, but I've been taking things that were owned by dead people, not goods that are wanted by live ones.'

'OK, so they were trying to take something from me. Or don't I matter? Aren't I important? Aren't I alive?'

'Of course you're important,' said Paul, slightly rattled. 'I just think you went too far, that's all. We can't have a community where everybody behaves like hooligans.'

'Who's the hooligan?'

'You are.'

'Why? Because I hit back when somebody tried to steal something that's mine? What would you have done if they'd have taken your car? Come on . . . what would you have done?'

'I'd have . . . I'd have tried to stop them,' said Paul.

'How?' There was a pause. 'Go on—*how*? By going up to them and saying, "Please don't take my car." Or, "Hey, please don't do that, or if you do I'll have to call the police." Go on— *what would you have done*?'

Paul was beaten and he knew it. He knew *just* what he'd have done, but it would have involved something a little more up-market than a leather belt. Sensing Paul's confusion, Derek rose to divert the conversation.

'Look, Kevin, no one is saying that you shouldn't have tried to prevent Lew getting your bike—but half-killing the guy isn't the right response either. As Paul says, it is illegal—even though there isn't anyone to enforce the law.'

'Well, maybe we'd better make some laws ourselves,' said Kevin. 'New ones, ones that don't favour people like Paul and victimise people like me.'

Paul was on his feet. 'I am not victimising anybody.'

'Yes, you are,' said Kevin. 'You're victimising me. You haven't got a way to prevent them taking what's mine, but you aren't going to allow me any means to defend myself.'

It was Martin's turn. His pacifist background came to the fore. 'We have to be civilised. We can't behave like hooligans.'

'Who says I was behaving like a hooligan?'

'I don't think half-strangling someone and beating him until he's nearly senseless is particularly civilised.'

'Nor is stealing bikes, come to that. It's ever so easy for you to be patronising when it isn't your bike.'

'Well, it wasn't yours originally, either,' said Paul, 'but we'll let that pass.'

'Now *you're* being patronising. *Everything* we're living on here is somebody else's. I didn't notice you passing up the opportunity to live in a nice big house.'

'Look,' said Derek, 'I think Kevin's got a point. It all boils down to this—how are we going to stop the bandits? We can't make our houses so secure that they can't get in and steal anything—that's impossible. Anyway, we had to break into most of the houses to start with, so they're already insecure. We can catch the bandits and lock them up—but then we'd have another set of mouths to feed, and they wouldn't do any work in return, so that's not very practical either.

'We could kill them,'—there was a sharp intake of breath from various places in the room—'but I don't think anyone here wants to do that, including Kevin.'

Kevin nodded.

'Or we can do what Kevin's just done and make the results of stealing so unpleasant that they don't try it again. When all is said and done Kevin has a good point. In practical terms there's not much else that we can do.'

Martin, agitated, was on his feet, surprisingly forceful considering his past mouse-like behaviour.

'I do protest at that,' he spluttered, his cultured voice sounding oddly high, almost like a child having a tantrum. 'I really do *not* think that we ought to regress to being barbarians. That really *would* be going back to the Middle Ages.'

From the back of the courtroom Mary agreed with him. 'We must have sympathy with the people who are trying to take things. They have just as much right to live on this earth as we have. We mustn't descend to the barbaric violence that we saw last night. We have to be gentle and kind. It's quite wrong to punish violence with violence. We have to educate them, change their social patterns; we have to understand what it's like to be on the outskirts of society.'

'It wasn't your bike, either,' observed Kevin loudly to no one in particular.

'All right,' said Derek. 'What are we going to do?'

Peter Abrahams got to his feet. As a former policeman he at least had direct experience of dealing with those who didn't want to obey the rules the rest of the community had decided upon. 'If you make rules, then those rules have got to be obeyed. If they're not obeyed you have to have a means of enforcing them. We have to decide what sort of punishments we're going to have. If we're going to make rules, we have to set up a legal system, even if it's only a small one. We have to have a system to decide who has flouted the law, and whether they did it deliberately or unintentionally. *Somebody* has to make the decisions and there have to be rules and regulations governing that, otherwise you've still got a free-for-all. And someone has to carry out the punishments. Now, do we really want all of this?'

'Why can't we all live together peacefully?' added Martin.

Mary was on her feet again. 'I agree,' she said. 'Why *can't* we all live together peacefully? Why do we have to have judges and juries and rules and regulations? Man is basically good. It's only when there are inequalities that problems arise. So long as everyone has a fair share then there shouldn't be any need at all for any legal system. If we provide everyone with a fair share we shouldn't need any regulations at all. The only reason why we've had laws in the past is because the people with money, the

262   After the Fire

landowners, the rich, have used them to oppress the poor. It's no coincidence, is it, that English laws were far harsher for those who destroyed property than those who harmed lives? Less than two hundred years ago people who had no food could get deported to Australia for stealing a single sheep: that's not just, is it? If we create a society here that's equal and fair then there won't be any need for laws.'

'I agree,' said Martin. 'You never get theft of those things that are free, where everybody's got as much as they need. You don't find people stealing air, do you?'

'Let's see if we can all agree to live in peace. It shouldn't be too hard,' continued Mary.

'*It wasn't your bike*,' said Kevin firmly.

'Talking of bikes,' said Paul, 'I think we ought to make it clear that we really can't tolerate people going joy-riding all the time. If you're going to continue as a member of the community, Kevin, you really will have to fit in a bit better.'

'Why?' said Kevin. 'Why do *I* have to fit in with *you*? Why don't *you* fit in with *me*? I *like* to ride my bike. It's fun. That's what being alive is all about—having fun, doing things you want to, not working more than you need. We don't have to work for the petrol—we can get it free from the petrol stations. Why should it bother you what I do with my life? Anyway Paul, you've got your own car and you like driving that, don't you?'

'Yes,' said Paul, 'but I very seldom use it just to drive. I usually go somewhere to do something, like to the aerodrome.'

'And how much does your car do to the gallon?'

'About twenty, I suppose.'

'Right,' said Kevin. 'Well, my bike does fifty, so for every mile you do I can do two and a half, and every time you take out your car I can take out my bike at least twice before I've used up the same amount of petrol.'

Paul was getting really rattled. He had thought he could dominate Kevin and he was finding out the hard way that it wasn't going to be as easy as all that. 'What does anybody else think?' he asked. There was a buzz of conversation.

'We think Kevin's got a point,' came a voice from the far side of the courtroom. 'It isn't up to other people to tell individuals what to do.'

'Yes,' said Derek, 'but we have to be careful that no one person uses up all the reserves that we'll all need. The fuel's got to run out some time. We can't go on mining petrol stations at our present rate for ever and ever. We'll need fuel for more important things than gunning up and down the bypass—operating combine harvesters for example. We'll look a bit silly if we can't bring in the harvest because we've used all the fuel joy-riding. I really think we ought to say to *everyone*—not just to Kevin, to *everyone*—that we've only got a limited amount of fuel, and when it's gone, it's gone. Let's be careful with it. And let's all try and live peacefully with one another, shall we?'

'It wasn't your bike,' muttered Kevin, under his breath.

Contrary to what everyone thought, it wasn't sheer cussedness that impelled Kevin to bring his bike to the meeting. He was sure the raiders would come back—probably in force—and he wasn't going to let his precious machine out of his sight until the threat had passed. So as the meeting ended, and dusk fell on that Christmas Day, Kevin and the three farmworkers—who by now had become his personal friends—went back to his house, parked the bike in the shed where it was kept, and then lay in wait, taking it in turns to sleep.

Christmas night passed, and nothing happened. So did Boxing night, much as Kevin had anticipated. The night after—which was the night on which Kevin thought the bandits would return—they did. At 2 o'clock in the morning, when the last quarter moon was just rising, Kevin watched as three dark shapes detached themselves from the undergrowth at the top of the hill, and scurried towards the house.

*   *   *

At 8 o'clock that morning the Market Square was treated to a sight not dissimilar from the Christmas Eve display, but this time there were three victims tied head down to the communal pump. It was a cold morning so Kevin had decided to add to his victims' misery by dowsing them with a bucket of ice-cold water. Then he went through the same routine with each of them, putting his face in front of theirs and watching their teeth chatter while he asked them again and again whose bike it was, and lashing them mercilessly every so often on their unprotected rear quarters.

A crowd came to watch, but again did nothing. This time no one tried to stop Kevin, except that when one of the bandits appeared to have lost consciousness completely, they prevailed upon Kevin to loosen the noose until he had recovered.

Kevin dealt with the minor members of the gang first. They received exactly the same treatment as Lew had received two days earlier. Once they had acknowledged, between gritted teeth, Kevin's right to the bike, they then received seven blows from the leather strap. It was obvious from their half-purple faces, chattering teeth and shaking limbs, and their frightened eyes, that they each thought that their last moments had come.

Then Kevin turned to Lew. 'So you thought you knew better,' he snarled at him. 'Whose bike is it?' Lew said nothing, so Kevin kicked him on the inside of the knee. Lew had to be picked up, or else he would have strangled himself, as he had collapsed, writhing, held up only by the noose. Kevin started on him again.

'Whose bike is it?'

Silence.

In went the boot on the other knee. Again they had to pick Lew up. Lew had hoped that he would be able to withstand the insults, embarrassment and the mental and physical torture that was being inflicted upon him, but eventually his pain threshold proved greater than his stubbornness and with teeth chattering and arms trembling he had to submit.

'How many lashes shall we make it this time?' asked Kevin. 'Seven, shall we say? No.' He savoured the moment. 'It was seven last time. Fifteen this time.' And with that he set about Lew until the blood ran again and Lew was screaming at him to stop, screaming that he'd do anything, just please would Kevin stop.

Kevin paused at twelve. 'You'll do anything, will you?'

'Yes,' blubbered Lew.

'Right—you go away and you don't come back. I don't want to see you or your cronies again—ever.'

'All right,' gibbered Lew.

'We've only got as far as twelve lashes,' said Kevin. 'How I do know that you won't come back again, like you did last night?'

'I won't, I promise,' said Lew.

'I don't believe you,' said Kevin and swung the lash again.

Lew screamed. 'I promise. I promise.'

Kevin hit him again.

'You'd better keep away. If I catch you again I'll half-kill you.'

The thought passed through Lew's mind that he didn't quite know what half-killing must be like if this was not being half-killed.

'I mean it,' said Kevin. 'You come back again and I'll do for you and your mates.' He raised his arm and then dropped it again. Lew heaved a sigh of relief, terminated only by a scream as Kevin, mustering all the energy he could possess, hit him with the leather strap. 'Remember,' said Kevin, yet again putting his face half an inch from Lew's. 'If I so much as see you again . . . Just get out. You've got the whole of the rest of the country to go to. Find your own bike somewhere else, preferably off somebody who doesn't want theirs any longer, like someone who's already dead.'

Lew was too weak to answer. Kevin wandered away, leaving the three of them strung there. Some of the crowd helped to untie them.

'He means it,' said one of them. 'Believe you me, he means it. We can't control him, and if I were you I'd get out of his way, and stay out of his way. We can't stop him: it's in your own best interests.'

The three raised themselves stiffly from their bent position, gathering their trousers up round them again. As they stood there shivering miserably it crossed their minds that someone might help them to dry out, but no one offered. Whilst none of the crowd really agreed with what Kevin had done, no one actually disagreed either. Certainly no one was going to break the spell by inviting them in for a rub-down, a change of clothes and a quick cup of tea. There was at least some solidarity within the community for Kevin's actions, harsh though they were.

Then, as had happened forty-eight hours before, the three were escorted over the brow of the hill to where they had hidden their motorbikes.

'Be grateful we haven't damaged them,' said Trevor. 'Next time we will. Got that?'

*   *   *

News of the repetition of Kevin's violence only reached Derek, Martin and Paul well after the event. They sat in the morning room at Dynevor, wondering how to get things back under control. Try as they might they couldn't think what to do. All the remaining options involved either giving in to the raiders' evils; or else giving in to Kevin's.

They tossed various ideas around in a fruitless search for an answer, any answer. Then there was a long silence. Eventually Martin reluctantly voiced their joint fears.

'Maybe we *are* going back into the Middle Ages.'

There was a pause.

'You may be right,' said Derek.

-44-

*T*hey were still bemoaning the new turn of events when there was a knock on the door. It was Kevin.

'We were just talking about you,' said Derek.

'I thought you might be,' said Kevin, completely unabashed.

'We're very concerned,' began Paul, 'that . . . '

'Oh shut up,' said Kevin. 'I came to warn you.'

'Warn me?' said Paul, prickling.

'Yes,' said Kevin blithely. 'They'll try again. Not to steal the bike, but probably just to do damage. They'll try to firebomb my house, if you must know, but they could just as easily take revenge on anybody in the community.'

'Which is precisely why we didn't want you to do it in the first place–'

'Rubbish,' interrupted Kevin. 'If you'd knuckled under they'd have taken you for everything you'd got. The minute your back was turned they'd come in, take whatever they wanted and disappear again. You wouldn't have stood a chance.'

Paul fell silent. The logic of it was only too clear. 'My method's the only one that will work,' said Kevin. 'Just wait—you'll see.'

'But you've just said you've come to warn us that they'll be back,' expostulated Martin. 'If your method's working, how is it that we've got to start taking defensive precautions?'

'If I'm right, they'll make one more try and if they fail again, with a bit of luck that'll be the last we'll see of them.'

'You're not planning to beat them up *again*, are you?' asked Martin hesitantly.

'No,' said Kevin. 'All we need to do is scare them off. They'll run, and they won't come back. They'll know just what'll happen to them if they get caught.'

'I wish I shared your optimism,' said Derek. 'All right. You've been right so far . . . in your predictions, that is. You said you thought they'd be back, so what do you think we ought to do?'

'We need lookouts on all the roads into Ampthill, and some near my house. Give each lookout a torch and a whistle. If they see a raider, they follow them quietly, get within fifty yards of them, shine their torches on them and blow the whistle. That ought to scare them off for good.

'If you don't post guards you may find that one of the houses goes up in flames. It's most likely to be mine, but it could just as easily be this one,' said Kevin, looking round for effect.

'How can you be sure they'll come?' asked Martin.

'They will. Believe me, they will. Only I can't tell you which night. We may have to have the guards out for a week.'

Paul thought for a minute. 'I think he's right,' he said, turning to the others. 'I think that's what they'll do. They'll come back for revenge and whatever we think of Kevin's method of dealing with them so far, we have to admit that he's always ended up the victor. I think we ought to do what he says. If we don't we'll only worry about it, and if they come and we scare them off that may well be the end of it all—which we'll all be happy about.

'And then,' he concluded darkly, 'we'll have to see whether it can be allowed to happen again.'

'Suits me,' said Kevin insolently and walked off without closing the door.

*   *   *

That night the community settled down to an uneasy sleep whilst twelve watchers hid themselves around its perimeter, to be relieved just after midnight by the second shift. It was a dark night: the last quarter moon didn't rise until about 3.00 a.m. and, being reduced to a half-moon shape, cast only a feeble glow on the countryside. The watchers quietly froze, and cursed Kevin for getting them into their present situation.

But as it happened they hadn't long to wait. The bandits came on the second night, at about 5 o'clock, when the moon gave just enough light to see what they were doing. Kevin and Trevor heard them first—a faint roar in the distance, to the north. From their vantage point on the very top of the ridge overlooking the Bedford plain they could see first one, two and then three pin-pricks of light as the bikes' headlights swept east to west across their field of view.

The growl of their engines faded, as the bandits switched the headlamps off. Kevin turned to his companion. 'Go and get the others,' he said. And then he checked himself. 'No. Not all of them. Let's leave a few on duty, just in case they're attacking from several sides at once.'

Five minutes later the reinforcements had arrived and staked themselves out in front of Kevin's house. They hadn't long to wait. The moon was temporarily hidden by a bank of cloud, but as the wind swept it away they could see five shadowy figures toiling up the hillside, going into the undergrowth at the approach to Kevin's house. The watchers retreated from their original positions and spread themselves out in the field between the undergrowth and the house, lying flat on the frozen ground so that they couldn't be seen.

The raiders came over the hill, through the bushes, five leather-suited figures creeping as quietly as they could towards the house. The lookouts waited until they were out in the open field, totally exposed.

'Now,' said Kevin and switched on his torch which shone straight in the face of the nearest raider, only twenty feet away from him. He blew his whistle furiously, as did the others and the raiders, taken completely off-guard, stood stock-still for a moment and then, as eight lights closed in on them and the cacophony of the whistles shattered the silence, they turned tail and fled.

Kevin came flying after them pelting them with clods of earth, stones and anything else he could get his hands on. There were muffled thuds and expletives as one or two found their target and then the raiders were gone, rushing headlong down the hill. The eight lookouts stood watching at the top of the hill in case the raiders regrouped and returned, but ten minutes later they heard the noise of the bikes starting up and saw their headlamps disappearing back towards Houghton Conquest again.

Paul, who had been among the watchers in the second shift, came up to Kevin and offered his congratulations. 'Very astute that,' he said, 'knowing they'd be back. Well done. What now?'

'I don't think they'll come back again,' said Kevin, 'but just in case, I think we ought to have the watchers out for another week.'

'Well, you seem to be the master strategist,' said Paul rather enviously. It takes one to know one, he added under his breath, thinking of the kinship that would otherwise have existed between Kevin and the bandits before the plague.

Kevin was right yet again. Although they mounted a full guard for the next week, and a token force for the month after, nothing further happened: the raiders had left, and peace returned to the community.

-45-

Although the human raiders had gone, Mary had raiders of a different sort. Coming out of her house one morning, she was concerned to see large numbers of chicken feathers blowing about in the breeze. She soon found the answer—five of her flock were missing. Three of them were at the far end of the garden, near the wood, their throats ripped out and bodies torn to bits, but of the other two there was no sign. The significance of

this took some time to dawn on Mary, mainly because she had
previously been a city-dweller. Perhaps one of the dogs or cats
she had seen roaming around locally had been responsible, she
thought. She did wonder whether Howler might have had
something to do with it, but he seemed to be quite unbothered by
the hens, and, in turn, they were unconcerned with him; so she
stored the information in the back of her mind and continued
giving them their food, having first disposed—at arm's length—
of the three chicken carcasses.

The next morning was the same—more chicken feathers.
This time six of the birds were missing; the remainder were
distinctly restless, and only one bird was still laying. On this
occasion four of the birds had been ripped to bits, and two more
had just disappeared. Puzzled, she sought out Trevor, who came
across from his cottage on Woburn Street to look at the bodies
and the feathers.

'That's easy,' he said. 'You've got a fox.'

'A fox?' said Mary, who'd only seen them in wildlife books
and on anti-hunt posters. 'Oh, how wonderful.' Trevor gave her
a sideways look. 'I've never seen a fox,' she continued happily.

'I don't think you want a fox around, somehow. Certainly
your chickens won't. How do you keep them safe at night?'

Keeping chickens safe from predators had not occurred to
Mary. As far as she was concerned, the only predators chickens
had were human ones, who tended to keep them boxed up in
undersized cages and at regular intervals killed and ate them.

'They're protected from the weather—in a coop,' she said,
proudly showing him. 'During the day they scratch around in the
garden getting all the nutriments they need. At night they come
in here away from the cold.'

'Where's the door?' said the farmhand.

'Door?' said Mary.

'Yes, to shut them in.'

'Oh I don't shut them in at night. I don't want to make them
prisoners. They're our animal friends. They have just as much
right to be on the earth as we have.'

'If you shut them in with a decent door you'll probably find
the fox won't get at them,' said Trevor, and stomped off down
the lane, scratching his head and thinking that this was the

weirdest keeper of chickens that he'd ever met.

Whatever she may have thought about the propriety of imprisoning any of God's other creatures, Mary did as he suggested and made a simple door to the coop. The next morning she opened the door of her house suspiciously, but to her delight saw no more feathers flying around the garden. She went to the cage and happily opened the door. Inside, feathers were everywhere. During the night the fox had dug his way inside, taken one chicken for food and torn the rest to pieces, just for fun.

*   *   *

While Mary was discovering the merits and demerits of being a chicken farmer, Derek was well into his studies. True to their promise the rest of the community had taken all other duties away from him so that he could get down to studying medicine as best he could. It gave a new meaning to the phrase 'practising medicine'.

Sensibly he had started with his home medical tutor and learned from that, giving himself a broad outline of the whole subject. After that he went a little deeper, discovering more of the anatomy—the structure, and the physiology—the function of each part of the body. Then he did a little pathology—the study of what happens when the body goes wrong, and pharmacology—how to treat it.

At the same time he began treating a succession of minor illnesses in members of the community—infections, burns, cuts, bruises, ear infections, sore throats: and each set of symptoms stimulated him to look up different aspects of each problem in the textbooks. Where necessary he was able to prescribe, and acting as his own pharmacist used the medicines available in the chemist's shop and in the pharmacy which he had discovered attached to the Health Centre. He started with simple antibiotics—he remembered some of their names from medicines he'd given the children in previous years: gradually he became more practised and able to use a wider range of drugs safely.

Initially he had debated within himself whether to operate in the old style and grand manner of the physicians of yesteryear— using a room that was part of his house as a surgery. He had the right house for it—one of the grandest in the town. On the other hand, he thought it might be clinically more appropriate to use a custom-built building such as the Health Centre, with all the attendant facilities—equipment rooms, screens, couches, shelves for medicines, examination equipment and so on—until he went down there one cold winter's morning and realised that no one in their right mind would ever want to take off any of their clothing in order to be examined. Like most modern buildings it was entirely centrally heated, and without electricity or oil it was as cold as the grave.

So, with a little help from members of the community, he transported back to Dynevor an examination couch, all the surgical equipment he could find, a surgical trolley and virtually every book in the place. Whilst scouring the Health Centre for the right equipment he came across something which intrigued and enthused him—a whole set of videos on medical subjects which, according to the list of contents on the covers, included demonstrations of minor operations, diagnosis of skin rashes, and joint injection techniques; but with no electricity they were useless, so he left them on the shelves, hoping that in the distant future he would be able to look at them and obtain, at first hand, knowledge from a real live—he suddenly realised what he was saying—doctor.

As well as the minor illnesses he also had to cope with one or two more major ones. By the end of February Jane was showing the first outward signs of her pregnancy and as the books said he ought to be examining her regularly he set about doing this. He found it a strange experience at first. Normally when medical students learn to examine people they start off on complete strangers: and even with an experienced physician, examining someone he knows quite well is strangely daunting, and can be extremely embarrassing for both parties.

Derek and Jane had no option. They both had to get to grips with the situation or face the possibility of disastrous consequences somewhere around the middle of July. Jane, surprisingly, didn't find being examined too much of a problem. After all, Derek was in his forties, and more like a father-figure than anything else: his relaxed attitude gave him an easy manner which, in earlier times, would have been ideal for 'the family doctor'.

On the other hand, Derek didn't find examining Jane easy at all. Suddenly, from not touching other people—especially other people's wives—he had to touch Jane in all sorts of ways that he would normally never dream of. Correction—that he often *did* dream of. Whatever Jane may have thought of him, Derek thought of Jane quite differently. Ever since that first evening in the White Hart he had been attracted to her, not so much by her sexuality as by her whole being and personality—her confident air, her quiet glamour. There was something about her that he found infinitely beguiling, and the fact that she was in the full bloom of her womanhood made her doubly attractive.

Had Derek had the impersonal introduction to examinations that most medical students have, he would have learned to pull down the barriers and—while examining her at least—treat her, physically speaking, as a piece of meat, to be examined and explored technically, without emotional involvement. Without this previous experience, Derek just couldn't cope. Initially, he was embarrassed when he needed to touch her: then he found he enjoyed putting his hands on her bare stomach; why did she have such sexy underwear, he asked himself?

None of this did he communicate to Jane, nor to anyone else. He was too ashamed. In physical behaviour he was the model of propriety: it was his mental behaviour that went where it felt like.

Nor did he say anything about it to Anne. He couldn't. Dear Anne, he loved her so much, but at thirty-eight she had lost the first beauty she had when they had married. Anne wouldn't like to be compared with Jane—not at all, not out loud. Anne was still beautiful—but in a different way. So he kept quiet, and had bad dreams instead, and always, after examining Jane, a bad conscience.

Jane was happy enough. The baby was growing steadily inside her and she had confidence in Derek's abilities—he had such an easy manner, she thought. He was so attentive. He made her feel so confident, so secure—so she enjoyed coming to consult him; her obvious enjoyment in coming for her antenatal care didn't help Derek one little bit, as it added even more to his awareness of her attractiveness.

Technically, the antenatal care was going well. Once Derek had discovered where the urine testing strips were kept he could at least do one part of the antenatal examination well—routine testing of the urine for protein, in order to detect impending toxaemia. Next he had to learn how to use the blood pressure machine. He tried it first on Anne, wrapping the cuff round her upper arm, pumping the pressure up to 170 on the scale; and then, placing the stethoscope over the radial artery just beneath the crook of the elbow, he let the pressure off the cuff and listened for the faint swoosh, swoosh as it dropped to the point at which blood could flow once more from the upper to the lower arm. That was the upper reading of blood pressure—the highest pressure in the system. Then, continuing to lower the cuff pressure even further, he listened until the sound of each beat faded and died away to where there was continuous flow. This second point was the highest continuous pressure within the system—a much more important value, especially in pregnancy.

To his delight he managed to get Anne's blood pressure the first time he tried. When next he saw Jane he tried it out again, and noted with satisfaction the reading was just what it ought to be.

His other big medical problem was Alison, but she, too, seemed to be making good progress, testing her urine on a regular basis throughout the day, in order to establish a profile of the body sugar levels. Derek had adjusted her insulin dose so that most of the time the test showed no sugar in the urine; just occasionally a little crept in. That was good control, thought Derek, correctly. The last thing he wanted was to overcontrol her and send her into another hypo—once had been quite enough for everyone.

The only other drama of the first two or three months of Derek's medical practice was Darren, Alison's boyfriend, who had managed to fall while helping at the farm and had an intensely painful wrist. Deprived of the means to X-ray Derek could only look for what the books said were the clinical signs of a fracture—pain, angulation, swelling, tenderness, loss of function. The wrist was painful at about the level at which a watch is worn—just where it ought to be for a fracture—but fortunately there was no change in shape, though Darren's arm was intensely tender and he couldn't grip properly. Derek had been unable to find anything resembling plaster at the Health Centre and rightly assumed that, as there was no X-ray equipment there, in the past any suspected fractures would have been sent to the local hospital. While deciding what to do he put Darren in a temporary sling, then went round to Paul's house and knocked on the front door.

It took quite a time for Paul to answer it. He looked startled to see Derek, but showed him into his spacious lounge.

'Do you want Jane?' he said, slightly thickly. 'I'm sorry . . . she's not here, she's gone out.'

'I've got a problem,' said Derek. 'Darren may have broken his wrist.'

'So,' said Paul. 'Plaster it.'

Derek looked at him oddly. Paul didn't seem to be quite normal; his speech was slow and just thinking seemed to be an effort.

'It's not that easy. Before the plague anyone with a suspected fracture would have gone to the hospital for an X-ray. The Health Centre never needed to carry any plaster of Paris. It'll all be at the hospital.'

'You can get plaster of Paris anywhere. Try the builder's yard.'

'It's not as simple as that. I've been looking it up. They used plaster-impregnated bandages, wet them, then wrapped them round and round. It's not just a matter of making a plaster mould.'

Paul looked at him with a slightly stupid expression on his face. 'I don't follow, what's the problem?'

'I'm worried about going into Bedford.'

'What, d'you think the ghoulies and ghosties will get you?'

Derek gave him a look and continued. 'I'm not sure how wise it would be: whether the corpses are still infectious. Almost certainly the hospital will be where the infection was worst and if I come out with the equipment I need *plus* Legionnaires' disease and bring it back here . . .'

'Ah,' said Paul, and went silent.

'I wondered whether you'd got any ideas?'

There was another pause.

'What about?'

'Whether it's safe to go or whether there's any other way we can do it?'

Paul thought for a moment, and then thought for another

moment. For once he seemed lost for ideas—lost for words, even. Derek suddenly had his own idea anyway, and before Paul had got any further chance to answer he jumped to his feet. 'I'm sorry to have troubled you, anyway. I didn't think anybody could really give me a final answer, but I thought I would just sound you out.'

'I haven't been much help,' said Paul, 'have I?'

'I don't know that anybody can give a good answer,' said Derek charitably, wondering just what had happened to Paul. 'Are you sure you're all right? You don't sound quite right.'

'Yes, fine,' said Paul. 'I've got a bad headache, that's all. I was asleep on the couch when you knocked.'

As Derek went out through the huge iron gates he knew what he was going to do—he would make his own bandages: plaster of Paris from the builder's yard, mixed with some ordinary roll-on bandages.

It worked. It made a wonderful mess, but it worked. By the time he'd finished there was plaster on Darren, plaster on Derek, plaster in Derek's hair, and plaster all over Darren's shoes, but Darren's left arm was held in a bright white cast that had set firm and to Derek's delight appeared to be neither too loose nor too tight. The book said that *'for undisplaced Colles' fractures the wrist should be in neutral position with the back of the hand continuing the line of the back of the forearm'*. Derek had managed to get this splendidly accurate. He also had to check that the plaster had not been put on too tightly: if it were, it would constrict the blood supply to the fingers, and gangrene might set in underneath the plaster. Not wanting Darren's hand to drop off quite yet, Derek thought that he would check rather carefully, and next day was glad to find that Darren's wrist was free of pain, that he could feel his fingers and that they were pink and not obviously puffy.

Later that morning Derek bumped into Paul, striding jauntily along the street towards Dynevor.

'You've got rid of your headache then?'

'Oh yes. It was rotten. I told you it would pass. When's Jane due to see you?'

'Not for another month now.'

'All going well?'

'Fine,' said Derek, guiltily.

The Old Rectory

*T*here is something about snow that brings out the best and the worst in people. It is such delightful stuff to look at, yet such a nuisance when it gets driven into the wrong places. It fell for the first time at the end of January. The night was quiet, with little wind, and no one really noticed it fall, except for Anne, who'd gone round to visit Jane and had come back into the warmth of Dynevor stamping her feet and shaking the flakes off her coat.

During the night the clouds blew away. By next morning the sky was crystal clear, and it was really cold—too cold to make snowballs, much to the disappointment of David and Sarah who had to content themselves with tearing down one of the hills in the park on a toboggan.

The snow put paid to most of the work. It was impossible to do any farming, because the ground was frozen solid, and the only duties that could still be carried out were milking the cows, supplying them and the sheep with hay, feeding the chickens and collecting the eggs.

Three days later, Derek trudged up Holly Walk towards Martin's house in the late afternoon. The brilliance of the crisp snow radiated everywhere, obliterating the dull green of the winter grass and the brown of the mud, like a white gown spread over the countryside. It was impossible for him not to feel uplifted by the sight, even though his fingers and toes were feeling the cold greatly.

He laboured up the hill between the rhododendrons, noticing that although it had been three days since the snow had fallen there were no footprints in it at all. Martin had neither gone out, nor received any visitors. Rounding the end of the drive, Derek could see the Old Rectory in front of him, the lawns pristine white, unmarked, untouched. A rook cawed up in the woods to the side, and in the distance he could faintly hear someone playing the piano. He shivered, and looked at the sky: the sun was setting fast, and it was getting cold very quickly.

Walking to the front door with its odd elongated porchway,

he knocked on it, stamping his feet while he waited. The piano continued faintly from within the house. He knocked again, more loudly, and the music stopped. There was a shuffling noise, and then the door opened.

'Oh it's you,' said Martin, wondering whether to let Derek in to invade his isolation.

There was a pause. 'You'd better come in.'

Without central heating the hall was almost as cold as the air outside. Martin was swathed in sweaters—including the appalling green and white one he'd had when they first met. Derek followed him down a dim corridor into what previously had been the dining room, which Martin had converted into a single-room bed-sit that he was able to keep properly heated by means of its woodburning stove. A large dining-room table with the remains of several meals stood in the centre of the room, a small upright piano against the right-hand wall, a bed—unmade—on the left, and a pile of empty bottles in the corner. The whole place was a mess—if it had been a person it would have been called dishevelled. Derek couldn't think of a suitable equivalent word for an inanimate object.

Martin looked thin, pale and uneasy, as though the ice outside had descended into his heart once more. The shutters had definitely come down again since Christmas Eve. He was only just about coping, thought Derek—a man on the edge.

'What can I do for you?' said Martin finally.

'I just came to see how you were getting on.'

'Why?'

'No reason.'

Martin shrugged. 'I'm OK, I suppose. I haven't killed myself, if that's what you mean.'

'I didn't, actually. Why, were you thinking about it?'

Another shrug. 'Does it make much difference if I do or if I don't?'

'Sartre.'

A lifted eyebrow. 'You've read him?'

'A little. *"If I pass a woman on the road, ultimately it makes no difference if I give her a lift or knock her down."* '

'That sort of thing.'

There was a pause. Derek nodded towards the piano. 'I
didn't know you played . . . ?'

'A little. I don't know why I bothered to learn, though. Not
much point, really.'

'Why not? I've always wanted to do it.'

'You soon wouldn't. What was there to play for before the
plague? No one wanted to listen: if *they* wanted to hear a piece
they just put on a CD. And if *you* want to listen to it, you'd have
put on a CD as well—far quicker than trying to learn to play the
piece, and you'd never be able to play as well as a professional
pianist. The only thing a pianist is good for is accompanying the
Sunday School, singing little ditties.' Bitterly he turned to the
piano and shut the lid with a bang.

'Spoken with fervour. Do I detect a frustrated musician?'

Another shrug.

'Anyway, that's all in the past. Now we haven't got electricity,
people like you would be in demand. What were you playing?'

'Some Brahms.'

'It sounded nice. Play me some more.'

'No.'

'Why not?'

'I've only just started practising it. I found it in the music
cupboard.' He indicated a cabinet that was half open, sheets of
music dripping out of most of the drawers. Dishevelled, thought
Derek again, and tried again to think of the right word.

'Play me something else, then.'

Another shrug. 'If you want.' He sat at the piano, fiddled
around uneasily with the books of music in front of him, opened
the lid of the piano, put his hands on the keys, then took them off
again and turned round to Derek. 'Are you really sure?'

'I'm sure.'

He turned back to the piano and shrugged again, as if to say,
'Your fault if I bore you stiff.' Then he started playing.

As the music filled the room for the next five minutes, Derek
relaxed into his chair and allowed it to flow over him, letting his
mind wander. Through the window he could see the last vestiges
of the orange sunlight on the snow. The music came to an end as
the afternoon faded.

'I liked that. What was it?'

'Beethoven's *Sonata Pathétique*. The slow movement. Sounds terribly grand, but it's not difficult to play.'

'It was nice. Do you know, apart from the Carol Service, that's the first piece of music I've heard for three months.'

'Have you missed it?'

'I don't know. Yes, I suppose I have.'

'*I* haven't.'

'Why not? *You're* the musician.'

'I'm glad to get away from all the noise and bustle, all the false enthusiasm—Musak, Radio jocks, jingles, pop—I haven't missed a single one. I rather like the silence. Do you know, I'd never been able to experience silence before I came here? There was always some noise around somewhere. If it wasn't some wally with his ghetto blaster, it was an unsilenced motorbike, or an aircraft going over: rush, rush, noise, noise—like being raped with sound.'

He opened the top of the stove and put another log on, then turned and lit a candle. Outside the light had gone, leaving that curious bright darkness that comes at night when there's snow all around—a grey-white light that somehow manages to be both dark and light at the same time.

'Perhaps it's a good thing that everyone died. At least it's gone quiet.'

There was a crackle from the logs, then a silence as they both stared, unseeing in front of them, thinking of what had been.

'I can't say I'm sorry to see most of it go,' said Martin finally. 'So much fuss and bother about . . . so little, really. What's the latest sound, what's the newest fashion, will England win the Test? Will United win the Cup? And what does it matter now, anyway? What does *anything* matter, then or now?'

'Sartre again.'

'Yes.'

'Didn't you think like this before?'

'You mean before I was a priest? I don't know. Maybe I became a priest in order to try to shut up the voice within me that said the truth was just an empty silence. At least I gave the appearance of having something to believe in, something beyond to aim for. It covered up the emptiness—for a bit. But it had the silence within.'

'I thought you said you liked silence?'

'I do. But there are different sorts of silence. There's an empty silence: no meaning, no God. And there's a positive silence—space to contemplate.'

'Like noise. Noise can be positive or negative—an intrusion, a distraction—or a message. You've just *played* me some positive noise.'

Martin shrugged again then, as if regretting having opened up a little, the curtain came down again, firmly. 'Was there anything else?'

'Not really.'

'Well, you'll need to be getting back or you won't find your way in the dark.' He showed Derek to the door, bade him goodnight, then shut the door again almost before Derek had got off the step—but not before he'd glimpsed in the cold night sky the crescent moon, peeping through the trees. By its feeble light Derek crunched his way back down the driveway, chilled to the marrow.

-47-

*I*f everything was not going well for Mary and her chicken rearing, neither was the lambing going without incident. Within a month of settling in Ampthill, Neil had organised a large cattle truck to pick up a flock of sheep from a farm in Houghton Conquest and bring them to Kings Farm in Maulden where it was more convenient to look after them. Many of the ewes were carrying and in February, in the middle of the coldest weather they had so far experienced that winter, the lambing began.

Within a few days it was obvious that they had major problems. Two days after the first six lambs were born only four were left, and the morning after that there were only three. There were no dead bodies either—they had just disappeared. To Trevor this spelled only one thing, a three-letter word—*fox*. Neil and Trevor consulted, then proceeded to search the farmhouses for shotguns and cartridges.

Mary was incensed. 'How can you do such a thing?' she said to them. 'The fox is such a beautiful creature. How can you hunt it?'

'Simple,' said Neil. 'It's either that or lose all your lambs. Do you want to lose them all? Such pretty little things with nice bouncy furry white coats . . .'

'You don't worry about that when you eat them, do you?'

*   *   *

Foxes are cunning, wily creatures, capable of immense stratagems. They are not just good hunters, they are cunning and devious as well. They also enjoy killing for its own sake and that, more than anything else, was the problem. Not content just with killing a lamb to feed itself and its cubs, a fox would get what it needed, and then go on a killing spree, just for fun—a vandal in a red fur coat.

Although the farmhands lay in wait on a number of occasions, freezing cold in the February snow, they didn't kill or catch it. On the fourth day Trevor spotted it and took a pot-shot at it, but the range was too long. He succeeded in scaring it off—and possibly even wounding it—but had no certainty of a kill. They tracked it back to its earth, but without trained dogs they couldn't force the animal to the surface and kill it there and then—but at least they had scared it off for the present.

*   *   *

Surrounded by snow in the silence and solitude of the Old Rectory, Martin was gradually starting to come to terms with the new order. In point of fact, he rather enjoyed the simple life—in many ways it was a great weight off his mind not to have to think about disarmament and international affairs, and as the initial shock of his loss of faith wore off and he began to adapt to his new-found world view, he found that a certain peace descended. For one thing, without electricity and a broadcasting service, there was no foreign news. Looking back he realised how much he had been disturbed by world events, especially as the more that news made the headlines the less likely was it to be good.

Then there had been the current affairs programmes which, in attempting to be impartial, stated arguments first for one side and then for the other, so that the viewer was left feeling that there was no answer to the question and that all potential answers had always got their detractors. Even when an answer *was* given, there was always an objection, as if by statute. 'The Government has announced an initiative to cut drinking and driving . . . *but* a spokesman for . . . said it was too little, too late . . . ' 'A campaign to help . . . *but* opponents of the scheme said it will . . . ' Whatever was proposed, however good, there was always an opposing view to be heard, always a critic available, always an objection. As a result the viewer ended up feeling that there was no way forward, no way out, no way to progress, that the evil was there, and there was no answer to it. It was mind-numbing, disheartening, debilitating.

Martin had always been concerned with the welfare of others, and as a result always became upset at sad and bad news; he also found that current affairs programmes which failed to provide any answer worried him even more deeply, so much so that in the past he would often go to bed and spend a sleepless night mulling over the problems that had been discussed, yet unable to come to any conclusion because the debate had shown that there were indeed no answers. If it wasn't the Middle East, it was the Far East and if it wasn't the Far East, it was Northern Ireland and if it wasn't Northern Ireland, it was local government and if it wasn't local government it was the economy . . . He'd had a six-month respite from it and he was much the better for the rest.

In any case the human mind cannot take in everything, and Martin had assumed in his ignorance that he could and should become knowledgeable on all subjects in the news. It hadn't occurred to him that in doing this he was actually trying to become omniscient—had he been challenged, he would have said that he wanted to develop an informed opinion, so that he should know what should be done. Omniscience is not an attribute of human beings. Because TV programmes invited an opinion on all subjects, from gardening to the Gulf, Martin began to assume that one man could take it all in. He can't. Martin had tried to play at being God, and lost. Yet here again was another turn of the screw: not only was the world in a state, it was uncontrollable because no one knew what the answer was, and not only was it uncontrollable, it was uncontrollable in every direction in which he looked.

After the shock of the first week after the plague, no one really missed the media—there was too much to do, and their very existence depended upon so much hard work that they barely had time to take breath between one day and the next. There was no question of anyone having time to waste watching a moronic game show. But the winter was different: with little natural light they couldn't do much outside—not that there was much to do in the fields except look after the livestock—and it was only when the depths of the winter frost struck that the members of the community had time to relax and seek entertainment.

At first none of them had known quite what to do with the time now that there were no televisions, newspapers, radios or record players—but then a remarkable thing happened. Instead of sitting round to listen to what a handful of people in studios up and down the realm had been saying or doing, the members of the community started talking amongst themselves. They started to make their own entertainment, too, so that instead of being passive they became active again. They met and discussed things actively, either in the White Hart, which by now had become the centre of much social life in the town, or else in each other's homes: there was much more popping in to chat than ever Martin remembered, and the older ones in the community said it was like going back to the '20s and '30s.

It was helped of course by the immediate crisis they had all to face—the plague, and how to live once it had struck. Derek had put it in a nutshell. 'We English are always very quiet in public, but give us a crisis and it brings out the community spirit immediately. The only time strangers ever talk in trains is when there's a breakdown.' And all those who had experienced going to work in complete silence in crowded tube trains nodded in agreement.

Something appeared to be happening to time, too. Although the first few months had been panicked and rushed, suddenly there seemed to be much more time available. For a start, in the absence of TV and trains they had lost their need to measure time that accurately. The public clocks on the clock tower and the church no longer worked, and there was little need to wear a wristwatch. Chris and Jane in particular noticed this the most, as their jobs had had to be accurate to the nearest second: when they had worn watches, and measured time in minutes or even seconds, they were much more aware of the passing of time. The need to time appointments, or catch the news or the weather forecast on the hour, had made them all slaves to their wristwatches: they had constantly to check their watches to make sure that they weren't late—or, as so often happened, weren't *too* much behind.

Like having the media constantly to hand, constantly having time to hand is, paradoxically, a mixed blessing. The more they were aware of time, the more quickly it seemed to be going away from them.

Before the plague, all their clocks had to be regulated by reference to a common accurate clock—the pips of Greenwich Mean Time. After the plague—well, everyone's clock showed more or less the same, but as the weeks and months went and the batteries ran out, significant differences crept in and no one knew which one of them had the watch that was correct. Eventually they stopped measuring time so exactly—and because there was no need to be that accurate they went back to measuring time by the hour rather than the minute—if they had to measure it at all. In many ways they were merely going back to what had been in the 1860s, before the advent of national railway timetables had required everyone's time to be the same, from town to town. England is quite wide, east to west, and the sun reaches its zenith slightly later in Cornwall than it does in London, so until the mid-nineteenth century time was measured by the local town clock, and each town would have its own slightly different point of reference for noon. The whole point of Greenwich *Mean* Time was to take an average for the whole country so that all clocks, whether in Cornwall or London, would show the same time throughout the land at the same instant, and the only reason for this was because of the advent of the railway. Differing local times would have made a nonsense of national timetables.

Now the need for accurate time had disappeared. In particular this brought a levity to Derek's soul—days seemed that much more languourous and there really did seem to be more time to stop and stare, yet at the same time each member of the community was actually working for much longer than he had previously been accustomed to. Their time was more productive—no one wasted three hours a day commuting, for a start. Work was always on the doorstep, or nearly so.

As a result of all these influences, the life of the community became slower, more cohesive and surprisingly much more genuinely productive in an emotionally satisfying way, even if not in absolute terms of what was once called gross national output. Paul thought wryly that GNP—Gross National Productivity— really ought to be replaced by GAP—Gross Ampthill Productivity. The two didn't compare at all—with no electricity nor outside infrastructure there was no way that absolute productivity could have been maintained. But as they lived their lives more simply, they didn't necessarily need as many of the products they had previously thought indispensable. They didn't need to travel, so they didn't need cars so much—and for the most part bicycles would do. If you don't need a car you don't need to pay for one, nor for the insurance. If you don't have a car you don't need a garage; if you don't have a garage you don't have to build or maintain it . . . And round and round it went.

This same unwinding happened in all areas. Somehow productivity became less wrapped up in itself, and although it was important—they had to work hard and long to eat and keep themselves warm—there wasn't the same frenetic chasing around that had been so much a feature of the times before the plague. The net result was to give a freedom to each member of the community that he had previously never experienced before.

In short, life on the treadmill had abated—at least for a while.

-48-

'Derek, why don't we get a concert together. We could have it in the big room upstairs.' Anne and Derek were sitting in the

morning room of Dynevor House, with the wind howling outside
in the night, intermittently battering the French windows with
rain. Derek had acquired a rocking chair, and was happily
reading a book on physiology, in the candlelight.

'Have we got enough talent around?'

'Does it matter? I was thinking over what Martin said, about
how there was no point in learning to play an instrument because
there was always better quality music on the TV or the radio.
He's right. It must have been very dispiriting to find your efforts
always being unfavourably compared with the very best. Now
there's no one to compete with, so budding performers can come
out of hiding. And we could do with some entertainment.'

Derek put down his book. 'Good idea. We've got the time,
too, while it's winter. But why upstairs? Why not in the village
hall? That's got a stage.'

'Where's your brains? Heat?'

'Ah.'

'Nowhere else big enough has open hearths. It's upstairs or
nothing.'

'All right, upstairs it is. Who can we get to take part?'

'Martin?'

'I doubt if he'll want to. I can always ask him, though.
Chris plays guitar.'

'I'll ask her. I can do a song or two, I suppose.'

'Maybe all the children can do a song or a short play or
something.'

'Good idea—they'll like that.'

And so their concert evening was born. Intended as a one-
off, it was so successful that they immediately agreed to put on
another, a month later. Many of the community came—and
those who didn't wished they had, when they heard how
enjoyable an evening it had been. Martin didn't play, of
course—Derek knew he wouldn't—but he came to listen, leaving
at the end without saying a word to anyone.

Although the technical quality of their work often left much
to be desired, the performers enjoyed taking part and they were
encouraged by the obvious enthusiasm of the audience. With the
absence of TV and radio, and all other forms of recorded sound,

suddenly average performers' talents were in demand—which was very heartening.

There is something about a bad performance genuinely given that draws the listener's attention to the difficulties of a piece in a way which a good performance doesn't. Good performers always make it look easy, until you try it—like ice dancing. The real artistry doesn't become apparent until the audience realises how difficult even the most basic of the performing arts can be. Like the definition of the saxophone—an ill wind that nobody blows good—it can be remarkably difficult to get good entertainment out of mediocre instruments, average performers, and staging without lights. But it was live entertainment, and they all enjoyed it.

Martin was right about the inhibiting effect of broadcasting, too. There's something about listening to an absolutely perfect piece or watching a near-perfect demonstration of the performing arts which totally disenchants the amateur. Now, without outside competition, the amateur artistes in the community began to flower.

It wasn't just the musicians, it was the actors too. Before the plague, few would have bothered to trundle down to the local hall to see friends and neighbours stage *Private Lives* when they could see it on video, in the comfort of their own home, done in full period costume by some of the best actors in the country. Now amateur actors and actresses could also express their talents to appreciative audiences, uninhibited by unfavourable—and unfair—comparisons.

The experience changed Derek, too. In the past he'd been something of a Philistine, content to put on the odd record at Christmas, or watch a variety show on the television, without ever needing or recognising the arts to any degree. Now, when he couldn't turn them on like a tap, he began to appreciate much more the work—and more importantly, the thought—that went into each performance.

He also started to develop a sneaking respect for Martin's opinions. Even though Derek couldn't empathise with Martin's loss of faith, his emotional withdrawal, or his drinking, nevertheless he began to see that Martin often had deeper and wiser thoughts than his depressed and sometimes puerile behaviour indicated.

The first thing that hit Derek with any force was the accuracy of Martin's predictions about the way the media can subjugate when they intend to enlighten, and depress when they intend to uplift; an interesting paradox of which he increasingly became aware. Martin also seemed to have a bee in his bonnet about the importance of expressing yourself creatively, and how, through creativity, you become much more human, much less of a number. At first, Derek thought this was so much hot air, but his attitude gradually changed as he watched the way in which the musicians and actors quietly developed a much richer and more satisfying approach to life which seemed to go hand in hand with the expression of their creativity in rehearsing and performing.

But although Martin wouldn't play in public, increasingly he did so in the privacy of the Old Rectory. Gradually the release of emotion involved in playing the piano started little by little to assuage some of his inner turmoil, and he slowly began to find an emotional space in which he could move.

-49-

Winter came and went, and it was with relief that they watched the slow arrival of spring. Frost, snow and gales are all very well with a warm, sheltered, centrally heated house to go to, but a bedroom with no heating throughout the whole of winter is not always the nicest spot on earth. For many it had been their first experience of scraping ice off the *inside* of the bedroom window in the morning, though the older ones remembered doing it when they were young. No wonder four-poster beds were so popular in the past—the curtains round the bed kept what warmth there was in, and draughts out.

Coming face to face with the vagaries of the weather had come as a brutal shock to most. Those who had been accustomed to outdoor work were less bothered by the changes in season, whereas those who had previously worked indoors were the ones who noticed the weather the most, and that year they had experienced winter with a vengeance. What intrigued the former townspeople the most was the way in which the seasons and the months of year seemed to be out of sync with one another—the coldest weather came well *after* the shortest day of the year. Winter *started* at the end of the calendar year. (But then, it always had done.) By the end of January many of them were saying that the winter was over, now that the first snow had melted and the slightly longer days had come: but the worst winter weather, as usual, came in early February.

But eventually the snowdrops arrived; then March came, and with it the daffodils, heralding the arrival of shorter nights and less cold weather. The blossom on the cherry trees was followed later by a sprinkling of green on the silver birches, as though they had been showered by a large green pepperpot, and above the verge opposite Mary's bungalow a kestrel claimed a patch of territory and began hovering, searching for signs of movement in the grass below. Then it would swoop and catch the creature in its talons. It stayed in that area a lot, that spring and summer—waiting, hovering and swooping on its prey.

With the spring came the work. They had had time to draw breath in the winter, as there was little to do in the fields, but once the growing season had started they found their work was cut out. There was sowing, and planting out and weeding, *always* weeding.

If it's difficult enough to keep a garden weed-free, try doing it to a three-acre field. The townspeople among the community suddenly found out at first hand just how much effort has to go into getting a field full of cabbages, or wheat. Weeds don't stop just because there's a crop growing, and hoeing, raking and harrowing are the only ways to keep them down—unless the farmer sprays weedkiller.

Mary, with an eye on a truly green environment, objected strongly when Neil said he was going to spray the vegetables— until she tried the alternatives. Hoeing is back-breaking work; and harrowing to uproot the weeds between the lines of drilled wheat isn't very accurate, and pulls up a lot of the wheat shoots as well. But she soon had her way, because their supply of weedkiller was quickly used up.

Then all of them had to join in on the fields in a desperate struggle to get the crops to grow unhindered by weeds, and Mary began to appreciate the difficulties of rural life once more.

She wasn't the only one. Many of the former townspeople had been keen gardeners and were looking forward to using their larger gardens in the coming spring and summer. They never got a chance. There was so much to do in the fields that by the time they were finished it was dusk—and in any case, they were exhausted. So the gardens became overgrown, and the flowers untended. Not what they had imagined it would be like—not at all.

It was at about this time that their stocks of non-perishables began to run low. Candles and batteries were the first problem. Although the nights were getting shorter there was still a great need for artificial light: in April there are still ten hours of darkness. Although they had found all sorts of stores at the depot at Elstow they hadn't located any candles. They could make their own tallow candles from mutton fat—smelly things that gave a dirty brown flame and the continuous aroma of burnt mutton—but there still weren't enough to supply their needs.

Every few weeks throughout the winter and spring Paul had taken the plane on reconnaissance and 'advertising' flights, and each time there had been a small but significant response. They now knew of some five hundred survivors, not all of whom wished to move to Ampthill, and discovered to their delight that they were but one of a number of communities that had come together during that first winter: there was one group at March in Cambridgeshire, another just south of Buckingham, one at Audley End, and possibly one at the north end of Harpenden, but about this one they weren't completely sure.

However, organisation of their own community was getting progressively more difficult. With so many members it was almost impossible to initiate a project without someone objecting that he or she had not been fully consulted, or had got the butt end of the work yet again; so eventually on the Saturday after Easter the six original members met in Dynevor House to discuss what to do next.

'It's the Kevin problem again,' said Paul, bitterly.

'You've still got your knife into that lad, haven't you?' said Martin.

'No, I haven't. Lots of others think the same. Why should

he receive the same as anyone else when he does so little? Why should he still use up petrol at a greater rate than anyone else? More important, who's going to stop him, and how?' He turned away from the window, and Derek noticed, not for the first time, the hard look in his cold grey eyes, with their tiny pupils.

'It does seem that things generally are getting out of control,' said Anne. 'It was all right when the community was small and everyone could have his say, but now there are just too many people. It's just not fair if one person works all day in the fields, while another lazes around doing nothing; but no one seems to be able to do anything about it.'

'I always said communism was a non-starter,' said Paul pointedly, staring out of the window again at the plum tree that was gloriously in blossom by the garden wall.

'No, no,' said Martin, 'we're not talking about communism, we're talking about *communalism*. Having everything in common like a kibbutz . . . or the early church, come to think of it. Mind you, that didn't last long.'

'No,' said Derek, 'and I can see why. It's easy to have everything in common when you're all working together, all pulling in the same direction and all doing roughly the same amount of work, but when life gets a bit steadier and you're not fighting for survival, then there's time to think, time to do things other than work, time to sit back and have a breather; and the trouble is some people like having longer breathers than others . . .'

'I hate to say this,' said Anne, 'but I really think we're going to have to introduce some form of financial system again. We've tried with people like Kevin and we don't seem to be able to get them to respond in any meaningful way.'

Paul nodded his head. 'Absolutely. I couldn't agree more. Then there's no argument. If someone spends extra time working for the community he benefits.'

'What are we going to do about those who don't do any work at all?' asked Martin anxiously.

' "Those who don't work don't eat", ' said Paul to him. 'Isn't that what it says in the Bible?'

Martin looked at his feet and went pink. It was one of those parts that he'd always found difficult to figure out, one that was best ignored, or at worst explained away.

'That was two thousand years ago,' he said. 'We know better now.'

'Do we?' said Paul. 'You're sure that isn't one of your eternal truths?'

Martin didn't rise to the bait. Besides he had a sneaking feeling that Paul might have a point.

'You see,' said Paul, 'it isn't very honourable to those who are working hard if they only get out of it the same as everybody else, including those who hardly do anything. What about all those who've loyally looked after the sheep these past two or three months, in the cold, during the lambing, protecting them, feeding them, nurturing them—often in the middle of the night— while other people have been in their beds? *They're* the ones who have a right to be cross with people like Kevin. And when it comes down to it, we can't force Kevin to do *anything* unless we tell him that if he doesn't pull his weight he can't receive any of the benefits. "*Those who don't work don't eat.*" Simple.'

'But you *can't* do that,' expostulated Martin. 'You can't really look Kevin in the face and say "No food", can you? Can you?'

By the look on Paul's face Martin knew that he could, and, in Kevin's case, *would* take quite a delight in doing it.

Anne as usual played the mediator. 'I don't think we ought to see this as some form of personal attack on Kevin,' she said, glaring at Paul. 'We ought to keep individual personalities out of it. But I think you're right. Unless we introduce some system of payment then the whole community is going to break down: people will either refuse to work or else will keep their produce to themselves and we'll end up with the same system anyway. Far better to try to keep the community together, peaceful and orderly, rather than let it fragment angrily.'

'Do you really think it will work?' said Jane, who was sitting in the rocking chair by the fire.

'I don't think we have any option,' said Paul. 'I really don't. The present system is creaking at the seams, simply because it's too large. Communism—all right, Martin, commun*ali*sm—is all very well in a small community, but it gets unwieldy when you have more people and it's impossible with a large group. We should really have done it ages ago—well before Christmas. It would have stopped all this bother before it even started.'

'Yes,' said Martin pensively. 'I think I'm forced to agree with you, though it goes against the grain. Isn't it a pity that people just can't be trusted to work conscientiously? Do you remember what Mary said in that meeting on Christmas Day? About people being basically good, and we all ought to be able to fit together. We should, we *should*. We've got the ideal opportunity here—no social inequality, no injustices. There ought to be no problems at all. *Why* can't we fit together?'

'Basic part of human nature,' said Paul.

'What—not fitting together?'

'No. Selfishness.'

'The materialistic society? I hoped that had gone for ever with the plague. People wanting more . . .'

'No,' said Paul. 'It's the other way round. In our case its people *not* wanting to do the work that's the problem, not people wanting to do too much. The ones who do a lot are doing it for the community, or at least they are at the moment, because they're not getting anything extra for it. No, the problem at the moment is the shirkers.'

'You know what the next problem's going to be,' said Anne. 'What do we do about those who say they deserve more money for what they do? Before we know where we are we'll be back to strikes and theft and a system of law and somebody to make the laws and judges and juries and . . . Oh, it doesn't seem worth it,' and she poked at the fire angrily.

'What doesn't seem worth it?' said Derek.

'People. We could have so much here, so much happiness, so much pleasure, so much companionship, so much enjoyment and what have we got? People not pulling their weight, people who are envious of what others get, people who have tried to steal.'

'You mean the raiders?' said Derek. 'They've been gone a long time.'

'No, I didn't mean the raiders,' said Anne, pointedly. 'I mean the people who don't work. They're the ones who are stealing—stealing from those who *are* working. Yet we don't seem to be able to encourage people to do what they ought to do. Why? *Why* can't people live in peace? Why can't people see that it's more sensible for each to do his own share? You're doing your own share, learning about medicine.'

'Yes,' said Chris, who had so far remained silent, 'but even so there are one or two who are saying that Derek's not really working at all and having an easy time, just reading.'

'They ought to see him,' said Anne, eyes blazing. 'They ought to see how many hours a day he puts in. Learning is hard work. It doesn't come easily. Who is it, who's been saying it?'

'I really don't think it matters,' interjected Derek, diffidently, anxious not to make a scene.

'No, I want to know,' said Anne. 'I want people to know just how much my husband is working. You were talking earlier about the people looking after the sheep. Well, I don't see Derek for fourteen hours a day. That's how much time he spends on it; and he worries about it a lot, the thought that he might end up injuring someone: and this is all the thanks he gets.'

'I really think you're overreacting, Anne,' said Derek quietly. 'They'll understand sooner or later.'

'No, they won't,' said Anne. 'They'll look at what you do and think it only took a few moments to work out what was the matter and prescribe something for it. It only took fifteen minutes to patch up that twisted ankle, or that infected finger. They won't think of all the time you've spent, studying just to get it right. They won't think of the worry you have. They won't think of *any* of it when they actually come to see you.'

Derek was silent.

'I had a friend once who was an electrician,' said Chris. 'My mother took a broken radio to him. He looked at it, fiddled with it for a quarter of an hour, tweaked one or two of the screws, handed it back to her in full working order and charged her £4.00. "That's an awful lot for just turning a couple of screws," she said. "All right," said the electrician, "I'll itemise the bill. For tweaking the screws in your radio set, four pence. For knowing which ones to tweak, and in what direction and how far, £3.96." I've always remembered that.'

'Skill is something you pay for as well as overtime,' said Paul. 'You have to pay for the time spent acquiring expertise as well as the time spent using it.'

'Talking of time spent acquiring skills,' said Derek. 'If we're all going to have to work for money again, what are you going to do about me?'

'We'll fix something up,' said Paul. 'You needn't worry about that.'

'No, I want to know now. Are you expecting I'll have to pay the money back?'

'Oh no,' said Chris, anxious not to have her plans for Derek destroyed almost before they'd begun, 'it's up to the community to pay for you to learn medicine.'

'All right then,' persisted Derek. 'Once I've "qualified" what fees am I going to charge and who should get the money for them? Me or the community?'

'Presumably you ought to get the same rate per hour as anybody else.'

'Fine by me,' said Derek, 'but I wonder whether the shepherds will want to get the same as everybody else when they're out in the fields at two o'clock in the morning, helping with the lambing.'

'I think we're getting into very deep water,' said Anne.

'And all because of Kevin,' added Paul.

'No,' said Anne, 'it isn't all because of Kevin. It's because of what you said before—human nature: people being selfish, not prepared to pull their weight, not prepared to trust each other or, if they do trust each other then finding that the other person isn't trustworthy. I don't have Mary's faith in human nature. Mine is a much more pragmatic approach.'

They fell silent. Anne turned and poked the fire again in an off-hand way.

'Our second problem is a purely practical one,' said Jane. 'We're running out of candles and batteries.'

'And I really ought to try to get some anaesthetic equipment,' said Derek with a slight glance at her, sitting by the fire, heavily pregnant. 'Just in case. All we need is someone to have a good-going fracture, fall out of a tree, come off a bike, that sort of thing—and we really will be back to the days of the old barber-surgeons.'

'Where do you think you can get it?' asked Paul.

'I don't know,' said Derek, 'that's the problem. I know we all ran the gauntlet of the corpses when we escaped from the plague, but I'm still not really convinced that we're safe to go into Bedford or Luton and that's where the hospitals are.'

'What are you most bothered about?' said Paul. 'Because we thought about this before we made our dash out of Docklands.'

'What worries me is whether the organism remains infectious inside the body after death. And whether, as the corpse decomposes, they get liberated and blown around by the wind, or spread by rats, cats or dogs. Once the corpses have decomposed completely I'm sure we'll be all right, but it's been winter, and cold, and although we've had some hot days I'm sure that there's a lot more than just bones still left on many of the bodies. I don't think it's fair on the others for us to go into Bedford and then come back.'

'Maybe we could request a volunteer to go into Bedford, get what we need and then stay outside the community for a few days until we're sure that there's no infection left,' said Jane.

'Yes, we could do that,' said Derek, 'but then is it fair to send somebody right into the middle of infection in a hospital? And who're we going to send? Shall I go?'

'No,' said Jane, wide-eyed. 'No, you will not. I need you. In about three months' time, rather badly—remember?'

'Well, who can we send?' asked Derek. 'I doubt if anybody else will know what an anaesthetic machine looks like. *I* hardly know what I'm looking for anyway.'

'Why don't we go to London?' said Paul, suddenly.

'You must be joking,' said Martin.

'Never more serious. London's empty in the middle— deserted. The bodies only start as you get near to the North Circular—from the inside, that is.'

'Aren't you overlooking one slight problem?' said Derek. 'Getting there in the first place?'

'No,' said Paul, innocently.

'What are you up to?' asked Jane.

'Simple. Why don't we fly in?'

'What?' said Derek.

'Yes. Fly in.'

'And land in one of the Royal parks?' said Anne. 'What if you hit something and turn over?'

'Much easier than that. I'd land at the Docklands Airport.'

They all looked at each other.

'That's absolutely brilliant,' said Martin.

Anne—practical Anne—had other ideas. 'Wait a minute.

What are you going to do when you're there—and more importantly, how are you going to get anything out? That aircraft won't carry much luggage.'

'No, but we could take a couple of bicycles. They're light; we could dismantle them and put them behind the seats: then we could cycle around the centre of London and find where the things we need are likely to be. If we find what we're looking for, *then* we can think of a way to get in to them.'

'And if we can't find what we need?'

'We won't have wasted too much time trying to get into the centre of London through a pile of what may or may not be dangerous corpses.'

There was a pause while they all considered it.

'Yes,' said Anne. 'That has definite possibilities.'

They settled down to make more detailed plans, and make lists of what they needed to get, but Martin fell silent. There was something bothering him, but he didn't know what. The idea that had come into his subconscious that previous Christmas Eve had been tickled into life again. An unformed sense of unease began tugging at him, but he didn't know what it was. It was something someone had said. It wasn't about the plane—he knew that—but there was something, *something* that was niggling in the background and he couldn't quite identify it.

Derek, too, had the same sensation, but for completely different reasons, and he too couldn't identify what was troubling him either.

It was something connected with Paul—what he'd said or done. He couldn't put his finger on it.

It was irritating.

-50-

*E*arly the next day Derek and Paul took off from Cranfield, having first loaded two bikes and some extra cans of fuel into the small space at the back of the cockpit. As usual they flew low in order to see the countryside below more clearly and to try to pick

out any signs of life. In particular they went directly over
Harpenden, but either there was no one there, or else they
somehow missed the postulated community, for they saw nothing.

As the plane droned southwards the countryside below
looked peaceful, with green shoots of wheat springing into life in
the fields and the lusher green of the meadows that had been
sown with grass, which was waving gently in the light breeze. It
was too early for the oil-seed rape to show its brilliant yellow,
but Derek could see that the fields sown with it were
considerably darker than the rest.

Most of the time they followed the M1 into London.
Although Paul knew how to fly, Derek didn't know how to
navigate and they both found it safer to follow the roads they
both knew so well. Going down the M1 was more or less going
straight into the heart of London anyway, and if it wasn't as
direct a line as it could have been, at least it was safe.

Although all the motorway junctions were blocked there
were long clear stretches with only the occasional crashed
vehicle, but as they began to pass over the northern outskirts of
London a wasteland of metal appeared beneath them—line upon
line of cars, immobile. When they came to the North Circular
they changed direction to follow it round, clockwise, but
nowhere was there any respite from the constant glint of sunlight
off windows and roofs of abandoned cars, and no hint of any
break in the traffic that might allow a vehicle access to the inner
part of London.

The previous October Paul had managed to get out of
London by a most circuitous route, and he was not sure that he
would be able to retrace his movements. Although he knew
exactly where he had crossed the North Circular road—at the
Hammersmith flyover—whether he could manage even to find
his way to the outer side of the flyover was quite another matter,
and looking at the maelstrom of cars below him he rather
doubted it. Getting back into London might prove even more
difficult than getting out had been.

They flew above the North Circular road until they came to
the Thames, but it was no good. There were no breaches in the
solid wall of traffic. They gave up, and turned eastwards: soon
Derek could see in front of them the runway of the Docklands

Airport crammed in among the houses and buildings. Although the strip was short for commercial aircraft, it was ample for the Jodel and Paul was able to land in less than half the available runway length. They pulled off the runway, parked the aeroplane, stopped the engine, got out stiffly and listened.

Silence.

Nothing stirred except for the seagulls. No sign of life: the city was just as they had left it—dead.

They assembled the bikes, then closed up the cockpit. Just to be on the safe side, Paul had brought a chain which he locked round the joystick, holding it firmly in the fully pulled-back position. They didn't want to end up stranded fifty miles from home with the prospect of having to find their way out of the city again.

Then having secured the plane against the unlikely prospect of thieves, mounting the bikes they cycled out of the airport and into the street. Thankfully the roads were almost completely empty of bodies, but Derek noticed how much more decomposed the few bodies were in comparison with those he had seen in Leighton Buzzard six months earlier. Many were no more than bones and hair with the occasional bit of skin. He preferred not to look at them.

Cycling to the City proved an easy journey. The weather was mild, but not too hot and with no traffic to get in their way, neither moving nor stationary, they made exceptionally fast progress. Their first port of call was to the area just north of Oxford Street, in the region around Portland Square: in the past Derek remembered seeing a number of shops there which sold medical instruments. He was right. They found several, and with the aid of Paul's cold chisel Derek was able to take a good look round. In the third shop he found what he was looking for—a complete anaesthetic trolley, with gas bottles, hand-pumped balloons and so on.

'That's the one,' he said. Paul mentally weighed up the chances of getting it home in the plane.

'No way,' he said. 'It's far too heavy—and bulky. Especially the gas cylinders. We couldn't possibly fly that thing out of here.'

It was what Derek had expected, but he made a point of

searching through the rest of the shop and found one or two other items of interest which were portable—a pair of Neville-Barnes forceps and a set of Keilland's forceps, both for use in maternity work, together with ten big packets of scalpel blades.

Their next port of call was Dillons Bookshop on Gower Street, about half a mile away. Although the Health Centre had a large number of medical textbooks, they tended to be on applied medicine rather than on pre-clinical subjects such as anatomy, physiology or biochemistry and Derek was desperately in need of a comprehensive pharmacology textbook. The shop was vast and dark. There was a list of departments on the wall by the staircase: an index to a shop, thought Paul. The medical section was down the iron staircase opposite, deep in the bowels of the basement. Here it was pitch-black; row upon row of books greeted them, glinting dull and yellow in the feeble light of their torches.

'Look at all this,' exclaimed Derek, excitedly running his fingers over the shelves and pulling down book after book.

'Hang on—there's a limit to what we can take, even if it's only books. Take one or two that you must have now, and we'll come back another day for the rest. Even if we can't bring a lorry, at a pinch we could always fly in again.'

'These will do for the moment,' said Derek, picking out one obstetrics and one pharmacology textbook. He waved the former in front of Paul. 'Specially for Jane.'

Next was the problem of the candles.

'Harrods?' suggested Paul.

'Could be.'

They must have made the oddest pair of visitors ever to that elite establishment—two trouser-clipped travellers who'd ridden there on bicycles and who were now using torches to illuminate the inner recesses of the store. There had been looting, but the thefts had been of goods that no longer had any real value in the post-plague world. Nobody had looted the candles, but it was obvious that much jewellery and other precious objects had been filched. Much good may it do them, thought Paul bitterly. The looters were probably all dead anyway, clutching their precious stones. Strange how something that is of immense value one moment suddenly ceases to have any worth apart from mere curiosity value. 'What a nice brooch!' thought Paul, 'Must have been worth two thousand pounds before the plague. Here, I'll swap it for a box of candles.' The old adage of 'you can't take it with you' was being revamped in front of their eyes. Things that were once precious had become worthless overnight now that a different set of priorities had supervened. In a world without electricity, electrical goods are worse than useless—they simply clutter up the space.

Nevertheless, they roved round the store looking at items that Derek would never have been able to afford in the past—and that neither of them wanted at all now, with a few exceptions. Paul had always fancied a good camera, but had never got round to equipping himself properly. He was just about to pick up a really expensive Nikon when Derek looked him in the eye and said, 'What about the film processing?' and suddenly Paul felt rather stupid.

'I could always use black and white. Set up my own dark room.'

'Yes,' said Derek pleasantly, 'and how are you going to power the enlarger?' Suddenly the Nikon was not a good idea at all and Paul put it down again. Maybe he'd pick it up some other time when the world was a little more organised.

They went through the other departments. The electrical goods were all useless, of course—the CDs, the televisions, the wall-to-wall stereos. The suits and other clothes were worth taking, but they were getting short of time and decided against trying anything on.

'We can always come back with a lorry,' said Derek finally. 'Maybe we ought to get a proper order book up. What about candles?'

They found some eventually, but they were mainly ornate ones, the sort that you put on the mantelpiece, but never light. What they needed were ordinary wax candles, and lots of them. They couldn't find any, and it was starting to get late.

'Sorry to disturb your plans,' said Paul, 'but we'll have to leave soon. We can't possibly fly into Cranfield in the dark, and we ought to take off by five at the latest.'

'We're probably looking in the wrong place,' said Derek. 'This is just the time when you want to ask a shop assistant where to go for that elusive item and she says "Try Tweedledums in Loughton Street . . ." '

'Why is it that there's never a shop assistant around when you want one?' said Paul, wryly looking round. 'Where can we get candles from?'

'We'd be better off at an ironmonger's in the East End.'

'You're probably right.'

They cycled back towards Docklands, through the City and into the East End, stopping at all the hardware shops on the way. They didn't find a single big supply, but most of the smaller shops had a few boxes lying around and they reckoned that a quick tour of the area with a lorry ought to provide a sizeable quantity to take back with them.

They got back to the airport at quarter to five. Paul's chaining of the joystick had proved either unnecessary or effective—presumably the former—because everything was exactly as they had left it. They filled the petrol tank from the jerrycans they'd brought with them, then dismantled the bicycles and stowed them behind the seats. Just before five o'clock Paul taxied onto the runway and then took off into the setting sun.

-51-

'*E*verything we need is there,' said Derek. 'It's just getting to it that's the problem.'

'You'd need something big to carry out the amount of stuff we saw,' added Paul. 'We couldn't do it with the plane; even a car would be too small; and if we were to take a lorry we'd never get it through the North Circular. We only just managed to squeeze the Porsche through on the way out.'

Outside Dynevor House the rain was falling, spattering the windows and stimulating the carp in the ornamental pool. Martin looked gloomily out of the French windows. The blossom on the plum tree was beginning to fall, making a white carpet on the ground.

There was a long silence while they thought, and the more they thought, the worse it got.

'So near and yet so far,' said Chris. 'Surely there must be a way. What about a helicopter? Didn't you say there was one at Cranfield?'

'Yes,' said Paul, 'but I don't know how to fly helicopters and I'm not practising now. I might just shoot up to two thousand feet, stay there and not know where the reverse gear was.'

'What about moving the cars out of the way with a JCB?' asked Jane.

'Too many of them. It's a long-term solution. If we ever wanted to use London again I suppose we'd have to, but it would take ages. In any case, we'd have to go past all those bodies, and as we said last time, we don't want to do that just yet.'

'Are you sure you checked all the crossings on the North Circular?' ventured Chris in desperation.

'Every last one of them. For good measure we even went round the South Circular on the way back. The whole lot's absolutely solid.'

Silence.

'It's a pity we're not on the Thames, upriver,' observed Martin mildly, looking at the carp. 'Then we could float down on a boat.'

'*But we are*,' said Anne suddenly. They all looked at her as though she'd gone mad. 'We *are*. We can go down the Grand Union Canal. It goes straight into the heart of London.'

It was so obvious that even Anne wondered why they'd not thought of it before. Discoveries are easy. Afterwards.

*   *   *

Forty-eight hours later two boats set out from Linslade. They didn't use *Willow* because—if nothing else—its sewage tank hadn't been pumped out since the Jones family had left it after their holiday and it was, well, just a little high. The normal method of emptying it uses a custom-built electric suction pump, so there wasn't much they could do about it, but in any case *Willow* was one of the smaller craft and as they wanted the largest storage space they could get, instead they took *Amethyst* and *Coral*.

Although the community didn't like to lose their doctor, they decided Derek really had to go on the trip, firstly because he knew how to steer and operate narrow-boats, and secondly,

because only he knew precisely what was wanted in the way of
books and medical equipment. To ensure they had enough
stowage space they took two boats, and Anne was the obvious
choice to steer the second. There was another reason: the whole
family wanted to go along on the trip. They hadn't been home
since starting on their holiday a week before the plague. Their
old home was only a quarter of a mile from the canal, and if it
looked safe and there weren't too many bodies about, they hoped
to moor the boat nearby so they could pick up some of their
personal belongings.

Jane also wanted to go, despite being six months pregnant.
She was anxious to go back to their flat—and besides she rather
fancied the idea of wandering through Harrods and having the
pick of their boutiques. She also felt safer knowing that Derek
was near at hand, just in case.

The last member of the party was Peter, who, true to form,
had come along to act as ship's mate, chief cook, bottlewasher
and stevedore. Any activity was better than none, and with
Dynevor House closed up for a time, there was little point in his
staying behind in his cottage in Church Square.

From Linslade, the Grand Union Canal goes towards London,
but the lie of the land forced its builders to go off to the west,
almost to Slough, before coming in to London. At London the
canal divides, one arm going to the River Thames at Brentford,
the other going round the north of London, through Little Venice
at Paddington, along the Regent's Canal through Regent's Park,
and on to Bethnal Green, finally entering the Thames at
Limehouse.

Their first plan was to take the Brentford arm, moor
somewhere near the centre of Osterley and walk from there to
their house. However, with fifty-six-foot boats they might well
not be able to turn in the canal. If they couldn't they would have
to go out into the Thames at Brentford, turn the boats round and
come back in again, a procedure which Derek was quite
concerned about. A canal is essentially a very elongated pond
with little or no current and navigating a narrow-boat on it is not
too difficult: but narrow-boats don't have keels and the Thames
at Brentford is tidal. Whilst narrow-boats are quite safe on
moving water if the skipper knows what he's doing, Derek was

not sure whether he had enough experience to be safe in tidal waters, and in any case they didn't know if the final lock into the Thames was electrically or mechanically powered. They might get all that way and find that they couldn't even get into the Thames. Narrow-boats can't be reversed—they go backwards all right, but they can't be guided properly—and the thought of pulling a fifty-six-foot narrow-boat six miles, backwards, to Cowley Peachy Junction, and up twelve locks in the process, did not amuse him. Eventually Derek put his foot down and refused to go down the Brentford section.

Instead, the whole family took bicycles, perched on the roof. There was no difficulty about this—in the days before the plague many a seasoned traveller on the canals used precisely this method to ensure that when he got to his mooring point for the night he was still mobile enough to get to the local pub, or explore the countryside in the immediate vicinity.

So they modified the plan. They would stop at West Drayton and cycle the six miles to their house either on the roads, or, if these were jammed, along the towpath. After this they would go on into central London and find a lorry to collect all the goods they needed and transport them back to the narrow-boats.

Derek led on *Amethyst* with Paul, Jane and Alison on board, and Anne followed, steering *Coral*, which held David, Peter and Sarah. As the two boats left the conurbation of Leighton Buzzard they immediately entered open countryside, rising slowly, lock by lock, to the Chiltern Hills. Travelling by canal had the same timeless quality about it as they had experienced on their holiday. It could have been before the plague, twenty years earlier or even —apart from the diesel engines thudding away underneath the stern—a hundred and fifty years before. They passed through the countryside, watched gloomily by the occasional cow, startled by their intrusion into its life after six months of complete calm. Soon they passed Marsworth Junction, then shortly afterwards the Wendover arm branched off on the right-hand side after a flight of seven locks.

At Berkhamsted the canal rose through five locks, running parallel to the main street along the length of the hill on which the town is situated. Berkhamsted was the first real town that they came to: shortly afterwards they encountered Hemel

Hempstead, after which they went through a gentle valley in which nestled Kings Langley and Abbots Langley with only the massive bridge carrying the M25 over them to remind boaters which century they were in. It hung over their heads, silent and ghostly, a remnant of the past, a vast frozen animal striding across their path and casting a gloomy shadow onto the boat. Shortly after passing the bridge they moored for the night, well satisfied with their progress.

The following morning they set off early, and immediately went back to the year 1805 for a few more miles: but Uxbridge marked the end of the countryside and from then on kept them firmly in the present day. Two miles further the Brentford arm split off at Cowley Peachy Junction and there they moored, in front of some old cottages.

The plan was for Paul, Jane, Peter and Sarah to stay with the boats while Derek and his family tried to reach their house. They weren't going to try too hard: if their way was blocked they would simply return. They could always come back on another occasion. It wasn't going to go away in the meantime.

Derek made an initial reconnaissance of the roads, but there were far too many cars, and more importantly, far too many bodies—so they chose the next best option which was to cycle the six miles to Osterley along the towpath. They had an uninterrupted journey and encountered no bodies—no one in their right mind flees from a plague along a towpath.

At Osterley they ascended from the towpath to the adjoining road, at a bridge. Thankfully they encountered few bodies in the street and were able to cycle the last few hundred yards with no trouble. Within a short time they were standing in front of their old house, in the middle of an attractive nineteenth-century terrace.

It was strange standing there in the quiet. They'd never known Isleworth without noise. Although their house was not on a truly main road it had been busy enough, with an almost constant thunder of traffic. In the absence of the low rumble of vehicles they were suddenly very aware of the high-frequency sounds—of the birds; of the branches and twigs rustling in the trees; of the gate creaking in the wind; of the tiny whisper the leaves of the plants in the garden made as they rustled together.

Anne wondered what the children were thinking. David was

trying to be brave, but from time to time his lower lip started to quiver. Alison was much more obviously affected and Derek could see a tear trickling down from the corner of her right eye as she surveyed their neighbours' houses, thinking of the people who'd lived there and who'd been so much a part of their life; the Jennings next door, old Mrs Kennedy in the little house at the end of the terrace, the Smiths with their two young children on the other side and Robert and Henry, the teenage sons of the McDonalds, at the far end of the terrace.

There and then Derek decided that they were not going to see what had happened in any of the other houses. The memories would have to be sufficient.

Treading on the weeds that had grown in the intervening six months, they walked down their own front path, looking at the straggly strip of grass and the unpruned rose bushes. Derek opened the front door and they entered the house, familiar yet strange, cold, damp, yet precisely as it had been when last they had seen it. Thankfully they had not had looters.

Alison went through to the kitchen at the back and looked through the window, then gave a little cry and turned away. On her right, in the garden of the house that had once held the Smiths and their family were two pathetic little heaps that had once been children. Anne put her arm round Alison.

'It would have been very quick,' she said. Alison nodded wordlessly, the tears running down her cheeks. It had been difficult thinking about her friends and neighbours when she had been in Ampthill, but then the sense of not knowing had distanced her from the misery. Now she could see, and now she knew. She had never really thought there would be any other answer, but the grim finality of it made the emptiness of it even more desolate.

Suddenly they all wanted to get away from the house that had once been their home. It held many memories, but now it was too silent. In Ampthill they had never known what had gone before, had nothing to compare their present state with. Here it was different. This was the house to which Anne and Derek had brought their first child, fourteen years before. This was the house in which, a year later, David had been conceived and to which in turn he had been brought back from the maternity hospital. This was where they had grown up, and where Derek had nursed his ageing mother until she died. The house had been the centre of their life, of their family, of everything they had lived for—and suddenly they wanted to get away from it. It had too many memories, and it too had died.

Suddenly they were not sure that they wanted to take any mementos: it might be better to leave the past behind completely. But they knew that if they didn't take their more precious things, sooner or later they would regret it. So each quickly filled his rucksack with the things most dear and irreplaceable; the photograph albums, the last letters from friends and relatives, the special gifts. After a lot of thought Derek took his address book, just in case.

They took the physical mementos too—the carriage clock that had been a wedding present, the brooch that had been Anne's mother's, and her grandmother's before her. Alison took two of her favourite books and her old doll, David his roller boots and his stamps.

Then, loaded up with their mementos, they went outside and shut the door behind them. The contents of four rucksacks is not a lot to take to show for a whole life, but there was nothing else that was worth taking. All the books they had could be obtained in the library in Ampthill; there was no point in taking their record collection—there was nothing to play it on. Nor did they need any clothes—they could get all the clothes they wanted, and more, from the deserted shops.

Behind them they left thousands of pounds' worth of things that were now of no value whatsoever; things that Derek had spent so long working to pay for—the house and its mortgage, the loans that bought the furniture when they were first married, the carpets, the clothes, the books, the records, the stereo, the television—all were suddenly valueless. They couldn't take them, and they didn't need them because they could have their pick of any of those things in Ampthill. The really valuable things, the really irreplaceable things were all the personal effects, the ones imbued with memories.

And so, as they closed the door, they left behind them a lifetime's work, a lifetime's earning, and a lifetime's memories.

Maybe they would come back some time in the future—and

maybe they wouldn't. If they did, everything would be there for them, just as they had left it—the chairs, empty in front of the fireplace, the dining-room table bare, the beds upstairs unslept in, the garden gradually reverting to its wild state.

Suddenly they were glad to be outside again and they found themselves pedalling as fast as they could back to the towpath as though pursued by all the ghosts and demons from hell. Without exception they wanted to leave behind the nightmare of what had once been and was no more.

*   *   *

Not two hundred yards away from their once-beloved family house another bundle lay on the ground, slowly decomposing, surrounded by feathers and pigeon droppings. No one, dead or alive, knew of the important, if unintended, part he'd played in the events of the past six months. When the evacuation of London had begun, Bob Harris, chief handyman and fitter at Southill Hospital, had stayed put. He couldn't have left his pigeons—not for anything.

*   *   *

They didn't remember much of the journey back to the boats. Jane, who'd been cooking in the galley, heard them first, came up on deck, took one look at their faces and exclaimed, 'Whatever's the matter?'

Derek told her. 'It never crossed my mind just how difficult it would be. I thought it would be like going home, but it was like going to another planet. It's all right going through areas that you don't know, but when it's your own street . . . '

'We saw the next-door neighbour's children,' whispered Alison, tears filling her eyes again, 'in their garden . . . ' Sarah, conscious of the emotion but not really understanding what had provoked it, sidled up to Anne and squeezed her hand.

'I'm glad you didn't die, Auntie Anne,' she said and gave her a kiss on the cheek. Anne smiled through her tears, and gave her a kiss back.

'Thank you Sarah. I'm glad you feel like that.'

Dusk was falling as they replaced their bikes on the roofs of the boats, and then boarded *Coral* for the meal Paul and Jane had

prepared. The craft was lit from the batteries that were charged
when the diesel engine was running, and it was a strange
experience to be able once again to put on lights with a flick of a
switch. It was too much like home used to be, the home that they
had just left empty and desolate . . . Anne began to wish that she
had never come, but then checked herself. After all, she'd been
able to pick up all the family mementos, the only irreplaceable
objects in the world as far as she was concerned.

The meal was a silent one. Jane was a good cook, but
somehow they didn't notice what they were eating: their
thoughts were too much in the past, and with what they'd seen.
Each of them felt terribly lonely, much as Martin had felt in the
vicarage that first awful night. For them it was the first time they
had been anywhere familiar that had been touched by the plague
and the contrast was too awful to contemplate.

They washed up in silence too, then went back to *Amethyst*.
Derek and Anne tried to read for a bit, and David idly toyed with
a game he'd rescued from his room, but their hearts were not in it
and they soon went to bed.

In the darkness, with the lights out, and the gentle rocking of
the boat on the water, Derek and Anne tried to sleep but their minds
were too active. In the other cabin they could hear Alison and
David quietly sobbing, until eventually they all fell unconscious.

About eleven o'clock a wind blew up and rain began to fall
heavily on the metal roof, and that night the tears of those inside the
boat mingled with the tears of nature outside as they all wept
together in sympathy for what had happened to the world.

-52-

A night's sleep often gives a different perspective, as though
the memories have been rearranged so that the emotional sting is
taken away. The next day was quite different: even the rain
clouds had blown away.

Jane and Paul had already revised their plans. Unlike Derek

and Anne their original flight had been from their own home, so they had already brought some of their personal effects. After seeing the effects of returning on the others, they soon decided that they had no further need to go back to the flat and would content themselves with the memory of how it used to be.

As it transpired, however, fate was not to let Jane off the hook that lightly.

Shortly after sunrise they breakfasted, and then casting off the mooring lines, began the slow four-mile-an-hour journey towards the centre of London. Soon a plethora of brilliantly painted craft greeted them; then they passed a white-painted lock cottage and under a beautiful Regency cast-iron bridge painted in blue and picked out in white, and they found themselves at Little Venice, a picturesque, triangular area of water with a central island, the whole area surrounded by tall residential buildings. Immediately they turned right into Paddington Basin, overshadowed by the yellow and red bulk of St Mary's Hospital, and moored at the north quay, the nearest point they could get to Oxford Street.

As with the plane, they locked up the boats—just in case— took the bikes off the roofs, and with empty rucksacks on their backs made for the shopping centre. The plan was to purloin a lorry to help carry the merchandise, but the streets were empty of suitable vehicles: there were cars here and there, but no lorries. Peter began to wonder how they would transport the things they needed without a vehicle.

He needn't have worried. Outside Harrods a delivery lorry, in Harrods' spectacular livery, was standing by the back of the store, and amazingly the keys were still in it. Peter looked in, half expecting to see a corpse huddled in the front seat, but the cab was empty. Perhaps the driver had left the vehicle for a moment—or more likely had been taken short coughing, got out, staggered a short way and then collapsed and died. He turned the key and on the second attempt the lorry started.

Although a visit to Harrods was on the list of destinations, it wasn't their first priority, and, loading the bikes into the back of the van, they set off to pick up the medical equipment that Derek had located earlier that week. The anaesthetic trolley proved heavier than expected and it needed two of them, straining, to load it into the van.

The next port of call was the bookshop where, under Derek's watchful eye, they gathered book upon book—pictorial atlases of anatomy, books on surgical techniques, on osteopathy, on allergies, orthopaedics, paediatrics. Whether he'd need any or all of them Derek didn't know, but at least if he'd got them up at Dynevor House they'd be available for reference if needed— warm, dry and undecaying.

Then it was time to go 'shopping' at Harrods. It felt odd to be stealing, and yet not stealing, from the most famous shop in the world. With the pick of the world's goods available to them they loaded everything they could think of into the van, especially those items that they couldn't get locally. But they chose carefully. Harrods is not noted for its downmarket approach, and it seemed silly to take up space with expensive, flimsy and totally impracticable clothing when what they really needed was warm, weatherproof working clothes.

Two hours later the van was full, and returning to Paddington Basin they loaded their booty on to *Coral*. Then they went hunting for batteries and candles, working their way slowly towards the East End. On the way they stopped outside several interesting-looking shops, the most useful of which proved to be an Army surplus store from which they retrieved lots of anoraks, heavy boots, thick sweaters and the like.

Candles were still a problem, but as they had found on their previous trip, by stopping at every ironmonger's in sight they were able progressively to load up with them. One shop had paraffin lamps: Paul decided to take them as well. They might well prove useful.

Two hours later the van, weighed down by another exceptionally heavy load, worked its way slowly back to Paddington Basin, this time to load up *Amethyst*. Then they made a third trip to collect more candles, returning just before dusk to load the boats for the last time.

*   *   *

Over dinner in *Coral* surrounded by cardboard boxes, clothes, books and paraffin lamps, Anne was pensive, though the others had enjoyed their day. Jane obviously had not been able to take much part in the physical exercise of loading and

unloading the lorry, but had rather enjoyed flitting around
Harrods, effectively with a blank cheque, as had the children.
David had come away with a saxophone and the most expensive
set of roller boots he could lay his hands on, whilst Derek had
discovered what expensive tastes his daughter had in perfume.

Paul, who'd been trying to attract Anne's attention for
several minutes without success, eventually waved his hand up
and down in front of her face. She started and looked at him.

'Sorry, I was miles away.'

'Penny for them.'

'I was just wondering if London will ever come back to life
again. All that history—and suddenly it's the dead centre of
England. The Houses of Parliament, Buckingham Palace,
Whitehall, the pictures in the National Gallery and the Tate, the
treasures in the British Museum and its Library, the Tower of
London—are we going to be the last to see them? What's
London going to do? Is it just going to decay and disintegrate?'

She fell silent and picked up her fork again.

'I'm sure it won't,' said Derek gently. 'It's the natural
centre of England. Like Rome, all roads lead there. It'll start up
afresh again, you'll see. All it needs is a bit of determination to
clear a path through the cars.'

'*We* didn't think it was possible, did we?'

'No,' said Paul. 'We didn't say that at all. We didn't think
it was *practical*. It certainly wasn't appropriate to carve a way in
just to get our hands on a few dozen boxes of candles, but if
you're going to use the place as a city once again, then a few men
with JCBs, and a bit of determination will carve a route into the
centre quite easily.'

'But who will want to live here?' asked Anne. 'What is there
to live for? Look around you. It's all pavements and concrete.
Londoners were never living on the earth, they were on a raft of
cement and stone. You can't grow anything here; you can't keep
farm animals. Everybody had to come here because it was the
centre—and it was the centre because everyone came here. It
would have been much more logical to disperse its industry out to
the provinces instead of having eight million people all trying to
get into the city to work at eight o'clock in the morning, and all
eight million going back on the same carriages and trains at five

o'clock the same afternoon. What an artificial life.'

'A black hole for people,' murmured Derek.

'A what?' said Paul.

'I know,' said David, looking up from fitting together the sax. 'Can I tell him, Dad? A black hole is a collapsed star, which is so big and so dense that its gravity is so strong that nothing can ever get out, even light, and it goes around sucking material in, getting bigger and bigger all the time.'

'Well done,' said Derek. 'I didn't know you knew about black holes.'

David bent down and pulled out a book from beneath his seat. *A Voyage Round the Cosmos*, it said on the front cover. 'I got this from the bookshop while you were down in the basement.'

'What did you say London was?' asked Anne.

'A black hole for people. Quite apt, really,' said Paul.

'Sad, but true,' said Derek. 'Having to live off the land directly has made me realise just how artificial civilisation can get. If you take away the administrative function and the tourists, there's precious little left in London. No port any longer, no farming, some industry, but mainly offices of headquarters—plus industries servicing all the people who come in to work at the offices . . . And everybody has to commute in because that's where the offices are, and everybody wanted their headquarters in London because that was the prestigious place to be. Not much point in putting it in Sturminster Newton.'

David tried a few experimental notes on the saxophone.

'Why don't we take a few hours just to go round and have a look at what's left?' said Peter. 'We're ahead of schedule—we didn't think we'd fill the boats until this time tomorrow. I doubt if there's likely to be any risk—there aren't many bodies around, and the ones we've seen are completely decomposed. Let's go and look round—we may be the last people to do it for a long time.'

'Or until Alison wants a change of clothes,' grinned Anne. Alison opened her mouth to protest, but Anne beat her to it. 'The trouble is they'll still have the same fashions in the shop windows next time you come.'

'We could do more than just look round,' said Paul, ever one to seize an opportunity. 'We ought to put up notices saying where we are—in Ampthill, I mean. London's a natural rendezvous point—that is, if people can get into it. We'd be silly not to indicate where we're living now.'

-53-

*N*ext day dawned, a glorious late April day with the bright sun picking out the brilliant colours on the boats in the basin and the red and white vastness of St Mary's Hospital towering above them on the opposite side of the water. After breakfasting they piled into the Harrods van, Jane waddling up to the passenger side. 'Getting bigger every day,' thought Paul with an odd mixture of interest and pride.

It was a beautiful day for sight-seeing, but a curious one too, going through the empty streets, past the occasional shop with a smashed-in window, avoiding a body here and there, and negotiating their way round the odd traffic jam.

At Trafalgar Square, Paul tied a large wooden placard to the base of Nelson's column. 'Survivors at Ampthill, Bedfordshire' it read. One hundred and sixty feet up Nelson continued to turn a blind eye to what was going on at his feet, looking instead up Whitehall to see if there was any intelligent life there. There hadn't been for a long time.

It was eerily silent in the square. Their voices and footsteps echoed off the buildings on each side. There was something very odd about the scene, even despite the absence of people.

It was Jane who noticed what it was. She suddenly looked up. 'Where are the pigeons?' There weren't any. The London pigeons which had been derived from rock-dwelling ones had become so domesticated, almost as pets living wild within the city, that when the human population left there was no food for them and virtually all the city's pigeons had died out, as a result of overadaptation and overdependence on an artificial supply of food. It hadn't been just the humans that had been changed by civilisation.

At Trafalgar Square they took the opportunity to look round
the National Gallery. Inside it was bright, most of the rooms lit
by large skylights. It was odd to walk among the galleries
surveying what had once been priceless works of art, but were
now financially worthless even though they had retained all their
beauty. Anne, who had not been there for many years, found the
sheer size and abundance of well-known paintings somewhat
overwhelming, rather like having a present of a box of chocolates
and eating one's way through the whole lot: however good it is,
eventually it becomes sickly. They stood in front of Constable's
Haywain, sensible that they might well be the last people to see it
for a long time: perhaps even the last people ever to see it, for in
the damp and cold of winter, and the heat of summer, the picture
was certain to decay more rapidly.

Then they drove up Whitehall towards the Houses of
Parliament. Big Ben loomed in front of them, its hands
permanently set to half past five, the time when London's
electricity had finally failed. Here Paul tied the second of his
posters to the railings overlooking Parliament Square,
deliberately choosing a spot that visitors would be attracted to,
were they to come searching round London. Looking up, Paul
saw the flag on the top of the Palace—the same one he'd seen
when he and Jane had come past while trying to escape. The
flag, now battered and torn, hung limp in the breeze. Then they
went inside the Palace of Westminster, and into the chamber of
the House of Commons, staring in silence at the green leather
seats that had been so familiar from the televised parliamentary
proceedings. Derek wrote out another note and placed it against
the back of the Speaker's chair. It seemed somehow appropriate
to put it there, at, literally, the seat of power for both the
Kingdom and, at one time, the Empire.

They went on to Buckingham Palace where Paul strapped
the third of his boards to the railings, and then they went back to
Paddington Basin. After casting off Jane thought they would
turn west, but as they started out of the basin and entered Little
Venice, Derek, in the leading boat, indicated that he was going to
turn east. He cupped his hands and shouted back to *Coral*.
'Let's go down the Regent's Canal: it's one of the nicest parts of
the Grand Union.'

It was. It starts at Little Venice with its clusters of boats and pubs and then passes through an avenue of trees, on either side of which are glorious Regency houses. It's one of the finest stretches of urban canal in the whole of England, beautiful and majestic. Almost immediately they went into the Maida Hill Tunnel, and then skirted the north side of Regent's Park, passing London Zoo with its curiously shaped aviaries, looking like offcuts from the Forth Bridge. There were no animals to be seen in the zoo: the cages were empty and silent. Anne at the tiller of *Coral* was left wondering about their plight when their keepers had fled or died and the animals and birds were left without water, food or means of escape.

After the flatness of Regent's Park and the zoo they turned left through a more urban landscape and came almost immediately to Camden Lock, once a timber wharf. It had a lock cottage in the form of a small castle, and craft shops around. Despite the emptiness it was still a beautiful place, redolent of years gone by and of a life on the canal that was no more. A beautifully simple Regency pedestrian bridge crossed diagonally above them just before they entered the top lock.

The two boats went through the lock together, and out towards the road bridge in front of them. It was a delightful day with clear blue skies, warm, and the previous slight wind had dropped completely: more like early summer than spring. As they came out underneath the road bridge Jane, who was at the front of *Amethyst*, gave a little cry and put her hand to her mouth. There on the right-hand side of the canal was a large building with plaster egg-cups on the ends of the ridges. It was AM-TV. Jane had not been expecting it, as they had come up on it from the canal rather than the road.

Suddenly, like Derek two days before, it was her turn to feel both nostalgic and threatened. She sat down with a bump on the seat at the front of the boat, hand still clasped to her mouth. Then she turned to Derek and shouted, 'I must go and see. I can't just go past.' Derek waved to *Coral* to indicate that he was going to moor.

Radio and TV stations are prone to hijacking by disaffected groups who get a lot of publicity if they can manage to break in during live shows. For AM-TV the canal formed a useful defence against this, a moat round the rear—except that is for

Hawley Locks which straddle the canal at the mid-point of the building. It is of course quite possible to cross a canal by walking across the top of the lock gates. AM-TV had made sure that any potential intruders couldn't do this.

Hawley Lock has two locks, placed side by side, and the architect merely replaced the gates on the lock nearest to the AM-TV building with a thin metal sheet that acted as a weir, keeping the water in, yet only allowing a quarter of an inch thickness for anyone foolhardy enough to try to walk along it. With a drop on one side into ten feet of lock water and on the other through eight feet of air into three feet of water, it was only somebody extremely brave or exceptionally foolhardy—or both—who would ever attempt to storm AM-TV from the canal side.

On the other hand it's quite easy to get to AM-TV by boat, so they just moored on that side of the canal, both boats nestling into the remains of the old lock. Then they simply stepped off on to the bank with the seats and tables that formed the open-air part of the canteen.

With her knees and hands trembling Jane peered in through the window. The canteen inside was just as she had remembered it—neat and tidy, but empty. She tried the handle of the door. To her surprise it opened, so she went back to the boat and picked up a torch. Paul, who had been on *Coral*, came up to her.

'Are you sure you want to go in?'

'I must, Paul. I've got to see what happened.' Memories of the last broadcast from AM-TV flooded into her mind; the desperate attempt to put out a programme with no cameraman, no one on the floor of the studio and Duncan collapsing and dying on air. 'I must go and see. It's would be like refusing to visit a friend's grave if I didn't.'

'Alison, you look after Sarah. David, don't do anything daft. And don't any of you leave the boat—is that clear?' said Anne firmly.

Derek, Anne and Peter followed a few paces behind Jane and Paul. The inside of AM-TV she knew would be bright with the sun streaming through the translucent panels of the roof, but in the dark interior of the blacked-off studio and galleries—where Jane knew she had to go—there would be no light at all. Out of the canteen they went, into the huge atrium of the main hall with

its little raised pseudo-walls on either side, and the vast central
staircase facing them, turning through a right angle as it ascended
to the first-floor level. It was quiet and still, and looked quite
normal, the same sort of normality, the same sort of quiet
stillness that it had always possessed at 6.00 a.m. each morning
when the show had started to go out. It could have been such a
morning, were it not that the sun was obviously high in the sky
and the shadows were in all the wrong places. As they went up
the stairs to the open-plan production office on the first floor
Derek noticed the computer terminals, the desks, and the way the
filing cabinets had neatly designed green tapering roof-pieces
that so elegantly stopped them looking purely functional and
allowed them to assume a more decorative aesthetic character.
Much better than the civil service ever got, he thought ruefully.

Surprisingly, there were no bodies. Nor were there any in
the more private glass-walled rooms that ran half the length of
the building on the side overlooking the canal—except, that is,
for one. At the far end, the office of the controller of news had
its door shut and behind the desk lay a body—Alan Fortescue,
who had collapsed during the meeting at the time of Hywel's
death. Obviously nobody had been brave or foolish enough to go
in and remove him.

It gave Jane a turn to see the body of someone she had once
known, albeit only distantly. She had never met death before in
anyone she had previously known, and it came as a shock. It
wasn't like the movies where deaths are dramatic but clean—
except for those where cardboard characters are made to 'die' in
the goriest ways possible. This was real death Jane was facing.
The end of a person and everything about him—the end of his
thoughts, his feelings, his emotions, hopes, dreams, talents,
aspirations. The end of a son, a father, a husband, a lover: the
end of a talent and a knack, the end of a 'nose' for news. The
end of a person. Looking at the collapsed grotesque figure
behind the desk, Jane wondered where it had all gone, all that
talent and all that personality. For a short time she stood looking
at Alan's body, then turned away with a shudder.

They went downstairs again, and turning on their torches,
walked through the low entrance way leading to the studios. On
the right was the entrance to the news gallery. Jane went in and

shone the torch round. It reflected dimly off the dozen or so TV monitors, but there was no one at the production desk and the news studio beyond was empty. Turning round, she walked across the passageway into the gallery of the main studio, the room where she had spent so many hours at work. There was one body there, in the director's seat, to the right of the one Jane used to occupy. The long hair showed that it was a woman, but Jane couldn't work out who it was from the white skull showing beneath the light brown locks.

She went out into the passageway again and, taking a deep breath, walked through the first of the 'sound lock' doors into the main studio area, remembering what it had been like when the show was running, with the dim light behind the scenery and the quiet voices floating over the top of the studio flats. This time there was nothing but sheer blackness and total silence. Jane walked carefully forward through the second door, the light from her torch picking out the seats for visitors waiting to go on, opposite the monitor at the back of the set that allowed them to see what was happening just the other side of the flats. Picking her way carefully in order not to trip over anything in the pitch darkness, she walked round the end of the studio set with Paul and the others close on her heels, their torches playing round the set which once was a light pinky beige but in the relatively dim light of the torches appeared little more than a slightly warm shade of grey.

As if attracted by a magnet the lights swung round to pick out the presenter's chair and the space in front of it and there, caught in the five torches like a stricken bomber in searchlight beams, was Duncan's body, crumpled in front of his chair, bowing as if in obeisance to the camera in front of him, the camera he had always worshipped and cultivated and in front of which he had ended his life sacrificially.

There was no mistaking that it was Duncan. The earpiece that he had been wearing lay next to the remains of his head and his dark wavy hair lay collapsed on top of the skeletal remains peeping out from beneath his pink shirt.

As she looked at Duncan and remembered his last few moments on air Jane felt a tear running down her cheek. They stood in a semicircle looking at him as if mesmerised. Such a well-known person, known to millions up and down the land, but now remembered by—how many? How short fame is, thought Jane. How quickly it passes until you're but a memory—and a short-lived one at that—as the people you once entertained and informed themselves died and the ones who were left replaced memories of you with other things more pressing and more urgent—like candles.

They stood in silence, looking, remembering. None of the others wanted to be the first to turn away: Jane had to decide the timing.

Suddenly she swung her torch round. 'I've done what I needed to do. Let's go back to the boat.'

They retraced their steps, out of the blackness of the studio that was Duncan's mausoleum and into the brilliantly lit atrium, through the canteen and on to the patio in front of the canal. The contrast couldn't have been greater—from darkness to light, from death to life, from gloom and sadness and memories of what had been, back to the present where there was life and action and hope. The sun on the water brilliantly showed up the bridge to their left and the willow in front of it: its leaves were just starting to come out, gracefully dangling into the water.

Jane was glad of the sunlight. Then she looked up and saw the eggs jauntily marching along each ridge of the roof, and the memories swept back over her again. She just made it to *Coral* before her legs gave way and she sat trembling on one of the seats in the prow. The children were in *Amethyst* so they were not party to Jane's immediate convulsive reaction of grief and sadness at all those who had died, all those who had gone. 'Where have they all gone?' she kept on saying. 'All that talent, all those personalities. Have they really all just disappeared into dust? How can a personality just disappear?'

Eventually she went inside to lie on her bunk, buried her face in her pillow and cried her eyes out. Paul didn't know what to do, but made her a cup of tea anyway.

Derek and Anne reversed the boats out of the old lock and managed, with a little difficulty, to turn them round. Canals are not built for turning long narrow-boats in—it's usually only possible at specially widened sections called winding holes, or else by reversing in and out of canal junctions much as a car backs into a side road. Just occasionally however, the natural layout of the canal forms an unofficial winding hole and this was true just above and below Hawley Locks. It was a squeeze, but Derek managed to turn round with a foot to spare.

The two graceful craft, engines roaring, spun on their axes and then headed off west, past the weeping willow, under the road bridge, up Camden Lock, and back towards the main line of the canal and Linslade.

-54-

*T*hey arrived at Linslade two days later, at midday. The weather was still good, but clouds building in the west threatened rain so they quickly got on with the job of unloading the two craft. The lorry they had brought to the quay was much larger than the Harrods delivery wagon, and much to their surprise all the cargo went in at one go. Their final job was to make sure that *Amethyst* and *Coral* were secured properly and shut down correctly; they were likely to make many more runs in to London in the future and would need to keep the craft in the best possible working condition.

On their arrival in Ampthill Martin came to meet them looking anxious and drawn, and smelling slightly of whisky. 'I'm glad you're back,' he said. 'We've had problems.'

'What's happened? Has somebody been ill?'

'Oh no, not that at all. It's Kevin.'

Paul wrinkled his nose in disgust. 'What's he done now?'

'He's completely out of control. In the past five days he's managed to enrage at least half of the community. He won't stop using his bike, he won't work and he won't co-operate with anything we try to do. He won't listen to anyone—Chris tried, and I've tried, but he just shouts obscenities. I can't cope with him. I'll leave him to you.' He turned on his heel and wandered slightly unsteadily back up the road to the Old Rectory, seclusion and alcoholic oblivion.

That they had to do something was obvious, but the problem

Gates House

was, what? And could all the members of the community agree
on it? An extraordinary general meeting was convened two days
later in the magistrates' court, but at least a hundred couldn't get
in and of the five hundred who were inside the court jostling for
space, it seemed that at least four hundred wanted to voice their
thoughts and had opinions—all different—about how Kevin and
similar problems should be managed. They moved the meeting
to the car park outside the courtroom, but it was still hopeless.
They couldn't agree on any single plan of action, and the more
they tried, the more others objected to details of their plans.

Eventually, after half an hour of hubbub and shouting Paul
got up on to the makeshift platform to speak. He had a
commanding presence—he was the sort of person one knows
instinctively is a leader—and a hush descended on the crowd
even before he opened his mouth.

'I think,' he said carefully, and in measured tones,
deliberately dropping his voice slightly to prevent it sounding
squeaky and ineffectual, 'like it or not, we will have to elect a
ruling body. Six months ago, when we first raised the subject,
we agreed we didn't need one, and we didn't *want* one, but now
we have six hundred members in the community and it's just
impossible for everyone to have a say on each and every part of
each and every decision. Unless we delegate our decision
making we won't be able to run the place at all.

'I suggest that we create a council of, say, ten or eleven
people who'll be responsible both for keeping order, and for
organising anything so urgent or needing such great resources
that it can't be left to individuals.

'If we don't do this I can't see us keeping an orderly society
going for much longer. We have to have some way of coping with
those who won't fit in, we have to have some way of protecting
those who are wronged and—most importantly—we have to
protect the community from those who are not prepared to use its
resources wisely and sparingly. We can't do this efficiently if we
have to wait for a consensus of six hundred people.'

He got down from the platform to applause which went on
and on. He stood up again. 'Can I take it that you agree?'

There was a murmur of approval and a nodding of heads as
above them the sparrows twittered. 'All those in favour please

show.' Practically every hand went up. 'All those against.'
There were just a few, of which Mary Harper and Peter
Abrahams were the most prominent. 'Would any of you like to
say why you are against a council?'

Peter was the first. 'You all know how unfairly I was treated
by the courts. Given power, people can use it quite unfairly, in
the name of law, order and justice. I don't want to see us go back
to any of that again. You're right, Paul—we *do* need to find
some way to keep order, so I'm not really against having a
council: but let's not create more injustice in the process.'

There were a number nodding their heads including some of
those who had voted in favour of a council.

'Mary?' said Paul.

'I feel exactly the same as Peter does. I don't like power
being concentrated in the hands of a few in case they manipulate or
misuse it. I want democracy and fairness, not remote committees.'

'I agree,' said Chris. 'I don't want to see any of these things
happen either, but we all agree that we have to do *something*, and
we can't do it by putting everything to discussion and a vote,
because with six hundred people all wanting a say we'll never get
any decisions made in time.'

'If we have a council I'd like Peter to be on it,' said Anne,
'especially in view of what he's just said. Maybe by having
someone on it who's experienced the rough end of justice we'll
guard against making the same type of mistake again.'

'Does that make you feel any easier?' asked Paul.

Mary nodded. 'I don't see what else we can do, really. But
we mustn't let it develop into an "us and them" situation. The
council *is* us.'

-55-

*T*he next day they voted for the council. There were no
nominations. Each adult member of the community cast five
votes and the eleven who got the highest number were to form

the council. Some of the results were predictable—Paul and Derek topped the list by a long way—but Martin, much to his surprise, came seventh. Chris, Anne and Peter Abrahams were all elected, as were Susan and Alan Rogers, Neil Rawsthorne, Mary Harper and Major Thornton. As it turned out, quite unintentionally the council was an interesting cross-section of the community, with a good range of abilities, education, age, sex and what before the plague would have been called political leanings.

Martin, reflecting on his election, ruefully thought that he was there as a token churchman and pondered on the parallel between Ampthill as it currently was and as it had been a hundred years previously when the Rector and the doctor were always held to be the pillars of the community—the Rector had been next to God and the doctor was next to the Rector.

There may have been something of that in the minds of certain of those who had voted for him, particularly the Major, but what Martin didn't realise was that, isolated, friendless and lonely as he felt himself to be, nevertheless he inspired genuine affection from many of the members of the community who respected him as a sensitive person and understood that it was this very sensitivity that had driven him to the brink of emotional collapse. They also respected his undoubted powers of thought. Had more of them known about his drinking they might not have been quite so keen, but he had been able to conceal his dependency on alcohol from all but a few—and none of those were the sort that gossiped.

As he wandered away to the Old Rectory that May evening, under the horse-chestnuts filled with their great white and pink candles of blossom, he was firmly of the opinion that either somebody had miscounted or that God was playing tricks with him. He stopped dead in his tracks in the lane. Funny, he thought, that's the first time for six months I've thought of God doing anything. He gave a wry little sniff, and headed home for the whisky bottle.

*   *   *

The council met the next week. Derek had offered the use of the large reception room at Dynevor House but Peter had been most unhappy at the prospect.

'If the council always meets at your house it will look as though it's in your pocket. We really ought to behave like the old council did—meet somewhere others are invited to come and listen, but without being able to interrupt.'

It seemed a sensible idea, so they agreed to meet in the magistrates' court, posting a notice of their intentions a day or two beforehand so that any of the community who wanted could come.

As expected, Paul was elected chairman.

'Right,' he said. 'Where do we want to start?'

It was Anne who spoke first—Anne the ever-practical. 'We've really just got to work out a few rules of behaviour, haven't we? We don't need to think of ourselves as anything too grand.'

'And sort out that brat Kevin,' added the Major, darkly.

'All right,' said Paul. 'Any ideas?'

'Are we right to do anything?' asked Susan Rogers. 'I mean, what law is he breaking?'

'It's odd,' said Derek, cautiously. 'We all talk as though the law of the land is still present, don't we—almost as if it's a physical thing with a life of its own. Yet there's no one to enforce it, is there? We know that the law says you mustn't steal, and technically there's still an Official Secrets Act. We really are still all constrained by those laws, aren't we? Now does anyone here know what those laws are? Do we have anyone within the community who has enough legal knowledge to tell us what the laws are, or where we can look them up accurately?'

'I know a bit about it,' said Peter, somewhat bitterly. 'After all, I used to be a policeman—before they threw me out. I can tell you all about the laws of theft, loitering, and vehicles, and the rights of suspects—but I don't know about most other laws, such as commercial law, or VAT. It wasn't my area.'

'Strange, isn't it?' said Susan. 'Previously if we'd done wrong the judge would have said . . . what was their pet phrase? Oh yes—"Ignorance of the law is no excuse." All citizens were expected to know the law and to keep within it. We're just hearing from someone who used to uphold the law that even *he* doesn't know what it is—and if *he* doesn't know, how could *we* have been expected to know how to obey it?'

'I take all that,' said Derek, 'and that's really what I was going to say. I think we ought to scrap all existing laws and start again. Firstly, *we* don't know what they were in detail; secondly, nor does anybody else; thirdly it was far too complex for its own good and lastly, as Peter has always said, law and justice are not the same thing.'

'But *can* we abolish the law just like that?' asked Susan. 'How do we know that there aren't lots of other survivors in different parts of the country, still using it? Anyway, the reason we're here is because Kevin won't behave, and now you're suggesting we get rid of the law rather than enforce it.'

'I didn't say that,' said Derek. 'I meant get rid of them all and start again.'

'I don't mind getting rid of the present laws,' said Alan, 'but what are we going to put in their place? Won't we end up building a system that's just as complex as the one we've thrown away, only worse, because we've built it up too quickly, and none of us has any legal experience?'

Then it was Peter's turn. Staring blankly ahead of him into the table, as though mesmerised, he started to speak, thoughtfully, slowly and with great feeling. He told them in detail what had happened to him on that dreadful autumn day—how, on a fine point of law, he had lost his licence, his job and his self-respect: how he had been pilloried in the local paper, and then in one of the Sunday tabloids; how the loss of his licence had stopped him getting other jobs; and all this even though he wasn't even in the driving seat of the car, and wasn't even awake at the time of the accident.

He wasn't a great speaker but the intensity of his emotion, the bitterness of his personal experience, and the fervour with which he spoke touched the hearts of everyone at the table.

'I've been thinking about the law ever since I was convicted and thrown out of the police force for something that, frankly, I didn't do. I've looked at the law and what it does to people— ordinary people, people like all of us here. I've seen its injustice —people made bankrupt by crooked company directors who can't be touched because of the insolvency laws; men whose wives have taken a lover, and the courts have forced her husband to leave the family house whilst the lover moves in—because "it's better for the children"; people sent to prison for punching yobbos who were throwing stones at their house—the youths were just cautioned, the man whose windows they were breaking gets put in prison.

'Why do we have laws, anyway? To stop people doing things we don't want them to—but all that happens is that the lawbreakers just ignore the rules, while good, law-abiding people get tied up in all the finicky regulations.

'Too many regulations make for bad law. And you don't make bad people good by giving them more laws to keep. Having lots of laws doesn't create more justice—it just makes lawbreakers of ordinary people, who find they've broken the law without realising it.

'And the more you make lawbreakers out of ordinary people by tripping them up over minor details, the less respect those people have for the law itself.

'And what about justice? You don't get more justice by having more laws. Anyway, you can't get justice—it costs too much. Ten thousand pounds a day it costs to hold a trial—ten thousand pounds! Who could afford this?—except big companies with legal departments. OK, so you can get your costs back, if you win. But maybe you won't—like I didn't. Maybe you'll lose—on a fine point of law, like I did. And after you've been denied justice, you may have to pay for your trial as well, especially if it's a civil case. It's like paying for your own executioner. So no one went to law—unless they had slick lawyers and a massive bank balance, or else they were on legal aid.

'This isn't justice. It may be law, but it's not justice. It may seem logical and consistent to the lawyers, but it isn't to anyone else.

'Parliament makes a law—let's say it's a good one. When it comes to court the lawyers get at it and turn it upside down, and make black into white and white into black. Then a judge makes a poor decision and establishes a precedent. In English law, whenever there is a precedent a succeeding judge has to follow it, so every time there is a bad judgement the law is whittled away—until it's impossible to apply, or even becomes the exact opposite of what it was originally meant to do.

'All right, so in theory a bad judgement can be changed on appeal, but it's so expensive to go there that most people—like me—wouldn't dare. It doesn't stop the big companies with their

large bank balances and retinues of lawyers who can bend the
law to their own ways, but it does stop the little man.

'Something else—lawyers have a habit of defining things out
of existence. They break laws down into smaller and smaller
pieces. It's like analysing a dive. Where are the diver's feet at
the point of the dive? On the diving board?—in which case,
that's before he's dived. In the air? That's after he's dived. Yet
we all know that the diver has dived. Splitting up the dive into
smaller and smaller fragments doesn't help us to see the overall
picture. But this is what the lawyers do, to try to get their clients
off. I've heard them. "The fact that this man was standing in an
open doorway doesn't mean that he was going to enter the
building, does it? Even if he did have a crowbar in his hand.
And he was wearing gloves because it was cold—it was a very
cold July, remember?" I've heard them. The guilty get off on
technicalities, and the injured get kicked in the teeth.'

Dead silence. He looked up at last. 'Well, that's what I feel,
anyway.' The anger and aggression of six months had surfaced
at last, been dissipated: he'd finally absolved himself.

There is nothing that stops superficial conversation as much as
a hurt personality revealing the real source and intensity of its pain.
Gently, very gently, Martin—who was sitting next to Peter—put
his hand on Peter's arm and said softly, 'We understand.' There
was a further silence, while Martin, suddenly becoming aware of
what he'd done, slowly withdrew his hand and started worrying
that the others would think he was stupid for doing it.

Anne broke the silence. 'Peter, you're completely right.
Whatever we do, we mustn't let something like this happen again.'

'How do you stop it, though?' said Paul in, for him, a
surprisingly gentle way. 'You're quite right, precedents can
make a mockery of the law. But if you don't have precedents,
then how does anyone know where they stand? One week, in
one court, a particular action is judged to be within the law. Next
week, it's judged to be wrong. Isn't that as unjust? No one will
know for certain how he stands.'

'Yes—how can you avoid setting up precedents?' asked
Martin. 'Surely a judge has to interpret the law and then the way
he interprets it acts as an extension of the law to show others
what to do.'

Peter shook his head.

'It doesn't work like that, Martin. Sometimes it can and sometimes it's good that it does, but usually precedents work by whittling away at the underlying justice of the law itself, a little bit here, a little bit there, until there's nothing left. Like the diver.'

'All right,' said Martin. 'How would *you* go about stopping it?'

'Simple,' said Peter. 'Make the court take note of precedents, but not feel bound by them. And especially— *especially*—take into account whether it's a fine point of law or not, when deciding the punishment. If you're obviously breaking the law—well, you deserve to be punished severely. But if, before the case, no one's sure whether the law's been broken or not, then the punishment must reflect that. It's not fair to punish someone heavily when beforehand there was real doubt as to whether what he did was outside the law or not.

'We can sort this whole thing out very simply. All we have to do is insist that at the end of any trial, the judge should ask himself, "Never mind the minutiae of the law—*is justice being done here*?" And his verdict and his sentence should reflect that.'

There was a silence, and a quiet nodding of heads.

'I'll tell you something else that may help,' said Peter. 'Do what the Americans did. They have—had—a Bill of Rights, which were over and above other laws. If any court decision infringed those rights you could call "foul" and the court's decision was invalid.'

'How does that help?' asked Anne.

'It means you can't whittle away at a law using precedent after precedent. There's a point at which somebody can say "Stop, this has gone too far, you've infringed the constitution." '

'But America was one of the most litigious societies ever,' said Alan.

'That wasn't the fault of the Bill of Rights,' interjected Derek. 'That was because of the way they paid their lawyers— on a percentage. The more they won, the more they got, so the lawyers went round positively encouraging their clients to sue. It gave the lawyers more money, and there was no risk to the client because he didn't have to pay up if they lost. It had nothing to do with the Bill of Rights.'

Peter looked up again from the table. 'What I would say is

this—let's scrap the law and start again. Begin with a statement of individual rights, and follow it with a simple system of laws that everyone can understand and that we try not to add to. Lawmakers love to have things to do. Let's try and set up a simple system that no one can fiddle with and that we can go away and leave working.'

There was a murmur of approval and the heads round the table nodded again, Mary's in particular. There were no objections—Peter was still speaking from the depths of his hurt personality, and no one wanted to break the spell, or its honesty.

'That sounds a good idea,' said Paul. 'Have you any idea what you'd like your Statement of Rights to contain, or do you think that we should go away and think about it?'

Peter gave a sad little smile. 'I've been thinking about this ever since my trial. How about this for starters? Some are freedoms and some are duties:

'Freedom of thought: The right to believe what you want, religiously and politically.

'Freedom of speech: The right to say and write what you want as long as it is not untrue or libellous.

'Freedom of behaviour: The right not to be interfered with physically or mentally against your will.

'Freedom to defend: The right to defend yourself, your family and your property against attack by other people.

'The right to a fair and open trial in front of a jury *without charge*—even in civil cases.

'The duty to restore what you have damaged'—but I think we'll have to be careful about that one, especially for people we ask to do risky things, like Derek here.'

There was another silence.

'Thank you for that last observation,' said Derek. 'I'd add something to your list, especially bearing in mind our present precarious existence: "the duty not to do things which are against the interests of the community"—though that's a hard one to define as well. The community must have the right to stop people who are damaging it.'

'That'll get Kevin nicely,' murmured Paul under his breath.

'People also have a duty to pay for what the community is organising,' added Major Thornton.

'Oh, that's another one,' said Peter: ' "No taxation without representation".'

'This is beginning to look good,' said Paul. 'It's simple, easy to understand, and it covers all our needs for the moment. For something as major as this I don't think we ought to make any decisions now. Let's go away and think about it and come back in a week or two.'

'What about punishment?' asked Derek, breaking the spell. There was a glum look round the table. No one really wanted to be the one who voiced the opinion that all of them felt. It seemed so much like reneging on civilisation and going back to a more unloving age. Eventually Neil grasped the nettle.

'I hate to say it,' he said, 'but I think Kevin had a definite point.'

'You can't mean that you agree with what he did?' expostulated Mary. 'It was barbaric.'

'No,' said Neil evenly. 'No, I wasn't thinking of what he did, I was thinking of what alternatives there were. The community can't afford to punish people by locking them up for year upon year as we used to do before the plague. We just can't afford a mouth that isn't working to feed itself. Nor can we afford to have people working only to look after those who've been locked up. There's just too much to do—I mean, I feel guilty just sitting here, because I really should be out in the fields.'

'So what do you propose?' said Mary, still flushed and angry. 'Bring back the stocks? Two thousand years of civilisation and within six months we come to this. What are we—savages?'

'I think it's quite a good idea,' said the Major. 'Don't see why it was ever stopped.'

Susan interjected, 'That's not how teachers are encouraged to exert discipline, Major Thornton.'

'What discipline?' snapped the Major.

'Any discipline,' said Chris. 'It's all very well talking about the good of society and the good of other people, but if people *won't* do what is right then what do you do about it? As Neil's just said, we can't afford to put people in prison. In any case I happen to think that prison is barbaric too. I can't think of anything more cynical than locking someone away for a couple of years—that's a thirtieth of his *whole life*—just leaving him there to rot. Is that civilised?

'And you talk about discipline in schools. Well, I seem to remember that before the plague schools could be divided into three, the ones that had no problems with discipline whatsoever, the ones that were totally out of control and the ones in between—and there were an awful lot of the latter. So your ideas about just using persuasion don't seem to be borne out in practice, do they?'

With that the meeting erupted. It took Paul nearly five minutes to restore order. When there was silence he looked round the table.

'Look,' he said. 'I think we have to forget our presuppositions. Maybe physical punishment didn't work before, maybe it did. Maybe putting people in prison is better than birching them and maybe it isn't. But our problem is what are we going to do *now* rather than what worked or didn't work then.

'Our problem is very simple. How do we stop Kevin and people like him from wrecking our somewhat precarious existence?'

Susan Rogers, ever the teacher, interjected crossly with 'Through education.'

'But we've tried that,' said Paul. 'We've tried till we're blue in the face. It may be right that Kevin shouldn't use up fuel unnecessarily, it may be right that he should pull his weight, but when it comes down to it *he chooses not to listen*. So what do we do, let him get on with it? Telling him yet again that he's doing the wrong thing is not going to help.'

'People are basically good,' said Mary. 'If someone like Kevin is behaving like this it's because of what's happened to him in the past. You can't blame him when he behaves selfishly if people in the past have taken away from him what was rightfully his.'

'Have they?' asked Paul.

'They must have,' said Mary, 'for him to be like that.'

'Isn't that an assumption?'

'Why should it be?'

'Why *shouldn't* it be? You're assuming that Kevin is the way he is because of what other people have done to him in the past.'

'When I was a policeman,' said Peter, 'I remember that there were some people I could just warn, and they'd learn and do something about it. Then there were others who were sure they were in the right—or wouldn't let anyone else tell them differently. These were the people who needed punishing, and sometimes they didn't reoffend–'

'–and sometimes they did,' said Mary, 'and where did that get you?'

'Ultimately you have to have some form of sanction,' said Anne calmly. 'I agree with you Mary, that it's a good idea to persuade people of the right thing to do—and with you, Susan, to try to educate people to see that what they're doing is wrong. But if they *won't* listen then there's got to be something else, otherwise anybody who wants to do something which is either criminal, in the old sense, or against the interests of everybody in our new sense, can do it with impunity and we can't stop them. We *have* to have some method of sanction.'

'Such as?' said Derek.

'There are three things that we can do. We can exclude him from the community, kick him out, tell him he's no longer welcome. Personally I doubt if that will help because that will just make him into a raider, a predator, anxious to get his own back; or even if he's not vindictive, he'll prey on us for food and the other things he needs—so actually we'd be making a rod for our own backs in the process.

'We can lock him up, but as we've all agreed we can't afford the manpower to do that.

'Or we can punish him physically. Now you're all shying away from this for various reasons. You, Martin, because as an ex-vicar you think that beating people is not going to make them reform; you, Susan, because you think that it's a matter of education; you, Mary, because you think that people are basically good inside. But I don't think we have any other choice, given our circumstances. I think we have to go back to what they used to do a couple of hundred years ago to people who were caught stealing . . . '—Martin spluttered something unintelligible—'No, I'm not thinking of sending them off to Australia or hanging them. I'm talking about putting them in the stocks or whipping them, giving them a short sharp lesson: showing them that others in the community don't like what they were doing because it offends and it hurts the community itself. But when their punishment is over, it's *over* and they go back to being a normal member of the community straight away, taking part in all the duties and responsibilities that they have.'

There was a reluctant silence round the table.

'It did work with the raiders, you know,' said Alan. 'I know it needed a couple of times, but they haven't come back, have they?'

'There's more to it than that,' said Peter. 'Being detected is also part of it. It took them three attacks on us to learn that lesson.'

'And the speed with which they are punished is important too,' interjected Derek. 'I've just been reading some psychology. If you put a rat in a cage with a lever that delivers a pellet of food every time it's pressed, the rat soon learns to press the lever to get food. If, now, you want to teach it *not* to press the lever when a light beside it is on, you can do it by giving it a tiny electric shock every time it gets it wrong, and the rat quickly learns not to press the lever when the light is on. But—and here's the important thing—if you delay the shock for more than twenty seconds, it can't learn to associate the punishment with what it did to deserve it. It gets shocks, and it can't work out why. Instead it goes neurotic, quivers, and won't press the lever at all, even when it's safe to do so.

'The longer you leave the punishment the harder it is for the animal to find out why it's getting one or the other, and what to do about it. It doesn't know how to modify its behaviour. It can't associate the two items: in other words, swift punishment is better than delayed punishment.

'I agree with Peter—but I think there's something else as well. Not only did the raiders find that every time they attacked us they were detected, they were punished *immediately*—within half an hour—so in their minds there was an immensely strong relationship between their illegal act and what happened to them. They did wrong, they were caught, they were punished and they were punished *quickly*. That leads to altered behaviour and we have the evidence for that in that they haven't returned to trouble us any longer.

'I'll tell you something else that I've learned. It goes back to what Chris said about locking people up and letting them fester. We don't remember physical pain, do we? We may remember that we hurt ourselves, but we can't remember the pain itself. You *can't* really remember what it was like to have toothache, can you? You can't create toothache just by thinking about it.

'The only type of pain that we *can* remember is mental pain, and we can recreate that any time we want by thinking of some embarrassing occurrence or some dreadful accident. By remembering what we felt at the time of the incident itself we recreate the pain, or the sadness, or the shame, or whatever it was that we experienced. Mental pain can be remembered, physical pain can't.'

'I don't follow you,' said the Major. 'Where does that lead us?'

'Quite simple. If you punish someone physically it's over and done with. They can remember that they were punished, but they can't recall or recreate the physical pain once it's over. But with mental punishments, the sort we used in our "civilised" '— he said the word with a sneer—'world before the plague, we went about punishing people in ways that they would always remember—like locking them up for a year or two—and *so they could always recreate and re-experience the mental pain they had*, long after the event. The advantage of physical pain, or physical punishment, once it's over, is it's over and done with. On the other hand mental pain can stay with you for the whole of your life.'

'So?' said Susan.

'So, far from being barbaric or uncivilised, physical punishment is actually more civilised than mental punishment.'

Mary and Susan shook their heads. 'I really don't think this is right,' said Mary. 'What Derek is proposing is barbaric.'

'Why is physical punishment cruel, but mental punishment not? If you don't like the idea of punishing people, fine—stop all forms of punishment: but we'll still have a problem with Kevin. On the other hand, if you decide that punishment is needed, then mental punishment is more cruel than physical punishment.'

'I don't see that we have much option at the moment,' said Paul. 'Why don't we try it and see what happens?'

'I agree. Let's try it and see if it works or not,' said Chris. 'Then we can make a better judgement. I don't see that we have much choice. We've either got to exclude people from the community, or carry out some form of physical punishment. We just can't afford the manpower to lock them away.'

'Unless anyone else can think of a way,' said Paul.

'I still think education's important,' said Susan.

'Yes,' said Paul, starting to lose his temper. 'I *agree*, but what after we've tried education, what then? What if they don't respond. We tried educating Kevin till we were blue in the face. You can see the difference it's made, can't you? He's exactly the same. He's not changed at all. *That's* the stage we're talking about. Have you got any better ideas?'

Silence.

'I don't like the use of violence any more than anyone else,' said Derek. 'But I can't think of anything else we can do, either.'

'I suggest that we close the meeting,' said Paul, 'and go away and think about it for a week. We'll make our final decision then.'

Susan grimaced.

'All right? Right.'

Susan grimaced again and remained seated whilst everybody else rose to leave. Anne went over to her.

'I hope we haven't offended you,' she said. Susan shook her head, holding on to the table, teeth gritted.

'Is something wrong?' Susan gave out a sigh and Anne could see beads of perspiration on her forehead.

'No, it's gone now. I had a pain in my stomach.'

'I'll get Derek.' Anne ran out of the room to the foyer where Derek was in conversation with Martin and Paul. He came back in.

'What's the problem?' The pain had struck again.

'Pain . . . underneath my ribs . . . here . . . After a few seconds she relaxed. 'It's all right, it's gone again.'

'I think I ought to examine you properly,' said Derek, frantically trying to think what might cause right-sided upper abdominal pain. 'Let's go across to the surgery, shall we?' He and Anne helped Susan out of the courtroom, and along to the Market Square.

Although at first he'd used Dynevor House as his surgery, Derek had finally decided to use one of the shops on the south side of Church Street, facing the square. Previously it had been an antique shop and before that—so Derek had discovered from some old papers—an office for one of the local newspapers. It had the advantage of a lot of light coming in through the bow-fronted window, and as an old house, had a working fireplace in the back.

As Susan went through the door she had another attack of pain and gratefully lay down on the couch. Derek examined her, pushing his hand high up into the area underneath the ribs. He could feel nothing. He tried prodding between the ribs and slightly below them and finally over the whole abdomen, but still he could feel nothing. There was no temperature either, just an enormous amount of pain. Duodenal ulcer? Gallstones? he thought to himself. He went across to his books.

'*Gallstones,*' he read, '*the mnemonic for which are the four "F"s, fair, fat, fertile and forty.*' '*Fair*' meaning the fair sex, that fits. '*Fat*'—he looked at Susan—fat. Very. '*Fertile.*' Yes, two children. '*Forty*'—forty-five, that fits too. He looked up the symptoms, the type of pain and the differential diagnosis. It looked very much like it. '*Treatment—pethidine is the drug of choice in the severe acute attack.*'

'Excuse me a minute,' he said to Susan, and went four doors up the road to the chemist. Before the plague the morphine-based drugs had been kept in a locked cabinet, which Paul had 'unlocked' for him with his cold chisel at the time they had been searching for the insulin. He opened it. In front of him rows of packets and ampoules of morphine, heroin and pethidine were stacked neatly. There didn't seem to be as many as he had remembered from the previous November, but then the mind does play tricks over the passage of time.

Picking up an ampoule containing 100mg of pethidine, and one of Buscopan, he went back to the surgery and injected them into Susan's right thigh. 'That should work in about twenty minutes,' he said. 'You'd better let me know if the pain continues.'

They didn't normally use cars now for short journeys, because of the petrol, but this was different. Anne brought the Peugeot round, put a now drowsy Susan in the back and drove her the short journey to her home in Woburn Street, then put her to bed.

*　　　　*　　　　*

The following morning Mary awoke to the sound of pigeons cawing in the trees. On the far side of the road the kestrel was hovering. It was a beautiful day, with a light wind which was blowing feathers all over her garden again. This time there were only ten hens left.

-56-

'Daddy,' said Alison after supper that evening. 'Why am I needing to take so much more insulin?'

'Are you?'

'Yes.'

'How long for?'

'Since about April I suppose. It's been gradually creeping up and up. I've been able to control my urine sugar, but only by putting up the dose a little bit each time.'

'How much are you using now?'

'About double what I started with.'

Derek thought hard.

'I don't quite see why that should happen,' he said. 'I'll look it up.'

*   *   *

After supper Anne walked the quarter of a mile up Holly Walk to the Old Rectory. It was a beautiful, quiet evening, but the house and grounds looked unkempt and overgrown, and somehow disturbed. Just like its occupant, she thought. The lawns were uncut, the hedges were overgrown, and there was a pile of debris outside the front door, among which bottles seemed to feature prominently. She tapped on the knocker. There was a long pause, then the door opened slightly.

'Hello, Anne.' He didn't open it any further.

'I brought you something.'

'Oh. What?'

'Something I thought you'd like. From London. I haven't had a chance to bring it to you before.'

Reluctantly Martin decided that he'd better let her in, opened the door and showed her into the lounge at the end of the gloomy

corridor. Anne hadn't been inside the house before. As they passed
the dining-room door she glanced in and saw that the dishevelment
outside the house was nothing compared with the chaos within.

'Do sit down.'

The lounge was light and airy—and neat. He probably never
used it, she thought, as she sat down in one of the chairs covered
in a soft blue flowery material. Reaching down into her bag she
brought out a pile of books.

'For you. I hope they're the right sort.'

Martin looked down. They were all piano music: a
complete set of the Beethoven Sonatas; a piano transcription of
the Brahms Symphonies; some Debussy; Rachmaninov's
Prelude in C sharp minor; and some Scott Joplin Rags.

A smile began to creep onto Martin's face and his eyes lit
up. Anne savoured the rare event.

'They're wonderful. I haven't got much music here—a few
bits and pieces, nothing more.'

'Play me something.' Martin got up to go to the dining
room, then hesitated, thinking of its state.

Anne seized the initiative and beat him to the door. 'In the
dining room, isn't it?'

'Yes, but I wouldn't go . . .' Too late. Anne surveyed the scene
again. Not a pretty sight, like a teenager's room, but five times
worse—clothes on the floor, old food on the table, dirty dishes on
the table from a week before. Martin followed her in, embarrassed.

'I'm afraid it's . . . not very tidy, is it?'

'Never mind that. Play me something.' She pulled an open
book off one of the chairs and sat down. Martin picked up the
Beethoven Sonatas and found the *Moonlight*.

'I used to know this once. I expect I'll be a bit rusty now.'
He got through the first movement, sight-reading, with a few
mistakes. At the end he sat back contemplating it. 'It'll be better
with practice.'

'What about the others?'

Martin picked up the Rachmaninov Prelude, tried the first
few bars and stopped. 'Too difficult to sight-read. It'll be OK
once I've worked through it a bit . . .' He tailed off. Anne was
looking round the chaotic room.

'Martin, when did you last eat?'

'I don't seem to be very hungry at the moment.'

She repeated the question.

'I can't remember precisely . . . I can't be bothered making food, if you must know.'

'You can find enough energy to play music, can't you?'

'Sometimes I think it's the only thing that keeps me going . . . I don't know why I'm telling you all this. I haven't told anyone else.'

'I'll tell you what. You play me some more of the music I've brought. Then you're coming down to Dynevor for a meal. And no arguments.'

Martin opened his mouth to protest, then thought better of it. He hadn't got the energy to argue: he'd not had any energy for anything, not since the plague. Everything was just too much effort—even clearing the table after a meal seemed an impossible task, so as often as not he didn't bother.

But he'd like some food, he thought, if only he could face the journey to Dynevor House; and walking back again to his empty, lonely house.

He didn't realise that he was crying until he felt Anne's arm round his shoulder.

'Is it really that bad?'

He nodded wordlessly, biting his lower lip, and gripping the sides of the piano stool. 'Everything seems . . . hopeless . . . too much effort . . . I can't be bothered . . . God knows, it wasn't like this in London . . . ' He shook his head and blinked back the tears. 'Do you think I like living like this?' he shouted suddenly, then subsided again. 'I'm sorry. I didn't mean to shout.'

'That's all right. Go on—play some more music, and I'll do a bit of tidying up, then that will be a bit of a weight off your mind.'

'You can't do that, it's not fair on you.'

'Yes I can. I've got the energy, you haven't. Play me some music.'

Martin played.

*   *   *

That night Mary lay in a sleeping bag on the step outside the back door of her bungalow, from which she could look out over the hen-coop. Fortunately for her it was a warm night, and

moonlit too. Inside the house Howler was asleep, having been
put in his basket long before. It wouldn't have done to have him
roaming the garden, not that night. The kestrel too had stopped
its hovering, and had retired to its perch on the topmost branches
of a tree at the back of her garden.

Mary settled down for what promised to be a long wait, lying
flat on her stomach, motionless, her eyes probing the blackness
of the trees behind the hedge for some slight movement, some
slight indication of life. At her shoulder the moonlight glinted
off the barrel of the shotgun. It was loaded and cocked.

*   *   *

That same evening Susan Rogers had another attack of pain.
Fortunately it settled after about twelve hours, but Derek was up
half the night trying to get the pain under control. He had read
up on the possible causes of her pain and decided that his initial
thoughts were correct—she probably did have a gallstone.

The gall bladder, he found out, is a small bag lying beneath
the liver on the right-hand side of the body, just under the
ribcage. It stores bile, which is made by the liver, and helps in
the digestion of fat. Sometimes chemicals crystallise out from
the bile to form small round stones, so that when the gall bladder
contracts to push its contents into the tube leading to the gut, the
stones get stuck. When this happens the pressure inside the gall
bladder rises quickly and causes intense pain, rather like the pain
from a pimple on the nose. With a pimple, once the top is taken
off and the pressure is released, all the pain goes. Exactly the
same happens in the gall bladder—if only the gallstone could be
got out of the way the pain would go immediately, as the
pressure inside the gall bladder drops.

Derek read about treatment: trying to avoid the formation of
stones by changing the diet—not very successful; or the stones
could be shaken to bits with high-frequency sound using a
lithotripter: but even in the days before the plague that sort of
medicine was only available at the biggest hospitals. The
commonest form of treatment was to remove the gall bladder and
stones together, an operation known as cholecystectomy.

He read on with a sinking heart, knowing that such an
operation was entirely beyond his capabilities. Or was it? Just

thinking about it made his blood run cold, not so much for whether he could do the operation, but whether the patient would survive his ministrations. He decided that now was not the time to start practising, and hoped that maybe he was wrong, that she was actually suffering from wind, and that the pain would go away never to return.

Bleary-eyed, he returned home just in time for breakfast.

*   *   *

Mary was similarly bleary-eyed. Lying outside her house at three o'clock that morning, she spotted a movement over at the back of the garden as the shape of a fox detached itself from the undergrowth and, illuminated in the moonlight, came padding softly towards the hen-coop. It looked up and sniffed the air. There was a slight breeze, but fortunately it was blowing from the fox towards the house and not the other way round, otherwise the fox would instantly have smelt Mary and rushed off.

From the verandah she could see the fox prowling round the cage and hear the cries of distress from the chickens inside as it started to dig underneath the right-hand side wall. Slowly and quietly she lifted the shotgun to her shoulder, aimed carefully and pulled the trigger.

In the quietness of the night the explosion was devastatingly loud. The fox keeled over on to its right side and lay motionless, having taken the full blast across its chest and head. Rubbing her right shoulder, Mary got out of the sleeping bag and walked warily across to the hen-coop. Inside all the hens were clucking and flapping about, disturbed both by the presence of the fox and the noise of the gun. Mary opened the door, let herself in and closed the door behind her.

'There there, my lovelies,' she said, trying to stroke their heads. 'There there. You're safe now,' and the hens who had over the weeks got to learn Mary's voice and smell were pacified.

She let herself out of the coop again and looked down sadly at the fox. What a beautiful creature, she thought, and felt immediate revulsion for what she had just done, but checked herself. Had she not killed the fox, she realised, all her remaining hens would have been dead by the morning. And maybe a sheep or two as well. She looked down at the great

brush spread across the grass, dark in the moonlight. Wily so-
and-so, she thought. I think we're all better off without you;
and picking the animal up by its tail she dragged it to the edge of
the garden and threw it over the fence into the woodland
beyond.

Far above the copse, the kestrel stirred, disturbed by the
noise and the movement, then went back to sleep in the branches
of the trees.

*   *   *

A week later Alison's insulin dose had had to be doubled
again: but even so she was showing sugar in her urine, and her
blood-sugar levels had gone back up from seven—just about
normal for a diabetic on insulin—to sixteen, which certainly
wasn't. Nothing Derek did seemed to make any difference. He
varied the amounts of insulin, he gave the doses at different
times, he used different types of insulin—long-acting, short-
acting, intermediate. Nothing did any good. Alison's urine
continued to contain sugar, and the blood-sugar levels rose
inexorably.

He consulted the textbooks. They said nothing about this.
Diabetes could *always* be brought under control, through
increasing the insulin to appropriate levels. There was no such
thing as a case which couldn't be brought under control, provided
one was not talking about controlling diabetic coma.

-57-

*I*t was mid-June and poppies showed in red profusion among the
uncut grass at the sides of the roads. The roads themselves were
starting to look overgrown—in the absence of regular traffic and
road sweeping, grit and soil had begun to accumulate at the edges
by the kerbstones, where there were sheltered air-pockets, and
these provided a place for weeds to grow. The hedgerows were
starting to get out of hand, too.

So far, the spring and summer had been as hot as the winter
had been cold. The first of the main harvests had been
gathered—hay for the cattle and sheep, ready for the next winter.
Neil had shown them how to choose the best time to mow the
grass, and how to leave it in the sun to dry, turning it from time
to time to ensure that it dried out thoroughly.

They used some of their precious diesel to cut and gather the
hay: it seemed an eminently sensible way to utilise what they still
had left. The weather had only to turn sour and they could lose
the whole crop; so for once in farming, speed was of the essence.

They had had the first of the soft fruit crops too. The
strawberries came into season for a short time in early June and
they all gorged themselves: the remainder they made into jam. It
was the only way they could keep them for later: no wonder they
used to be called preserves.

Out in the garden at the back of Dynevor the three children
were playing in the sun. Alison wasn't feeling well, so she just
lay on the grass teaching Sarah how to make daisy chains, while
David was climbing trees. Eventually, exhausted by the heat, he
too plopped himself down by the pond and started sucking a
piece of grass.

'What wouldn't I give for an ice cream,' he said wistfully,
idly stirring the water and causing the carp to vanish with a flick
of their tails.

'Me too,' said Alison. 'Only I wouldn't be allowed one
now, even if we had any.'

'I'd like an ice cream too,' said Sarah. 'A strawberry one.
Yummy.'

'What else do you miss?' asked Alison.

'Bananas,' replied David. 'Bananas and oranges and kiwi
fruit. And apples. What do you miss?'

'Records and discos. And magazines. We've got
strawberries, though.'

'I think I'll be sick if I see another strawberry—we don't
have any, at first, then we get them all at once.'

'I miss apples,' said Sarah. 'Why can't we have apples?'

'Yes,' said David, 'why can't we? We grow them here.'

'But ours are only ready in the autumn,' said Alison. 'All
the rest have rotted. In spring we used to get them from

The Maulden Road

abroad—like South Africa or New Zealand, where the seasons are the other way round to ours.'

Derek wandered into the kitchen to see jam pans bubbling on the stove, making an already hot day even more so.

'It's a pity you have to work in such a temperature,' he said to Anne.

'I can't do it any other way,' she said, sweat pouring down her face. 'We've got to do it when the fruit's ripe—strawberries go off so quickly. Even in the larder where it's cool we can't leave them more than a couple of days: and we can't freeze them without electricity.'

Then the penny dropped. Derek sat down on a chair with a bump. Question: Where had they found the insulin? Answer: in the fridge in the chemist's. Where was it now? In the fridge in the chemist's—as a suitable storage place rather than to keep it cold. And what was the temperature inside the storage cabinet? Far, far too hot. The insulin itself was going off. It was nothing to do with Alison or her disease.

He stood up abruptly, without speaking, and with Anne watching open-mouthed, rushed out of the house leaving the door wide open, down Church Street and into the chemist's. Inside the shop it was pleasantly warm. Inside the fridge it wasn't so much warm as just not cold. He grabbed the vials of insulin. Written on each was the sentence: '*Store at four degrees centigrade. Do not freeze*', followed by an expiry date which was August that year. Even if it had been kept cool it would soon be going off significantly on its own. Why hadn't he thought of it before? he asked himself, clenching his fist. If it was so sensitive to heat why hadn't it gone off sooner? he thought academically, and then realised that without heat in the shop the insulin had kept cool until the warm weather began in mid-May—which was when Alison had first noticed the problem.

If it was warm in the shop it wasn't warm inside Derek's chest. An icy hand gripped at his throat as he realised the implications. There would be no more insulin—not here, not anywhere—because no refrigerators were working any longer. Going to other pharmacies wouldn't help—he would find the same warm conditions. It wouldn't help even if he went to the suppliers or manufacturers.

Dynevor House: The garden

That hot afternoon Derek sat down in the shop and watched his daughter's life evaporate away in front of his eyes. How do you make insulin? he thought, and then remembered what the books had said. Originally it was obtained by purification of the pancreas of cattle and pigs, but now it was—had been—obtained by growing bacteria that had been genetically changed to contain a copy of the gene for making human insulin, so the bacteria themselves produced human insulin artificially.

Where did they manufacture it?

Could they find any of the bacteria? He picked up the box of insulin. The address of the drug firm was in Welwyn Garden City. He put the rest of the insulin back in the fridge. Habit, he thought to himself, what good is it there? Then he ran out of the chemist's front door, up Church Street to the huge iron gates of Paul's house and banged furiously on the door. Paul answered the knock, and Derek blurted out the story to him. 'Could you go and look for the factory?' he asked. 'See if you can find how to do it—bring back some of the bacteria?'

'Wouldn't it be better if you went?'

'No fear,' said Jane, who'd just come in from the back garden where she'd been resting in the shade, 'I need you here!' Despite the heat, and her heavily pregnant shape she looked elegant and cool, her blonde hair drifting over the shoulder of her sundress.

'I've got to look after Susan as well, Paul. She may need me at any time, too. You shouldn't find it too difficult to find the laboratory: I mean, no more than I would.'

'Yes, but what am I looking for when I get there?'

'I don't know,' said Derek, bitterly. 'I haven't a clue. Vats? Samples in refrigerators? I really don't know any more than you.'

'I'll try. It sounds a tough job, but I'll try.'

'How are you going to get there?' asked Jane.

'I could use the Porsche—but Welwyn's on the A1. It will be difficult to get to.'

'What about the plane?' said Derek.

'I'd already thought about that—but where am I going to land? I could try a playing field I suppose, but there won't be anybody on the ground to tell me if things are safe, nor even which way the wind's blowing and if I have an accident, hit a rabbit hole . . . no one would even know.'

Jane winced.

'I suppose I'll just have to swallow my pride.'

'Why?'

'Best way in? Motorbike. Who's the only motorcyclist we know of round here? Kevin. I'll ask him if he'll take me. I'll go and eat humble pie,' and with that he walked out of the door.

'You look as though you could do with a drink,' said Jane. Derek suddenly realised that his hands were trembling. 'Whisky?'

'Thanks.' He sat down with a bump on a chair in the hallway. She pressed a tumbler into his hand: Derek took a swig and put the glass down, the perspiration glistening off his forehead.

'Does Anne know?'

'Not yet. I've only just found out.'

'Well, wait here until you're feeling a bit better,' she said, sitting down. 'You must feel dreadful.'

'It's rather hard to contemplate the death of one's daughter,' he said. 'Slowly.'

'Is there nothing else you can do?'

'Nothing. Young diabetics like Alison don't produce any insulin at all. With older diabetics you can multiply the effect of the insulin they produce using other tablets, but in young diabetics it's all-or-nothing: either they're given insulin or they die. Before they discovered insulin that was what happened to every single one.'

'Can't we make some here?'

'In theory, maybe, in practice, no. We haven't got anybody here who's a chemist and even if we had, think of all the chemicals and apparatus that we'd need. It's probably extremely complicated.'

*   *   *

They went to tell Anne, both of them, that fine sunny June day. Then Derek went to get Martin, because she needed a priest. As he worked his way up Holly Walk the sunlight seemed to be hard and impersonal, and the laurel on either side of the track was grim and unyielding. Implacable nature, thought Derek, and hoped Martin was still sober and would agree to come to Anne. He was, and he did. He stayed a long time. He even called again, later that day.

*   *   *

As the shock began to wear off, Derek had begun to think
more calmly. After all, there was still a chance that Paul would
find what he was looking for.

'What about your idea that we wouldn't go back to the Dark
Ages because we'd always still have knowledge?' said Martin.
He was standing with Derek in Dynevor's elegant study, looking
out over Church Square and the houses opposite. It was a
beautiful room, elegant and cool, and filled with antique furniture.

'We *do* have the *knowledge*. We just aren't able to put it
into practice very easily. In theory we still know how to put a
man on the moon: but we couldn't do it now because it's far too
complex, even though we could look up all the computer
guidance programmes, and find out how to make space suits.'

'Surely making insulin isn't anything like as complicated.'

'True, but it still demands a lot more people than you might
think. You see the one thing we have lost since the plague is
interdependence. Two hundred years ago life was like it is
now—everything they wanted had to be made, usually within the
same village. They'd have had to go to market for a few
things—iron goods or pottery for example—but they'd make or
grow anything else they wanted. They didn't depend upon other
people, so villages and towns were mainly self-sufficient. They
even worked their own iron—each village had its own smithy.

'But things got more complicated. You didn't heat with
wood from the nearest coppice—you bought coal shipped from
Yorkshire or South Wales; and the pottery came from Stoke.
The more complex society got, the more specialised it became—
electrical goods; cars from the Midlands. By twenty or thirty
years ago *everything* was interconnected. Anything you wanted
had to be made in a special factory—manufacturing in plastic, for
example—and the plastics originated in oil from the Middle East.
But you couldn't get the oil without huge drills—made in places
like the Midlands.

'Then there were all the chemical works making plastics and
paints and solvents and paint strippers and cleaning agents, all in
one big chemical works on Merseyside or in the north-east: and
what about the oil refineries? And so it goes on. Everything was

interdependent. You can't do one thing without requiring help from elsewhere. What about electricity? We can't even make that locally. Or gas? In the past each town had its own gasometer.' He pointed out of the window, down the road towards Maulden. 'Once upon a time Ampthill had its own gasworks, out there, two hundred yards away from here. Yet before the plague everyone got it piped from the North Sea.

'Two hundred years ago the smallest unit that could exist without outside help was a village: then it got to be a town; and just before the plague things had become so interdependent it needed a continent the size of North America before you got a unit that could exist without outside help.

'The *knowledge* is still there all right. It's just the ability to put the knowledge into practice that's the problem. And that's going to remain true for a very long time. What's true of insulin now will soon become true for all other medicines that we use like the anti-depressives I put you on. Most of them are produced by complex chemical processes—no doubt using chemicals from many different chemical factories. We won't be able to get that lot going again in a hurry, I can assure you.'

'What did they do for medicines a hundred and fifty years ago?' asked Jane, coming into the room.

'They grew herbs. They were quite good at using them. I've got a book somewhere about herbal treatment. I think some of them work, but generally they're not as powerful as the modern medicines, though a lot of modern medicines come from herbs and plants of one sort or another—Digoxin for example—that's a heart drug. It's extracted from foxglove leaves. Then there's feverfew, for migraine.'

'Shouldn't we be collecting and growing them so we've got something for the future, when the medicines run out?'

'Yes, we should really. It's just that I'd never thought of it before today.'

He changed the subject. 'Is Anne all right?'

'Yes. She's sleeping.' Jane put her hand on Derek's. 'What do you think are the chances for Alison?'

'Do you really want to know? Nil. I don't think we'll find any viable stores of insulin nor any means of making it: at least, none that we can follow.' He bit the side of his lip, desperately

trying to remain calm, detached and professional. 'If it's made
from bacteria then the bacteria will be dead by now. All the
cultures will be dried out. Remember it's eight months since the
plague. There won't be a thing left, I'm sure of it.'

He was interrupted by a knock on the front door. Martin left
the room quietly and answered it, leaving Derek struggling with
his emotions. It was Alan Rogers.

'Is Derek here? It's Susan. She's got the pain again.'

'I'll come straight away,' called out Derek from the study,
blinking back the tears. 'I'll just get my case.'

He hurried off. Jane watched him from the window as he
turned the corner into Church Street, outlined in the warm
sunlight, and then put her hand on her stomach as the baby gave
her a kick.

-58-

*P*aul came back two days later having spent a whole day
searching the factory. Kevin had taken him there on the Harley-
Davidson—why, he didn't know, except perhaps that he felt a
sense of loyalty to Derek—and had scavenged local stores for
food while Paul did his best to make head or tail of the
information in the laboratory. It was next to impossible. Only
someone who actually worked there could have found his way
round in less than two weeks, and only then if he was lucky and
had a degree in industrial chemistry. Eventually, by sheer
dogged persistence Paul found out which part of the laboratory
housed the insulin production line; but when he got there he
found that the whole wing had been destroyed by fire.

He surveyed the blackened charred mess, and in an odd way
felt relieved. If there had been any faint chance, he knew Derek
would have spent hours trying to culture bacteria and extract
insulin out of the dried mess on the Petri dishes. In many ways it
was cleaner and neater that everything had been destroyed. He
knew in his heart of hearts that Derek would never be able to make

purified insulin on a scale big enough to keep his daughter alive. Perhaps it was better that she would die sooner rather than later.

On his return Paul broke the news to Derek as gently as he could. He needn't have worried—Derek knew already. He couldn't see himself extracting and purifying insulin successfully, either.

So there was nothing that could be done. Derek went into Alison's bedroom, where she was lying in bed weak with the return of her thirst and frequently needing to pass water. Alison knew the answer by the look on her father's face and she bit her lip and turned her face to the wall. Darren, who had loyally stood by her all the time, was sitting on the chair next to the bed holding her hand. He looked as though he was about to cry too, Derek thought. He sat on the bed by his daughter.

'No luck?' she asked hopefully.

'No,' said Derek. 'There's been a fire in the factory. Everything's gone.'

'Oh.' Her eyes filled with tears again and she buried her face in his shoulder.

'I'm sorry, Alison,' he said. 'I'm sorry.'

*   *   *

When it came, the end was mercifully quick. Alison developed a summer cold which, in the sugar-rich secretions in the lining of the lungs soon progressed to a chest infection. Any infection makes a diabetic much worse: twelve hours after starting the chest infection she was unconscious.

Derek had to look on, helpless. He tried antibiotics, but inside he knew that it was pointless and that sooner or later the diabetes would get her, so much so that he half wondered about the wisdom of using up some of the precious remaining antibiotics on a hopeless case. In the end he gave them to her, feeling that he couldn't live with himself if he hadn't tried. Had it been someone else's daughter, he reflected, he might have had the strength to say no, in the knowledge that he wasn't going to affect the outcome, but being a doctor to one's only daughter is a bit different. Subjectivity is always dangerous in medicine, and you can't remain objective when treating your own family. Derek tried the antibiotics and it didn't work.

They buried her the next day in the little cemetery to the north of the parish church, no more than a hundred yards from Dynevor House. Most of the community was there, either because they knew Alison well or out of respect for her father as both leader and doctor to them. It was a sunny day again—hot and humid, with the leaves in the trees rustling gently, high above them.

Martin came out of retirement for a second time to conduct the service. Strangely, he found it easier than he had expected, and easier than he remembered it being in the past. Burying a child had always been difficult for him. He could never understand why God had allowed the death of a child to happen and such times had proved the nearest occasions to real doubt he had experienced. Now, with his loss of faith, deprived of the need to apologise for God, strangely he found he could conduct the service with a completely clear conscience. It made sense that implacable nature would carry off the weaker of the species, the less genetically fitted, leaving only the strongest to continue the line. No longer was there a crisis of belief engendered within him, as there had been in the past.

On the other hand there was no hope either, neither for Alison, nor for her family: and it was when he read the words 'I am the Resurrection and the Life,' that his own doubts recurred and redoubled.

He comforted the family as best he could, including Darren, who was quite distraught, standing at the foot of the grave with tears pouring down his face.

Eventually the mourners left the churchyard. Martin took off his vestments and wandered back up the path to the Old Rectory and the inevitable bottle of whisky. The weather which had been hot and sultry became even more close. He felt some spots of rain and heard a rumble of thunder as the skies closed over and the weather broke.

*   *   *

Dynevor House was a very different place after that. It's hard to lose one's daughter: but it's even harder when you know that you could have saved her, but didn't have the means at your disposal. Derek's mood was not helped by the weather which had suddenly turned. The two brilliant sunny months had suddenly stopped and in their place was rain, teeming down, battering the crops, flattening the corn. The weather seemed to fit Derek's mood as he watched the skies anxiously. Nature, it seemed, was taking it out on them.

In the past, whenever rain had threatened or the weatherman prophesied a front moving up from the Atlantic, Derek had merely glanced at the television for confirmation and taken a raincoat with him to the bus. For most citizens before the plague, rain had been an inconvenience, something that ruined a holiday or a day out, something to make the coat shapeless or the feet sodden and cold. Before, not many had spared a thought for the farmer who needed rain at the right time and needed sun at other times, but now suddenly they were all aware of their dependence upon the vagaries of the weather.

If this continues, thought Derek, we'll lose the whole of the wheat harvest. And up and down the town, anxious faces peered out each day at the grey skies, the cold winds and the rain coming down in sheets. Suddenly Derek's feeling of vulnerability was shared by the whole community—except for Neil, who'd always been accustomed to living with the insecurities engendered by the English climate.

Derek was glancing at the skies yet again when there was a furious hammering on the door. It was Paul. He'd only come seventy-five yards up the street but already he was drenched. 'It's Jane,' he said. 'The baby. It's started.'

'I'll get my bag.' They splashed back to Gates House, Derek experiencing a slight thrill of excitement and apprehension. He'd been present at the birth of both of his children and marvelled at it; and here he was, going to deliver a new life, the first one for the community. But the apprehension was there all right. Had he learned everything? With no one to teach him as an apprentice, he'd found it very difficult, but he'd managed to acquaint himself enough with obstetrics to make him feel that he could cope with most things. He'd practised using the forceps with a dummy baby and pelvis just in case; he'd found them in the shop selling medical equipment. He'd even taught himself to use Keilland's forceps to rotate the head of a baby that was stuck high up in the birth canal. But there was much that could go wrong, he thought, especially in someone who's never had a baby before.

The first part of the labour was absolutely textbook, the contractions coming quite regularly at first, every ten minutes, then more frequently and more painfully. Eventually he gave her 50mg of pethidine to ease the pain. He had another vial of pethidine ready in his bag, just in case.

The first stage lasted six hours, which wasn't bad. The baby was lying in the normal position, heartbeat normal, the rate dipping down as each contraction occurred, then going back up again afterwards, as usual. Jane seemed in good shape too.

Regular internal examinations helped Derek keep track of the progression of the labour. Finally the neck of the womb became fully dilated and he told Jane she could start pushing, and with each successive contraction he could feel the baby begin to move down.

Ten minutes later nothing further seemed to have happened, so he did yet another internal examination, to feel for the suture line on the head and get the exact position of the baby in the birth canal. He couldn't feel it.

'I've got another contraction,' said Jane, gripping the bed.

'OK,' said Derek, stopping probing. The contraction obviously hurt Jane this time, but there was no progression of the head downwards even though she was obviously pushing as hard as she could. A little finger of suspicion waved inside Derek's mind and he felt for the suture line again. Not there. He ran his fingers down the centre of the skull and felt it go into a little hole. His heart leapt into his mouth. What on earth have I done, he thought. I can't have put a finger straight through the baby's skull, can I? He pulled his finger out and carefully felt around. There was a small ridge, and then another hollow. Derek suddenly realised that he was feeling the top of the baby's nose. But it shouldn't be there! The baby was trying to come down the birth canal forehead first, rather than head first, and the words of his obstetric book stood out clear in his mind, as though he were reading it. *'Brow presentation is undeliverable and requires an immediate Caesarean section.'*

Oh no, not again, thought Derek. Oh God, not again. Not a brow presentation. Oh please, not a brow presentation. Jane shrieked as another contraction hit her and she strained and

strained, but nothing happened. He gave her the second dose of
pethidine and tried to think of something to do, but nothing
would come. In between contractions he tried to rotate the
baby's head, first with his hands and then with the Keilland's
forceps, but it was stuck firmly. He listened for the baby's heart
but it was faint and irregular and didn't come back to its normal
beat in between contractions.

The anaesthetic machine had been ready in the house for
some time, and he switched on some nitrous oxide and oxygen
and held the mask over Jane's face until she was drowsy, then he
ran round to the other end and tried to manoeuvre the baby whilst
there was no resistance and no contraction from Jane. It
wouldn't shift. Panic-stricken he rushed to the mouthpiece and
gave Jane another couple of whiffs of gas before struggling yet
again to try to move the baby's head into a better position. It
wouldn't budge.

He couldn't possibly do a Caesarean section. He would kill
Jane, and probably the baby as well in the process. Again he
listened for the baby's heart with a foetal stethoscope, but
couldn't find it. He tried again, visualising the baby inside the
womb slowly asphyxiating, its umbilical cord trapped between its
own head and the side of the pelvis.

Again he tried to shift the baby's head, this time pushing it
upwards towards the centre of the abdomen in the hope that
maybe he could bend it to a better position where it could be
delivered. Nothing moved. He was scared to continue the
anaesthetic for any longer so he left the mask off and allowed
Jane to wake up, which she did, screaming in pain. He had no
more pethidine left in the bag. He listened again for the baby's
heart. Nothing. Paul came back into the room, alerted by Jane's
scream. He looked at Derek's face.

'What's happened?'

'I . . . I don't know yet,' said Derek. 'Things aren't going
too well. The baby's not in the right position and I've run out of
pethidine. I'm just going across to the chemist's to get some
more,' and so saying he tore off his rubber gloves and rushed out
of the house. Entering the pharmacy, he flung open the door of
the cupboard in which the dangerous drugs were kept. There in
front of him were the rows of pethidine boxes.

He opened the first one. It was empty. Odd, he thought, surely I hadn't used that much on Susan. He threw it in the bin and went to the second. That was empty too. So was the third, and with a chill in his spine he went through each and every box of pethidine and morphine and diamorphine. Every single one was empty.

He rushed back to Dynevor House, found Anne and told her to go to the chemist down in Flitwick, break into the dangerous drugs cupboard, get some pethidine and bring it back to Gates House.

Anne ran off to get the Peugeot. Derek went back to the bedroom where Jane was in great distress.

'Have you got it?' said Paul looking up at him.

'No,' said Derek. 'Someone's pinched the lot, all the pethidine, all the morphine. It's all gone.'

'You what?' said Paul, wide-eyed.

'Every little bit of it has gone,' said Derek. 'Every last drop of morphine and pethidine and every one of the dangerous drugs. All empty.'

'Kevin,' said Paul. 'That . . . . . . Kevin.'

Derek put on another pair of gloves and examined Jane again. No progress. Everything was as it was before. Ten minutes later Anne came into the room in obvious distress. Two pairs of eyes looked up at her.

'Did you get it?'

'No,' she said, 'there isn't any. Someone's been there before us and broken into the dangerous drugs box. There's nothing there, just empty cartons.'

Jane gave out a shriek as another contraction hit her.

'Try somewhere else. Shefford. Aspley Guise. Anywhere . . .' Anne ran out to the car again.

'What are we going to do?' said Paul, panic written all over his face.

'I don't know,' said Derek. He did though. He remembered what the doctors in the past had done when presented with a problem like this. Faced with a dead baby and a dying mother they dismembered the baby, cutting it apart piece by piece, and delivered it that way. Sometimes they saved the mother's life that way. The thought of doing something like that made Derek feel sick. Why, oh why, he thought, why do I have something like this for my first delivery? Another contraction hit Jane. She gave a shriek and passed out.

Derek pushed on the baby's head as hard as he possibly could and suddenly something gave and the head moved into the right position. He put the Keilland's forceps on and pulled and slowly the head of the baby came into view, purple, and very dead. He delivered the head. The umbilical cord was wound tightly round the neck, and it was this that had asphyxiated the baby so quickly.

He undid the cord, delivered the rest of the baby and waited for the next contraction to deliver the afterbirth. It came away on the end of the cord, looking like the roots of a tree and immediately after it followed torrents of bright red blood as Jane exsanguinated—a postpartum haemorrhage, the most dangerous emergency of the lot.

Derek tried to make the womb go into spasm by rubbing up a contraction, but still the blood came out. Quickly he pulled out an ampoule of ergometrine, found a vein and injected it. It seemed to make no difference and Paul and Derek watched as Jane, now unconscious, grew paler as her blood spread out onto the bed and dripped onto the floor.

Derek felt her pulse at the wrist. It became weaker and weaker and then more irregular and finally stopped altogether.

'Can't you do mouth-to-mouth resuscitation?' screamed Paul at him, but Derek shook his head. There was no point. Without any blood to pump there's no point in keeping the heart beating. Paul began to get hysterical, shaking Jane and calling for her to wake up. Finally, the awful truth sank in and he became silent. Eventually he turned and wordlessly left the room.

Derek placed the body of the baby at the bottom of Jane's bed and pulled a sheet over both of them. The sheet turned crimson as it touched the blood that had oozed everywhere over Jane's lower parts, and onto the bed. He took off his gloves, collected all the debris of the ampoules, needles and syringes together and packed his bag up.

He'd intended to go straight home, but he never made it. The trauma of losing first his daughter, then the baby and then Jane proved too much for him. His legs buckled and he

collapsed on to the stool by the dressing table, buried his head in
his hands and, surrounded by the debris of two lost lives, and the
guilt of his secret feelings for Jane, sobbed his heart out.

*   *   *

They buried Jane the next day, next to Alison, in the old
village tradition with mother and baby sharing the same coffin. It
was raining as they had the service in the church, but it stopped
before they went out for the committal. If Martin had found
himself untroubled by the previous burial because he no longer
needed to ask why God had allowed a child to die, illogically,
exactly the reverse applied to Jane's funeral, and when he came to
'I am the Resurrection and the Life' it was all he could do just to
get the words out. You swap one problem for another, he thought.
Ashes to ashes, dust to dust, but where did the ashes come from in
the first place? Where did the universe come from? Where is
Jane now? What is Jane now? *Is* Jane now? And the questions
and the problems raced round his brain in a great turmoil, sapping
his energy again like a huge electrical short circuit.

He finished the committal by the skin of his teeth and went
back to the vestry to disrobe. As he went up the lane back to the
Old Rectory he was in a daze. A few of the community greeted
him as he left the church, but he made no response, and trudged
up the lane as if in a dream. Underneath it all was a renewed
sense of total loss—loss of God, loss of peace, loss of love, loss
of the first person he'd spoken to after the plague and with whom
he'd shared the front seat of the car on his way from London.
Loss of a friend, loss of the new life of a baby, loss of hope.
Loss for Paul. Loss for Derek, loss for them all. He turned into
the drive of the Old Rectory knowing that that evening he was
going to get more drunk than he'd ever been before in the whole
of his life.

*   *   *

Derek meanwhile had left the grave and turned in the
opposite direction, back to Dynevor House. He too was in a daze.
He had something to say to the council, but he'd been pre-empted.
The council also wanted to say something to him and to Kevin,
and had called a meeting for the next morning at ten o'clock.

Seeing Derek was in no fit state to offer assistance to Paul, Anne decided that she ought to visit him. She went through the large iron gates, up the steps and across the pea-gravel path to the front door and banged on the knocker. There was no reply. She tried again more loudly. She was pretty sure that Paul was still in the house, but still there was no reply. Anxious to make sure that he was all right she banged a third time and after an interval there was the sound of the latch being drawn as Paul opened the door. He looked vacant, distant.

'How are you feeling?' said Anne gently. 'Can I do anything?'

Paul swayed slightly. He must have been at the whisky, too, thought Anne. He started mumbling something incoherently and staggered slightly, his glazed face pressed against the edge of the door. 'No . . . All right . . . Want to be alone . . . Thanks anyway,' and he smiled an odd cracked smile at Anne and slowly and erratically shut the door on her.

Anne turned away. Better leave him to it, to do his mourning in his own way. Of all of the community, Paul had lost so little before, she thought. Only now had he started to lose what had really been precious to him, because even after the plague he'd still had Jane, and the two of them had formed a cohesive solid unit. He would be like a man with one leg, she thought as she opened the massive iron gate leading onto the road and closed it gently behind her. He won't have anything to live for, not now.

-59-

*I*t was raining again the next day as the council met. Neil, who'd spent the last weeks anxiously looking up at the sky and muttering, was getting more and more worried. If this weather continued they were going to lose the whole of their wheat crop. He kept glancing out of the window, but there was no break in the cloud. It was bitterly cold for a July day, with a high wind to make things even worse.

In the courtroom the council decided to hold a brief investigation into the circumstances surrounding Jane's death, but this led to a few tricky problems of protocol. Both Paul and Derek had to be excluded as having a particular interest, while Martin was in no fit state to take the chair—in fact he was in no fit state to do anything, even think straight, having succeeded in giving himself an even bigger hangover than the one he'd had on the day he'd first bumped into Paul and Jane.

Susan would have been the next choice, but she wasn't well either and declined the offer. Anne couldn't take the chair because of her relationship to Derek and so it was eventually decided that Chris would hold the gavel.

She cleared her throat. 'I'm sure none of us want this to become too much like a formal court hearing, but we ought to investigate the circumstances surrounding Jane's death, and see if anything should have been done differently.'

There were nods round the table.

'It isn't appropriate to conduct a witch-hunt. When the council was first formed we said that we didn't want to create all the paraphernalia of law, and that we wanted to keep things simple. Well, let's do just that. Are we agreed?'

It was agreed.

They called Derek first. He told them how, at his first obstetric case, he'd been faced with a baby in a position that was impossible to deliver; how he'd tried as hard as he could; that someone had ransacked the chemist's supplies of pethidine and morphine, and of how Jane had been in agony as a result, finally bleeding to death from a post-delivery haemorrhage. He spoke accurately but flatly, without emotion, staring at the table-top in front of him.

Afterwards they asked him a few questions. Was he sure there was nothing else he could have done? He was sure. When he got back did he have a look at his books? Yes he did. Had he remembered what to do correctly? Yes he had. Did they say there was anything else that he should have done? No they didn't.

Then the council called Paul as a witness, and he corroborated everything Derek had said. They asked him why he suspected Kevin of stealing the pethidine.

'Because he's that sort of person,' flared Paul. 'Can't you

see? He does what he wants, when he wants. It's where he came from before the plague. That sort of person is the sort of person who's into drugs, just the right sort of person to take heroin . . .'

'Heroin?' asked the Major, sitting even more bolt upright than normal. 'Who said anything about heroin?'

'Heroin and diamorphine are the same thing, Major,' interjected Anne, 'and pethidine is a close relative.'

Paul continued. 'It'll be Kevin all right. He'll deny it, of course, but we'll all know.'

There were nods round the table again, particularly from the Major, who cleared his throat. 'Paul, I . . . that is . . . we . . . want to say how sorry we all are about Jane. And I'm sure that we will all want to find and punish whoever stole the drugs.'

A row of bobbing heads indicated the council's approval. Chris, who had had her position slightly usurped by Major Thornton's declaration, rather pointedly asked Paul and Derek to leave the room, then giving Major Thornton a stare she asked in turn for everyone's opinion. They were unanimous—Derek had done his best, having been faced with an impossible task, and should be totally exonerated from any blame attached to Jane's death. Paul was to be commiserated with: and Kevin was to be sent for immediately, to be tried by the council that afternoon.

Derek and Paul were brought back for the verdict. Derek listened without emotion, whilst Paul seemed even less affected by the proceedings, more distant even than Derek—but then he was the more recently bereaved of the two of them.

After Chris had delivered their verdict Derek indicated that he wanted to speak.

'I've been thinking,' he said. 'I really can't be your doctor—I'm not cut out for it. The stress is just too great. You've been very kind to me in what you've said, but I really do feel very responsible for Jane's death. I feel I should have been able to do more.' For the first time that morning he raised his eyes and looked at them. 'I can't be a doctor, I just can't. The strain is too great, the responsibility too demanding. I don't really know what I'm doing, and there's no way to find out. I just can't do it any longer. I can't continue.'

There was a ripple of 'No, no' round the table. Susan was the first to speak.

'Derek, we know how you feel, but you mustn't blame yourself. It was fate, nature—'

Or God? thought Martin in his hangover haze. No it couldn't have been God, God doesn't exist. Or if he did exist, he only makes problems for everyone. So he was either an unloving God who did exist, or a loving God who didn't. Not much choice there, he thought, and dreamed of the whisky bottle again.

'—it was nature that caused the problem, not you. When we first asked you to be our doctor you said you'd only do it as long as people didn't hold you responsible if things went wrong. Well, we haven't held you responsible, and we aren't going to.'

'But you've held an inquest, haven't you?' said Derek. 'What would you have said if you thought I *had* made a mistake?'

There was a sudden silence. Susan continued, ignoring the riposte. 'I—we all—think you've done splendidly so far, under most difficult circumstances. You haven't anyone to guide you and you've had to do it all from books. You've looked after me very well, too, and I'm grateful. But don't expect too much—of yourself, or of others. Life now is more precarious than it used to be. We'll all have to get used to living like this.'

Alan Rogers, acutely conscious of his wife's need of Derek's skills, took up the same theme. 'We all know you feel cut up about Jane, and you must be devastated about Alison: but don't make any decisions now, because you're too shocked to make sensible ones. We really do understand the stresses facing you, you know.'

There was a murmur of approval. Derek returned to staring blankly at the table in front of him.

'No, you *don't* understand what it's like,' he said, dully. 'It's the most isolated feeling I've ever had. To be responsible for somebody else's life and not to know what you're doing . . . I just *can't* take the strain of it any more.'

'I agree with Alan,' said Chris. 'I don't think you're in a fit state to make any long-term decisions. Wait for a bit, then see how you feel.'

'Can I make a different point?' asked Alan. 'Whoever's our doctor, and whatever happens, sooner or later we're going to run completely out of drugs and we won't be able to manufacture any more. Wouldn't it be sensible to start collecting and growing the herbs that the old apothecaries used? At least that way whoever becomes our doctor in the future will have a renewable supply of medicines; and we won't have to eke out the stocks we have before they all go over their expiry dates.'

Derek nodded his agreement in a blank sort of way.

'That's an excellent idea,' said Chris briskly. 'Neil, can you give some thought to organising it? And on that positive note, I think we'll end the meeting.'

-60-

*K*evin, protesting, was frogmarched from his house to the court-room amid scenes reminiscent of the French Revolution. The community wanted blood, they wanted expiation, they wanted a sacrifice and they were going to get it. It didn't matter how many times Derek said Jane's death wasn't caused through lack of pain relief: they all felt that Kevin was responsible.

'So now we know where you've been going on that bike,' said Paul who was back in the chair, and had also cast himself in the role of chief prosecutor, and with a bit of luck hanging judge as well. 'Raiding chemist's shops.'

Kevin shook his head sullenly.

'I don't believe you,' said Paul. 'Nor does anybody else here.'

'It's not true,' said Kevin, staring at his feet. Cries of 'Rubbish' echoed round the courtroom.

'All right,' said Paul. 'Prove it. Prove you didn't take it.'

Martin made as if to protest and then thought better of it. In a previous court of law that would have been the wrong way round. Kevin shouldn't have to prove his innocence: Paul should have to prove Kevin's guilt. We've gone back to medieval times, he thought: we'll have trial by ordeal next. He was going to say something about it, but the banging inside his head was too great. No one would have listened to him anyway.

'How can I prove that I *didn't* take it?' said Kevin to Paul, with a snarl. 'It could have been any one of us in the community.'

'You're the one who's most likely to want to use it though,' said the Major.

'Why? Why pick on me? I tell you I didn't.'

'As I said, prove it,' said Paul, menacingly.

'All right,' said Kevin. 'What makes you think *I* took it? Where's your evidence? Has anyone seen me going into the chemist's?'

'You could go in the middle of the night,' said Paul. 'Nobody would see you.'

'Well I didn't, see.'

Paul turned away with an expression of total disgust and disbelief.

'What would I want it for anyway?'

'*You're* asking *me* that?' said Paul.

'Yes.'

'Well, what does anybody use pethidine and heroin and morphine for? Injecting of course. Intravenously. It's easy enough for you to get the apparatus. Just go down to the Health Centre. There's thousands of needles and syringes down there.'

'So if I use morphine and heroin I'd be injecting it? Right?'

'Right,' said Paul, 'that's what you did, didn't you?'

'Well, I'll show you something,' said Kevin, rolling up his left sleeve. 'Look.'

He showed his arm to the council and then to the rest of the audience. There were no marks on it. He pulled up the other sleeve. That was clear too.

'Don't give me that,' said Paul, obviously taken aback. 'Just because you don't use it now doesn't mean you didn't use it in the past. It's all run out now, hasn't it? That's why you keep going off on your bike to try and find more supplies.'

'No,' said Kevin. 'No I don't, but I tell you what,' he said, changing his gaze from Paul to Chris. 'Why don't we ask everyone in the community to show their arms to the council, and see who's got needle marks?'

'*If* anyone else has needle marks, you mean,' said Paul in an irritated tone. 'You're just playing for time.'

'No, I think it's a good idea,' said Chris. 'It would be easier if everyone in the hall were to bare their arms and show them to their neighbours, and then if anyone has anything that looks like needle marks they should come forward and Derek can examine them.'

There was a general swirl of clothing as sleeves were pulled up, sweaters taken off and forearms and elbows displayed to the people nearby. There were one or two cries of 'show it to the council' as vigilant eyes spotted odd lesions of questionable origin. They were brought to Derek, who gave each a careful inspection.

The first was Stephen Porter, a lad of eighteen, with obvious eczema on the inside of his elbows, whose itching had caused him to scratch: he had a number of straight scratches where the irritation had proved too great, but they were obviously not injection marks. Derek moved on to the second man, the burly Trevor Smith, whose arms were covered in light scratches as a result of an argument with a hawthorn bush—the hawthorn bush had obviously won. Two more sets of arms were shown to Derek, but after a brief look he shook his head and asked their owners to go back to their places.

'You see,' said Paul. 'No one else has been shooting heroin. Just because you've stopped, doesn't mean you didn't do it before.'

'Oh no,' said Kevin with a leer. 'We haven't excluded everybody, have we? *What about the members of the council?*'

A silence fell on the room and suddenly an icy hand gripped Derek's heart as all the pieces of the puzzle fell into place, and he knew, he *knew* what was going to happen. One by one the members of the council rolled up their arms to show the assembled community. Derek and Anne, Chris, Major Thornton, Alan and Susan Rogers, Mary, Neil and Peter, which left only Martin and Paul. Martin shrugged and pulled up his right sleeve. The skin was clean. He pulled up the left sleeve. That was clean too.

And all eyes fixed on Paul.

'You don't really think it was me, do you? After all it was Jane who died, you know. I know we weren't married, but . . . Oh well, if you must.' He rolled up his left sleeve. The skin of the arm was completely unmarked. He imitated an imaginary syringe being injected into the left arm. 'See. Nothing there. Now will you believe me that it's Kevin who stole the morphine?'

'No,' said Chris evenly, 'not until you roll up your other sleeve. You're left-handed.'

'Oh, come on,' said Paul, 'this charade has gone on long enough.'

'Roll up your right sleeve, Paul,' said Chris firmly. With a shrug Paul reached down, unbuttoned the right cuff and rolled up the sleeve. The arm was covered in needle tracks.

Derek sat back in his chair, his worst suspicions confirmed. That was why Paul had been so odd on occasions, with his slurred speech, his incoordination and his pin-point pupils. Then, hard on the knowledge of Paul's guilt came the realisation that if only he, Derek, had been quicker he'd have spotted it earlier and saved Jane some of her agony.

And then Derek watched the humiliation of his friend, outside his family the one to whom he was closest in the whole community, the one on whose advice he had so often relied, the man who'd driven him hard enough to work out how to diagnose and treat Alison, and give her those extra precious months of life. In front of the whole of the community their leader, their thinker, was brought low, the man who had so powerfully analysed and prophesied what needed to be done and had encouraged and driven them to organise themselves properly.

'There you are,' said Kevin with a surprising lack of rancour. 'Does anybody mind if I go now?'

'Yes,' said Chris, still looking shocked. 'Yes *I* do. Kevin, I want to say on behalf of us all that I'm very sorry for what we've just done. We distrusted you without any real reason, and misjudged you completely. I'm sure you'll agree that in the past relationships between you and the rest of us haven't been easy, but it was quite wrong of us to assume that because you were not toeing the line in other directions, or else'—she glared at the Major—'because of your background you should necessarily be the one most likely to have committed a crime like this. Please will you accept my apologies personally, and on behalf of everyone here. We are very sorry.'

There was a shamefaced murmur of agreement from the whole of the council mirrored by a murmur from the audience.

'Now that you have your real culprit, are you going to punish him?' asked Kevin. 'Bearing in mind of course that he is the chairman of the council and one of the boys.'

'Yes,' said Chris, riled, 'we will. We're not going to have one rule for the council and another for everybody else. Justice is justice and it applies equally to everyone. Paul, I think you have some explaining to do.'

Paul stood up, defiant. 'For the record,' he said, 'all I've done is used some morphine and pethidine—that's all. When I worked in the City I was in the habit of snorting cocaine from time to time. I could handle it. When we came here life was a bit dull by comparison, but the night that we went into the chemist to get the insulin for Alison I saw the drugs there, so I started using it again. Not often, you understand, just from time to time, when things got difficult or I needed a pick-me-up. I wasn't really hooked, but it was nice to have it. That's all. And I haven't done anything wrong, you know, because we agreed to abolish all the laws and start off afresh, didn't we? So we haven't got any laws about using drugs.'

The members of the council looked at each other in consternation. Paul was right. 'In any case,' he said, 'who's to define what's a drug? What a good job we don't call alcohol a drug, especially whisky.' He threw a quick glance at Martin, who flushed.

'What about Jane?' said Chris.

'Can I remind you that Jane was my wife in all but name? I'm not a fool. I know that I hurt her by not leaving a big enough supply behind in the chemist's, and I wish to goodness that it hadn't happened like that, but it isn't against our new law to use drugs.'

'No,' said Chris. 'You're right—it isn't.' There was a rustle from the audience, who were having a hard time swallowing what they were being given.

'Nor,' said Paul, 'is it against our law to take things which were the property of someone else before the plague—otherwise everyone here would be guilty of theft. I haven't taken anything that was the property of anyone else here. It belonged to the chemist before the plague. Nor was I responsible for Jane's death. I admit that my actions may have caused her some extra pain, but I didn't plan that, and I certainly didn't realise that I'd used up the last of the stocks. We can always get more from chemists in other towns. There'll be no problem about that—I'll get it myself if it makes you happier. I haven't done anything that you can charge me with under our new laws, so if you don't mind, I'd like to go, too. I don't like remembering Jane's death any more than anyone else and thinking about it means more pain to me than it does to any of you.'

'You're right,' said Chris evenly. 'You haven't stolen from anyone here, and as Derek said you didn't cause Jane's death. That was an act of God, or nature, or chance, or whatever you want to call it. And you're right that the drugs were no one's personal property. And you're right that there is no law against taking drugs in this community.'

Suddenly her voice went steely hard. 'But you are wrong when you say that you haven't broken any of our laws. We have a new law which you agreed to and which you knew all about: that every member of the community has a duty not to do anything which would harm any other member of the community or the community itself—*and you broke that law*. You broke that law by taking from our communal supply of drugs, unnecessarily.'

'So did Kevin with the petrol,' interjected Paul.

'I know, and we've already remonstrated with him about that. But there's a lot less morphine available in comparison to the amount you took than the amount of petrol that Kevin has used *and* you left the supply in a dangerous state—if you'd only thrown away the empty boxes perhaps we'd have realised that we needed to replenish them. But because you left them in place, hoping that no one would notice, you made it harder when things came to a head.'

'They could have been replaced very easily,' said Paul. 'There's a chemist four miles away in Aspley Guise. I haven't been near that one.'

'I know,' said Chris, 'and bearing in mind what happened to Jane, we could overlook all of this. You're the one who's going to have to live the rest of your life with the memory of Jane's screams. That should be penalty enough. *But you tried to blame Kevin* and that, Paul, is unforgivable. Whatever else you may or may not have done, accusing Kevin was a direct attempt to shift blame, and inflict harm, quite unfairly, on to someone else: and you nearly succeeded. There is no question that you are guilty of that. Everyone in this room heard you.'

For once Paul was silent. He stared stony-faced at the council, his self-composure visibly fraying.

'I suggest therefore that the council meets privately to discuss a suitable punishment.'

While the main courtroom buzzed with conversation, the council retired to the magistrates' rooms, ten of them crammed into a room originally intended for the deliberations of just three people.

'Well?' said Chris. 'Where do we go from here? This is our first case. We'd better get it right.'

'Flog the little whipper-snapper,' interjected the Major. 'Disgusting man: I've always said so. Make him an example. Drug addiction . . .' He shook his head.

'That's exactly *not* the point,' said Alan Rogers, angrily. 'Let's get it right. We're *not* punishing him for using drugs as such. It's for taking away the stuff in the first place, when others might need it, and then trying to blame Kevin. We're not punishing him for using it, whatever any of us might feel about the rights and wrongs of that.'

'What punishment do you suggest then?' asked Chris. There was a silence. 'Anyone?'

'Flogging's about the only punishment available to us,' said Neil, after a time. 'The only question is—how much?'

'Seven strokes?' suggested Chris, tentatively.

'No,' said Anne, 'more. Two for the theft, and seven for trying to get Kevin to take the blame.'

Derek looked sideways at his wife. 'I thought you were one of the "love and understand them" school,' he murmured.

'Do you really think a hug would work in Paul's case?'

There was a silence.

'Are we all agreed?' asked Chris. 'Major? Martin? Susan?' They each indicated their assent.

'Peter, what about you? Do you think what we're doing is right?'

Peter had said little throughout the trial: his thoughts had been of another trial, in another time and place, and now, it seemed, in another world; of the magistrates who'd been discussing him, in a similar room, and delivered such an unjust result. He cleared his throat.

'Let's try and forget what we've seen of the law in the past. I've got just two questions: are we sure he's guilty? Well, yes, there's no doubt, is there? Secondly, does the punishment *really*

fit the crime? Will it punish him properly? Will it prevent him
doing it again? Will it warn others what they can expect if they
themselves do wrong? I think it does.'

'But Paul's a member of the council,' interjected Susan.
'Shouldn't we add on punishment for that alone? Paul should
have known better, so he should be punished more.'

The Major nodded vigorously.

'*No!*' shouted Peter. 'I . . . I'm sorry, I didn't mean to shout,
but do that and you make out that those on the council are
different—better than—anyone else in the community, so we
should have a bigger fall. Well, we're not better than anyone
else. We've just been given a job to do, and if we go against the
rules we should be punished the same as anyone else, not more.
It doesn't matter that Paul's our leader; all that matters is what
he's done, and what is needed to stop him—or anyone else—
doing it again.'

The Major shook his head.

'I agree with Peter,' interjected Derek. 'We *all* have to abide
by the same law. There can't be one law for the rich and one for
the poor, one for those on the council, another for the rest.
Everyone must be treated the same.'

'All agreed?—except Major Thornton, that is?' asked Chris.
There was a murmur of assent.

'And when it's over it's got to be forgotten about, too,' said
Peter, impassioned. 'No harking back to it, no late recriminations.'

'I'm sure that goes without saying,' said Chris. There was a
further murmur round the table. 'Then we're all agreed—nine
lashes. Now who's going to administer it?'

A few minutes later the council returned to the main
courtroom and a hush descended.

'Paul, you will stand in front of us,' said Chris crisply. 'You
have been found guilty of one of the worst possible crimes in our
community, that of hurting another member of it. Stealing from
our meagre supply of drugs was bad enough, but deliberately
trying to push the blame onto Kevin was even worse. You will
receive nine lashes . . .'

Paul went white. Kevin gleefully started unbuckling his belt.

'. . . which will *not* be administered by Kevin. We will draw
lots to decide who will administer the punishment—from among

all those in the community aged between eighteen and sixty-five.'

As luck would have it the lot fell on the barrel-chested Trevor Smith, who also happened to be one of Kevin's particular friends. Paul blanched again, as Kevin rubbed his hands with glee. 'We will *not*,' said Chris to Trevor, 'we will not go overboard. He will be tied to the market pump, and you will whip him across his bare back nine times.'

They pulled Paul, kicking, struggling and protesting, up Woburn Street, Trevor gripping his left arm, Peter the right. Someone produced a length of rope and at the stone pump they took Paul's top clothes off and tied him so that his arms went round the pillar with the rope completing the circle. Then Trevor began the punishment. At each blow Paul gave a short cry as the welts showed up on his back, larger versions of the scars now so prominently displayed on the inside of his forearm. He was no coward, but he still cried out with each blow and a little trickle of blood ran down his mouth where he had bitten his lower lip in an attempt to keep from shrieking.

When the sentence had been duly carried out, Trevor handed Kevin back his belt.

'Now I want everyone to know,' said Chris, looking round at the crowd, 'that the council has determined that this is to be the end of the whole affair. We are still a community and, Paul, we still care about you and want you as one of our number. You have been punished for the reasons you know all too well, but it is over and we hold no further anger or recrimination against you. Let this be an end to it,' and with that she untied the rope that was tethering Paul's wrists and handed him his shirt. She turned round again to the watching crowd and raised her voice slightly. 'Now I suggest we all go away and get on with our work.'

No one in the crowd could remember Chris being as firm as she had been that day, and no one felt able to suggest anything different. They rapidly dispersed leaving just Chris, Paul and Derek alone in the square. Paul winced as he put his shirt back on.

'Paul, I think you ought to stay at our house tonight,' said Derek. 'You can't go back to your own house, not after this: not after Jane, not on your own.' Then, looking at the blood that was occasionally staining Paul's shirt, he added, 'In any case, you look as though you need patching up.'

Paul nodded ruefully.

'Paul—I didn't enjoy doing what we did today,' said Chris.
She had visions of having made an enemy for all time, particularly
with Paul's reputation. Paul looked up at her and half-grinned.

'I don't blame you. I'd have done the same in your place. I
suppose I shouldn't have done what I did, so I can't blame you or
anyone else for reacting to what I've done, can I? No hard
feelings, eh?' and unexpectedly he held out his hand to Chris.
She accepted it gratefully.

'Let's forget about it from now on, shall we?'

'Fine, but I think I ought to resign from the council.'

'No,' she said firmly, 'forgetting about it means *forgetting*
about it.'

'I hardly think I can continue as chairman.'

'I don't see why not,' said Derek. 'It would be going against
what we've just said.'

'Just at the moment I doubt if anyone will have much
confidence in my decisions.'

'If you're referring to your bereavement, yes—for a bit. If
you're thinking about today's events, I would hope no.'

Chris left them, and the two men walked slowly back to
Dynevor House. As they passed Gates House Paul suddenly
stopped and stared at his home through the railings.

'Why is it that we only become aware of what we've got
when we haven't got it any more?' he asked, almost to himself.

'Jane?'

'And everything else, I suppose. Respect . . . contentment . . .
responsibility . . . power . . . money . . . society . . . It's all gone.'

'But mostly Jane?'

'Mostly Jane.'

'It hadn't really hit you before, had it.'

'No.' There was a pause. 'I was too concerned trying not to
get found out, I suppose. But it's all gone now. Everything. I
can't even leave and start again somewhere else . . . Well, I
suppose I could try to see if I can make contact with another
community, but it would be difficult . . .

He swung round to face Derek. 'How am I going to talk to
people again, look them in the eye, after this? Always, *always*,
I'll know what they'll be thinking, and it won't be about what

I'm saying, they'll be thinking "There's Paul, the drug-taker, the one who killed his wife . . ." '

'I doubt it. Time will change things. And you're low at the moment—it's natural that you should take a pessimistic view. You heard what Chris said—forgive and forget.'

'Can you really see it making any difference?'

'Do you think what's happened is going to affect our relationship?'

'Oh no . . . well . . . not much.'

'Or with Anne?'

'. . . no . . .?'

'Or Chris?'

'But what about the Major? Trevor? Neil? And all the others I don't know as well?'

'Let's deal with that if it happens. I hope it won't be necessary. Come on, back to Dynevor. Food beckons. I think you need some.'

They walked the hundred yards to Dynevor House in silence. The grieving process had begun.

-61-

Derek also was grieving, first and foremost for Alison, of course, but also for Jane; and with very mixed emotions, too. Although he had never told anyone of his feelings for her, he still felt guilty about them: why, he couldn't quite say, as he didn't have any religious beliefs. It wasn't logical to feel guilty, but knowing this didn't seem to make the feelings go away.

Anyway, he missed her. He missed her as a friend. He missed her attractiveness, her glamour, her conversation, her presence. And though Derek had forgiven Paul for removing the pethidine, he couldn't get Jane out of his mind, he couldn't forget the baby, he couldn't forget how she'd died, nor could he escape that supreme sense of isolation and desolation at having failed them both.

But worse was to come. At the council's next meeting Derek

once again broached the subject of their finding someone else to
be their doctor, and was surprised by the stiff reaction he got.

'But you can't give up,' said Chris in an irritated tone. 'We
told you this last time. We haven't got anyone else.'

'I know that,' said Derek. 'Not at the moment that is. But
there's no reason why someone else shouldn't get trained. After
all I can teach some things to whoever takes over—so they
wouldn't have to start quite where I did.'

'Had you forgotten?' asked Major Thornton testily. 'We all
arranged to do your work for you so that you could learn how to
be our doctor. We didn't do it for fun, you know.'

'I'm well aware of that, Major,' said Derek, 'but the truth of
the matter is I'm an engineer. I'm not cut out to be a doctor. I
didn't realise this at the time you all asked me. It's not the
intellectual learning or knowledge side of it that's the problem—
it's . . . it's the strain, the pressure of knowing that I'm
responsible, yet not knowing whether what I'm doing is right or
not—and often not having the resources to do what I'd like to do
anyway.'

'Surely you could have foreseen this?' asked Chris.

'Not really. I don't think until you've done any job you can
see what the emotional pressures are going to be. Everyone
thinks they'd make a jolly good job of being Prime Minister'—he
corrected himself—'everyone *used* to think that they could make
a go of being Prime Minister, but would they have stood the
pressure? The jibes? The comments of those who criticise from
a distance without ever having to take responsibility for *their own*
actions?

'It's easy to look only logically at someone else's job, and
forget that there are emotional strains as well. I just didn't realise
what the strains were going to be. Had I known I wouldn't have
accepted your invitation. I know what they are now and I know
how difficult they are to face.'

Susan, who was fortunately well enough to attend the
council that day, chipped in. 'But Derek, we never expected you
to be perfect: don't you remember? You made us promise not to
hold you responsible if things went wrong, and we haven't. We
didn't blame you over Jane's death. We didn't blame you over
Alison's death–'

'No,' interrupted Derek, 'because there was nothing to blame me for, because I did all the things that I was supposed to. But what would you have done if you'd found something that you thought I should have done differently. That would have altered things, wouldn't it?'

'Well—' began Susan.

'No, it's not a matter of "Well",' spat out Derek angrily. 'That's what would have happened. If you'd thought that what I'd done had killed Jane you'd have been very quick to blame me. People have very short memories for promises, and very long ones for mistakes. I don't mind doing my best with cuts, bruises and scrapes, but dealing with people's lives is a different matter. One slip and they're dead . . . perhaps. Or else permanently injured. All I've got to do is get a dose of a drug wrong, or mix two drugs that I shouldn't, or get the wrong diagnosis, or set a bone incorrectly and the patient's in trouble and *I'm* in trouble.

'Don't forget I've got no one to guide me, *no one*. No one else in the community is in that position. You've all got a trade or a craft or a profession that you're busy using or teaching to other people; or else there's somebody in the community who's actively teaching you. Look at those who are helping on the farms: most of them have had no previous experience, but they're learning fast from you, Neil, and from those who were farmworkers before the plague. I've got no one to teach me— just books: for something as complex as medicine books are just not enough, at least not to get the subtle things right first time.

'No, I've had enough, and I'm quitting. I'll go back to earning my keep on the farm or doing engineering, my old trade.'

'You can't quit,' said Chris bluntly. 'We own you. We've paid for you to learn medicine for this past eight months. We've no one else. You can't escape from your responsibilities. All we can do is to repeat once again that we won't hold you responsible when—if—things go wrong—'

'Like heck you won't,' murmured Derek under his breath.

'—and we'll all give you our assurance that we will not conduct a witch-hunt if you make a mistake. We just want you to use whatever skills you can acquire to help us all. Does everyone in the council agree?'

There was a firm murmur. 'I'm sorry, Derek. I do understand what you are experiencing, but we don't have any other choice: I don't think you have a choice, either, because the next time somebody falls down and breaks his wrist you won't be able to stand by doing nothing. Whatever happens you will always have six or eight months' start over anyone else that we might train. Try as you will you can't get away from your responsibilities. And let it be said—we do also appreciate the work that you're doing,'—Susan smiled and nodded enthusiastically—'we really do. We're sorry that you found it so difficult and we all agree you've had a baptism of fire. We *will* be sympathetic, but you *must* continue.'

*   *   *

For Derek, the summer was sheer hell, and for the first time he began to experience something of how Martin felt—lost, isolated and alone. Gradually a deeper bond developed between the two of them. For all the superficial differences between them, Derek found in Martin someone who could listen to him and understand the intensity of the problems besetting him; and likewise Martin found in Derek a kindred spirit, intelligent, rational, and above all a realist, prepared to face the truth—any truth—head-on.

The awful truth was of course that there was no one else to take over from Derek. Despite the paucity of his teaching, he knew more about medicine than anyone else in the community. This knowledge merely served to increase the pressure on him: even if he wanted to give up, he couldn't. Only Susan's grateful face, as once again he managed to relieve the pain of her gall-stones, kept him from throwing in the towel completely.

Over the next few weeks Derek gradually began to see more of Martin, and often wandered up Holly Walk to the Old Rectory of an evening to talk, over a drink or two. Derek wasn't going down the same alcoholic road that Martin had travelled, but he now shared something of Martin's sense of loss and isolation, even though the substance of each one's loss was quite different. Martin had lost his God and all purpose in living. Derek had lost his daughter and his confidence in any medical abilities he might possess.

They sat in the front garden of the Old Rectory when the weather was fine, and in the lounge when it was not. And they would talk, usually over a bottle of whisky, of which Derek would consume a twentieth and Martin attempt to down the rest. They talked of everything—of the world, of morals and ethics, of knowledge, of science, of religion . . . And they talked about the community, and the problems facing it, and about themselves, and their own reactions to life and living, of the stresses each faced and of strategies for coping. After a time it was hard to decide who was helping whom the most: the truth was that they were both supporting each other.

Being a member of the council, Martin had been party to their decision that Derek had to continue as a doctor: but that didn't mean he wasn't aware of the effects of their decision on Derek himself.

'The trouble is,' said Derek one evening as they sat watching the shadows lengthen on the hills in the distance, 'that I feel so isolated. I've no one to turn to, yet I'm caught in a trap and I can't get out of it. I'm sure I'm going to fail—and not just let down myself, but other people as well, probably rather badly. And now I've got Susan to deal with I feel even more helpless.'

Martin listened. He was a good listener. He'd had years of practice at the vicarage, listening to old ladies chattering on about their families and their grandchildren, and old men talking about the war and how the young people were so different today. He'd learned to listen without showing boredom or offence, even when the most outrageously silly or trivial things were said. But he was also a good listener in detecting what was driving someone onwards; he was good at discerning the excuse that lay behind the reasoning, the real motive that clouded the apparently guileless one. The only difficulty with being perceptive to this degree was that he could also see his own motives only too clearly—so while he was listening to Derek voicing his self-doubts and failings, he was forcibly and painfully reminded of how he himself had failed completely just when others needed him. He could have left the security of the vicarage to look after those who were lost, those who were ill, those who were dying. He could have—but he hadn't. And the more Derek talked about the impossibility of fulfilling what was asked of him, the more Martin came face to face with his own inadequacies; and ironically his one source of contact with the outside world was the very thing that was also driving him back to the solace of the whisky bottle.

But it was not all gloom—had it been, Martin couldn't have stood it. They talked of other things by the hour—ideas, principles, ethics. More than once Martin's belief in pacifism came up.

'Why did people have to be so warlike?' he said one day, as they sat on the lawn in the warm evening air watching the sky gradually turn from red to deep indigo. 'Why couldn't people just let their natural goodness come out? Where has war got us anyway? Think of the dead, think of the maimed, think of the injured—Vietnam, Korea, Beirut, the Gulf . . .'

'But you must agree that there are just wars?'

'Why must I?'

'Don't you think there were some that were worth fighting: Hitler, for example?'

'The Nazis came to power as a reaction to what we did to Germany after the First World War, and the First World War was triggered off when someone threw a bomb at a minor member of the Austrian nobility. What a waste of all those people: two world wars, courtesy of a single anarchist's bomb. If we hadn't fought at all, think of the difference it would have made. We wouldn't have laid waste Europe: we could have spent our efforts improving the quality of life for everyone, beating disease, stopping poverty.

'Peace is much better. I do think Jesus was right, even though I don't believe in him any more—at least, not in a supernatural form—when he said "Love your neighbour and turn the other cheek." If we all did this wouldn't the world be a much more peaceful place?'

A bat scudded along the line of the trees silhouetted against the darkening sky, its flip-flopping flight distinguishing it from that of a bird.

'It's an attractive theory.'

'It's not just a theory—it works. Live at peace with everybody. The Buddhists seem to do it quite well.'

'I'm not sure how far it got them in Tibet.'

'It would have been worse if they'd resisted, wouldn't it?'

He poured another drink for himself and offered Derek a refill, but Derek put his hand over his glass and shook his head. 'Live at peace with everyone, that's what I say, and it works. It really does. Not that many people have tried it consistently. All people need to do is not react when insulted or threatened—that's all. Then there'd be no battles.'

He looked at the far hills and grimaced. 'Do you realise that the whole of the world—everyone out there—died because of war?'

'I don't follow.'

'The plague. That was a weapon, wasn't it? They didn't learn. They wouldn't listen. We *told* them germ warfare was stupid. We said sooner or later there'd be an accident: now look at it.' He waved his arm a trifle overexpansively at the horizon. 'All dead. All gone. Just because they wouldn't listen.'

'But it was a natural disease—at least that's what they said in the papers I read.'

'Lies. Lies. It was a cover-up. Of course they said it was natural. They would, wouldn't they? But we all knew. Sir Richard . . . Porton Down . . . Southill . . . we all knew the connection, even if no one was admitting to it.'

'So you like conspiracy theory, too?'

'It wasn't a theory, it was a fact. Sir Richard's wife admitted it. The Porton Down connection. Genetic engineering. Well, look what it did.' He spat out the words and waved his arms at the horizon again.

'What if I told you it wasn't like that?'

'I wouldn't believe you.'

'Why not?'

'Because . . . '

'Do you really not know me, even after all these months? I wouldn't lie to you.'

'Yes, but what do you know that's so special?' Martin hesitated. There was something about Derek that he couldn't quite fathom out and a certain hesitancy came into his voice. 'You're just repeating the excuses you've been told . . . aren't you?'

'I haven't got any reason to lie . . . '

'I didn't say you were lying—just repeating an untruth that someone else had concocted.'

' . . . and I've no reason to cover up for anyone, either . . . '

Martin stopped talking. There was silence for a moment.

'You know something, don't you?'

'Yes.'

'What?'

'How do I know you'll believe me if I tell you?'

'Try me.'

'I've *been* trying to.'

'And?'

'You didn't believe me.'

'Didn't believe what?'

Martin was alert now, leaning forward on his seat. Strange how the alcoholic befuddlement could leave him so quickly, thought Derek.

'The plague wasn't genetically engineered. Porton Down had nothing to do with it . . . '

'Oh, don't give me that again . . . How would you know, anyway? You weren't even aware there *was* a plague until after it had happened.'

'No, but remember what I used to be.'

'A civil servant. In the patent office.'

'Before that.'

'I thought you'd always worked there?'

'I was attached to the Ministry of Defence before that. Do you know what the relationship between Southill and Porton Down *really* was?'

There was a pause. 'No . . . ' said Martin uncertainly. 'But I have the feeling you're going to tell me, and I have the awful feeling that it's not what I thought it was.'

'You're dead right. It's what no one thought it was—except those in the know. Do you know what Southill was doing for Porton Down in that infamous liaison two years earlier? . . . Eh? . . . *Testing safety suits for laboratory workers.* To make sure that the lab technicians didn't get accidentally inoculated with Lassa fever, Green Monkey disease or the like.'

'*Testing lab suits?*'

'Yes.'

'Why didn't someone say?'

'They did. They said it until they were blue in the face. They said that there was no connection over germ warfare between Porton Down and Southill. No one believed them.'

Visions of the last days of Parliament flitted through Martin's mind, and of the reception the Commons had given the Secretary of State when he tried to tell them that the plague was a natural phenomenon.

'Then the media lied?'

'No, they didn't. They just sowed doubt.'

Unbidden, the sound of Hywel's voice rose into Martin's consciousness. He was asking questions. Hywel was *always* asking questions: 'But can we be sure that . . .?' 'Is it *really* the case that . . .?'

There was a long silence.

'No cover-up?'

'No cover-up. Things sometimes have to be taken at face value. And the media don't always get it right.'

Martin looked down, his face contorting, biting his lip. 'It was all a natural disease?'

'I assure you, Southill and Porton Down weren't working together on anything remotely connected with genetic engineering.'

Martin suddenly looked ashen and drawn. 'So it's God's fault then . . .' he said under his breath.

'What?'

'Oh . . . I'd just started to begin to believe that God might be there after all . . . and that the plague was man's fault . . . but now it seems it's not, it puts me back where I was before . . . ' He took a large swig from his glass and let out a long sigh. Over behind him a pigeon rustled out of the foliage and swept across up into the trees on his right.

'I'm sorry . . . '

'It's not your fault. The truth will out, and all that . . . ' He stood up suddenly. 'I don't want to talk any more,' he said, turning on his heel and going indoors, leaving Derek alone on the lawn. Derek looked at his retreating figure, and shrugged, then drained his glass and stood up to leave.

Down in the town Susan's pain started up again.

*   *   *

Not only did Susan have an attack that night, she had a further one the night after, increasing Derek's sense of helplessness. Although he could quell the pain a little with injections of pethidine, he couldn't get rid of the underlying problem. Such a pity he thought, feeling her stomach for what felt like the thirtieth time that month. The cause of the problem was only an inch or two below his fingers. If only he could get those stones out she'd be free of pain.

He could anaesthetise her, he thought, using the equipment they'd acquired in London, but could he then manage to perform the operation to remove the gall bladder? If he'd looked at his surgical textbook once, he looked at it a hundred times, and the more he read the worse it got. The anatomy of the gallbladder region could vary, and even experienced surgeons, it seemed, could muddle up the vessels and tubes in the area—so if proper surgeons could make mistakes like that, what chance had he?

Despite this he still mused over the problems of operating— of trying to stop the bleeding, of knowing where he was inside the body, of the dangers of severing nerves by accident knowing that they would never grow again, of cutting into a vital organ, of hitting an artery and watching Susan bleed to death.

The more he thought about it the more he knew two things: firstly that he had to do something, and secondly, that he didn't have the expertise to do it. The more he thought about it the worse the dilemma seemed.

Derek wasn't the only one with a problem he could do little about. Although it was late July, the weather was cold and rainy, the countryside green and dripping—and Neil had virtually given up hope for the wheat. The vegetables and fruit were coming along fine—the extra rain filled them out wonderfully—but the wind and rain had battered the green corn flat: worse still, there was no indication whatsoever of any change in the weather. But they would only get one wheat harvest—unlike previous years there was no chance of buying in grain from elsewhere if the local harvest failed. Their own wheat harvest was all they would have—and if it failed, their stocks of flour wouldn't last beyond Christmas. And still it rained.

In desperation Major Thornton and one or two of the more staunch churchgoers began to pray in earnest for fine weather: Martin was not one of them. Derek, who had never had any belief in God, merely regarded such activities as harking back to the obsessionalities of childhood and a childish belief in magic; an extension of the idea that daddy could get rid of all hurts and ills, like all daddies can. Derek wasn't openly critical of Major Thornton or any of those who met in the church: he was tolerant of their beliefs, but just didn't think that their prayers had any meaning or importance. But the prayer sessions continued anyway, and Neil went on looking anxiously at the western sky and shivering in the cold wind.

Chaos theory shows how dynamic systems can sometimes be exquisitely sensitive to their starting conditions: so minute changes at the beginning can have massive effects later: the flap of a butterfly's wings in China really *can* affect what sort of weather Britain gets ten days later.

Perhaps the butterfly flapped in the right direction, or else the prayers worked, but for whatever reason the appalling weather gradually abated, to be followed by a more settled warm spell, and while Neil and the others held their breath and got cricked necks from looking up at the sky, the sun actually came out and August began as a proverbial scorcher.

At least Neil had been given a ray of hope. Derek had not been so lucky. Despite his protestations at not wanting to stay as the community's doctor, he had been obliged to continue practising medicine. If nothing else, Susan was needing his ministrations at increasingly frequent intervals. It was seldom that more than a few days went by without a call to her bedside.

At least he had pethidine for her, which relieved the worst of her pain. Immediately after the trial he had replenished their stocks from some of the more remote pharmacies—and had taken the precaution of locking the vials away in his house, just to be sure. Nothing left unguarded would have been safe against Paul's cold chisel. Derek didn't really think he was likely to use it—but even so he felt that temptation would be better out of the way, and took no chances.

He needn't have worried. For all his protestations, Paul found he *had* been addicted—but like so many addicts didn't realise to what extent he'd been addicted until he tried to stop. Then he had three weeks of sheer hell going through withdrawal, but Paul being Paul, pig by name and pig-like by nature, he refused to do anything but grit his teeth and get it over with.

And get over it he did. His extreme moodiness lifted and he began to be get back to being something like his old self—except that nothing could bring Jane back, and now he missed her more than he would ever have believed.

He couldn't bear to live in Gates House any longer—it held too many memories, and reminded him daily of what had once been—so, to the delight of Major Thornton, Paul swapped residences with him. The Major had always fancied Gates House as a place to live—and in any case, had always felt that really *he* was the one who should be squire in Ampthill.

Within a few days of Jane's death Paul had transferred his belongings to the Major's old thatched cottage, opposite the courthouse. As it happened, the cottage next door to it belonged to Trevor, who—surprisingly—treated him as though nothing untoward had happened in the past. What Paul didn't know was how heavily Chris had leaned on Trevor to persuade him that enough was enough, that Paul was bereaved, and that his bereavement would be hard enough to bear without any sly remarks from Trevor, thank you very much.

There in his tiny cottage, Paul clawed his way back to a more stable existence and gradually got some peace back into his life again.

It wasn't to last for long.

-62-

'No, I am not prepared to have him back on the council,' the Major flared. 'It's totally disgraceful. Not only is he a drug addict, he's a liar and a cheat. What amazes me is that some of you don't just want him back on the council, you want him to go back to being chairman as well. I think it's appalling.'

He sat back in his seat, his bristling white hair and moustache contrasting with his perspiring red face. It was hot in the courtroom and tempers were running high. Immediately after the trial Paul had tendered his resignation, and the council was debating whether to accept it or not.

'But he's served his sentence. It's over and done with,' said Alan Rogers. 'That's what we agreed when we sentenced him— no looking back: it's over. Finished.'

'Absolutely,' said Peter. 'Don't you remember—we *all* said that once he'd served his sentence, that was the end of it.'

'Oh yes,' replied the Major. 'Yes—as far as the offences themselves were concerned. *That's* all over and done with. But we're still left with the personality of the man, obnoxious as it is. He's displayed his true colours now. He won't change those—he *can't* change those. He's shown just how totally unfit for office he is. I *won't* have him back as chairman and that's final. You've got his letter of resignation. Let's accept it here and now.'

Chris sighed with exhaustion. They'd been at it like this for two hours and they were going round in circles.

'Major, it's not for you to say who will and who won't be chairman. That's a matter we put to the vote,' she said. 'And you've talked about Paul's true nature: well, we elected him to the council because we thought he was the person to do a good job, a man with the right talents. And he has—mostly. Look how well he organised us at the beginning. Where would we be now without him? Anyway, we all make mistakes.'

'Some mistake,' snorted the Major. 'More like a personality defect.'

There was hubbub round the table. Half the council was in favour of accepting Paul's resignation, and half against.

'What do you think, Martin?' asked Chris. 'You've not said much so far.'

'Oh . . . er . . . no . . . ' said Martin, vaguely. For once he hadn't had a drink, but it didn't seem to make his mental processes any better.

'It seems . . . it seems a bit hard on Paul, don't you think?' he began pleasantly.

The Major fixed him with a glare.

'Of course . . .' he continued swiftly, 'I can see the Major's point, too. But we need to look at this calmly, and with kindness and love . . . It's a very difficult situation. Very difficult. One wants to help Paul—not to lay the blame at his door for ever, so to speak. But I can quite see the Major's point . . . It's very difficult. Very difficult . . . ' He tailed away into silence.

'Thank you Martin,' said Chris in a reflex response, adding an irritated 'for nothing' under her breath. 'Look—it's getting late, and we've made no progress. I think we ought to put the matter aside until the next meeting. We're never going to get a consensus even if we stay here until midnight.'

'I'm not going to change my mind,' said the Major, 'not even if we wait till Christmas.'

'Maybe not,' said Chris firmly, 'but doubtless there are others who would like to give it further thought. We'll bring it up next time. I'll tell Paul myself.'

*   *   *

Chris conveyed the news to Paul that evening, at his cottage. Paul stared at the empty grate and grimaced.

'I suppose half of me thought they would reject the letter immediately, give me a vote of confidence, and have me back.'

'And half of you thought they'd accept it.'

'Yes.'

'That's just about how the council saw it, too. Half and half.'

Paul stared at the grate again, blank, lost for words.

Chris put her hand on his arm. 'I'm sorry.'

'For what?'

'Sorry you're being put through it again, after all we said about the punishment being the end of it. Peter was most insistent upon that at the trial, you know.'

'He would be, with his background, wouldn't he?'

'And the rest of them agreed with him—at the time. He's not letting them forget it, either, even if some of them want to.'

'It's nice to know Peter's on my side.'

'But he's right. And the Major's wrong.'

'That's not what a lot of them think.'

'It's what I think.'

'Thanks.'

'And it's what most of the community thinks, too, if you must know. They want to forget it all, as well. They want you to start again.'

'That's nice of them.'

'It's not just nice—it's self-interest, too. We need you. We value you.'

He turned away from her and touched his eye as though there was something in it.

'It's true. We do value you.'

'Me or my brains?'

'Both.'

'Ah.'

There was a pause. 'Trevor's been remarkably polite to me, considering.'

Chris said nothing.

Paul sighed. 'I'll just have to wait, I suppose. *"You're forgiven, but you can't make amends for it."* That's the Major's line, isn't it? Oh well, I'll just have to live with it. Thanks for coming to tell me.'

'That's all right. It's important.'

-63-

*T*he fine weather continued into August and while the whole community waited anxiously, the corn at last began to ripen. It was hot—very hot—the sort of heat that it's nice to get out of: certainly not the sort of heat in which to work in the fields. In the evening the air was warm and humid; the windows and doors were left open, even throughout the night, in order to catch any breath of wind.

The only subject of conversation was the weather—there was little else talked about. One question was on everyone's lips— would the fine weather hold? Would the corn ripen in time? And how would they live over the coming year if the harvest failed?

Each day, without exception, the first thing each person did on waking was to look outside—not, as in the past, to see if it was fine enough to do without a raincoat or an umbrella, or else to see if it was a good day to go to the seaside or play out—but because their very lives depended upon it.

During that month the whole community seemed to hold its breath, waiting, watching, hoping—and also, in the case of Major Thornton and his little group, praying.

By the middle of the month the weather had still not broken and each day, little by little, the corn ripened until it glowed golden in the summer haze. Although to the layman it looked ready to cut, it wasn't—not yet. It needed more time to ripen fully.

On the twentieth, Neil wandered through the fields in the sunlight, pulling at stalks of corn, rubbing them between his hands to extract the grain, sniffing it, chewing it, examining it. It was nearly ready, he decided. Two more days of sun would do it, though a quarter of the corn was still standing at a most precarious angle and a small percentage had not recovered at all from the battering it had received and was still lying flat on the ground.

Just two more days . . . It was baking hot. Anxiously he looked up at the sky. There were a few clouds, but nothing too great. Would the weather hold? he wondered, and wished he still had access to the weather forecasts that had been so useful in the days before the plague. Although the weather couldn't be predicted with any certainty beyond three days—chaos theory saw to that—three days is a long time, especially in farming. If they started cutting now the grain would be just too damp and would quickly go mouldy—but at least they would have some harvest. On the other hand, if he left it two more days and the weather broke, they'd lose the lot . . . He shuddered, and shared some of the isolation that Derek felt. It all depended on him, and he didn't have enough information. He would have to make a guess—an educated guess—but thanks to the lack of weather forecasts, a lot less educated and knowledgeable than the one he'd made routinely the year before.

Neil stared up at the sky again, calculating, thinking, wondering. He bent down to look at another ear of wheat, then straightened up. He would risk it. He would wait two more days; then they would start.

*   *   *

The next two days were the longest the community had ever experienced. Anne had arranged a concert for the day before harvesting was due to start, and there seemed no reason to cancel it. There was nothing to do but wait, anyway.

They held the concert, as before, in the magnificent first-floor reception room at Dynevor, in the early evening. It had been a sultry day, humid, with the threat of rain and the odd roll of thunder, and many an anxious eye was cast to the heavens that afternoon in case a storm came to ruin the harvest that was so nearly ready.

The room was packed. The furniture had been turned round from its usual direction so that the piano, which was at the end away from the fireplace, was now the focus of attention.

Most of the artistic people in the community had come with some form of offering—whether it was a song or a solo, a recitation or a poem. After the first three items, to Derek's surprise Paul and Chris moved to the front. Derek hadn't realised that Paul had any musical pretensions and it was with some considerable delight that he listened as the two of them performed a Django Reinhardt number as a guitar duo. The way that Paul and Chris played was so neat, so together, and the piece such an up-beat number that there was tumultuous applause at the end. In terms of music at least Paul and Chris obviously thought as one.

'A bit of a dark horse, aren't you?' murmured Derek as Paul passed him, having taken his bow.

'I've always played the guitar. I learnt it at school. I've just not had the opportunity since. Chris plays well, doesn't she?'

Other items followed—Anne played and sang a couple of songs from the old musicals; David played a solo on his newly acquired saxophone—very passably Derek thought—and Sarah recited a poem about two butterflies.

Then it was Martin's turn—the first time he'd put in an appearance at one of the concerts. Nervously he settled himself at the piano, fiddling with his music, adjusting the piano stool. Beyond him, Derek could see the yellow corn brilliantly outlined in the light from the setting sun and above it the sky becoming darker and more threatening, as if nature knew that something was about to happen. There was a rumble of thunder in the distance and then Martin started to play.

The change in him was amazing. From the fingers of this shy, insecure man suddenly poured music of an intensity that Derek had never heard before. Martin had chosen Rachmaninov's

Prelude in C sharp minor and into it poured his own special dramatic melancholy.

The piece begins with three dramatic notes played *fortissimo* in octaves, followed by mournful bell-like chords, like funeral bells tolling in the distance. There is something about the music—so obvious, once heard—that it cannot be conceived of in any other way. Just as the doommongers should have been able to predict the end of the world but didn't, yet wondered afterwards why they hadn't, so those hearing the Prelude for the first time that night wondered why they had never imagined it before—it was so logical, so obvious, like a perfectly formed pearl.

The Prelude contains all the profound Russian melancholy of Rachmaninov, and into it Martin put all his own anxieties, anguish, emotion and fury. He played like a man transformed.

There is something about live performances that can grab the audience, transporting them into a rapport of incredible intensity. It can't be predicted, it just happens, and it doesn't happen necessarily because the performance is technically good: it happens because—who knows?—ESP perhaps? But the audience and the performer and the piece merge into one, transported beyond what is being played, lifted out of themselves, touched by raw emotion. Such moments occur only seldom. Afterwards everyone remembers the experience, but cannot really recall the piece of music or the play or the recitation or the poem: they remember only the mood and its effect—that it happened, and that it was unbelievably moving.

And so it was that evening as Martin crouched over the piano, with the sun playing on the corn in the distance and the thunder rumbling in the background; and as the huge tolling bell-like sounds came thundering out of the piano, all the anguish Martin had ever felt was put into his performance that night.

And all the anguish that the listeners had felt went into their response, too. Martin attacked the restless middle section like a whirling dervish. Technically it wasn't his best performance: there were missed notes and one particularly excruciating E flat that should have been an E, but it didn't matter. No one noticed—except Martin. The music, the mood was what counted and as he approached the final section, recapitulating the bell-like sounds of the beginning, but with increasing intensity, the minds

of those in the room went back to the sadnesses that they had
experienced, the loved ones whom they had lost and the lives
they had left behind, and as the music tailed away at the end into
its crushed silence, so those in the audience were left crushed
with the intensity of their memories; and as the final
disintegrating chord sounded Anne put her arm around Derek and
her head on his shoulder and sobbed great heaving sobs—for the
world, and for Alison, and for Jane.

Others in the room did the same; some crying out loud,
some with tears silently running down their faces. Paul was
sitting on a windowsill, staring outside, his head turned away. At
first Derek thought Paul was unmoved, but then he saw a little
rivulet glistening on his cheek as Paul made a point of carefully
studying the crab-apple tree in the square below him.

As the last chord faded into nothingness the silence in the
room was broken only by Anne's sobs. Over in the distance the
thunder rolled again.

Martin didn't know what to do. He'd never played a piece
where nobody had clapped—if only politely—and in a strange
way he'd not really been aware of what he'd just taken part in.
All he could think of was that wretched E flat that should have
been an E.

Uneasily he stood up, shuffled the music together and
walked away from the piano, feeling terribly awkward and
wishing to goodness that he'd done what he really wanted and
not taken part in the concert. He was about to leave the room
when Derek put his arm across the door, barring his way.

'Again, Martin. Play it again.' Not a request, a command.

Martin didn't know what to make of it all. He looked
uneasily around the room, then slowly went back to the piano,
looking at the audience as if for confirmation. Sixty-two heads
nodded as if in unison.

'Play it again, Martin,' said Paul firmly from his window
seat, making out that he had a small piece of dirt in the corner of
his eye that had to be extracted with his little finger.

As he began the *fortissimo* three octaves, for the audience it
was like going back to sleep and reinhabiting a dream that they
had had to break off on waking; there and then they rejoined their
emotions. Again Martin was transformed from the shy retiring

priest into an emotional whirlwind. Again it was not a perfect technical performance—but then nobody was counting. Again the music and the performance expressed what every one of them felt, and like the slow resolution of a fever or the slow winning of a battle, the music touched to the depths the emotions that had been locked up since that fateful October week when the plague had first struck.

If anything, Martin attacked the middle section like an even bigger whirlwind, the whole audience hanging on to every note, willing it not to finish. And then as the bell-like theme returned, louder, but not more triumphant, and the desolation of the last few chords rang out and faded into the distance, they sat open-mouthed, tears pouring down their faces.

And then they roared. They clapped, they shouted, they went across to Martin and hugged him, they cheered, they danced. Again, Martin didn't even know what he'd done and rushed to get out of the room. This time it was Anne who grabbed him and with the remains of the tears still streaming down her face she held his arm, looked him straight in the face, and then kissed him on the cheek. 'Thank you Martin—that was incredible. Unbelievable.'

Martin could only think of the E flat. Why, oh why had he made such a stupid mistake?

'You're only saying that to be polite. There's no need. I know I didn't do it well the first time. That's why nobody applauded.'

'No . . .' said Anne to Martin's retreating figure as he ran down the grand staircase. 'No, Martin, I *mean* it.'

The front door slammed, and as the next performer started to play her piece, through the open windows Derek could hear the sound of Martin's feet crunching up the gravel of Holly Walk, heading for the Old Rectory, whisky and oblivion.

There wasn't much point in listening to the rest of the concert. They all did so for politeness' sake, clapping gently after each item, but each and every one of them really wanted it to end there and then, so they could savour the majesty of the music that they had just heard, savour the emotion they had just tasted, and re-experience the catharsis of the emotions they had all bottled up for the past nine months.

*   *   *

After the concert, as the light began to fade, Derek followed
Martin's path up to the Old Rectory. It was silent and gloomy,
and the bats had started flitting about in the warm, sultry twilight.
He knocked on the door and the house echoed back to him.
There was a pause, a shuffling noise, and then Martin appeared.
    'What d'you want?'
    'I just came to say thank you.'
    'I don't believe you.'
    'Can I come in?'
    'If you want.'
    They went into the dining room. There on the top of the
wood stove lay the music of the Prelude, crumpled up, waiting to
be burned.

-64-

*T*hat night Neil didn't sleep at all. He tossed and turned,
listening to the thunder rumbling in the distance, and on more
than one occasion he thought he heard rain. It was hot and close,
and at two in the morning, exhausted yet unable to sleep, with
sweat sticking round the collar of his pyjamas, he got up to look
out of the window yet again, worrying that really he should have
started the harvest two days before.
    Dimly he saw a movement in the street below him, and the
adrenaline started racing even more furiously. Burglars? The
raiders back again? Then he realised it was Derek, accompanied
by Alan Rogers. Susan was in trouble again, obviously.
    Neil went back to his rumpled sheets and lay there listening.
He heard the last of the thunder, grumbling away in the distance:
shortly after that he fell asleep, only to be disturbed by the dawn
chorus, and especially by one pigeon that had taken a fancy to the
gable above his bedroom, jarring Neil each time it squawked
unpredictably. Half an hour later he heard Derek's weary
footsteps going back along the empty streets to Dynevor House
and bed.
    And then Neil could stand it no longer. Wearily he got up

and dressed in the dim light. Today was the start of the harvest:
the day he'd been working towards for the past nine months.
What would the weather be like? He pulled back the curtains:
the sun was—shining!

*   *   *

They had to wait while the sun heated the ground and
dispersed the damp air: but from mid-morning onwards it was
baking hot, and dry. Trevor filled the combine harvester with
precious diesel, and at last began to bring in their first wheat
harvest. They had a lot to choose from—many fields had been
set to wheat in the month before the plague, so there would be no
shortage of grain—providing only that the weather held long
enough for them to get it in.

As in the old days, everyone joined in: that was what the
long school summer holidays had originally been for. But it was
easier than it had been two hundred years ago: scythes and sickles
were no longer required and instead the combine carved great
swathes through the fields. They still had to transport the grain,
though, and collect the straw for bedding the animals during the
next winter. Neil flatly refused to use any more of the diesel to
drive a baler. They had the manpower to collect the straw by
hand, and the less diesel they used now, the more there would be
available for the combine harvester in the years to come.

It was hard work, but rewarding, as little by little they cleared
the standing corn and collected the straw as bedding for the
animals. Nor was it just wheat they harvested, but barley and oats
as well: for themselves but also to provide cattle and horse fodder.

Neil still had a crick in his neck from anxiously staring at the
sky. More than once there was a rumble of thunder in the distance,
and on each occasion every member of the community, whether in
the fields or not, looked up in fear. All they needed was a single
downpour and the harvest would disintegrate in front of their eyes.

Evening came all too quickly—the days are much shorter at
the end of August—but it was still warm, and as long as it wasn't
humid they could continue harvesting. Anne thought that Neil
would stop when it got dark, but she was wrong. Through the
night they worked, the combine's lights blazing far into the
darkness and the moon—that precious harvest moon—flooding

the fields with its pinky-white light, letting them continue harvesting right through the night.

On and on they worked, day after day and, where possible, night after night. Fourteen hours a day in the fields—cutting the corn, carrying it away to be stored, gathering the straw for the animals.

Straw is surprisingly heavy, thought Paul, flinging yet another pitchforkful on to the very top of the horse-drawn wagon he was using. Then he stopped and wiped away the sweat that was running down his forehead. Rural idylls? he thought. No way, and bent his aching body to the next forkful. Behind him Peter, Chris and Martin were doing the same. Kevin was there too, deriving great pride from being strong enough still to throw the straw up on the top of the cart when the others had reached their limits.

On and on it went, in the heat of the sun and the warmth of the evening. Gradually they completed each field, gradually they transported the grain into safe dry storage, gradually they got the harvest in.

*   *   *

Ten days later they were exhausted—but they had the grain they needed. Only then, as he stood at the edge of the last field, his face yellow in the light of the setting sun, did Neil *really* stop worrying. He looked round at the shaved stalks where the wheat had been, and at the darkening sky above him, now heavy with rain clouds. It had been a close-run thing. It could rain all it wanted now, he thought, as he turned his back on the last field and strode out towards the town.

He alone knew how close they had been to disaster. The rest of the community had learned a lot about farming in the past year, but even so none of them really knew just how close it had been. Had the wet weather not changed, had the rains returned too early . . . Neil shuddered. It didn't bear thinking about. They would have starved, slowly and progressively.

But now the harvest was in and he could relax. The other harvests—the vegetables, the fruit—didn't depend upon continuous dry weather at this time of year. *Their* critical time was in the spring, when the flowers were on the trees and the fruit was setting—and not many people had noticed that either. Only Neil knew and, in his phlegmatic way, he wasn't letting on to anyone else.

But Martin knew. In the isolation of the Old Rectory he'd gradually become more attuned to the weather, more aware of nature generally—being on his own, he'd not had as many distractions as the others. But he'd also worked in the fields with the rest of them, and he also knew all too well how close they'd come to disaster.

But he knew something else, too. That little seed of an idea which had popped into his mind the previous Christmas Eve was still there—growing larger, and giving off shoots.

But it wasn't ready for harvesting—not quite yet.

-65-

*T*he harvest was home! Neil thought he was going back to a well-earned bath and a rest, but the rest of the community knew differently. They were waiting to welcome him, and as he entered Ampthill from the east he found himself walking past a veritable guard of honour. *Everyone* had come to cheer him back. The whole community was there, lining the streets, cheering, shouting, singing 'For he's a jolly good fellow' and clapping him on the back.

He tried to get through to his own house which was diagonally opposite Derek's, but the way was blocked by smiling people who ushered him on towards the Market Square, and into the White Hart. A great cheer went up as he entered.

Chris and Kevin between them had organised a party: Kevin and Peter had taken a lorry and raided one of the more distant pubs to provide a good supply of beer and wine. They'd decorated the inside of the bar, too and—amazingly—had used some of the precious petrol to run the generator for a few hours so they could have electric lights and run a CD player: extravagant, yes, but it was such a special day, and there was so much to celebrate.

The harvest was home! They were safe for a further year. It could rain all it wanted now.

And rain it did. Halfway through the evening the heavens opened as the storm that had been threatening for so long erupted and the warm rain cascaded down into the square. But no one cared. Trevor even went out and danced around in it, singing, stripped to the waist, glass in hand, his floppy hat still on his head, the rain running in rivulets down his nineteen-stone bulk.

There was much jollity that night: it was the party to end all parties—not because it was particularly outlandish, but because it involved *everybody* in the whole town—old and young alike, children, teenagers, pensioners—everyone came.

Except two. Halfway through the evening Chris found Derek. 'Have you seen Martin?' she shouted against the din.

'No,' he mouthed, his voice lost in the tumult, 'nor Paul.'

'We can't let them cut themselves off on a night like this,' she replied. 'They *must* come. It'll do them good.'

'You get Paul, I'll try and get Martin.'

They left the White Hart to go in opposite directions. It had stopped raining by then, but the streets were still running with water as they splashed on their way.

Twenty minutes later Derek returned triumphantly with a slightly sheepish Martin who had consented to join in the merriment. At first he looked his usual awkward self, his gangling features spread out everywhere as usual, the lock of hair falling across his face as always, but then he lost his self-consciousness. It was good to see him enjoying himself, thought Derek: so much nicer than on that first awful night when they'd met in this same room, after the plague. It seemed so long ago now . . . Nice to see him happy for a bit, he thought. Derek left him to it and went back to David and Sarah who were dancing in the corner with the other children.

But of Paul and Chris there was no sign—except that Trevor, on returning to his cottage next door long after the party had finished, noticed that there was a candle still lit in Paul's lounge; and the chink of glasses and the murmur of contented conversation floated quietly out of the open window.

For Derek, the sense of jollity and relief disappeared at three o'clock that morning, an hour after they'd all finally got to bed. The clanging of the doorbell from deep within the hall told him that, once again, Susan was in trouble.

She was really ill that night—in so much pain that the pethidine hardly touched it, but eventually the attack passed and the pain left her. Sleepless and haggard, Derek trailed back to Dynevor House.

The next night was the same. And the next. And the next. Wearily Derek attended to her, thinking all the time, dare he operate? Dare he? It would be foolish—but if it worked . . .

And what if it didn't?

And could Susan stand pain like this for much longer?

Could he do it . . . ? *Dare* he . . . ? What if . . . ? Round and round in his head went the alternatives, all of them impossible, all of them insoluble.

*　　　　*　　　　*

For the rest of the community, the euphoria had still not worn off, though the weather had definitely turned cooler and autumn was obviously drawing near. 'Season of mists and mellow fruitfulness', Keats had called it, and season of mists it certainly was: for the first time since going on their canal holiday, Anne was aware of the beauty of nature rather than its hostility, as each morning she rose to see the sun playing on the mists that washed around the fields and the trees before being dispersed as the day became warmer. It was a mellow time, too—the greens of summer were slowly changing to the red and purple of berries and flowers, the gold of the cut wheat and the brown of the leaves. Now that the harvest was in and the immediate worries over, for once it felt good to be alive, even if the raw cold of winter was just around the corner.

Although it was nearly a year since the plague had first struck, new arrivals were still trickling in. Sometimes the

newcomers had just stumbled across Ampthill but increasingly
travellers' movements were becoming more purposeful, now that
the whereabouts of surviving communities was better known.

There were also a few people coming back from the far
north, where they had fled to escape the plague; they were now
trying to get back to their old haunts. It was not an easy journey
for them—the main roads were blocked as far as the Scottish
Lowlands, and a year without traffic had meant that the roads
were growing weeds and becoming obscured at a quite alarming
rate. Nevertheless, a small but steady trickle of travellers
continued to come through the town.

Around mid-morning, ten days after the harvest had finished,
the sound of a heavy diesel engine came from the west, and a few
minutes later a lorry with high sides and a closed-in top came
over the brow of Woburn Street and down into the Market
Square, to be followed by a petrol tanker and a Range Rover with
a large caravan in tow.

If the group of vehicles was out of the ordinary, what was
even more interesting was the man who stepped out of the Range
Rover. He cut an imposing figure, about forty-eight years old,
tall, alert, with black hair swept almost directly back, a slightly
jutting chin and immaculately tidy clothes.

Chris was walking through the square at that moment and
went across to greet him.

'Hello,' said the new man in an obviously public-school
voice. 'Nicholas Poulton.'

'Chris Wilson. What's your ... er ... entourage ... ?'

'We travel around the country, finding communities that
have been set up to see if they need help.'

'Oh,' said Chris, interestedly. 'What do you do?'

'I'm a doctor—a surgeon to be precise.'

Chris nearly fell through the floor. Her face must have given
away at least something because Nicholas immediately went into
his best salesman mode.

'Do I detect that you've been looking for a medical man for
some time?'

'You could say that.'

'Ah. Well, I'm glad I'm here to be able to help. What can I
do for you?'

'Er . . . I think you'd better come and meet the chap who is doing our medicine at the moment.'

'Oh, so you've got a doctor then.' The disappointment was obvious.

'Not a proper one. One of our community is learning all about it.'

The look of disdain on Nicholas' face said it all. 'You can't learn medicine like that, out of a book. Don't be silly.'

'He's doing quite well.'

'That's probably because he's had easy things to deal with. How's he going to get his experience? Doesn't he know that a medical student needed six years walking the wards before he was even allowed to *start* practising on patients?'

'He's doing tolerably well, you know.'

'How many people has he killed then?' Chris winced, then told Nicholas about Alison and Jane.

'I could have saved Jane,' said Nicholas. 'What a pity I wasn't there at the time. I must speak to this barefoot doctor of yours. It sounds as though he's had quite an interesting year.'

'Well, I'm sure he'll be glad to meet you,' said Chris somewhat testily. As they walked towards Dynevor House, Nicholas told Chris of where he'd been on his travels. It seemed that by judicious use of the east–west roads and also by a certain use of force—Chris realised that the front of the lorry had a makeshift plough on it—they'd been able to clear a way through the traffic jams and so traverse vast tracks of the countryside. Nicholas had much to tell about conditions up and down the country.

They rounded the corner into Church Square. Chris yanked the antique mechanical bell and its ring from somewhere within Dynevor House was soon answered by steps in the hall. Derek opened the door.

'You know you wanted a proper doctor,' said Chris.

'Yes?'

'Here he is.'

'Er . . . Do come in,' said Derek, for want of anything better to say.

'No,' said Nicholas, 'you come and see what I've got here.'

They walked back to the Market Square exchanging

pleasantries. Chris took a closer look at the V-shaped plough welded onto the front of the lorry.

'You like it?' said Nicholas. 'We call it the car plough. Put the point of it between two cars, push with the lorry and it moves cars out of the way like a knife through butter. It's not much use for getting along a line of traffic, but it'll get you *across* a jammed road in minutes.'

What an interesting idea, thought Derek, dropping back into his previous life of being an engineer. Why hadn't he thought of that?

Nicholas went round the back of the lorry, undid the lock holding the rolling tailgate and lifted it so that they could see in. Derek gasped. Inside it was kitted out as a complete operating theatre with lights, a central operating table, and on the far wall an autoclave for sterilising the instruments.

'D'you like it?' asked Nicholas, superiorly. Derek was astounded.

'How come you've got all this?'

'I used to be a consultant surgeon in London. I was out of town visiting friends in Norfolk at the time the plague occurred: they died, but I knew I'd be all right as I'd already had Legionnaires' disease a year or two back. I tried to get back to London, but I couldn't, because of the traffic jams.

'Then I realised that I was probably the only surgeon left alive in the whole of England so it seemed sensible to kit out a lorry with equipment and go round offering my services. Most of the equipment came from the Norfolk and Norwich Hospital—there was no one alive to miss it. And that was when I devised the car plough, too.'

Chris was fascinated. Derek wasn't really listening—all he could see was an operating table and theatre lights, and all he could think of was Susan. Nicholas launched into his salesman pitch, public-school accent to the fore. 'Now doctor,' he said looking down his nose at Derek, 'what patients have you got for me?'

'There's one woman I think has got gallstones.'

'Ah,' said Nicholas.

'Other than that, nothing.'

'No hernias, women needing a hysterectomy, broken bones that haven't healed properly and need resetting? Breast lumps?'

'No,' said Derek, 'none of those. Just one lady with gallstones.'

'Well, you'd better lead me to her,' he said, reaching inside the Range Rover for his bag.

Derek led him up Woburn Street to Wisteria House. He introduced Nicholas to Susan, and then they went upstairs to begin the time-honoured process of generalist and specialist consulting over the passive body of the patient.

-67-

*M*artin, meanwhile, had been to Trevor's to borrow a shotgun. A flock of pigeons had been damaging the crops over at Kings Farm and help was required. Martin fancied pigeon pie for supper, so he thought that he would kill two birds with one stone—to make a tidy mess of a metaphor, he thought, wryly.

As he strode up the rise to the top of Woburn Street he was looking forward to his morning's shooting: his pacifist leanings didn't extend to the animal kingdom, which was where he parted company with Mary. As he drew near to Wisteria House, just before the descent into the Market Square, he noticed Chris patiently waiting outside. Chris didn't often stand and wait for anything, so it must be important, he thought.

It was. Chris told him enthusiastically about Nicholas. Won't that be a relief for Derek, thought Martin with delight. Won't that be a relief for Susan as well, he added, mentally kicking himself for not thinking of her first.

The pigeons could wait. It wasn't every day a doctor turned up! As Martin stood with the gun broken over one elbow, looking every inch the local squire about to go on a pheasant shoot, Derek and Nicholas came out of the house, deep in conversation.

'Quite simple,' Nicholas was saying. 'A completely routine operation—that is of course if you're accustomed to doing operations. I'll need help of course; perhaps you'd like to . . . '

Derek agreed that he would, very much, then looked up and

Wisteria House

saw Martin. He introduced him to Nicholas.

'You've got some medical books?' enquired Nicholas. 'Good.'

They walked down Woburn Street and across the square to the surgery.

'I'll show you what we'll be doing,' said Nicholas, picking up Derek's copy of *Gray's Anatomy*. Finding the relevant pages he showed Derek how he planned to carry out the operation. Chris and Martin watched with fascination, aware also that Derek was deeply interested and, now that he had someone else to turn to, was actually enjoying himself. Martin was glad to see Derek relax: he was obviously looking forward to being involved in the operation.

'Good,' said Nicholas, closing the book with a bang. 'That's all organised. All we've got to do now is discuss the fee.'

'Fee?' said Derek warily.

'You don't think I do all this for nothing?'

'How much?' asked Chris.

'A tankerful of fuel,' said Nicholas without batting an eyelid.

'*You what*?' expostulated Chris.

'A tankerful of fuel. Petrol and diesel.'

'But that's outrageous. I doubt if we could get more than two tankersful from the whole of the surrounding area.'

'What a pity,' said Nicholas, 'it would have been such a pleasure to have taught you how to remove a gall bladder. Ah well—such is life. You have no other patients I think? In which case I'll be on my way.'

'Wait a minute,' said Chris, thinking of Susan doubled over in agony, 'do you mean to say that you would leave someone in pain just because they couldn't pay?'

'Things cost,' said Nicholas. 'You can't expect to have something complex like a cholecystectomy done without expecting to pay for it—now can you?'

'Our community couldn't possibly afford that amount of fuel,' said Chris. 'The small amount we have has to be kept for important vehicles such as the tractors and the combine harvesters—to help us grow our food for next year.'

'Then I'm sorry you're in such dire straits,' replied Nicholas.

Martin agitatedly opened his mouth as if to speak, then thought better of it.

'Couldn't you take something else?' asked Chris.

'It's a tankerful of fuel or nothing.'

Chris continued undeterred. 'We may have other produce that you would like instead.'

'No,' said Nicholas. 'I'm a little low on fuel at the moment, so fuel it is.'

'We can't possibly afford a tankerful,' said Chris, 'and that's final.'

Martin opened his mouth again and tried to say something, then thought better of it. Out of the corner of his eye Derek could see him shifting uneasily from foot to foot and biting his lip.

'Can't we barter?' asked Derek.

'No,' said Nicholas flatly. 'Well, if you're not going to pay my fee then I'll be off. I have other things to do.'

'Do you mean to say that you're prepared to leave Mrs Rogers to suffer just because we can't pay your fee?'

'Oh no,' said Nicholas, 'it's not that you *can't* pay, it's that you *won't* pay. You just don't value my time enough and you don't value Mrs Rogers enough. If you really cared about her you'd pay.'

'Half a tankerful?' said Chris in desperation.

'A tankerful. That or nothing.'

Chris heard a soft click behind her, but couldn't quite identify what it was. Martin stepped forward to Nicholas and looked him in the eye. 'I have to say that I don't think much of your ethics.'

'It's nothing to do with ethics,' said Nicholas. 'It's whether you're prepared to pay.'

'Are the rest of the medical profession like you?' asked Martin, eyeballing him.

'What d'you mean?'

'You know what I mean. Are they all as avaricious as you?'

'I've told you,' said Nicholas smoothly, 'it's nothing to do with avarice. I just need paying for a job well done and you're not prepared to do it.'

Martin leaned forward and Nicholas felt a sudden pressure on his right foot which seemed stuck to the floor. He looked down. Martin had put the left-hand barrel of the shotgun against Nicholas' right big toe and was leaning on the gun, jamming Nicholas' foot between the barrel and the floor. Chris suddenly realised that the click had been Martin cocking the gun and looked up to see Martin's face, suffused with anger, two inches away from Nicholas'. Martin had a strange look in his eyes, a determined look that Chris had never seen before. With cold deliberation he said very slowly, 'Mr Poulton, I consider you to be a selfish, avaricious person, unfit for the worthy name of doctor or surgeon. The fact that you won't perform an operation unless you're paid appals me, so I've decided that this time you're going to do it for free.'

'And if I don't?' said Nicholas.

'Then I'll blow your right big toe off.'

'I don't believe you.'

'Try me. You have ten seconds. Ten . . . '

'Don't be ridiculous.'

'Nine . . . '

'I'm not used to being threatened.'

'Eight . . . Well, you should be.'

'Well, I'm not.'

'Seven . . . '

'Would you stop him being silly?' said Nicholas to Chris and Derek. 'Tell him to go away and calm down. He's making an idiot of himself.'

Neither Chris nor Derek replied.

'Three . . . ' said Martin.

'You wouldn't dare,' said Nicholas.

'Try me. Are you going to do the operation?'

'No.'

'One . . . Are you sure?'

'I'm sure,' said Nicholas and to Chris and Derek's astonishment Martin pulled the trigger.

-68-

*I*nside the small room the concussion of the explosion had been tremendous. Nicholas let out a yell and looked down in disbelief at his right foot which was hidden from view in smoke, dust and debris. When it cleared he could see an inch-wide hole had been blasted into the wooden floorboard just adjoining his shoe. Martin eyeballed him again.

'You will notice,' said Martin slowly, 'that I have the *left* barrel over your big toe and that the first barrel of a shotgun to discharge is always the *right* one. Now there's only the left one remaining. Are you going to do the operation?'

Nicholas swayed. He could feel himself getting light-headed as he wondered what kind of a maniac he had come across.

'Nine . . . '

'All right, all right. I'll do it.' Anything to get out of the way of this madman. He could do the operation and be away in an hour and a half. It would only cost him a little bit of anaesthetic, some swabs and a few surgical blades—anything to get this crazed man away from him.

'I *am* glad to hear that,' said Martin, smiling thinly. 'You'd better get ready,' and with a slightly exaggerated movement he broke the gun open, took out the remains of the spent cartridge and inserted another one. He left the gun broken open across his arm. 'I think I'll stay and watch . . . to make sure you don't change your mind. Derek, you'd better go and tell Susan.'

*   *   *

They completed the operation that afternoon. For all his avarice, Nicholas was a top-flight surgeon and had a first-class set of equipment. He had decided straight away that there was no point in trying to escape or pull the wool over Martin's watchful eyes. He would make the best of a bad job: at least that way he'd escape with his feet intact. So with one of his drivers who had been trained to anaesthetise, and Derek acting as his assistant, he soon had Susan unconscious on the operating table.

Having first prepared the skin by swabbing with an antiseptic fluid, he began the incision. Derek was fascinated. He had never seen an operation before, not even on television. *Your Life in their Hands* had been one of the more popular television programmes when he had been young, but even as a child he'd been too squeamish to watch. Now, however, he was enthralled; intrigued; fascinated.

Nicholas obviously had what all good surgeons have—tissue

sense. Like a gymnast who always seems to know where he is in
three dimensions, Nicholas always knew where he was inside the
body, even when it was anything but obvious which layer of tissue
he was in. The outer wall of the abdomen isn't a simple single
layer. First there is skin, then fat, then layers of tough fascia which
coat the muscles, like shrunk plastic. Next there is the muscle, and
on the other side of the muscle another layer of fascia, and finally
the peritoneum, a tough layer like a transparent plastic glove,
coating the whole of the inside of the abdominal wall.

Only when this had been breached were they truly inside the
abdomen. To Derek's surprise, the next thing Nicholas did was
to insert his arm up to the elbow through the incision line, hands
exploring, feeling, checking all the abdominal organs just in case
there was some other abnormality that had so far not been
noticed. Satisfied that all was well, he turned his attention to the
gall bladder. Derek tried to remember the complicated diagrams
from the books and was fascinated to see how unerringly
Nicholas found the right tubes to cut. Derek reflected ruefully
that he was right not to have attempted to do the operation
himself. He could never have managed it. There were so many
little tricks Nicholas used that Derek would never have thought
of: how to stop bleeding points; how to cut into a tube so that
none of the contents spilled out; how to free the mangled
remains of the gall bladder sticking to the underside of the liver
by blunt dissection.

In planning the operation—fantasising, rather—Derek
mentally used a scalpel most of the time. Nicholas hardly ever
did. Instead he would put a clamp on either side of the line to be
cut, then use scissors to cut the tissue between them. Most
surprisingly of all he used scissors the opposite way round:
inserting a pair of blunt-ended scissors, blades closed, between
two organs that he wished to separate, he would open the blades,
neatly pushing one organ from the other, gently separating the
thin connective tissue between them without any danger of
cutting into either organ. Blunt dissection like this was a
revelation to Derek, who had never thought of using scissors in
that way. It didn't cut into anything, it just pushed organs to one
side, or opened up the space between them. So simple, so
obvious and yet so unexpected.

Holding a retractor, he watched as Nicholas identified the gall bladder with the stones inside and deftly tied the duct coming from it, twice. Then, cutting between the two ligatures he freed the gall bladder, brought it out and put it in a stainless steel kidney dish. For once he picked up a scalpel. 'Watch,' he said, slitting the plum-sized bladder from top to bottom. Yellow bile poured out and with it a heap of fine stones, looking like polished black grit. 'There you are, that was what was causing the pain.'

Putting the kidney dish to one side, he picked up a needle-holder and having put a rubber tube in to act as a temporary drain, began to stitch the abdomen together again, layer by layer, in the reverse order: peritoneum first, then the muscles, the upper layer of fascia, the fatty layer and finally the skin. Susan was left with a neat scar about four inches long, just under her right ribs.

'Most impressive,' said Martin, who had also donned surgical garb and had been watching from the end of the table.

'Yes,' said Nicholas eyeing him warily, still aware that he appeared to be dealing with some sort of homicidal maniac. It was a good job he didn't know Martin's previous profession and beliefs—he really *would* have had doubts about Martin's mental state.

'Thank you for showing me that,' said Derek.

'It's a pleasure,' said Nicholas, meaninglessly.

'We ought to pay you for this,' said Martin.

That was the last statement that Nicholas expected to hear.

'I thought we'd been through that.'

'No, you'd tried to be extortionate. We ought to pay you, but *fairly*—for both sides. Now what do you want? We could pay you in petrol, to a reasonable degree—we must certainly reimburse you for the petrol you've used in your mobile generator for the lights and the autoclave—and you can have some of our produce: whatever you want, so long as it's a reasonable amount.'

Nicholas really was taken aback. He'd not expected this. His plans had included operating on the patient as quickly as he could, then getting out of Ampthill as soon as possible, and preferably never coming back.

'Derek, what do *they* pay *you*?' asked Nicholas.

'They do all my farm work for me so I have time just for medicine. We get by.'

'Don't you think you're a bit underpaid?'

'Not really. I don't think I know very much yet. And in any case, it's all that the community can afford. I'm contributing what I can they're giving me what I need.'

Nicholas sniffed. 'Communism rearing its ugly head in the Home Counties, eh?' He untied his mask and started taking off his gown.

'Not really. In a small community there isn't much left over for anyone else. I think what they're doing is quite fair.'

'You won't later on, not when you find that for all that hard work you put in they still want to pay you the same amount. And what happens if you want to go somewhere else?'

'They've already thought of that,' said Derek darkly as he got down from the trailer. 'They won't let me. They won't even let me stop being a doctor—not that I could. I just couldn't stand by and let people suffer—so it looks as though I'm stuck with it.

'Now—what are we going to pay you?'

-69-

'So what happened to you, then?' asked Derek, sitting with Martin in the garden of the Old Rectory that evening, watching the bats. For once Derek had a glass in his hand and Martin hadn't. 'After all, here are you, the great CND supporter, love thy neighbour as thyself, turn the other cheek, pillar of the church, and you go around threatening to blow people's feet off. It is—shall we say—not quite in character.'

Martin grinned. It was a nice smile. Derek hadn't seen him smile like that in all the time he'd known him. He looked like a man who'd had a weight removed from his shoulders, all at once.

'Shall we say, a lot of things suddenly fell into place.'

'Like what?'

'Like I think I've been working under a completely false set of premises. Tell me, do you think man is basically good or basically evil?'

Derek thought for a moment. 'A bit mixed really, a bit of each. Basically good, I suppose.'

'That's what I used to think—that man was basically good, that given the right circumstances he'd do the right thing, the good thing, the loving thing, the kind thing, and that it was only upbringing or social circumstances that turned people into criminals or made them behave badly. And nations were just the same as people. Give them their rights, behave honourably to them, don't try attacking them and in their turn they'll behave peaceably, rationally and in a friendly manner.

'Mary put it in a nutshell, you know, at the first meeting of the council. Do you remember? She said just what I believed—at heart, man is good. Give him the right environment and his goodness will blossom. If someone is doing wrong it's only because of what's happened to him in the past.

'Only it's wrong. She's wrong. I was wrong.

'I learned a lot of things the day the plague broke out, you know, though it didn't feel like it at the time. I learned how selfish people could be in a crisis—the way they trampled over one another; the looting. And I was the same. I didn't go out to help those who'd been injured, or those who were ill, so I was no better than anyone else.

'When we got to Ampthill life seemed a lot better—at first. Everybody was working together, supporting one another and it was wonderful, really friendly.'

'I'm surprised you remember, the amount you were drinking at the time.'

'Oh, I do remember it. I wasn't happy, but I could see in everyone else a sense of direction, a sense of purpose, a sense of getting on and living in a way that I'd never seen before. Everybody clung together and pulled in the same direction and I thought, at least this bears out what I think about human nature. Given the right surroundings man will show himself for what he is—basically good.

'Then we had the raiders. They didn't need to do what they did. They could have come in and been part of the community and we'd have welcomed them with open arms. We'd have helped feed them and they could have had any number of motorbikes, but no, they wanted to steal; and when they found they couldn't have Kevin's bike they would rather have destroyed it than let him continue to enjoy it.

'Then it got a bit nearer. There was Kevin who wouldn't work, even though everyone else did. He'd no reason to behave in that way. He had lots of freedom; he could do what he wanted—within reason—but he just wouldn't fit in.

'It got even closer. It wasn't just the people on the outside of the community: it was those right at the centre—Paul, taking the pethidine. He knew he shouldn't, but he still did it. He knew what he was doing was against the interests of the community, but still he carried on. You'd think that someone in his position would have known better, but no, he didn't.'

Derek thought once again of Jane; and her death; and of his unspoken feelings for her. He shivered.

'And finally there was Nicholas, a kind, gentle, considerate, courteous doctor, who is also avaricious beyond belief. I thought, why is it that some doctors get like that? Even members of the caring professions, the ones we always looked up to, even they seem to have this streak inside them as well.' He fell silent. Derek sipped his drink as another bat flopped past in the gathering twilight.

'So?' said Derek. 'I don't quite see what you're getting at.'

'Well, wait just a bit longer, because there's another strand to it. As I've said, that day of the plague I sat in my room and watched the people go past. They just barged past each other. They only looked after themselves. They didn't care whom they mowed down, so long as *they* got away. All politeness and manners were thrown to the winds. Civilisation disintegrated in front of my eyes. And I got to think about civilisation and what it is and what it does. We used to think that we lived in a civilised society, didn't we?'

'Well it was, wasn't it?'

'All right: what does civilisation mean to you?'

Derek thought for a moment, sipping his glass of wine.

'Architecture . . . music . . . art . . . courtesy . . . manners . . .'

'So where do you see civilisation at its highest? At the

National Gallery perhaps? Glyndebourne?' He was tempted to say 'in our system of law and government', but remembered the TV broadcasts from Parliament and decided that maybe government wasn't civilised. Then he remembered what had happened to Peter Abrahams and decided that maybe the law wasn't a good example either.

'Look at what happens in a "civilised" existence. There's always someone at the bottom doing the dirty work. Go into an up-market hotel—and at the bottom of the pile there's an immigrant worker washing the dishes or sweeping the floors. Civilisation isn't civilisation for everybody: often it's only civilisation for a few. Often society is only civilised for a proportion of people in it. The rest have to work to support that society, that style of existence.'

'Hang on a minute,' interjected Derek. 'Aren't you just mixing up civilisation with selfish consumption? The two aren't the same, you know.'

'I know,' said Martin. 'They don't *have* to be the same, but most of the time they *are* the same. As you say, it does depend very much on what you mean by the word. Civilisation can mean some good programmes on TV, but some pretty unpleasant ones as well.

'There's another side to it. Civilisation and good manners just paper over the cracks. You saw it as soon as people started fleeing from London and the looters came in. Isn't it strange that in our society—the richest we've ever had—there was an insistent demand for more, more, more? Less than a century ago there were people in England who didn't even have piped water. Then look what we had, before the plague: televisions, videos, cars—not just one per family, but several per family—washing machines, telephones—and *still* we got looters and thieves.'

'So we had a very sick civilisation.'

'No, don't you see? It's not the civilisation that's sick, it's the people. *That's* the problem. That's why it's all gone wrong—because people are basically not good. It's people who make civilisation sick, not the other way round. Civilisations will *always* be sick—just because they're made up of people.'

'You're not trying to say that people are all evil?' expostulated Derek.

'Of course not. They're not evil through and through. There's tremendous good in everyone—at least potentially. But it's like a crown-green bowl. Have you ever seen one?'

'I can't say I have.'

'Each bowl has a lead weight on one side so that as it goes along it's gradually dragged across to one side, so that the player can make the bowl curve round in a 'J' shape round his opponent's ball, so as to get near the jack. It's only a little weight. It only drags a little bit, but by constantly pulling on one side, it makes a bowl, which at first is going straight, gradually veer off a little to one side, then a bit more, and a bit more—until after a time it's going at right angles to its original direction.

'Man's like that. Only a little bit of wrong; only a little bit of selfishness; but gradually it pulls him away from what he ought to be doing, and the direction he ought to be going in.'

'In other words you're talking about original sin.'

'You could call it that if you wanted, but sin is such a . . . *loaded* word isn't it? Let's just say that we've each got the capacity to be selfish and that sooner or later that capacity gets expressed. Nobody's perfect. *Nobody*.'

Derek looked out across the lawn to the darkening trees on the far side. He drained his glass.

'It all sounds a bit academic to me. People are people. Does it really matter if they are basically all good or mostly good or a little bit bad? Why don't you just take things as they come?'

'But that's the point,' said Martin, his eyes dancing, 'that's the whole point. If you try to live your life on the assumption that man is basically good then you'll get it all wrong. And what's worse, if you create *society* on the assumption that everyone is basically good, then you'll get that wrong as well. For a start—what happens with crime and punishment? If we constantly excuse people who are bad "because it's their background" we deny the existence of evil. So we don't punish wrong-doing: we treat it like some psychological abnormality that just needs straightening out. And it doesn't work because it isn't true.'

'You're not saying that background and upbringing don't matter?'

'Of course not. They're both important in their place. But wrong is wrong and needs to be treated as such. Remember what

I said about the looters? Compared to people in the Third World
we used to live like millionaires. I could have understood the
looting if it had been by people who were poor—but this was by
people who were rich and *still* wanted more. It wasn't their
background that did it—it was their selfishness; their choice;
their evil.

'Exactly the same happens between nations as between
individuals. I used to work on the assumption that if you treated
everybody as though they were nice they would be nice back. It
doesn't work that way with individuals, because actually they
aren't made quite like that: and it doesn't work that way with
nations either for the same reasons.'

'So what happened to the great pacifist and CND supporter,
then?'

'I'm coming to that. I used to have a great problem with the
story of the cleansing of the temple—do you remember?—where
Jesus made a whip and drove out the merchants that were
desecrating the place by their sharp practices. And I always
thought, why didn't he just *reason* with them? I always thought
that that was a flaw in his character, that he'd lost his temper, that
he'd been violent and shouldn't have been. The man of peace
who wasn't peaceful.'

'That's original sin for you,' said Derek cynically.

'Actually it's not, it's not at all. I suddenly realised why he
did it. It was because there was no other way, that these selfish
people were quite prepared to rook their fellow countrymen, and
what's more, do it in the name of God, and what's worse, do it in
the temple. They couldn't be got rid of by any other method.
They weren't going to listen to sweet reason. If they'd been
listening to reason in the first place they wouldn't have been doing
what they were doing. No—there was no other way. Jesus *had* to
force them out. He came proclaiming peace, but sometimes
needed to use force as well, when there was no other way. And
then I got to thinking, if Jesus was right to force them out of the
temple, then who am I to say that the use of force is always wrong?

'Then it dawned on me that having a peaceful society
depends not *just* on yourself, but on what others do. It was like
that over the raiders. We had a peaceful society until the raiders
came. Then Kevin dealt with them. I thought at the time he'd

done something absolutely appalling, but now I'm not so sure. We wanted a peaceful society, but the raiders didn't want us to have one. If we'd kow-towed to them and let them have what they wanted they would ultimately have ruled us, and made our lives sheer hell. They'd have been pure parasites.

'My attitude, which at the time I thought was Christian, was to turn the other cheek. I was wrong. The more I think about it, the more I'm sure that Kevin taught the raiders—and me—an important lesson.'

'I'm not sure that half-strangling a chap while you beat him up is a particularly Christian way to go about things,' said Derek grimly.

'I agree. I'm not talking about the method—I'm talking about the principle. There's a great paradox here. Being a peacemaker may involve being violent. Odd, isn't it? But it's far better to be a true peacemaker by using a moderate amount of violence than it is to be an appeaser, use none—and create more violence long-term. In a selfish world, sometimes force is necessary to stop a greater evil developing.'

'Which is why you threatened Nicholas.'

'Right.'

'There's an awfully fine line between the two,' said Derek. He shivered.

'Shall we go inside?' asked Martin. 'It's getting cold.'

They went into the lounge and Martin lit a candle. 'Do you want another drink?'

'Yes please,' said Derek.

'I think I'll have one now,' said Martin pouring himself half a glass.

Derek looked at him, then at the glass and back up at Martin again. Martin read his thoughts. 'No, I don't need it any more. I drank to blot out the pain, the emotional pain. Nothing fitted. Everything I tried to think about was at odds with everything else. I couldn't make sense of the world. Now I can, and because I can, I don't have the turmoil and because I don't have the turmoil, I don't need to anaesthetise myself with this stuff any longer. I can just drink it to enjoy it, instead of drinking it to blot everything out.'

'Well, it's obviously made a difference to you. I still don't see why what you've said has changed you so much.'

'I'm coming to that. The point is this: civilisation just papers over the cracks of original sin. Civilisation—at least in the way that we both used to think of it—is really quite false. It gets in the way. You know this yourself. How many people in a previous "civilised" society ate meat, but couldn't bear to go into an abattoir? How many people were protected by "civilisation" from realising just how precarious their existence was on the surface of the earth?'

Martin looked out of the window for a moment, then a thought occurred to him. 'Do you know where the word "civilisation" comes from?'

'Not really.'

'It's from the Latin—*civitas*, meaning "city". "Civilisation" is all about city life: about people who've got out of touch with the country, out of touch with nature.

'Before the plague, how many people like Mary hadn't the vaguest idea of what nature is *really* like? She says she doesn't want to kill in order to eat "because we must live in harmony with nature". Yet this goes against everything we know about nature. You look at what nature is *really* like—the fox getting the chickens; Mary's kestrel killing the fieldmice. Nature isn't the nice kind thing that in a "civilised" world we liked to think it was.'

'You're right there,' said Derek, slowly. 'I remember, at the end of our cruise, before we knew about the plague, looking out over the countryside and thinking "Isn't it charming?", and a week later I was saying to myself "What a wilderness: how are we going to exist in this?" You're right—civilisation often does give us a totally wrong view of life.'

'Nature's pretty raw when it's left to itself,' said Martin. 'Except that we're a special case. Do you realise we're about the only animal that doesn't have a natural predator? Almost all other animals have. Yet before the plague many "civilised" people used to think that being vegetarian was somehow good, right, proper and natural. It may be nice, but it's the most unnatural thing ever. And the plague. That was natural too.'

'Man doesn't have big predators, just very powerful microscopic ones,' observed Derek. 'Interesting. I hadn't thought of it like that before.'

'The plague was quite an eye-opener, wasn't it? Afterwards we learned that when you lose "civilisation" you behave in a different way. In some ways it was easier, wasn't it?—a simpler life really does make people happier sometimes. But it's brought us all face to face with life in the raw—how you can't get your shoulder of lamb without butchering a sheep, how you can't get milk without taking the calf away from its mother.'

'But it was *always* like that,' said Derek. 'Nothing's changed.'

'*That's the point*,' said Martin. '*Nothing's changed*. We *always* got our meat that way, we *always* got our milk that way. It's just that because we dissociated what we got from how we got it we thought that somehow civilisation meant an absence of all those things that we disliked, and so we all ended up living in cloud-cuckoo-land, with abattoirs and factories that were walled off so we couldn't see them—just as the Victorians shut away mental patients in asylums, so they weren't disturbed by them.

'We took it to crazy lengths, you know. We even had protest meetings because we didn't want factories or mines on our back doorsteps—but we still demanded cheap manufactured goods and we still wanted coal. Where did we think it would come from, then? The more we went on, the more we divorced ourselves from reality.'

'I still don't see why this has made such a difference to you.'

'Simple,' said Martin. 'Or rather, it's because it's simple that it's made the difference. Previously I couldn't understand the world. I didn't understand the Bible, I didn't understand God. They all seemed at odds with each other. I couldn't make them fit. When the plague came finally it was the last straw—everything fell apart.

'Today I realised the mistake I'd made—why I couldn't fit it together. I saw in good, kind, upstanding, avaricious Nicholas the greed that was prepared to sacrifice another human being for gain, and I realised, just as with Jesus in the temple, that unless I faced up to it and was prepared to use force to stop it then it would *never* be stopped and evil would continue. I learned today that however good man may seem to be on the surface, underneath there is always this little bias like the bowl, and that if you don't stop it, it will gain the upper hand.

'And suddenly everything clicked into place. I understood

human nature, and with that I understood what the Bible was
saying: that at heart man is sinful and God is perfect. And
suddenly the idea of God sending his son to earth didn't sound so
stupid to me after all, to live among us, to show us what a
perfect person really was like—and that perfect person could get
quite forceful when it was really necessary.'

'So where does that leave "turning the other cheek"?'

'Where it always was. Where Jesus had it: very appropriate
on the right occasion—but not necessarily the response for *every*
occasion, that's all.'

Martin went to the window. It was a bright clear night. Out
in the west just beyond the trees he could see Venus shining
brilliantly. Up above them was the Milky Way—stars, hundreds
more than he remembered seeing as a child. He opened the doors
and led Derek out into the garden. 'Look at that,' he said. 'Have
you ever seen such a display?' They both gazed up at it. 'Did
you see them before the plague?'

Derek shook his head.

'They were there all the time. We just couldn't see them.
Do you know why? We couldn't see them because our own
trivial little light that we used to illuminate our streets and our
cities blotted them out. Civilisation got in the way of seeing the
stars as they really were. They've always been like that. We've
just been blinded by what we've produced ourselves. Get rid of
the side-effects of "civilisation" and you can see things with
much greater clarity.'

Derek saw.

-70-

*N*ext morning, with a certain amount of trepidation, Major
Thornton made his way up Holly Walk towards the Old Rectory.
He hoped he was calling at a good time as, from experience, he
knew that Martin was usually less drunk before two o'clock. He
tapped on the door and was surprised to see the bounce in

Martin's step as he answered the knock.

'Come in Major, what brings you here?'

'We were wondering if you could possibly bring yourself to celebrate Harvest?' began Major Thornton rather hesitantly, expecting the worst.

'I'd be delighted to.'

'Just the once you understand: we wouldn't want you to do two services . . .' He suddenly realised what Martin had said.

'Yes,' said Martin putting his hand on Major Thornton's arm. 'Yes, I'd be delighted.'

*   *   *

Things were different when next the two men met.

The following day the council had to decide Paul's fate. Although there had been many discussions behind the scenes, nothing had been resolved, and it seemed that deadlock would prevail yet again, with all its attendant acrimony and disappointment.

They met, as usual, in the courtroom. Susan, of course, couldn't be there as she was recovering from the operation, but Alan managed to come. Shortly before they were due to start the Major stormed into the room and banged his papers firmly on the table, obviously ready to do battle. The others came in more gently, wondering what was going to happen.

'We all know what was said at the previous meeting,' began Chris. 'Has anyone got anything new to add?' She looked round the table. 'Peter?'

'Every time I think about it I get angry,' he replied. 'We said after the trial that it was over and done with—well, over and done with it should be. No follow-on. No further repercussions. The whole matter should be closed. When Paul is ready—I mean, when he's got over losing Jane—then he should be welcome back on the council again.'

'Rubbish,' snorted the Major. Chris ignored him.

'Alan?'

'I agree with Peter, on principle. Anyway, we need Paul's advice. He's the best planner we have.'

'Neil?'

'I can see the Major's point. Will we ever be able to trust Paul again?'

428 After the Fire

'Yes of course . . . '
'No, we can't . . . '
'How can you say that . . . '

On and on it went, just as it had done the previous month, with the Major getting more and more infuriated with those who disagreed with him: but gradually more and more *were* siding with him, albeit reluctantly. Paul was a liability, it was true. He couldn't really be trusted any longer—that was true, too.

Only Martin remained silent, but, unlike the previous meeting, his silence was positive, not negative. He waited patiently until everyone had vented their anger. Finally Chris turned to him.

'Martin, you've said nothing so far.'

'I was listening. I *would* like to say something if you don't mind. Actually, I'd like to *ask* Major Thornton something. Major—you feel that Paul has blotted his copybook once and for all, don't you?'

'Most certainly I do, yes.'

'For ever?'

There was a pause. 'Well, for a very long time, at least.'

'How long?'

'I . . . er . . . wouldn't really like to say. Long enough for him to learn to change his ways.'

'So he's *not* blotted his copybook permanently, then?'

'No . . . er . . . yes . . . er . . . '

'Come on, I want an answer. Has he or hasn't he?'

Another silence. The rest of the council listened intently. This was a different Martin they were listening to. They'd not known him like this before. In the past he'd always vacillated.

'I'm waiting. Has he or hasn't he blotted his copybook permanently?'

'I'm not sure. Anyway, what does it matter? He's certainly done it now.'

'I was just wondering—that is, if you feel he hasn't ruled himself out permanently—how long you feel he would have to wait before he could be allowed back?'

The Major paused. 'I don't know. Years. Five or ten years . . . at least.'

'Why?'

The Major raised his voice angrily. 'Because he's not suitable, that's why. We've already gone into that.'

'What if he's reformed? Does he still need to serve his five-year "sentence"?'

The Major saw the trap too late.

'It's not what he's done. It's his personality,' he blustered, 'and whether he's likely to do something similar in the future.'

'Such as?' asked Martin innocently. 'What sort of thing do you have to do to blot your copybook, then, Major?'

'It's not what you do, it's the sort of person you are . . . what we used to call a cad. Selfish; thieving; immoral—that sort of thing.'

Martin looked at the Major for a moment, then away for a moment and then back at him.

'It's what you are rather than what you do?'

'Definitely.'

'Hmmm. So the rest of us here are all right, are we? We're OK to be on the council?'

'Yes.' The Major thought of mentioning a certain ex-priest's alcoholic tendencies, but decided against it.

'So we're perfect, are we?'

'No, but there are degrees of behaviour.'

'Is being envious part of being a cad?'

'I suppose so.'

'Being proud?'

'Yes.'

'As you're a churchgoer,'—the Major flushed with pride—'you know the prayer of general confession, don't you?'

'Of course.'

'Before you've confessed your sins you're at odds with God, aren't you? And after you've confessed what you've done, you believe your sins are wiped out?'

'Of course.'

'Without any punishment due to you?'

'Yes.'

'And all this, knowing that by the same time next week you'll probably have done the same things again? Because we're all sinful people.'

'Well, yes.'

'Then aren't you being a hypocrite?'

Martin sat back in his chair and waited for the expected storm.

It came.

When the Major had quietened down somewhat, Chris interjected. 'That wasn't a fair comment, Martin, and I don't see what it has to do with Paul.'

'No, it *is* a fair comment,' replied Martin evenly. 'The Major is quite prepared to confess to his own mistakes and have them forgiven, even when he knows he's going to do them again, but he won't allow someone else to be forgiven at all, even after he's been punished.'

'That's not the point at all,' expostulated the Major.

'Yes it is,' said Martin coolly. 'The point is—we all do things we'd prefer others not to know about. You, Major— you're not exactly unhappy to be in Gates House, are you? You always did think you ought to be squire in the community, didn't you? And you've just said that pride and envy aren't particularly good attributes—well, you've been exhibiting them. Maybe we shouldn't have you on the council either? But where do you stop? Do you throw a man off the council because he's a thief? Even when he's reformed? Do you get rid of him if he's immoral? No one is perfect—*no one*—so where do you draw the line? Each of us has things we don't want others to find out about, things of which we're ashamed.'

Derek thought about Jane and tried not to flush.

'So just what disqualifies anyone from being on the council? Being found out? I suspect *that* is actually the criterion. It certainly was in the past. You know the eleventh commandment, don't you—"Thou shalt not get found out?" It's all right if you do it in secret, but once it becomes public . . . And *that's* hypocrisy as well, because it's not what you do that determines whether you're a fit person, it's whether you're found out or not.

'OK, so Paul did something wrong. He was a good council leader before you found out about his use of pethidine; but he was using it at the time you still thought he was a 'good chap', and he was still making good decisions. Just because you found out about him hasn't altered the fact that he did his previous council work effectively; in fact, now he's off the pethidine he ought to be *more* effective, not less, but it's *now* that you want to remove him—which is somewhat illogical. Paul knows now that he shouldn't have tried to blame Kevin, and regrets it bitterly. He's not going to do it again.

'The reason I suggested that you're a hypocrite is that obviously you have one list of misdemeanours which you think are good to confess to, and another which you think are bad. Well, that's hypocrisy. Things are either good or bad—if you like, in the church terms we were talking about before, sinful or not sinful.

'Now don't get me wrong—I don't mean any personal nastiness by what I've just said. It applies to *all* of us, including me. If it comes to that, I more than anyone else should be off the council, because half the time I wasn't thinking very straight as a result of the amount of alcohol I was consuming. But I hope that now that's behind me you'll feel more like having me on the council, rather than less: well, apply the same logic to Paul. None of us is perfect—but it's wrong to pillory one man rather than another, just because he's been caught, and especially when what he's done bears no relationship whatever to the quality of the work he carries out.'

Martin looked over towards Peter, who nodded silently.

There was a pause while the Major took this all in. He opened his mouth to say something, sighed and looked at Martin. 'I think I've just made a fool of myself,' he said.

'No,' said Martin gently, '*I* don't think that. You're just repeating an idea that's been handed down for generations: it's wrong, it's illogical, it's unfair, but it's easy to believe in it, for all that.'

There was a silence, and then a peace that spread throughout the room: suddenly everyone there knew what to do.

'Anyone disagree with Martin?' asked Chris.

Silence.

'Do I take it then that we're all agreed that Paul is welcome to come back when he's ready?'

There was a nodding of heads—including the Major's.

'Then I think that concludes the meeting.'

*   *   *

'No hard feelings, Major?' enquired Martin.

'No, but it'll take me some time to come to terms with it.
It's quite a change from what I used to believe.'

'I know. Take your time. No one's rushing you.'

-71-

No one who has lived in a city all his life can even begin to
imagine Harvest Festival in a rural community. Previously, most
of the inhabitants of Ampthill had been city dwellers. If they'd
bothered to go to church at all on Harvest Sunday they came with
tins of food to be sent to the Third World to atone for their sin of
being English and rich and having food when others didn't; or
else they sent the food to those in Britain who were less fortunate
than themselves. So instead of Harvest Festival being a
celebration of the fruits of the earth, a rejoicing that the harvest
really was safely home, it became an expiation, a lament for a
lack elsewhere. In the past, Harvest had been turned into
something that was negative, not positive.

But for the whole of the Ampthill community that year
Harvest Festival took on a new meaning. They all knew just how
near to disaster they had come: that they had been within a
whisker of having nothing to celebrate at all. But now the
harvest really *was* home, and all really *was* safely gathered in;
and the relief and exuberance—ecstasy even—were abundantly
evident in everyone's mind. They were relieved, they were
joyful, and above all they were *thankful*—to God, nature, fate or
whatever, they weren't always sure—but they were thankful. It
could have been so different, and they knew it.

That Sunday the church was packed, decked out throughout
with sheaves of wheat, vegetables, loaves, flowers and, at
Derek's suggestion, books—a celebration of the harvest of
knowledge as well as of the fruits of the earth. They'd worked
out how to operate the organ in the old manner, with bellows
instead of an electric pump, and young David proudly had the job
of making sure that the air in the wind-box never got too low—

not an easy job when the organist is playing with all the stops out. By the time they'd reached the end of 'Come ye thankful people, come' he was looking just a little pink about the cheeks and breathing almost as noisily as the wind inside the organ.

Unlike previous occasions when Martin had merely been the official to guide the service through, taking as little part as he possibly could, it was obvious now his heart was thoroughly in it. He even gave a sermon. It was short, sharp and to the point.

'We're here to celebrate Harvest—to give thanks for our food. How different from last year! Last year we didn't really see what we had to thank God for, because the harvest seemed to be under *our* control. How much we've learned since then!'

Then he told them what he had already told Derek, five nights earlier, about the sky and how easily it could be obscured by—of all things—light, not darkness. He related how, sitting in his vicarage window he had for the first time realised the sheer power of moonlight; yet, in the past, he had only been aware of the first half of the verse in Genesis which talked of God creating the sun to rule the day and the moon to rule the night.

'You know, civilisation affects us so much,' he said. 'It gives us clean water, drains,'—there was a little titter of laughter—'art and music, and I'm sure that many of you here know how much I appreciate those last two. And these things are all good.

'But civilisation also gets in the way. It gives us false ideas about nature itself. It shields us from death; it stops us being aware of the precarious nature of life on earth. It makes us think we're in control of the universe—yet nothing could be further from the truth.

'Life *isn't* like that—we all know that now. Life is raw, difficult, precarious. And death is very real to us all as well.

'If we're separated from what life is really like, we won't appreciate much of what the Bible says, either. The Bible was written by people who knew about life as it really is—because they lived in it. They knew about the contrast between light and darkness—we didn't. They knew about life and death in its rawness—we were shielded from it. They knew how precarious our existence on earth is—we took it for granted.

'Before the plague, we were encouraged to think about life in a particular way. But because civilisation distorted our view of events, sometimes we ended up with the wrong end of the stick. Then we didn't see how God fitted in. We cut great chunks out of the Bible because we didn't understand how that fitted in, either. It didn't seem to fit in with our "civilised" philosophies; but often we'd lost touch with nature to such a degree that we didn't even see what the Bible was *actually* saying—like "the moon to rule the night".

'Now there are many things about civilisation that are good, and I don't want to minimise it. But sometimes its conclusions are wrong—sometimes it leads us in the wrong direction. So it looks as if we may need to rethink our approach. In some ways the plague, awful though it was, may have helped us to see life more clearly.'

He paused, then became aware of a strange sensation. *Everyone* was looking at him, not with glazed eyes as so often in the past, but obviously alert and interested. For once, after all the years he'd spent in the pulpit, he was actually saying something they found helpful, something they could relate to, something that was relevant.

'Let me tell you what *I'm* going to do—and don't forget, I'm just as much a learner as any of us. I'm going back to my Bible, and I'm going to read it through again, having first taken off my twentieth-century blinkers. And then I'll be looking at it through eyes that are experiencing life as it *really* is—as we're living it now.'

*   *   *

After the service Derek invited Martin to Dynevor House for lunch. They stood in the sunlight on the patio watching the golden carp in the pond, and then wandered up the grassy lawn at the back of the house underneath the trees. 'What did you mean by that last bit?' asked Derek. 'About seeing the Bible through different eyes?'

'Something that you'll appreciate,' said Martin calmly, neatly flicking a twig with his foot: Derek was reminded once again how much his friend had changed in the past few days. He seemed to have lost ten years of wrinkles, but gained twenty years in maturity and sureness of purpose.

'All through the Bible there are references to things that we've forgotten about, or don't use now. Light in contrast to *real* darkness, for example. The sense of not being in control of things, such as the weather. We know now what it's like to be at the mercy of the elements; when the crops fail; when the rains don't come, or come too much.

'There are lots of other hidden things, though. Do you remember when I first started milking, I nearly put my back out, lifting the pail in my right hand all the time? So I made a yoke—a milkmaid's yoke just like you see in old paintings—and I found I could carry twice the weight with ease, because it was well-balanced.

'So?'

'Do you remember the passage where Jesus says, "My yoke is easy and my burden light"?'

'Vaguely. I'd always thought that was about animal yokes, though.'

'It may well have been, but the principle's the same. I found out at first hand that a well-balanced yoke actually makes work lighter, not harder. It wasn't the imprisoning thing I'd previously imagined. Just experiencing it myself turned the meaning of the whole verse upside-down in my mind.

'Let me give you another example—something *you'll* particularly appreciate. In the past I never really thought about what it meant to Mary when the angel came to her at the annunciation, to ask her to become pregnant with Jesus. I've always thought: "Oh a little bit of pain at the end when the baby is born—nothing too much—and what a wonderful privilege." It never occurred to me that by agreeing to carry God's son, Mary was actually risking her life. It was only after Jane died that I realised the importance of it—how women would say, "My time has come" with a mixture of eagerness and dread. Mary was risking her life to have Jesus, just as Jane was risking hers in being pregnant, though she didn't know it at the time.'

Derek looked down at the ground.

'You haven't got over her death yet, have you?' said Martin.

'No,' said Derek, 'but I'm a lot better. I now know that there was nothing more I could have done—Nicholas told me that. It was a great help having him, you know.'

'I shouldn't think he'll come back,' said Martin ruefully. 'Not after what I did to him.'

'Oh no,' said Derek. 'It's funny, you and your original sin. It works the other way round you know. Just because somebody is wicked in one area doesn't mean they're going to be wicked all through. Nicholas is coming back on a regular basis, just to see how I'm getting on, to teach me, and to do any surgery that's necessary.'

'I should think you feel relieved about that.'

'Not half. It was very encouraging being shown how to do things. We had quite a chat afterwards, and he put me right on some areas where I'd got the wrong end of the stick completely. It put one or two aspects of medicine in a totally different perspective.'

They walked slowly round the garden, then stood for a moment at its highest point, looking down towards the house, the house that had seen so many changes in its three-hundred-and-fifty-year existence.

'I know just what you mean about seeing things with a different perspective,' Martin mused as they wandered again under the trees, lost in thought, their faces dappling in the autumnal sunlight coming through the leaves.

After a few moments more, Derek spoke. 'We'd better go back into the house,' he said. 'Lunch won't be long. Would you like a sherry? There's still some left.'

They went down the hill of the lawn, past the pond with the goldfish lazily basking in it, and were just entering the house through the morning-room French windows when there was a loud knock on the front door. Derek crossed the hall and opened it. Outside was a Range Rover, its bonnet creaking gently as it cooled down. On the steps was a dapper man of about fifty-eight, immaculately dressed.

'Hello,' said Derek, 'you're new here, aren't you? What can I do for you?'

'How do you do? May I introduce myself? My name's Courtauld—Henry Courtauld—and you appear to be living in my house.'

'. . . after the fire a still small voice.'

The saga will continue . . .